Convergence

ISBN: 9781495940255

Genesis 1:26-28

Then God said, "Let Us make man in Our image, according to Our likeness. They will rule the fish of the sea, the birds of the sky, the animals, all the Earth, and the creatures that crawl on the Earth." So God created man in His own image.

Chapter 1

Did I wake naturally, or did something wake me? It's an important question when you are the only person inhabiting a star ship. The cabin was full of the normal comforting noises made by the air conditioning system. Noises that one soon learns to ignore. I searched my sleep drugged brain for what had disturbed me. Then it came, the residual memory of that gut churning feeling of the Hyperspace drive operating. But we were not due to exit Hyperspace for another two weeks; Had I just dreamt it? I had barely sat up in my bunk before the whooping of the alarm shattered the peace and shocked me fully awake.

My body switched to automatic and I convulsed off my bunk and headed for the Bridge. There was a series of remote thumps and the ship lurched ominously. I launched myself down the corridor, bouncing off the walls. As I dived into the pilot's seat, I could see that the Control board was lit up like a Christmas tree; alarmingly with very few green lights. Red and yellow predominated.

My brain engaged belatedly.

"Alfred what is happening?" I yelled, frantically pressing buttons. In reply, there was a series of bangs and thumps from the outside of the ship, as if we were being hit by meteors, and the ship lurched again. I was about to call the ship's AI again when he finally responded in his usual calm and mellow tones.

"We have a problem with the Hyperspace Drive Paul." It was unlike Alfred to be so vague.

"Could you be more specific Alfred?"

"It has disconnected," he said.

"Disconnected?" I gaped at the Technicolor control board, but it did not enlighten me. "How...what..?" I began, feebly.

"There was an overload when we came out of Hyperspace and the automatic safeties detached the Hyperspace drive from the body of the ship."

"Those thumps were the Hyperspace module detaching?" I asked.

"Yes," he replied.

"And what were those other bangs?" I asked.

"That was the Hyperspace Drive blowing up," replied Alfred in his usual polite English Butlers monotone, as if announcing that Tea had been served. For a few seconds my brain seemed unable to comprehend English.

"Blowing up? You mean in bits...destroyed."

"Yes, in very small bits, and quite destroyed," replied Alfred taking me literally as always. I slumped back in my seat. With no Hyperspace Drive, there was no way to return home. Earth was thousands of light years away, totally unreachable without the magic of the Hyperspace Drive. A dozen questions crowded my mind but the sheer finality of the disaster made them all pointless.

"That's it then, we are dead, no way back."

"Not strictly true Paul," responded Alfred. "There is no way back, but we are not dead."

"Come on Alfred," I groaned "Don't be pedantic, it's just a matter of time "

"Paul, take a look at the screen," responded Alfred cryptically. The screen flashed and displayed a new image. I expanded the magnification to maximum and there was no mistake. A beautiful blue green planet hung in the star studded blackness of Space.

"I take it back Alfred. Maybe we are not quite dead."

"As far as I can determine, we are seven hundred and thirty five light years from what should have been our destination," explained Alfred. "But by incredible good fortune, we have re-entered our Space-time 2.5 million miles from the fourth planet of the star SG24536 otherwise known as Perseus ".

"Good fortune indeed," I agreed. Now, those of you who are familiar with the operation of the Hyperspace Drive will know that the HD can only operate at a minimum distance of 3 million miles from any Planet or 50 million miles from any Star. Any closer and unpredictable things like explosions and meltdowns are likely to occur.

"The navigation co-ordinates for the last jump were incorrect and we have entered normal Space too close to the planet. That is why the HD detached prior to exploding."

"Yes, yes Alfred I get the picture," I said. "But how did such an error occur, it's unheard of."

"It is unheard of because no one has returned to report this malfunction," retorted Alfred, which was not at all comforting. "As to how it could have happened, I am continuing to investigate the causes."

Two point five million miles, I thought, that really is a 'bulls eye'. We were very lucky to survive re-entry to normal Space so close to a planet. The up side was that we could reach the Planet using the ship's reaction drive, which, as Alfred had pointed out, meant we were not dead. Not yet. But if the atmosphere of Perseus 4 was poisonous, then we were dead, just a bit later.

"Alfred , have you conducted an analysis of the planet's atmosphere?" I asked

"Under way Paul." he responded "Initial results look good - very Earth like, oxygen, nitrogen , carbon dioxide , no poisonous gases, gravity 95%

Earth, surface area 60% ocean 40% land mostly equatorial with two small landmasses in the northern hemisphere and one large landmass in the south. The Planet is slightly further from its sun than the Earth so the Equatorial climate should be very agreeable. Polar climates are more extreme."

"Vegetation, Animal Life?"

"Vegetation is widespread except in the extreme polar regions. There are a few desert areas around the equatorial regions."

"Right Alfred, set course for Perseus 4." I had an alarming thought. "Wait, we need to check that there has been no damage to the rockets."

"There looks to be no damage as far as the diagnostics are concerned, but it's possible that the HD explosion may have done some structural damage to the ship which does not show on the sensors." retorted Alfred.

"Hmm... exterior examination needed?" I asked

"It may be safer."

I set about preparing to detach the EE Robot, a small self propelled device that would navigate around the ship under Alfred's control beaming back full colour video. This was a fairly straight forward job that involved removing the Robot from its dustproof storage, checking its power pack and communications electronics, running a diagnostic for its simple control computer and then physically manipulating it into the air lock. Alfred took over from there and I sat back to examine the video.

It was always sobering to see the *Lisa Jane* from the outside. She was a big ship, but she looked small and frail against the vast starry backdrop of deep Space. Scout ships are built for speed and endurance, not for good looks, and she looked like a combination of power station and chemical plant, which in essence, she was. She was bracketed by five huge cylinders of water that held the fuel for the rocket engines. The front was truncated; that was where the missing HD should have been. *Lisa Jane* was not designed to land on a planet, she was strictly a Space faring girl. Nestling in her bulky rear was the *Epsilon 2*, the atmospheric shuttle that would fly us down to the Planet's surface. Despite the massive power of her two fusion reactors, in the emptiness between the stars she was just a feeble bubble of warmth and life, relying on her immensely complex machinery to navigate and cross that unimaginable vastness; Complex machinery which had let us down, marooning us far from home.

The external examination was problem free and after retrieving the EE robot we prepared to start up the reaction engines. Alfred started the countdown and I settled into the acceleration couch. The precaution was not strictly necessary, the ship would accelerate at barely a quarter of a G (one Earth Gravity) but for the initial firing of the reaction engines procedures required strap in and all equipment stowed. The starting muffled rumble of the rockets seemed smooth and trouble free and the feel of weight after weeks of weightlessness was reassuring, somehow as if things were returning to normal. The acceleration phase would last some hours while the ship built up speed and then we would cruise for three days before braking to orbit Perseus 4.

When Alfred declared the all clear I prepared my own meal. The thought that I may have seen the last of the human race led me to ponder the circumstances that had led me here. Why had I joined the Space Exploration Service? It was well known that only misfits and eccentrics were able to tolerate the months of loneliness and isolation. The closest similarity was probably to single handed around the world sailors. Except that if you broke a sail you called the emergency services and they would have you home for tea in no time! I could call home as well, but the message would not be received for more than two thousand years.

I had never considered myself a misfit as such, but a succession of bad jobs and bad relationships had convinced me that a break from the Human race would be a relief. The SES will eventually send a search and rescue ship to our original destination, but we were not going to be there. Whatever we found on this planet was going to be our home.

The SES had been set up about two hundred and fifty years previously. After the first hundred years of Space exploration, it had become apparent that planets that were suitable for colonisation were few and far between, and the job of finding them was going to be more difficult than expected. Instead of having a small number of very large ships, the SES had decided that a large number of very small ships would be a more efficient way of going about the job. The *Lisa Jane* was a typical Scout ship, designed to house only one human passenger and therefore minimising the food, water and accommodation requirements. The other 'passenger' was the ship's Artificial Intelligence Computer. The ship's AI was one of the most advanced Computers ever built, endowed with an intelligence that was almost Human. Although I was nominally Captain of the ship, and the ship's AI was my 'crew', we were in practice partners, sharing all decision making.

The Human member of the crew got to choose a personality for his or her ship's AI. Most male Scout Ship Captains preferred to choose a female voice and personality, sometimes motherly and comforting, sometimes youthful and sexy. I am not sure why I chose the 'Alfred' personality. Perhaps having grown up in England, I nursed that very typical English dream of having my very own Butler to wait upon my every whim! Sadly for me, Alfred did little to humour my fantasy.

Life on a Starship has a routine based on a normal Earth day. We kept to a 24 hour day, slept for 6-8 hours, woke had breakfast, started work. End of the day was the time for food and recreation. Of course, one was always on duty, but Starships are highly automated and the AI Computer ran most things. Why have a Human on board? I sometimes think it's just to declare ownership. This is a *Human* Starship, got it? Not just a machine, but inhabited, a little piece of Earth. Truth is, Alfred could do everything. There were a number of Robots on board which could act as his hands. He (It?) did not need me. But despite his great intelligence and massive processing power, AI's could still not quite duplicate the human brain and robots were not as flexible and intelligent as a person. So we still had a job. For now, but who knows for how long!

It was nice to have a bit of gravity and I used the opportunity to get some exercise. Very soon we would have to cope with .95G and that was going to be hard after 6 weeks without gravity

Alfred busied himself building up a mass of information about what was soon to become our new home. So far he had found nothing alarming and so at least it appeared that I would not die in space. I was feeling a mixture of excitement and trepidation. I kept telling myself that I was not going back home again, I would not ever see another human being again, but somehow it did not seem to have an impact. I was too busy, there was too much to study and do and the familiar surroundings of my ship lulled me into a feeling of denial. I kept thinking that the reaction would come later, and was grateful to put it off.

Perseus 4 grow larger in the screen, and we were able to see more and more detail. I started to discuss a possible landing site with Alfred and we identified a number of possibilities. I examined maps and displays and thought, how do you decide where to live when you have a whole planet to choose from? A nice warm dry place near a clean river perhaps? On top of a hill to be protected from predators? What about food? I had a sudden thought.

"Alfred, what are the prospects of us being able to eat the local fauna and flora?"

"It is very unlikely Paul." replied Alfred in a non committal sort of voice. It was all right for him , he was not concerned with such gross bodily functions .

"Five planets have so far been discovered with life." he continued in his best schoolmasterly voice "All have slight variations in the basic proteins of life. It's possible some of the vegetation may be edible, but animal protein may be hard to digest. As you well know Paul, we have supplies for six months. But we also have seeds from which you could grow crops to extend your survival indefinitely"

"Ah yes" I nodded "Join the SES and become a farmer...!"

"You will have the assistance of the mechanoids" retorted Alfred . The mechanoids in question were half a dozen robots of various sizes, some designed to carry out specialised tasks on the planet, such as collecting samples and other more general duties.

"I guess we can put off selecting a place for a permanent habitation until we have surveyed the planet in greater detail, and perhaps made a number of landings," I mused. "We do seem to have plenty of time."

"Yes, we do," agreed Alfred.

"Well I'm off to bed," I yawned. It had been a hard ten hours or so since I had been dramatically awoken and I needed to catch up with my sleep.

"Sleep well Paul, I will of course continue surveying the planet." I had another thought.

"Alfred, should we give the planet a name? I mean, we can't just keep calling it 'The Planet' or Perseus 4?"

"I could pick one at random," suggested Alfred .

"No, can't have that Alfred. We have to live there so we may as well choose a name we like."

"If it makes you happy Paul, then it's fine with me."

"OK, more in hope than anything else , let us name it 'Omorphia', after the Greek word for beautiful."

"That seems most appropriate Paul. 'Omorphia' it is."

Sleep was slow in coming, but it had been a long tiring day and it came eventually. I do not know how long I slept but I awoke to hear Alfred's voice seemingly coming from the bottom of a deep well.

"Paul, Paul, wake up. We have a problem!"

My first thought was…. 'just when you thought it couldn't get worse…'

"What is it Alfred." I said with a deep sense of foreboding.

"I have detected an object orbiting Omorphia. It is clearly artificial."

Chapter 2

A succession of confused thoughts crowded my brain. An object orbiting Omorphia? What sort of object? How did it get there? Then of course, the really scary thought. As far as I knew, I was the first Human to come to this place. I realised Alfred was still waiting for a response.

"Are you sure Alfred?" I said lamely.

"Sure of what Paul, whether the object exists or whether it's Artificial?"

"Er...both." I replied.

"Yes to both." Alfred responded.

"Any chance that it could be one of ours?" I asked.

"It is possible Paul, but I do not recognize the object, it looks like a starship but the design is unfamiliar."

Without bothering to dress, I hurried to the Control Room.

"Put it on the big view screen Alfred." The object that appeared on the view screen was at first glance quite innocuous. But Alfred was right, it did not look like any human ship that I had ever seen. The bulbous front end looked like a Hyperspace Drive. It was attached to a long spindle, at the other end of which was a sphere. The resolution was poor, there was little detail present. "Any measure of the size Alfred?" I asked.

"I will display the *Lisa Jane* next to it for comparison." A graphic representation of the *Lisa Jane* popped up next to the Alien ship; it was five times the length of the Alien, and larger in girth and volume. If the Alien was a starship, it was a pretty small one. Literally 'little' green men I wondered?

"This is a turn up." I muttered to myself. "But we have seen no signs of habitation on the planet." I was making a statement, but Alfred took it as a question.

"No signs of large cities. And no radio transmissions of any kind."

"That may imply that they are visitors. Like us," I mused.

I paused for a moment; something was bothering me about the Alien ship, I looked again at the long spindly object. It did not look much of a starship, hardly big enough to transport any appreciable number of individuals.

"Alfred, either the Aliens are very small, or that ship is not a starship," I continued. "It's too small, and there is nowhere to hold reaction mass." The '*Lisa Jane*' was completely surrounded by the massive cylinders, five of them, which held the thousands of gallons of water used by the Nuclear Reaction Drive. "There is also no sign of anything that looks like a

Reaction Drive." I added. "That ship is not capable of moving under its own power."

"You appear to be correct Paul," replied Alfred "But why the Hyperdrive, if it is a Hyperdrive?"

"Yes, that's the question, is it a Hyperdrive?" I examined the ship closely. More detail was now appearing and the massive doughnut with its central spindle at the front of the alien was clearly visible. "Its a Hypedrive all right, can't be anything else," I muttered. Then it came to me! "Alfred , it's obvious. It's a Hyperspace Communications Device - that's why it's so small and there is no Reaction Drive." A few moments passed while Alfred considered my suggestion.

"Your deductions appear to be correct Paul," he responded. "That would also explain its synchronous orbit."

"Absolutely" I replied "But you know what that means?"

"Yes, it would be logical to deduce that the Aliens have established a base on the planet, in line of sight with the satellite."

As Alfred said, the Aliens had no doubt established a base on the planet and left the HCD in orbit as a permanent connection with their home planet. It remained to be seen how extensive their settlement was. Was it a fairly new exploratory base or was it a permanent settlement? Alfred's scans of the planet had not shown widespread habitation. No towns or cities, no major areas lit up at night to show extensive built up areas.

"Alfred, continue scanning the planet, particularly beneath the HCD."

"Should we make any attempt to hide our approach?" questioned Alfred.

I considered for a few moments "Let's just go straight in. No stealth, establish us in orbit next to the HCD and put up a big sign, Earthmen have arrived, lock up your daughters." I chuckled at my attempt at humour. "Their daughters are probably as ugly as sin!" I added.

"That has never stopped you in the past," quipped Alfred and I did a double take.

"Alfred," I laughed "Are you developing a sense of humour?"

"It's no laughing matter!" he retorted. I snorted my amusement.

I returned to my quarters and decided that any further sleep was out of the question and prepared some breakfast. Over coffee I pondered the mind boggling possibility that I was about to make contact with Alien life forms. The thought suddenly occurred to me that if there were Aliens out there, they could give me a lift home! But there was a problem; Procedures dictated that under no circumstances should the Galactic location of the Earth be revealed to any Alien Civilization. The Ship's AI and Computers were programmed to cover up the location of our home star system. Space navigation used Galactic co-ordinates unrelated to Earth. Paranoia walked hand in hand with Procedures back at SES headquarters!

Procedures were also very explicit about Alien contact; the Scout would minimize contact, setting up a meeting with the Aliens at an agreed location and time, and hightailing it back to Earth to report to his superiors. Sadly, this was something I could not do.

After a leisurely breakfast I made my way back to the Control room again. The alien ship was still displayed, with increasing detail.

"How are the scans of the Planet's surface going Alfred?" I asked.

"They are proceeding well," he replied.

"Let me rephrase that, have you detected any signs of life on the planet?" I re-iterated. Sometimes I forget that Alfred is just a Computer.

"There appears to be some constructions on the surface, immediately beneath the alien HCD. Resolution is poor at present, if they exist, the structures are small."

"Constructions!" I exclaimed in shock, "Bloody Hell!" then I collected my thoughts. "It's not a city then?" I asked.

"No, just a cluster of structures, five or six, covering a small area."

"How small?"

"One to two hundred metres square."

"Put them on screen Alfred, and show location on the map." One screen displayed some fuzzy images, a group of pale oblongs arranged in a square, with one large oblong in the middle. On the other screen, the coastline of one of the equatorial continents was displayed, and then zoomed in to one part of the coastline, a deep bay with low mountains behind it. The alien structures were at the neck of the bay, with the mountains immediately behind.

"How high are the mountains?" I asked

"Very low, two thousand metres or less."

Hardly mountains I thought. It sounded a very pretty location. "Probably an alien holiday resort," I muttered to myself.

"It does not look like a holiday resort Paul," retorted Alfred, taking me literally. "It is more likely to be a base for exploring the planet and its biosphere. The vegetation is very rich there and there is no doubt an abundance of wildlife." I thought about this for a few moments because something was bothering me. Then it came to me; "Alfred, do you see any aircraft at the settlement?"

"No aircraft." he replied.

"They may not be home," I suggested. "Out and about exploring no doubt."

"I have adequate resolution to detect an aircraft either in flight or on the planet's surface," replied Alfred.

"Hmmm, that doesn't make sense," I muttered to myself "Keep looking Alfred, maybe it is on the other side of the planet. It's bound to turn up eventually."

The hours passed slowly, and gradually details of the planet and the alien settlement became clearer. But still no aircraft of any shape or size. We were due to make orbit in three hours and were now braking heavily, adjusting speed and direction to slip into a synchronous orbit next to the alien HCD. I passed the time checking out *Epsilon's* flight systems. The shuttle was a beautiful craft, both in an aesthetic and technical sense. She was sleek and streamlined, with swept back delta wings. She was equipped with an immensely powerful fusion reaction drive as well as atmosphere jets which also operated in vertical take off mode, allowing the ship to hover and land without use of a runway. She was also designed for both manual control and automatic control, under Alfred's guidance. I spent a couple of happy hours checking out her systems and then, not having heard from Alfred I wondered back up to the Control room to see what was happening.

The alien structures were now clearly visible; six oblong structures arranged in a square with a single square one in the middle. There was a flat area surrounding the structures, extending down to the beach at one end. The buildings were set up on a raised section of land extending from the beach back to a sheer rugged rocky cliff that was the start of the rocky mountains. It was a protected and secluded spot. But there was no runway, and, inexplicably, no sign of an aircraft of any type. There was also something not quite right with the buildings.

"Alfred, can you zoom in on those buildings" I asked. The buildings expanded to fill the screen and I could not restrain a gasp of surprise. "Shit look at that, Alfred those buildings, look at them!"

"What am I looking for Paul?" inquired Alfred.

"They are falling down man! Look, there are holes in the walls and roof, that one on the left, the big one, its almost completely collapsed."

"They do look in a bad state of repair," responded Alfred.

"Yes, more than that, they must have been abandoned a long time ago to have collapsed like that." I didn't know whether to be happy or disappointed. Clearly the settlement was abandoned, which explained the lack of any aircraft.

"No aliens Alfred, they have all gone," I said wistfully.

"Yes there does seem to be no activity on the site," responded Alfred. "I have seen no movement of any form.".

"But why leave a HCD in orbit about an abandoned planet?" I mused. "Perhaps they intended to return, but never made it?" Alfred recognised that I was thinking out loud, and did not respond. "Perhaps they could still return?" I added. Clearly more questions than answers here!

"Still, those buildings do look as if they have been abandoned a long time," I went on. Was I trying to reassure myself ?

We were now very close to a synchronous orbit and approaching the orbiting Alien 'ship' from above, just a couple of hundred miles away. I could not see the object with the naked eye yet, but Alfred's electronic 'eyes' were much sharper than mine and the detail on the screen was becoming clear and distinct. It had the characteristic shape of a Hyperspace starship. The doughnut of the Hyperspace switch was at the front, at the end of a long pointed 'nose'. This Switch established the field that allowed the ship to exit from our space-time. Unless the Aliens were also very small, it did not seem to be a practicable Starship. The more I saw of it, the more I was certain that it was a HCD.

"No sign of little green men yet Alfred?" I asked superfluously.

"No sign of life of any sort, green or otherwise," he retorted. "Synchronous orbit has been achieved," he announced, "We are just fifty metres from the alien craft."

"Well, if there was anybody around they would have seen us by now," I remarked, "What do you think, shall I carry out an EVA to have a look at it?" I asked.

"It would be safer and more instructive to use the EE Robot," he retorted. I pondered this for a few seconds. Alfred was certainly correct that more information about the alien would be gleaned by using the EE Robot, which was equipped with far more sensors than me, and far more sensitive ones as well! It has visual, electromagnetic and radiation monitors. It also had touch sensors which could be placed in contact with the alien ship to detect audio and heat sources.

"You are right Alfred," I agreed, "The EE Robot has to go, but there is any reason why I should not accompany it?"

"What is to be gained?" asked Alfred. I sensed that he was not going to be very obliging here.

"Well, this is the first alien object ever discovered Alfred. I would like to go across and have a figurative look through its windscreen and kick its tyres."

"I understand," he replied, "If we were able to return to Earth I would advise against an EVA. Safety would be the paramount consideration. But since this is now not possible, you may satisfy your curiosity if you wish." I was not quite sure what to make of his reasoning, was he saying that since I was now as good as dead, then getting myself dead in practice would make no difference? AI logic was sometimes remorselessly indifferent to Human feelings!

"Um thank you, I think!" I replied.

We began the preparations for my EVA after I had again prepared the EE Robot and sent it on its way. I agreed with Alfred's suggestion that we should carry out a thorough examination of the alien object using the EE Robot, before I went anywhere near it. I sat and watched the pictures and data from the EE Robot with interest for a while, and then started to suit up. Spacesuit technology had progressed enormously since the early days of space travel, and my high tech suit was comfortable and light. Throughout the EVA I would continue to be connected to my ship by a safety line, although my suit had a built in mobility unit under Alfred's control. He would jet me across to the alien ship, and only then allow me to manoeuvre myself using the fine controls of the suit.

The excitement of a space walk, particularly when in planetary orbit, is something that never fades. The stunning beauty of the blue green planet beneath, set against the star studded blackness of Space never fails to kick the adrenalin into action. But, as I floated out of the airlock, my eyes were not for the planet, but for the metallic shape of the alien artefact floating in Space beside us. Seeing it close-up, it was indeed small. The main body was barely any bigger than a large bus or lorry, its nose extending about ten metres from the body with its characteristic Hyperspace doughnut. As I came closer, I could make out a number of hatches and protrusions, one that looked large enough to be an airlock. The EE Robot was latched on to the surface of the alien, carrying out audio and heat tests on the surface, as well as a metallic analysis of the surface material.

"Anything going on internally?" I asked Alfred.

"The object is powered up , but there is no movement or signs of operation."

"Bloody Hell!" I exclaimed in surprise. "Powered up, how do you know?"

"Its ambient temperature is well above zero. It is emitting heat. But there is no audio activity from inside, nothing moving." I pondered this rather shocking news for a few seconds. If this was an alien HCD, and it was still powered up, it could not be so old. Its owners may well return to reclaim it, or perhaps just to service it. I was floating next to it now, and reaching out I placed a hand on the alien machine and gave it a pat. I could not feel anything of course, the material of the space suit insulated me from any contact.

"What is its temperature?" I asked.

"Minus one hundred and twenty degrees Celsius," replied Alfred. Just as well the material of the space suit was highly insulating. At that temperature, my skin would be immediately welded by the cold onto the metal.

"Warm and cosy," I muttered, "Nice shirt sleeve weather for nitrogen breathing aliens."

"The internal temperature would be much higher," retorted Alfred, "Between minus fifty and minus ten."

"Mmm, so we can discount the possibility that anything organic is living inside?" I asked.

"Yes, it is almost certain that this is an automated machine which has been left on standby," replied Alfred.

I made a few rotations of the alien object out of curiosity, closely examining its construction and engineering. There seemed no way of gaining entry to the ship, no buttons or control panels that I could see. It was all fruitless, the alien object refused to respond to us, so after half an hour of pointless experimentation I reluctantly made my way back to the *Lisa Jane*.

"Nothing much to be learnt here Alfred," I said, "Tomorrow we'll get down to the planet and have a look at those buildings."

Chapter 3

We decided to hold off going down to the planet until the morning, that is, morning at the landing site. This was in twelve hours time, being late afternoon at this point. This gave us time to finish the shuttle checkout, load up supplies and get some sleep. My thoughts turned to the possibility of meeting hostile Aliens. It was a quixotic thought, because the Epsilon was not armed, but she was equipped with two under wing cartridges of missile, eight in each cartridge. These 'Surveyor' missiles, with programmable charges, were for rock sampling. A small controlled charge would vaporize rocks and allow analysis of the gasses. In addition to the missiles, we were equipped with a couple of hand held missile launchers for the same purpose. A rifle and two small pistols to defend ourselves against over inquisitive predators completed our armaments.

I would also be taking two of the ships robotic staff; I called them Butch and Sundance (after the famous western gunfighters of the same name – for those of you who have not seen the film!). They were not fighting robots, they were built to assist in observation and analysis and had innumerable instruments built in. But they were also able to defend themselves and their human master. In this context they were a formidable pair; Butch *was* butch, broad and massively build, his job was to take samples of the environment and analyse them in situ. His square body contained gas chromatographs and analysers, as well as drills, scrapers and scoops to take samples. He was also armed with a small projectile weapons, bolted to his barrel 'chest' . Sundance looked like an insect and was incredibly agile. He was not armed, relying on speed, agility and outstanding sense organs to avoid trouble. He could intercept and grab any predator before I even moved a muscle. With those two guys next to me I felt as safe as houses.

Sleeping was a problem. I'd given myself a thorough physical workout in the ship's small Gym and treated myself to a couple of brandies after dinner, so eventually I drifted off. I woke early and felt far too jittery to try to sleep more. I showered dressed and loitered over coffee and toast. At last it was time to suit up and go. I would be wearing a light protective suit atmospherically sealed and carrying my own oxygen. We had no idea what sort of nasty bugs and poisons lived in the atmosphere. Butch and Sundance would collect and initially analyse samples of the biosphere, but these could optionally be returned to the *Lisa Jane* for further analysis. It would be days before Alfred gave the go ahead for me to go surfing!

Suited up, I made myself comfortable in the Pilots seat, although I would not be flying the shuttle until we came to touch down. Re-entry was Alfred's bag! I was still on ship's air, the helmet would be worn when I stepped out on the planet's surface. We worked slowly through the launch procedure with me double checking Alfred's countdown. *Epsilon* was released from the main body of *Lisa Jane* and drifted gently out from the rear. Great care needed to be exercised at this point not to come into contact with *Lisa Jane's* huge water cylinders which completely enclosed the shuttle. As we cleared these my screens lit up with a display of the planet beneath us. I realised that in all the excitement I had not actually seen the planet in its full glory. It was beautiful and so Earth like I found myself trying to trace the outlines of the continents. But there was no Africa or Australia here, the continents were quite different. There was the alien HCD again, gleaming metallic against the black backdrop of space, enigmatic and silent.

There was no time for rubbernecking though as Alfred pressed on with the countdown to firing the retros. All checks proceeded smoothly, the whine of the pumps was followed by ignition and the rumble of the reaction motor pressed me gently into my seat. The *Lisa Jane* displayed in one of the screens started to shrink into the distance. She appeared to be accelerating away from the shuttle, but in fact we were slowing down, to begin the drop into the planet's atmosphere.

"See you Alfred, don't get up to no good while I'm away."

"The possibilities are fairly limited," he responded dryly. "The same applies to you also Paul. "

"I'll try to avoid the local night life," I promised.

I started to read off the altimeter and speed to Alfred, just to confirm that our instruments matched. We had enough fuel to slow the shuttle down to a comfortable re-entry speed. There was no need for a spectacular and dangerous high speed entry into the planet's atmosphere. We would slow down to less that mach 10 before entry into the atmosphere and then rotate the shuttle around so that we were pointing forwards. I would then start the atmosphere jets and by the time we were at sixty thousand feet we would be flying like a jet aircraft at mach 5.

I sat back and thought of what may be in store for me. This was my third scouting mission. The other two had been to "dead." systems, that is, neither of them had planets with life. Disappointing, of course, but most all missions would be like that. Planets like Earth and Omorphia were rarities, one in a hundred Star Systems would have such a planet. So I was very lucky to have found one on my third trip. It was unfortunate for me that I would not be able to return and report my discovery. It was also very unfortunate for the human race to lose such a beautiful Earth like planet, but I guess the human race, unlike me, would survive. Sometime in the future another scout would arrive at Omorphia and find *Lisa Jane* and my remains. And the Alien remains, I remembered. Would they wonder if I had met the Aliens I mused? I could become posthumously famous as the first Human to make possibly contact with Aliens. It was a possibility that left me singularly unimpressed!

The time passed and Alfred's warm tones interrupted my musings.

"Hello *Epsilon* please respond."

"Hello yourself Alfred," I responded. Formality seemed superfluous given that only the two of us were here "All systems green."

The ship was still flying backwards and we needed another burn to slow us down to mach 10 before entering the atmosphere. The shuttle was still five thousand miles from the landing site. The second burn proceeded smoothly and I rotated the shuttle so that we were now facing forwards.

"I calculate one minute to atmosphere," Alfred reported but I could already hear the first sighing of air. I gently made some experimental movements as the sighing of air increased and she began to respond. The shuttle had proper windows and the planet started to become a landscape. Soon we were flying and I started to make out details, mountains and rivers scrolled beneath. Lower we went , down below ten thousand feet and our landing site now just fifty miles away. Speed had dropped drastically to below mach 1 and I dropped her nose and throttled back even more. Alfred called the numbers and I gradually re-directed forward power to vertical thrust, We were now flying below the shuttle's stall speed, she was now transforming herself from an airplane to a helicopter. Below I could see the sea on my left and the coastline on the right. Around that bend in the coast was the inlet where the alien buildings were, And there they were, beneath me and to the right. I was now on ninety five percent hover and five percent forward thrust and gently I manoeuvred her over the landing spot, the flat cleared land between the buildings and the sea. Forward thrust to zero, vertical thrust down a notch and she began to fall gently. There was a thump as we touched and I throttled down the engines quickly almost to a stop. We had decided that I would keep them turning over for a few minutes so that, if I was suddenly set upon by bloodthirsty aliens I would be ready for an instant take off .

"*Epsilon* has landed," I declared triumphantly. Shame there was only me and Alfred to hear!

"Most competent piloting Paul," came Alfred's response.

"Thanks old bean, couldn't have done it without you."

"I know," he retorted. From a human that would have been smug, from Alfred, it was just a statement of fact.

The shuttle was facing parallel with the coastline and the buildings were to my right. I looked eagerly out of the window. They were fifty to eighty meters from me and clearly visible. I could see the back of one of the main buildings on one side and then a gap and another of the buildings sideways on. They looked deserted and ramshackle and I confess that my guts rumbled queasily and a cold shiver ran down my spine.

"No action down here Alfred, quiet as the ...um well quiet," I added nervously.

"I see no sign of movement either," came the response. It was comforting to think of Alfred hovering above and keeping a keen eye out for trouble.

"Shut down engines then?"

"Affirmative."

The final shut down of the engines bought a blissful silence. It was a bright sunny day but a couple of little clouds were visibly moving across the sky, so it was windy. The sea was choppy, the waves quite high as they broke against the shore, Not quite surfing size though, I will have to try elsewhere for that. To the front right I could see the march of the coastline as it curved back out to form the bay. Further to the right, the low mountains were covered with trees and vegetation. It was all so Earth like I thought for a moment I had gone in a circle and come home without realizing it, Were those buildings human after all? Alfred's matter of fact tones dispersed my fantasy.

"Prepare to deploy Survey Mechanoids," he intoned. These were of course good old Butch and Sundance and I unwound myself from the Pilot's seat and set about preparing them. Their job was to trundle up to the buildings and have a good old nose around, before I even set foot on the planet.

Butch and Sundance were very advanced robots, their computers were almost at AI level. Because of this, they could perform their own checkout, in conjunction with Alfred. I just activated them and stepped back, well back. I confess that they both made me more than a little nervous. They did not have Alfred's affable character, being more direct and purposeful. There was no room in their programming for adding any sophisticated human interface, since their job was to collect and analyse samples and report to Alfred. They were anyway always under Alfred's command and control, their own volition coming into play only when they were disconnected from Alfred's control. Butch ran on tracks and Sundance had four skinny insect legs and two long insect like arms with multiple wicked looking claws and fingers. Sundance did all of the above ground collecting, feeding samples into Butch's various analysers. Butch was equipped with various drills to take below ground samples. Both were equipped with multiple eyes, cameras , infrared and ultrasound detectors and other gadgets whose names I could barely pronounce and whose function was comprehensible only to bearded monk-like individuals in University labs.

Butch and Sundance pronounced themselves fully functional and I was not going to disagree! I obligingly led them to the airlock and opened the inner door. It would not be necessary to pump out the air. The airlock was also designed to be completely impermeable and on returning both Robots would be sluiced with boiling hot acid water, dried with superheated air and bombarded with ultraviolet radiation. This would hopefully prevent any viruses, bacteria or other nasties entering the ship. Once we had established that the planet was safe, it would not be necessary to go through this procedure. This was why I could not set foot on the planet until Butch and Sundance proved it safe; the cleansing process would kill me just as surely as it would kill any alien life forms!

Alfred and I would be able to view whatever Butch and Sundance were viewing from their multiple sense organs. The airlock external door had opened and the ramp lowered. Butch trundled out first, followed by Sundance. The two trundled up the slight incline towards the buildings. I returned to the flight deck where I was able to view the outputs from the Robots cameras. I put Butch on one screen and Sundance on the other. The Robots veered to the right as they approached the buildings to move through the gap between the two buildings. As they came close the ground levelled off and became smoother, the surface was coated instead of just levelled.

"Alfred, instruct the robots to examine the material from which the road and buildings are constructed."

"Affirmative Paul.".

Butch had paused and started examining the ground closely. A drill was lowered beneath his body and a sample taken from the road surface. At the same time Sundance was examining and taking a sample of the building wall. The robots proceeded around the large building and into the central section between the external quadrangle and the central square building. We could see the quadrangle clearly; the large building was on our left and a smaller one to the right. Both looked in bad shape, riddled with holes and with huge chunks missing.

"A preliminary analysis of the building material indicates a silicate base with some resinous binding agent." he replied.

"In other words" I mused "made from local rock with a binding agent?"

"Yes," replied Alfred.

"How durable is this material?" I asked

"Extremely hard and durable," replied Alfred "This sort of material should last hundreds of years in this sort of climate."

"Is it possible that this site is thousands of years old?" I asked.

"It is possible, but we need to find other artefacts to confirm this."

"Press on then, where to next?"

"A look inside one of the buildings may be instructive."

Butch and Sundance moved towards the larger of the two buildings. I looked out of the shuttle window and I could no longer see the robots. They had turned the corner and were hidden behind the larger building. The wind moaned louder and the shuttle shook slightly. The wind was picking up and there were some dark clouds moving in our direction. Butch and Sundance would not be bothered by a bit of rain. Meanwhile Butch was focusing on the front door of the larger building, which was hanging on its hinges. Clearly the building had never been intended to be airtight, this was just a normal door. While Butch covered him, Sundance moved forward and forced the door open, clearing away some rubble to allow Butch access. Butch then eased himself forward, turning on an incredibly bright searchlight he lit up the doorway and then moved through it, guns at the ready. Inside the building was a mess, rubble everywhere. It was completely open, with a broad table fully thirty feet long down the middle. There was also a bench running down one wall and what appeared to be desks and chairs arranged in clusters along the other wall. Under the rubble could clearly be seen piles of electronics equipment, display screens and gadgets. There was also what clearly looked like a microscope.

"Its a bloody laboratory," I gasped. Then I thought, why should I be surprised? If aliens had come to explore the planet, then of course they would need a lab. Then I realised what was bothering me. I had immediately recognised it as a laboratory, a place of work. The benches and equipment, the tables and chairs looked the same as their human counterparts. Whoever the aliens were , they were not very different from us, in shape and size.

Chapter 4

It took the Robots three hours to fully explore the buildings and
surrounding area. They took copious samples of the flora and fauna,
photographing a number of animals of different sizes, from a sturdy puma
like creature to a large number of small creeping crawling jumping flying
and swimming creatures of all shapes and sizes. Nothing too large or nasty
looking though.

The alien buildings were our first priority of course and the robots spent
the first couple of hours exploring all seven buildings in detail. They were
exactly what we would have expected an Earth exploratory base to be.
There was the large Laboratory, that was the first building we saw,. The
larger building opposite was the dormitory and living accommodation.
There were three storerooms for mechanical, electrical and building
machinery and components. The fourth store contained sealed plastic
packages containing food. This was very exciting because analysis would
provide us an insight into the aliens physiology. It also indicated that the
base had been fairly recently occupied, which was a serious shock. The
final building housed a small nuclear generator to supply electricity to the
camp. All were damaged, pockmarked with what looked like bullet holes,
and with large holes blown out of the walls and roofs. Behind each large
hole in the walls, the interior damage was consistent with a projectile. The
conclusion was unavoidable; the base had been attacked, probably from the
air, with bullets and light shells. There were no bodies.

It was whilst exploring the accommodation block that we found the
photographs. They were the sorts of prints that people would take with
them on a long trip. Pictures of the wife or husband and the kids! Up to
that point, despite the subtle differences in the design and construction of
all the fixtures and fittings and machinery, I was becoming convinced that
the camp was human, so uncannily normal everything was.   The entrance
to the accommodation block led into a hallway which opened up into what
was clearly a common room, with comfortable chairs arranged in facing
groups, small tables scattered about and what seemed to be a bar or food
preparation area in one corner. A corridor led into the private rooms.   The
first one the robots looked into had a bed, a cupboard with clothes still in it
and a small desk with a computer on it. On the wall hung a large print of
what I guessed was home, a rustic country scene which could have been
Earth, with small circular and oval buildings arranged in clusters around
small courtyards, planted with flowers and bushes. It was charming and
pretty, and I thought to myself that we could have a great deal in common

with such people. On the table were two framed pictures and as the only human present I was the only one to gasp with wonder and amazement. It was no wonder that everything around us was so familiar, the creatures looking out at us from the framed prints were humanoid to an uncanny degree. Two arms and legs and one head , which was a good beginning! The faces contained two large eyes, a prominent nose and a wide lipped mouth. No eyebrows, but two curved bony ridges where the eyebrows should be. The ears were small and triangular, set at eye level and well back on the scalp. There was thick wavy hair coating the scalp and around the ears and down the neck. The eyes were large and wide set . Altogether not what I expected aliens to look like!. Other pictures displayed the aliens standing up and in various poses. They were remarkably human looking, the shoulders more narrow but deeper set, the chest deep, the waist narrow but the thighs and legs long thick and powerful looking. There was an air of elegance and supple power about their bodies.

I expressed my amazement to Alfred. 'How is it possible for them to be so human in appearance Alfred? Surely the chances of that are incredible?"

"Science would say that form follows function in biology as well as in design. It may be that intelligence develops best in a humanoid form, that is, an upright body with the brain and senses close together at the apex. Two arms and legs contribute balance and agility. Of course I should add," he went on in his best school masterly tone "The fact that the only two known intelligent species are humanoid, does not prove that all possible intelligent forms are humanoid."

"Sometimes Alfred." I retorted "You sound like the small print on the bottom of an insurance form!"

"I am simply presenting the facts," he said and actually managed to sound miffed.

"I take your point," I agreed, "Two out of two does not make a law. But still, they are amazingly human. Not just that, they are cute. They have no right to be so cute. They should be green and repulsive with half a dozen tentacles!"

After three hours, I was itching to get out of the cramped shuttle. The weather outside was great, sunny and hot, and I could not wait to get out and breathe fresh air. Eventually, after interminable tests of the air, water, plants and animal life, Alfred declared it safe. He would have preferred further tests and a longer incubation period for his experiments, but I argued forcibly that I had very little choice anyway; It was either live on the planet or die when my food ran out!

The outer air lock door opened and the sounds and smells of a real world drifted in. As I stepped off the ladder to the ground I paused for a moment, but no momentous thoughts popped up in my head. The wind ruffled my hair in a friendly fashion and I nodded a greeting.

"Hello to you Planet. Greetings from the people of Earth." "I walked up the slight incline towards the alien base then turned around to examine the shuttle. She looked sleek, sturdy and familiar, and in gleaming condition. I was wearing communications equipment and Butch and Sundance were in attendance, twenty yards away up the incline

The walk up the incline to the buildings was a short one, the gravel crunched beneath my feet and the wind whistled off the sea as I marched up, Butch and Sundance keeping twenty yards ahead and on either side. As I turned the corner, the other buildings came into view. The big central one was the accommodation building, and to my left was the laboratory building. I was fascinated by the accommodation block and headed towards it. Butch went before me and Sundance behind and we stepped from the hot sunshine into the cool shade of the building, through the entrance hall into the common room. I gazed with fascination around me, imagining the aliens relaxing here, seated on the chairs and sofas, chatting eating and drinking, relaxing after a days work. I moved through and explored the individual rooms, marvelling at the pictures and wall prints. I came upon a collapsed portion of the wall and stopped to examine the destruction carefully. That part of the outside wall had disappeared for an area of five feet, and the internal walls and room behind it were rubble. An examination of the rubble revealed traces of blackened deposits. "Alfred, have we taken samples of these deposits?" I asked.

"No Paul, the mechanoids will take some samples now and carry out chemical and biological tests."

I was able to climb over the rubble and continue exploration of the building. It was a part of the building that the robots had not yet examined. Butch was unable to climb over the rubble and I was accompanied by Sundance only. There were more rooms, and at the end of the block, what appeared to be the toilets and bathrooms, so similar to Earth equivalents they were easily recognisable. At the end of the block there was another massive hole in the wall and we were able to climb out of the building into the courtyard. We sent a message to Butch to join us and headed for the Laboratory block. I wanted to examine the machinery there in more detail.

Seeing the inside of the Laboratory in live detail was much more revealing than by remote camera. With the robot's assistance we cleaned up and examined a number of the pieces of lab equipment which were provisionally identified as possibly being an Electron Microscope, a Gas Chromatograph and a soil chemical analyser. The workmanship was of a very high standard, constructed in light composite materials and beautifully finished. There was an artistry about them, with fine engravings and polished edges and surfaces which spoke of more than functionality but of pride in beauty for its own sake. This reinforced the overall impression I had gained from the accommodation block, where the furniture and fixtures and fittings, and decorations spoke of functionality graced by art. These people were highly sophisticated and enjoyed fine things around them. I wondered whether an equivalent Earth environment would have had such fine touches. I rather thought it would have been utilitarian and functional.

There was no doubt that this was some sort of scientific base for exploring the planet. But what had happened to these graceful and civilised aliens. What tragedy had overtaken them. Had they been victims of an interstellar war, a struggle over possession of Omorphia? And if so, where were the victors? Had they destroyed the base and then disappeared without occupying the planet? I puzzled over these and other questions as I rummaged around the desolate buildings, looking for clues to unravel the mystery.

Sometime later, Alfred interrupted my investigations with a report on the black powder stains we had scraped up from the accommodation building.

"They are the residue of an explosive similar to military grade Semtex." he reported, "I can give you the formulation if you wish," he added. I jerked in shock and surprise.

"Explosive you say? Damn!" I muttered to myself in disbelief. "So there was violence here. That explains the destruction. Is this quite an advanced explosive Alfred?

"No Paul," he replied "To the contrary, it is quite basic. In fact, very inferior to the explosives we have. Actually, we no longer use chemical explosives for military purposes. The programmable shaped micro Fusion warheads we have in our missiles are hundreds of times more powerful and can be programmed to deliver the precise and directed force required for each specific operation."

"Hm yes," I muttered puzzled by this anomaly "I can see why the shells did so little damage to the building, comparatively," I added.

"The building material was very hard and highly resistant to blast damage, and, yes, the explosives used were relatively weak," said Alfred. I wondered about this. Maybe the attackers had purposely held back from using more destructive weapons. Perhaps they did not want to take more lives than necessary. Which means that the attack was meant as a warning? Had the residents of the base hightailed it off the planet after the attack, beating a hasty retreat back to their starship and returning home? Or did they have no way of returning home? In which case, they were either all dead, or some of them, those who were not killed by the attack, were still here.

But the fact that we had found no bodies indicates that they had taken their dead back to their home planet. Or had they just buried them? There were too many questions and not enough answers. Frustrated I stomped around , looking into corners and cupboards, looking for clues until tired and dusty I called it a day.

"Alfred, there is a big mystery here" I mused as we headed back to the shuttle for a well earned shower and some food and drink. "Have we searched the surrounding area for any graves?"

"Not specifically Paul," replied Alfred.

"Hmmm, let me re-phrase that Alfred, have we seen anything in the surrounding area that may be a grave, for example, a mound of freshly dug earth, or the earth disturbed anywhere?"

"I have not specifically carried out this type of scan Paul. Would you like me to do so?"

"Yes Alfred. Also look for any signs of fire, the aliens may cremate their dead rather than bury them. Or indeed, anything that looks like an artificial disturbance of the earth or the forest, outside of the base area of course."

"Very well Paul. It will take a few hours. Since it will be dark soon, we shall have to complete the task tomorrow."

"OK Alfred." Then, I had another thought.

"Have we done an analysis of the aliens food packets?"

"Yes Paul. The material is composed of carbohydrates, proteins, fats, vitamins and minerals."

"That sounds like food," I mused "Is it edible, I mean could I eat it?"

"You could Paul, but some of the vitamins and proteins are different from their human equivalents. I believe that they are not poisonous, but it will not be a balanced diet for you and may cause you digestive problems."

"Well, I didn't literally mean could I eat it," I replied "I'm not that desperate yet! I meant, how close is it to human food. But you have answered my question, thank you Alfred." Which reminded me that I was starving so we made speed forthwith through the shuttle airlock, putting up with the de-contamination procedure, and I set about preparing supper.

After a good meal I poured a small scotch from my diminishing stock strolled up to the flight deck to chat with Alfred about the day's findings. Although I could chat with Alfred anywhere, I felt that while I was there, in the ship's control centre surrounded by screens, machines and computers, I was at work. Anywhere else, in the galley and living area, I was relaxing.

"We have a mystery Alfred," I began. "What happened here, where are the aliens and are they likely to return? Have we blundered into someone else's war?"

"Which question would you like to address first Paul?" inquired Alfred .

"The first one I think. Before we speculate, we need to be sure of what we actually know. Let me summarise and see if you agree." I paused for thought. "These buildings here are clearly a base for carrying out a scientific exploration of the planet. It housed around twenty five individuals, going by the accommodation. It has been attacked, from the air and maybe from the ground, and the buildings seriously damaged. Some of its personnel were hurt, maybe killed, we do not know how many. The attack was very recent because the food rations are still in perfect condition and the undisturbed rooms are still relatively free of dust. I would say the attack may have even been a few weeks ago. What do you think Alfred?"

"I agree," he replied "The organic remains that we have been able to recover indicate as you say, a number of weeks."

"It seems incredible coincidence that we should arrive here at this precise time," I mused. I dismissed the idea as being far fetched and continued. "Other facts that we know," I continued. "The damage to the alien base is not so great as to indicate that all the aliens died in the attack. There is also no sign of an alien shuttle on the planet."

"The conclusion would be that those aliens still alive after the attack took the shuttle and fled after the attack," added Alfred.

"Yes," I agreed. "But I wonder why they left the HCD behind?"

"Perhaps they were still under attack and abandoned it," retorted Alfred.

"Seems reasonable," I agreed. "OK, if that's what happened to the aliens and that's where they have gone, so are they likely to return?" I asked "And what have we blundered into?"

"It would seem reasonable, and prudent, to assume they will return."

"Prudent, what do you mean Alfred?" I suddenly felt uneasy.

"There has been an armed conflict here," he responded tersely.

"Yes, but what does that have to do with us?" I asked, feeling somewhat defensive.

"It is impossible to predict how our presence will be interpreted by whichever group of aliens returns first. It is possible that they may recognise our innocence. It is also possible they may not."

"There goes my peaceful retirement!" I groaned. This did rather put a new complexion on the situation; A horde of avenging aliens on my tail did not make for a comfortable retirement! It seemed prudent, as Alfred had expressed it, to assume the worst and do our best to prepare for it. The shuttle windows were now completely black, we were in the tropics and night had fallen in its usual precipitate fashion.

"Alfred, we need to think hard about how we are going to meet the aliens. We do not know which group will return first, the Base aliens or their attackers. Either way, as you say, they may take unkindly to our presence. What are the possibilities?"

"There are not many Paul."

"Not what I wanted to hear Alfred!"

"The main decision is where you and the shuttle should be. The *Lisa Jane* is now redundant, but the shuttle is an important resource. And you because the main objective is to prevent your death."

"You get to the heart of the matter as always Alfred!" I couldn't help but agree. "Say we all take refuge in the *Lisa Jane* and wait for them."

"Not good to put all of our eggs in one basket!" was Alfred's rejoinder. I nodded in agreement

"Right enough! Particularly this little egg here," I said patting my chest. "So that means I stay on the planet. The shuttle? We should hide the shuttle. If the Aliens are hostile it would be a sitting duck on the ground."

"If the Aliens are not hostile, hiding the shuttle may be misinterpreted," retorted Alfred.

"They could not believe that we were responsible for the attack?" I exclaimed, finding the idea shocking. I was surprised that Alfred could be so suspiciously devious.

"Hopefully not. But we should be prepared for all possibilities. If there have been hostilities and we are in the middle, we should be prepared. Keeping the shuttle hidden would be prudent."

"It sounds like you've done this before Alfred."

"Out of interest I have read a large number of what are called 'Detective' novels. Sherlock Holmes for example. I have learned that finding the murder weapon is crucial." I grinned at the thought of Alfred curling up in front of the fire with a good book!

"You will also know that the other most crucial aspect of a murder is motive. We do not have a motive for attacking the alien base."

"I know that, and you know that. But the aliens do not know that," he retorted.

"Yes, and we need to buy enough time to persuade them," I said thoughtfully. "If they see the shuttle and its weapons, we will have a hard time doing so."

"Remove the weapons from the shuttle?" asked Alfred.

"That would be putting us completely at their mercy. I am not too keen on that. We need to hide the shuttle, on the ground camouflaged, but able to take off quickly."

"And yourself?" asked Alfred

"No point trying to hide me. I am banking on them being surprised to find only one individual and wanting to question me instead of putting me to death instantly in a slow and painful fashion. Questioning me would need time for us, well you actually Alfred, to learn their language. This would give us the time to persuade them that we are just innocent bystanders."

"What if the first aliens to return are the attackers?" said Alfred.

"Then they would know we are innocent. And all the more reason to hide the shuttle.'

"But how secure would you feel about handing yourself over to the aggressors? They may not be interested in communication and kill you out of hand as an unwanted irrelevance," insisted Alfred.

"I have been described as a few things," I muttered "But never an unwanted irrelevance!"

"Nothing personal," retorted Alfred impassively.

"You're probably about to say that they would not destroy you because they would want to study the technology," I said accusingly.

"That would be reasonable," he retorted smugly.

"Yes, it's a reasonable world when technology is worth more than human life," I said sarcastically.

"I was describing the logic of the situation," said Alfred in his most reasonable voice. "Not my own ethical system, which of course puts human life above all other material things."

"I know that Alfred, I was just having a moan. But that does raise the question of whether you should remain in the *Lisa Jane*, or move to the shuttle." Physically, Alfred was housed in a large drum equipped with its own power supply and completely detachable. There was a duplicate interface for him in the *Epsilon*, the idea being that if the starship was crippled in some way, he would have an alternative home. We both pondered the possibilities for a few minutes before coming to a conclusion.

"The *Epsilon* I think Alfred, more mobile and easier to defend.?" I suggested.

"I agree Paul," he responded. "I will take the shuttle up tomorrow with Sundance and make the move."

I got up and stretched. "Sounds good Alfred. Well I'm ready for bed , its been a long day. Let's plan the details tomorrow. "

"I can plan the details while you are sleeping Paul."

"Um so you can," I muttered "OK, I want you to find a nice spot for the shuttle, hidden from view from space, but with a clear space for take off. Say, an overhanging cliff facing the sea. Not too far from the alien Base. I will take up residence here at the base, with just Sundance for protection. Leave Butch with the shuttle. I want supplies for a couple of months, including hand weapons, food, water , clothing etcetera, we'll go over the details tomorrow. I would like to repair the accommodation block and live there. Meet them in their back yard, no point in skulking around. What do you think?"

"A good plan Paul. I suggest you leave Butch as well. He will be very useful in clearing rubble and repairing the accommodation building. He can be disarmed if you think that will be less suspicious to the aliens."

"Done deal Alfred, see you in the morning."

Chapter 5

The next day we arose early and prepared the equipment to refuel the shuttle. Lengths of light flexible plastic tubing were unrolled down to the stream and the shuttle's tanks were pumped full. The return to the *Lisa Jane* and the relocation of Alfred went without hitch. The crippled starship would remain in synchronous orbit acting as our comms satellite.

And so it was, two days later, after some heavy work repairing and rebuilding, I decided to spend the first night in the alien accommodation building. The hole in the wall was repaired by Butch in a bit of a makeshift fashion, using local stones cut and shaped to fit. I congratulated him on his handiwork, saying it was charmingly rustic and he thanked me politely. Rubble had been cleared away and the place cleaned up. We had no power for the moment but the robots were working with Alfred to restart the alien generator. This would be a great boon as it would also allow use of the toilet and shower facilities. I decided to sleep in the first room, nearest the common room.

It did feel very spooky and I was having second thoughts about living in the desolate and abandoned building. I expected to turn a corner and bump into one of the aliens at any time, and found myself creeping furtively about, looking carefully around corners and down dark passage ways! The presence of Butch and Sundance clanking about and busily cleaning and tidying like a pair of bizarre chamber maids was very reassuring though

We eventually settled on a secluded spot to hide the shuttle, a little further from the base than what I would have preferred but otherwise perfect, providing total cover from the air and ease of access. We watched from the top of the hill as the shuttle rose on its powerful jets, lifting gently straight up and then accelerating powerfully up and out to sea. She would circle around the headland , heading fifty or so miles down the coast to its hiding place.

As it vanished into the distance I could not help feeling a stab of loneliness and home sickness. I decided that a swim was what was needed to cheer me up. Down on the beach, which was beautiful white sand, an alien tropical paradise, I pulled off my jump suit and headed for the surf. The sea was warm and inviting and bought back to me memories of happy times, holidays with friends and family. The water was delightful but I came out after half an hour feeling even more melancholy. Scout's are picked for their self sufficiency but I would be less than human not to feel lonely and isolated , God knows how many million miles from the nearest other human being.

"Let's get up to our new home and see what there is for dinner." I mused strolling up the beach and wistfully imagining my favourite fragrant meals, washed down with a fine bottle of wine. Sundance was still working on getting the power up and Butch was finishing off fixing the front door. There was no culinary feast to greet my eyes so I settled for some reheated ship's rations. I pulled a chair and table outside to enjoy the cool evening air and wondered how I was going to pass the time. I almost wished the aliens would hurry up and arrive in order to break the monotony. When dusk fell I moved inside and switched on the temporary lights that the robots had rigged up. The power was supplied by a lightweight chemical power supply that had a lifetime of some weeks. After that, it would have to be returned to the ship for regeneration, but hopefully we will have got the alien power system working by then. The robots had rigged up alarms at various distances from the camp, and with Butch outside and Sundance inside the house I felt more than secure. Nevertheless, it took some time for me to drop off to sleep. I dreamt that a ravishing alien women enticed me to her bed and then started operating on me, removing my organs one at a time and examining them carefully. I seemed to have an inexhaustible supply of internal organs and their removal did not cause me any discomfort because she then took me to her home where she introduced me to her family, declaring me to be "one of us"!

The days passed and life was not too unpleasant, although lonely. The robots started up the alien power supply and with light , power , hot and cold running water and cooking facilities I had all the comforts of home. After some experimentation we actually found some of the local flora that was edible and even tasty. They did not have all the vitamins and proteins so I could not live on them, but they supplemented my diet and added freshness and variety. In the long run I would have to grow Earth vegetables to survive but I was not going to bother with that yet. I did manage a little fishing, but could not bring myself to try and eat any of the remarkably ugly creatures I had caught, preferring to throw them back instead.

I explored further a field with Sundance, heading around the headland in both directions .The countryside was very pretty, the low rugged mountains were covered with a variety of trees and shrubs, numerous streams running down to the sea. It was rich with wildlife, birds and small animals in abundance but there was no evidence of anything larger and certainly no evidence of intelligence. This was a beautiful planet, virgin and untouched. It was not hard to imagine what the human race would do to this lovely coastline, but I preferred not to think about that. There was no real need to explore since we had examined and mapped the terrain in detail from orbit. I knew that over the other side of the low mountains stretched a flat plain for over fifty miles to another taller range of mountains. But it was a very pleasant way to pass the time, and I took to staying out the odd night under the stars. It was also good exercise and after a few weeks I was tanned and fitter than I had been for a very long time. Sundance had trapped a few animals and taken samples of protein, which were pronounced as fit for human consumption, although missing some necessary proteins, but Sundance was not programmed to prepare and cook raw meat and I could not face skinning and cleaning animals. This was a bit too "Robinson Crusoe." for me yet. Maybe later I said to myself.

I also spent considerable time examining the alien laboratory instruments and machinery, with a view to gauging their level of technology. The Power generator was a compact fusion device, smaller and lighter than anything we had, but not by much. The Laboratory instruments and other machinery was finely made, with quality materials and solid construction They were also beautifully decorated with designs, carvings and bevelled edges. Again, technology was similar to ours, but much more care had been put into their construction. It indicated a technology not far in advance of ours. But what did the more elaborate and well made construction and decoration mean? Was this a culture which valued beauty and quality instead of throw away functionality as we did? I couldn't help feeling approval if this was the case.

In between my other pursuits I spent considerable time with Alfred reviewing various strategies we could adopt when the aliens arrived. We had no doubt that they would arrive. In particular, our first concern would be to establish a basis for communication. This was obviously an important part of Alfred's programming, and an important part of our job as a scout team. Our masters back on earth had anticipated, indeed, hoped, that first contact would take place via a trained team such as us. Innumerable scenarios had been worked through as part of our basic training, involving everything from psychotic man eating monsters to weird introverted life forms barely able to communicate in ways that were familiar to us. Our aliens seemed reassuringly normal by comparison to these sorts of extremes. Knowing that they were humanoid, with senses similar to ours simplified our planning enormously.

The first and most basic part of communication was to establish an electronic connection and protocol that allowed the exchange of recognisable information. This would be carried out by our cybernetic servants, Alfred and his alien equivalent. They would then have to move on to learning each other's language. Alfred had been programmed to use an artificial language, created specifically for this purpose   Alfred had been working on building the basic routines to establish communications and to explain what had happened to us. The idea was to get these processes done before the aliens arrived on Omorphia. That is, between coming out of Hyperspace and travelling the remaining three million miles to the planet, a period of three to five days. Although I was confident that Alfred was right, I was concerned that, if we encountered unexpected problems, we needed a 'plan 2'!

After some discussion, we came to the conclusion that a second camp was needed, hidden in the woods as far as possible from the alien base. I would equip this was the basic elements of survival, and with Sundance for company, head for the woods at the first sight of the aliens. If Alfred was successful in establishing communications and the aliens were peaceful, I would return to the base camp to meet them. If not, I was to remain hidden. How long I could remain at liberty was anybody's guess, but I had a little more chance than if I remained a sitting duck at base camp.

I set about preparing the basic materials for what I called my 'boy scout' camp; A small tent, a selection of clothing including winter clothes, knives, guns, and survival gear and a food supply.

We set off the next day with Sundance to establish the secondary camp, which was to be ten miles down the coast in the direction of the shuttle and inland over the mountains to a valley with plenty of running water, vegetation and game. The weather was hot and humid and the trek took all day. We set up camp in some sheltered rocks overlooking the valley, and spent the night there before heading back. We left the tent pitched, with all the survival equipment inside. Since we had seen nothing around there bigger than a sheep, we were confident it would be undamaged.

The trip back was easier as we were no longer loaded down with supplies and equipment. I enjoyed the rugged and beautiful scenery as we trudged down the mountain to the sea to head back along the coast to the base camp. I was looking forward to a return to the comforts of the base camp, a good shower, and a comfortable bed. One thing the aliens did know how to build was a comfortable bed! We were now ready, our plans laid and our preparations made. As I gazed down on the sea breaking against some rocks, following Sundance's trail there was a click in my ear and Alfred's fruity tones interrupted my reverie.

"Paul, a starship has dropped out of hyperspace, two and one half million miles from Omorphia."

Chapter 6

My heart jumped and a shiver ran down my spine despite the humid heat of the day. I stopped dead in my tracks. "This is it then?"

"It is what we had expected," replied the imperturbable Alfred.

"Expectation is one thing," I muttered "Realisation is a different smelly kettle of fish!"

"We must be calm and follow the plan," replied Alfred. "They must now have seen the *Lisa Jane*. Shall I proceed with initial contact?"

I realised that I was breathing heavily and my heart was racing. I tried to calm myself. "Yes Alfred, proceed as planned. In the meantime, should I return to base camp or to my forest hidey hole?"

"It is your decision Paul," responded Alfred "We have three to four days before they arrive so there is no urgency."

"True," I muttered "I'll return to base, pick up some more supplies and then decide in a couple of days what to do. Good luck Alfred."

"Luck is not relevant Paul."

"I was wishing you success with the Contact Protocol."

"I understand. Thank you."

"Keep me in touch."

"Of course."

I continued to trudge down the hill following Sundance. The sea was to my right the mountains to my left. I walked but my attention was elsewhere. After a couple of minutes, a hiss of static and then;

"I have sent initial hailing signals on a range of frequencies." The hailing signals were basic binary and mathematical sequences. It took a couple of minutes before the next response.

"The signals are being returned on a range of frequencies," said Alfred. I smiled to myself. At least they were talking to us!

"I will proceed with the program," said Alfred. He was now going to proceed step by step through the program to agree a common communications protocol. Without this we could go no further.

It took hours to set this up, much longer than expected. The aliens appeared to have been taken unawares or their computer/AI was not programmed for first contact. Alfred took the lead, but his leads were often not interpreted or understood. A number of attempts were needed, using different ways of presenting the information before they caught on. But by the time Sundance and I walked into base camp Alfred was reporting that a communications protocol was established. We had a common basis for exchanging pictures, voice, text , graphics and digital.

My first job on getting back to base camp was to power up the satellite screen linking me to Alfred. There was a big digital display with associated storage and retrieval facilities at the alien base and Alfred was displaying the data coming and going to the alien ship. On seeing this I could not help being startled and gasped with surprise. In one corner was the received signal from the aliens and it showed what appeared to be a control room with a number of people at work there. Facing the screen were two aliens. With bated breath I examined them closely. They looked exactly like the individuals whose photographs we had found on the base. These then were the base aliens I thought; unless the attacking aliens were the same race, in which case we were no wiser! But that was not the only problem.

"The aliens are trying to communicate the idea that they require the exchange of visual information. They want to see what we look like."

"I'll show you mine if you show me yours!" I murmured facetiously, but thinking furiously. There was a video cam mounted above the screen, but to enable that would be to show them where I was. Would that matter? I guessed it would be better to keep my location secret, but on the other hand we needed to establish some trust.

"What do you think Alfred? Shall I switch on the video cam here?"

"I see no harm in that Paul," he replied. "I am commencing the language program. In a few hours we should be able to communicate at a simple level and explain to them what we are and what happened to us. I cannot see why they should react with hostility." I nodded.

"I agree Alfred. I am switching on the video cam now. I will take them on a tour of the base, pointing out the damage and showing them what we have repaired." This was what I proceeded to do. When I first switched on the camera and Alfred broadcast the image, there was agitation from the aliens. They jabbered and pointed at the screen, and other faces appeared for a look. One of the aliens started punching buttons and talking into a microphone agitatedly. I nodded in what I hoped was a reassuring manner, although as far as the aliens were concerned I could be insulting them! I removed the camera from its mounting and called over Butch. I fixed the camera into one of his appendages and instructed him to follow me around, keeping me on camera. I then proceeded to give them a guided tour of the site, showing them the repaired and cleaned up accommodation building and the working power systems, the holes in walls and the destruction. Whilst walking around I could not see the image from the alien ship, but Alfred informed me that they were very agitated. After a half hour of doing the 'tour guide' act I decided that would do for now.

"Alfred, I'm closing down the video cam for now. Let me know when we can talk with the aliens."

"It will be a few hours yet Paul. Get some rest," suggested Alfred.

Sometimes he was just like my mother. A shower and some food got me through the next couple of hours after which I decided to check in with Alfred before bed.

"How is progress Alfred?" I asked.

"Very good Paul," he replied. They were very quick to comprehend our Language Compiler and we have been making good progress. We can exchange some basic ideas now."

"Alfred, shall we attempt communication now or wait until you have built up a more sophisticated language capability?"

"If you can wait until tomorrow, it will be much better," he replied.

"Fair enough , I will get some sleep and speak to you in the morning," I responded. I treated myself to a night cap from my receding bottle of Scotch before bed. Sleep was slow in coming. I was excited and hyped up, my head buzzing with ideas. I drifted off eventually because I was physically very tired and slept very heavily.

The morning arrived and I awoke to the sun streaming through the window. I lay still for a few minutes savouring the morning peace before getting myself up and about. I did not want to rush talking to Alfred because I was afraid he would say everything was ready and I could talk to the aliens. I was not ready for that. "Would I ever be?" I asked myself. After ablutions, dressing and breakfast I could put it off no longer.

"Good Morning Alfred, how was your night?"

"Good Morning Paul, my night was very productive. How did you sleep?"

"Better than I expected," I retorted "And ready to rumble."

"Rumble?" he enquired.

"Fighting fit," I explained.

"I hope there will be no fighting," he retorted disapprovingly.

"No fighting," I agreed "There will be sweetness and light across the Galaxy."

"You are relieving the tension again," he observed.

"Right you are!" I agreed, "How did your language lessons go Alfred?"

"I have a substantial vocabulary," he replied "It is interesting that I had to take the lead in building a communications and language interface. It seems that they have not done anything like this before, and were not prepared for it."

"You have to remember Alfred," I said "We are a specialist team with highly sophisticated systems for alien contact. That is our job. They are just a bunch of guys out on a mission to see what happened to their exploration team. The onus is on us."

"That is true Paul," he agreed

"And you have performed most admirable," I said

"It is a vindication of my design and programming," retorted Alfred modestly. "They will be very pleased back at the Space Exploration Service that the design has been so successful."

"Enough of these self congratulations. let's put your interpreter skills to the test."

"Connecting," said Alfred. A blank square appeared on the top of the screen, and a picture of what we were transmitting on the bottom. In addition to the audio video link Alfred also had a number of other microwave digital links to the aliens. One of these alerted the aliens that we wanted to talk and a couple of minutes later the top screen lit up to display the control room we had seen the previous day.

Two individuals were displayed on screen, quite different from each other. About the same height, one was whipcord lean, with a long thin somewhat lugubrious face, the chin long and drooping, the mouth a slit and a gleaming huge bald pate. He wore a dark uniform, very Official and Military in appearance. It looked like military men throughout the Galaxy had a liking for uniforms! The individual next to him was the complete opposite. Although the same height, she wore more casual garb and loose fitting, She had black hair which cascaded down from a high marble forehead. Her face and body were plumper than the man and her eyes a startling violet colour. She was also dressed elaborately in a loose finely embroidered gown. Behind them was clearly the ships control room, with a number of uniformed individuals working at control stations. The room was large and well appointed, without the pipes and cables that crawled all over the walls of a human ship. It looked more like the control room of an ocean liner than a starship.

"Paul, you may talk," Alfred whispered in my ear. I started and cleared my throat.

"Um..my name is Paul Constantine and I am from the planet Earth. For the last day you have been in communication with my partner, the Artificial Intelligence Computer which I refer to as 'Alfred'. We are the crew of the Earth exploration ship that you see in orbit about this planet." There was a pause while the translation process took place, then the aliens turned , looked at each other and the woman spoke.

"My name is Manera Ka Hatekam , Science Director of the Verana exploration Team. Verana is the planet your ship is orbiting . This is Smetronis Ne Pashmateri , the Captain of this ship." She paused for a moment. "Why are you inhabiting our exploration base?"

"Our starship suffered a fault which destroyed its Hyperspace drive. We are unable to return home. Because our physiology was so similar, your base seemed a ready made and comfortable habitation. We were puzzled by the damage to the base. What became of its inhabitants?" I finished with a questioning tone. The Captain now spoke for the first time.

"The base was attacked by an alien craft and the scientific team fled. Some were hurt. Did you witness this barbarous act?"

"No," I replied quickly. "We found it the way it is now, apart from the repairs we have carried out to make it habitable." The Captain spoke again, looking directly and sternly at the camera.

"Since you are on the Planet, I presume you have a shuttle craft. Where is it?"

I did not like the direction the conversation had taken and I had to pause to think of my reply. He detected this and turned to whisper something to the woman. Bugger, I thought. He is suspicious.

"We were concerned that you may think we were responsible for the attack to the base and we took some precautions," I said , not trying to give too much away.

"Like hiding your shuttle craft?" he asked looking agitated.

"Why would we attack your base and then stay here?" I asked, avoiding the question. He looked angry and the woman turned to him, laying a hand on his arm and whispering something under her breath.

"Captain Paul Constantine," she said. "This is an auspicious moment, the first contact of our people and yours. We do not wish to spoil it with suspicion." She glanced quickly at the Captain when she said this. "We have two of the Scientific team who survived the attack and witnessed the aircraft responsible. We also have some recordings of the attacking vehicle, imperfect and out of focus but adequate to prove whether it was your shuttle, if you are prepared to trust us."

"That will be excellent," I said with relief. "Your photographs and witnesses will certainly prove that we are not the attackers. Can you make the photographs available?"

"Yes, we will transmit them later. Now, I am very excited to learn more about your species. Have you discovered other intelligent species in the galaxy or are you alone? Tell me about your history, how long have you been a space faring race?" She was visibly unable to contain her excitement and curiosity. I smiled sympathetically at the screen.

"Yes. I also am very excited. We as a race call ourselves Humans and we have had Interstellar travel for two hundred and fifty of our years. We have explored a few hundred or so star systems and colonised a number of planets other than our own. We have not met any other intelligent life forms." Protocol required that I did not reveal the exact number of planets explored or colonised by Humans.

"Only two hundred years!" she exclaimed in surprise "You are very new to Interstellar travel!"

"Ah," I said cautiously. "And how many years has your race travelled the stars?"

"Many thousands of years," she said equally cautiously and I could not help the twitch of my eyebrows and the widening of my eyes in surprise.

"We call ourselves the 'Hianja' and I am from the planet 'Mesaroyat'. This planet, which we call Verana, was discovered some years ago by an exploration team and this base was established last year to assess the planet's suitability for settlement."

"I see," I replied thoughtfully, still shaken by the thought that the Hianja had travelled the stars for thousands of years. "Are you at war with any other race?" I asked. "Or are you in competition for this planet with anyone who could be responsible for this attack?"

"I have already stated that we have not made contact with any other alien race. And, it would be quite impossible for any Hianja to attack any other, whatever the pretext!" she said emphatically.

"Mm!" I grunted "You seem rather certain that no other Hianja could be responsible?"

The female's head came up in surprise at this and she replied rather haughtily.

"Violence is completely alien to our nature," she explained "There has been no act of violence between Hianja for thousands of years." The military individual was scowling in a very unfriendly fashion.

I was baffled by their reaction. Why should it be so incredible that other Hianja had attacked the base?

"That is remarkable, and very gratifying," I replied. "We on Earth have the same philosophy. But nevertheless," I continued. "Someone or something attacked your base and injured some of your people." I had an afterthought. "Was anybody killed?" I asked. Both aliens inclined their heads.

"No deaths," said Manera-Ka. "But a number of injuries. "

"They made no attempt to shoot down the shuttle or attack the mother ship?" I asked

"That is correct," responded Manera.

"And the damage to the base was minimal," I continued. "We were able to repair the accommodation building and restore power and water. All in all," I concluded. "It's as if the attackers were trying to frighten off your people, without excessive casualties."

"There would be no point in doing that," said Manera, who seemed to be the senior spokesperson. "If they wished to make a claim on the planet there are clear protocols available. If they were Hianja, we would have agreed to share the planet equitably. It is inconceivable for Hianja to attack Hianja for this reason . "

I was becoming frustrated by their insistence that the obvious was impossible. Since we were not responsible for the attack, and no other alien race was in evidence, then clearly it must have been Hianja. The real problem was, what was the motive? However, it seemed a good idea to get away from this sensitive subject for now.

"Shall we leave this mystery until you arrive at , er Verana, and carry out your own investigations?" I suggested. "Perhaps you can tell me a little more about your civilisation?" I asked. "How long have you been a space faring race and how widespread is your civilisation?

"I see no harm in revealing this information," responded Manera courteously with an incline of her head. "The Hianja invented the Hyperspace Drive Twenty thousand of your years ago." I could not prevent a sharp intake of breath.

"Twenty thousand years!" I gasped in amazement. "But..!" I said, struggling to organise my thoughts. "You must have spread throughout the Galaxy by now! Why have we not met before?" I restrained myself from saying "Where have you been all my life?"

"The Galaxy is a big place," said Manera and I caught a glimpse of what could have been a smile on her lips. A dimpled quirking up of the lips, straightened out very quickly. "We have explored a tiny part of it so far, just a few thousand stars. We have settled a few planets..," she inclined her head slightly as if listening "Seventy three on the last count."

"Bloody Hell!" I muttered to myself. I thought of the Human race's Earth plus a measly three planets and how proud we were of our "Empire."! What a joke that's going to be when they find out about these guys!

"Fifty asteroids, two hundred moons and two hundred and fifty six artificial settlements," she said, dead pan. I could almost swear she was enjoying this.

"Um...that is remarkable," I was somewhat overawed by this revelation, and my excitement was tempered by a frisson of fear ! What wonders would you see? They had populated asteroids and moons. Built huge Artificial Worlds no doubt housing hundreds maybe thousands of people. But their military power would also be immense. Alfred's voice in my ear rudely interrupted my thoughts.

"Paul, the aliens have just transmitted to me photographs of the ship which attacked their base. There is no doubt, it is human."

The bottom dropped out of my world, taking my stomach and all my innards with it.

Chapter 7

There was a moment of sheer terror, until I remembered that the aliens had no idea that the attacking ship was human. They had not seen our shuttle yet.

"If you will excuse me now, Alfred tells me that he has received your pictures of the attacking ship," I said hastily, "We will examine it to see if it is familiar to us. This incident is unfortunate but I would like to say what an honour and privilege it is for me to be part of this contact with your great race. I hope this will be the beginning of a long, peaceful and mutually beneficial cooperation," I bowed courteously.

"Thank you Paul Constantine for your fine words. I also hope the same, and look forward to further conversations." She did a little Japanese bow as well. Her tall companion inclined his head stiffly and the picture blacked out.

"Christ!" I gasped. "I wish you had waited until I had finished talking to them before telling me that Alfred! I nearly gave the game away!"

"I thought the quicker you knew that the better," he responded

"It was a bit of a shock. Put the pictures on screen," I said.

"These are the best three pictures," said Alfred and three blurred images flashed up on the screen. I examined them carefully. They were of a dart shaped aircraft, seemingly identical to *Epsilon 3*.

"Have you tried enhancing the images Alfred?" I asked

"Yes Paul, they were quite high resolution, but they were taken from a moving aircraft and not in focus. The first picture is without reconstruction, the second one is with."

"What is reconstruction Alfred?" I asked.

"A process of artificial enhancement of an image," explained Alfred in his best schoolmasters voice. "Without reconstruction the object is just cleaned up, with reconstruction it is rebuilt to look as new. Some degree of extrapolation is necessary to reconstruct the original."

"I see," I said examining the two side by side images. The first was fuzzy, only the major features were clear. The second could have been a shiny new aircraft, straight out of the factory. "Looks like you used a lot of extrapolation ."

"There was enough detail in the original to identify the craft," responded Alfred. "It is a Scout shuttle , Raytheon class."

"Wait a minute Alfred," I protested. "Raytheon class shuttles were used for the first generation of scout ships. We are talking one hundred and fifty years ago now. Before you and I were born. They went out of use one hundred years ago. There have been five generations of shuttle since then."

"Correct Paul, actually Raytheon were the second generation, but your dates are effectively correct."

"Damn!" I muttered "What the hell is going on here? Alfred, how sure are you about the reconstruction?"

"I am ninety percent sure."

"OK," I said "Let's leave aside for the moment the question of how this came to be here. How similar is the Raytheon class to our shuttle? Can we show that the two shuttles are completely different animals?"

"If they accept my reconstruction, yes, they are not the same," said Alfred "If they do not , the unreconstructed image looks very similar to *Epsilon*."

"Well, we are just going to have to sell them the reconstruction," I said emphatically.

It was still early in the day and the aliens would not arrive on Verana/Omorphia until tomorrow afternoon. I was hungry to learn more about them and their civilization, but just talking to them seemed slow and clumsy. I asked Alfred if they would release information to us, historical, archaeological, biological, social and so on, that I could read and browse through and Alfred agreed to ask. I took a break and took a walk. I strolled along the beach, throwing stones at the sea as people have done from time immemorial and cogitating on our situation. My stomach was churning with excitement and there was a little voice at the back of my head which was babbling hysterically and incoherently. I silenced the voice severely, but every now and again it broke through!

I wanted to know as much about the Hianja as I could before confronting them with the *Epsilon*. If they were a peace loving people as they claimed, I had to persuade them that we were the same. The female, Manera, seemed sympathetic, but her companion, the saturnine Smetronis was less so. When I returned from my walk, Alfred informed me that the material we had asked for had been supplied. The aliens were happy to reveal themselves and their civilisation to us, and had asked for similar information from us. This presented us with a problem, in that I was not happy to reveal Man's warlike past to the aliens. Not yet, not until they had at least had the chance to appreciate our better qualities! I asked Alfred to provide factual information about our biology and evolution, about our different Nations and their Cultural, Philosophical and Religious inheritance, and our scientific history, the history of ideas. We agreed to include a sketchy overview of our Science and Technology, since most of it was obvious from what they had already seen. But nothing that would reveal Man's blood thirsty past, the wars and religious conflicts, the Genocide and Ethnic Cleansing which blotted our history. When I considered all that, for the first time in my life I felt ashamed to be Human. Surely I thought, the Hianja must have similar episodes in their past? We, like them, had left these things behind us. The United Nations, re-enforced and given teeth in the 21st Century had ceased to tolerate Tyranny and had acted with sanctions and military force if necessary to enforce Democracy and Human Rights across the Globe. The oppression, inequity and exploitation that had characterised the previous three thousand years of man's recorded history had slowly come to an end.

After some lunch I settled down with excited anticipation to study the Hianja.

"What have they sent us Alfred?"

"Biological, Historical, High Level Scientific and technological. We have a list of all their Planets and settlements and can examine them in overview."

"That's a lot of info!" I said "I would need weeks to get through that lot."

"Would you like me to provide an overview , and you can then choose which items to study further?" offered Alfred.

"That sounds good Alfred," I agreed . "Go for it."

"OK Paul," began Alfred "General info first; The Hianja have an immense History, going back thirty thousand years. They originated on one Planet, funnily enough called 'Hian', which is still inhabited and is in fact the centre of their 'Empire', if they can be said to have an Empire. In fact it is a loose Federation of Planets, self ruling and Independent, but , seemingly, peaceful and peace loving. Our friends originate from the planet 'Mesaroyat' as they said, which is at the edge of the Hianja Federation. It is a planet which has fairly recently been settled, by Hianja standards, some three thousand years ago. It seems that our friends can be almost considered as hardy 'Frontier Folk' by the Hianja in the older worlds. There are two other Hianja worlds within 'spitting' distance (a few days travel in Hyperspace), otherwise the next closest world is twenty days away. The Hianja 'Federation' covers twenty thousand Light years. The Hianja do not use the same Hyperspace Universe that we do, which is why we have not met before. Theirs is half the size of ours, so their travel times are correspondingly shorter. Biological information; The Hianja are Bi-Sexual, like Humans, but their method of reproduction is different."

"Oh?" I interrupted Alfred's flow. "Different? In what way?"

"They have sex organs similar to Humans, but the male is sterile."

I did a double take, then asked the obvious question. "Sterile? How do they conceive...?" I began.

"It is an artificial process," explained Alfred. "Genetic material is taken from the male and implanted using in-vitro fertilisation. The baby grows up in an artificial 'womb'. As to how reproduction occurred prior to this, they have not released that information."

"That's bizarre! The whole process of reproduction is artificial! So these people do not have a sex life as such then?" I asked.

"Surprisingly, they do, not too different to Humans. But the male does not fertilise the female."

"Not too different you say? So there are differences?" I tried not to sound as if I was interested in prurient details.

"Hianja lack a continuous sex drive. Either Evolution, or Genetic accident has dampened down their sexuality to the point where drugs are needed before copulation can take place."

"I am surprised that they provided that level of detail," I mused.

"The information is buried away in some biological detail and they may have overlooked its presence," Alfred replied.

I mulled this over for a few seconds before continuing. "We would have to believe that some time in the past, the male must have been fertile and they would have reproduced naturally. Do you think infertility may have happened slowly, say as a result of pollution?" I asked.

"Possibly," answered Alfred. "We have seen a similar fall in male fertility on Earth over the last few hundred years due to the contamination of the Environment by pseudo organic materials."

"But this fall has stabilized recently?" I stated rather than asked.

"Yes," replied Alfred, "But only as a result of the rigorous cleanup of the environment undertaken in the late 21st Century ."

"This is all very interesting Alfred," I said "but we must move on to wider things for now. How about their Science and Technology?"

"One very interesting and major difference Paul," began Alfred. "They are not substantially in advance of us in most areas, although their technology is more sophisticated in most areas. They do however have one major technology which we do not; They are able to generate an artificial gravity field."

"Artificial gravity? How effective is it? What can they do?" I asked, unable to restrain my excitement.

"They are able to generate a focused and directed Gravity field or gradient. It can be used to counteract a Planet's natural gravity, or to accelerate a ship in a required direction. Their shuttles for example do not use rockets. They do not need to carry thousands of tons of reaction mass to allow planetary landing and take off. "

"Gravity Control. The Holy Grail! What they would pay back on Earth for that!" I mused.

"It would certainly transform Earth's economy," said Alfred, taking me literally.

"Any other technological titbits Alfred?"

"It would also appear to have been more successful in conquering biological ageing. The average individual can live for more than three hundred years before irreversible senility sets in."

"Incredible," I murmured, awestruck. "It's something we have dreamed of and they have made it come true!" Human lifespan had been increased over the last two hundred years to well over one hundred, but no solution had been found to senility. Brain cells died off and were not replaced, so although the body could be kept healthy, the mind gradually died. The world's oldest woman was one hundred and seventy five years old, and the average was one hundred and fifty, so great progress had been made. But to live for hundreds of years, that was incredible. What effect would that have on a person's psychology? In fact, what effect would that have on Society I mused. Earth scholars would go ecstatic with delight studying the Hianja.

But then, I thought, the Hianja have had more than twenty thousand years of civilization. I would have expected these great advances, in fact, been surprised if their technology was no more advanced than ours. Alfred continued with his summary of Hianja technology but there were no more major surprises. They had made advances in automation and construction techniques, allowing them to build huge ships and artificial space stations, inhabited by thousands of people. They had made advances in Bio Technology and Nano Technology, Computers and AI, Fusion Power and compact electrical storage mediums, the list was endless. I was impressed by the scale and magnitude of their achievements. But mostly, I was impressed with the thought that these people had built a superbly advanced civilization, *that had lasted 20000 years*! It was a testament to their sanity and stability.

The hours passed and I suddenly realized that it was dark, and I was tired.

"Alfred, let's call it a day ," I said, stretching and leaning back in my chair. "Tomorrow let's have a meeting to discuss our strategy. We have to prove we are not responsible for the attack on the base. The problem is, we may not be responsible, but a human ship certainly was. How do we get out of that?"

"Paul, that ship has been lost for one hundred and fifty years. We do not know where its been in that time, and we do not know who is flying it now. There is no evidence that it is under Human control."

"All true," I agreed "It is a mystery Alfred!"

Chapter 8

The next morning I took my time in rising and preparing for the day. I wandered down to the beach for a relaxing swim. This was followed by a light breakfast and I was ready for the day. I settled myself in front of the screen and contacted Alfred.

"Progress report Alfred? What's the aliens ETA?"

"Sometime this afternoon Paul," came the reply. "I am able to examine their craft in more detail. It is impressively large, two hundred to three hundred meters in length and fifty in circumference. It had the hyperspace drive doughnut at the front, and another circular protuberance in the middle which I am guessing is the Gravity Control device. There are no Reaction engines of any sort, it looks like all non-Hyperspace travel is under Gravity control. There are five tanks around the rear section which I am guessing hold water for biological use."

"Aha," I said thoughtfully. "Visual available?"

"On screen," replied Alfred and a picture of the alien craft appeared on the display. I examined it carefully but there was no more detail to be seen other than what Alfred had described.

"OK Alfred," I said decisively. "About the shuttle problem. The choice is that we keep quite about the Raytheon class shuttle, claim that it is completely unfamiliar to us, and concentrate on showing that the attacking ship was not the *Epsilon*, leaving us and the Human race in the clear. Alternatively, we can admit that the attacking ship was human, but prove it was not us. This still leaves the human race implicated."

"If you do not wish to reveal the Raytheon it is possible to carry out image enhancement without using the Raytheon specifications," suggested Alfred.

"Do it Alfred."

"Processing," he replied. The shuttle image appeared on the screen and started to shimmer, firming up here and there and finally becoming sharp and focused."

"Display *Epsilon* next to it," I requested. I examined the two images carefully. There were obvious differences between the two, in size and shape. The two craft were clearly not the same.

"There you go Alfred. That is what we will do. Say nothing about the Raytheon class, show them these enhanced images and we are home and dry. Get them on line now and let's do it."

"Connecting," responded Alfred. The control room of the alien ship appeared, showing a number of individuals active in the background. I turned on my Video cam and settled back in my chair. The image from the alien ship blanked out, and was replaced with a different room. In the foreground sat Manera and Smetronis again. Manera was looking excited and eager, Smetronis was looking stern and impassive.

"Hello Paul Constantine," said Manera with an incline of her head. Her hair was combed differently today and she wore what looked like some very expensive jewellery in her hair and around her neck. She and Smetronis were dressed in beautifully embroidered robes, light and silky and cool. I felt tatty and basic in my one piece blue jumpsuit. Next time I'll dress better I thought, before realising that I did not have anything better! The Scout Service had seemingly not considered appearance as an important factor in alien relationships!

"Good Morning," I tried to appear affable and relaxed. "I hope you are both well."

"Thank you, we are well," responded Manera and the Smetronis nodded, his face fixed.

"We have carried out an examination of the images of the attacking aircraft, and Alfred has enhanced and processed the images to improve the clarity. The aircraft is not ours and it is not of a type which is used by Earth. Alfred will transmit to you the enhanced and processed images, and for comparison, a picture of our own shuttle, which is currently on the planet."

I paused to allow Alfred to carry out the transmission. "I have no idea who would have used this aircraft to attack your base, or indeed why they would want to do this," I added. I leant back, smugly pleased with my choice of words. All strictly true I thought!

Smetronis leant forward and looked coldly out of the screen.

"You say this aircraft is not in use by Earth, has it ever been used by Earth, in the past?" My smugness evaporated and I struggled to contain my shock.

"I have no information on past models," I managed to stammer. "But the attack on your base was recent, was it not?"

"Yes," replied Smetronis. "Is it possible that some piratical members of your race have got hold of this old armed aircraft and decided to appropriate a Planet for themselves?"

"You are assuming this is an Earth made craft," I pointed out. "There is no evidence for this. And if it was, we have no idea who was flying it. It could just as easily have been Hianja."

"We have already said that Hianja would never attack Hianja!" exclaimed Smetronis angrily.

"With respect Smetronis, you accuse Humans of carrying out an armed attack, but deny that your own people could be responsible. I believe this is one sided logic."

Smetronis started to say something and then stopped himself. Manera held up a hast hand .

"These accusations without proof serve no purpose," she said, looking accusingly at Smetronis. "It is enough for now to see that the attacking ship was not yours. To prove that I hope you will display live pictures of your shuttle as evidence," she said.

"Of course," I said. "Once you have landed on Omorphia, you will see it."

"Why not before," exclaimed Smetronis.

"Smetronis," I said carefully. "I am one individual, with a disabled starship and one shuttle. You have a large and no doubt armed starship and a number of aircraft, no doubt also armed. I cannot be sure of your intentions, although I believe them to be peaceful," I added hastily. 'It is not unreasonable for me to be cautious."

There was another pause and Manera nodded. Smetronis scowled.

"It could be construed as guilt," he said.

"You will have to wait and see," I replied. We proceeded to spend the next two hours discussing and elaborating on the information we had both provided about our respective civilisations. It was an absorbing two hours and the sparkle in Manera's face and eyes revealed her own excitement and fascination. Smetronis did not seem to be interested and left after fifteen minutes. I was not too distressed by his absence! I grew to respect Manera as our discussion progressed. She was incisive and sharp, and her memory photographic. I quizzed her on this.

"Manera, you have a remarkable memory for detail. Is this natural to all Hianja or are you exceptionally talented?"

"Sadly I am not exceptionally talented, not in this area anyway!" she said with a twinkle in her eyes. "All Hianja are genetically enhanced to improve memory and other cognitive functions."

"To improve intelligence you mean?"

"No, we consider such manipulation as undesirable. Not just cheating, but taking away from the child its uniqueness. We have used genetic manipulation to ensure that no diseases or defects exist, and to enhance memory and language abilities to some extent. These are considered 'neutral' characteristics. They do not change the individual's personality, but rather allow it full expression."

I nodded in approval. "That sounds very mature and sensible. Sometimes Science is like a table loaded with delicious food. It is too easy to eat too much and make ourselves sick!" She inclined her head in a gesture which I had come to recognise as showing agreement.

"I speak from experience," I continued. "The Human race has been guilty of misusing Science and Technology."

"So have the Hianja, in the distant past," she said "But I am pleased to say that for many thousands of years we have been very careful to use technology wisely."

"But, how do you prevent fanatics and extremists from getting their hands on technology and misusing it?" I asked.

"You cannot," she replied. "The only answer is to ensure that there are no extremists or fanatics."

"How is that possible?" I asked. "A race of totally like minded individuals is not possible, not without sacrificing individuality and freedom."

"We have no fanatics or extremists that would use violence to achieve their aims."

I looked at her with disbelief. "Do you use Genetic Engineering to achieve this?" I asked suspiciously.

"Certainly not!" she said emphatically. "Tampering with people's minds in that way would be wrong. No Hianja would use violence against another."

"Never?" I asked in disbelief. "Under no circumstances? It has never happened?" I insisted.

"Of course, during primitive times there was conflict," she seemed to hesitate at this point, before continuing. "But for thousands of years now we have pursued a path of strict non violence in all aspects of our lives and relationships."

I leant back in my chair. "That's remarkable," I murmured, almost to myself.

"Do I understand that it is not the case with Humans?" she asked. I tried to read her expression but failed. "That you do not have inhibitions to the use of violence?"

"Certainly we have inhibitions to the use of violence!" I protested. "A civilised society cannot function otherwise."

"But it was not always so?" she said insistently. I realised that I had already given the game away, and there was no point in lying.

"No," I admitted. "It was not always so. Humans have been prone to violence in the past, at a personal and social level. But we have worked hard to control this, to make it unacceptable." I realised I was almost pleading. There was a few moments quiet, and she looked impassively, and almost, I thought, accusingly, at me.

"But it still exists does it not?" she asked quietly. I felt as if I had been caught by my mother reading a Porno magazine in bed!

"Yes," I said "Unlike you, we have not fully eradicated it. At an individual level humans may still react with anger and violence. There are also extremists and fanatics who resort to violence to achieve their aims. They are a tiny minority, but they do exist," I admitted.

"So what Smetronis said, that a group of Human dissidents could have stolen or found the Scout ship with its armed shuttle and used it to attack our base, that is possible?"

"Yes, I have to admit that it is possible. But I think it very unlikely. They surely cannot believe that they can frighten off an Alien race with one ship? You have returned with a superior force and they would be foolish to confront you. So what was the point of the attack in the first place?" I protested.

She nodded. "It does not seem to make sense."

I shrugged in dismissal. "Manera, this first contact is so important to our two races, that we should not let this bizarre incident affect us. We must trust each other. Do you agree?".

"Yes I agree!" she said, inclining her head.

"I get the impression that Smetronis may no be so agreeable," I said carefully. "Why is he so suspicious, is it his nature?" Her face was impassive as she replied.

"Smetronis is the representative of the Central Security Commission of his planet." She paused for a second and a tight smile quirked her lips. "It is his job to be suspicious!" she finished.

I nodded. "Fair enough. We will try to satisfy him as well." I got the impression that Smetronis may well be listening in to our conversation. Better play it safe and diplomatic I thought.

When translating, Alfred mimicked the voice of the original speaker. When he was himself, he used his own distinctive English Butler's voice. Thus when he translated Manera, I would hear Manera say her thing in her own language, and then magically, Manera's voice would repeat it in English. He would have a great career on the stage as a ventriloquist I thought!

"I am happy to hear that . Now we must make preparations to enter orbit and arrange a landing. We will be in touch. It has been pleasant conversing with you," she nodded, and the screen went blank.

I sat back and replayed the conversation over in my mind. Manera seemed to be sympathetic and positive, and clearly, as a scientist, hugely excited by the scientific possibilities of the situation. But what was this fixation with violence? They seemed to have a pathological hatred for it, which was very laudable of course but I had to wonder how that hatred had come about. My Aliens may look very human, but it was beginning to become apparent that appearances may be deceptive.

Chapter 9

The next day I was still trying to digest the information we had acquired. The previous evening they had arrived in orbit, and Alfred had sent close up images of their starship. Manera had revealed that this was a relatively small vessel, built for scientific missions. The largest passenger ships were ten times bigger, vast ships as big as ocean liners and carrying hundreds of people. But this was the morning when they were due to land on the planet and we were to meet face to face. I was excited and nervous, as well I should be. This was a truly momentous event and I intended to record every second via my trusty robots, if the Hianja did not object! I was up early, before daylight and was ready for them by the time the sun was up. But they did not make contact until the sun was well and truly up and the heat had climbed to a sultry 35 degrees. Alfred's message was short and to the point.

"A shuttle craft has exited from the starship and is on its way down. Expect them in a few minutes."

"Alfred," I protested "They can't arrive from orbit in a few minutes!"

"I believe they can Paul. Remember, they have gravity control. They can kill their orbital velocity in a few minutes, and float down like a feather."

"Very poetic Alfred," I grumbled. "I am ready for them." I wondered out into the bright sunshine

"How should I meet them?" I thought; With a smile and a bow, or straight faced and solemn? This had never been done before and there were no precedents. "Dr Livingstone I presume?" I muttered frowning thoughtfully. Alfred's voice broke my reverie.

"The shuttle should be within sight very soon Paul." I strained my eyes into the bright blue sky, shading them with one hand against the glare. It appeared as a dot, very high up, and expanded very rapidly. They were falling quickly, but as they came closer, they slowed rapidly until they were hovering a couple of hundred feet up. A few final positional adjustments and then the shuttle descended vertically, settling as gently as a feather on the dusty soil. Not a puff of dust was raised.

"Impressive stuff this gravity control!" I muttered. I walked a little further towards the ship, stopping a hundred feet away. It was substantially bigger that the *Epsilon*, built like a bumble bee, dumpy and business like. It was clearly not designed for high speeds within the atmosphere, but with Gravity control they did not need it. The craft could rise vertically up out of the atmosphere and then, once in space, accelerate to any speed, then descend vertically down to its destination. Quiet, efficient and comfortable. But it was clearly not a military craft. I could see no guns or rockets, or other signs of armaments.

A large hatch opened on the side, unfurling to the ground to provide a ramp. I walked slowly forward, my heart thudding, butterflies busy in my innards and my knees shaking. I felt like a schoolboy on his first date. I cleared my throat a few times and made some experimental noises. It would not do for my first words to come out as a croak. A figure appeared in the hatch and then three more followed. They descended quickly and took up positions to either side of the hatch. They appeared to be carrying weapons, short stocky rifles at the ready.

"That's a bit unnecessary!" I muttered in annoyance "Against one unarmed man." A further figure appeared in the hatch and, after pausing a few seconds to look around, made its way down the ramp. I recognised Manera, but there was no sign of Smetronis. I walked forward slowly, and so did she, flanked by her armed escorts. We both stopped about ten feet apart and just looked at each other saying nothing. She was dressed in a sumptuous two piece outfit, comfortable loose beige trousers, ornately embroidered and a baggy sleeved beige and gold blouse, again elaborately embroidered, with a high collar, tight around her slim waist, but full in the arms. A flashing diamond encrusted head band held back her thick black mane. She looked like an exotic eastern princess. I was of course wearing my best silver and blue Exploration Service uniform, shoes polished and gleaming, with my dark blue beret carefully placed in a jaunty angle. I had shaved off my beard, and trimmed my hair, but I still felt like the plumber who had come to clean the drains!

"Alfred, are you with me?" I muttered, Soto voce.

"Yes Paul, I am in contact and able to translate," came the reply. I cleared my throat and stepped forward.

"Hello Manera, it is a great pleasure to meet you," I said, loudly.

She replied in a musical warm contralto, and Alfred's voice whispered the translation in my ear.

"Hello Paul, I am also very pleased to meet you at last," she said. "What does your race normally do on first acquaintance?"

"It varies," I said. "Some races would bow, others would shake hands, and others would embrace. How about the Hianja?"

"We would normally touch shoulders with both hands," she replied.

"That seems very agreeable," I replied. A small perking of the lips indicated that she was smiling and she moved towards me until she was only two feet away. Close up, she was even more impressive. The quality and cut of her clothes, the texture of her skin, the glossy and sumptuous fall of her hair over her pale forehead and the sheer impact of them huge azure eyes was overwhelming. Looking at her in person I could see more clearly the differences between her and the Human physiognomy. What I had taken to be faint eyebrows was actually the 'V' shaped bone structure of her forehead. She was as tall as me but the proportions of her body were different. Her upper body was small in proportion to her lower, and her head looked too big for her body. Her lower half looked stocky and powerful and she moved with an easy grace. Manera's eyes were examining me closely. She came close and raised both arms, placing her hands gently on my shoulders. We were about the same height, so this caused her no strain, but it bought her very close to me. She dropped her arms and I copied the gesture, placing my hands gently on her shoulders. I was aware of the swell of her breasts (there seemed to be two!) and her shoulders were square but narrow. Her face was longer than a human face, the forehead high the eyes huge and set wide apart. The nose was long and Grecian, the cheekbones high and the mouth broad with full lips and a firm lower jaw. By human standards it was not a beautiful face, it looked alien, the proportions not quite right but it was not an ugly face. The lips were full and expressive and the eyes were stunningly beautiful. Her lower body was more amply proportioned than her upper, her legs looked long and powerful..

I released her shoulders and dropped my arms. In unison we both took a step back.

"Paul Constantine," said Manera formally. "On behalf of all Hianja, let me say how excited we are by this first contact. We have waited twenty thousand years to find another intelligent species in the Galaxy, and this is a momentous event. I hope my people and yours will build a great friendship, based on mutual respect and understanding."

I could listen to her musical voice all day I thought. I wonder if all Hianja are so charming I asked myself. Then I remembered the grumpy Smetronis and answered my own question.

"I echo those remarks Manera," I replied. "My race has not waited as long to find another intelligent species, but I am sure the excitement will be intense." She inclined her head in agreement.

"Tell me," I went on, "has news of this been sent to other Hianja worlds?"

"Yes," she replied. "We could not keep this to ourselves. A Hyperspace message capsule was transmitted to our world, and it will arrive in a few days. We can expect a reply soon after that, and I am sure the Governing Council will send other ships and officials. Prepare yourself for many questions!" I grunted my agreement.

"Fortunately my tireless friend Alfred will be able to answer most of them."

"Yes, your AI is a very advanced machine. I am impressed that you have such advanced technology. It has taken us thousands of years to develop our AI's to this level of sophistication," she replied.

"True, but you are more advanced than us in many other areas," I said. "For example, we have no Gravity Control," I pointed out.

"That discovery was made soon after the Hyperspace Switch, some eighteen thousand of your years ago," she replied.

"Only eighteen thousand years ago!!" I laughed. "Human Civilisation only goes back three thousand years. Before that, we were savages living in caves!" She shook her head and looked at me with a peculiar expression.

"Yes, that is amazing to us, that you have made such incredible technological progress in such a short time. But I have to tell you, it is a worry. Smetronis believes that your technological progress has not been matched by equivalent psychological progress. He maintains that you are like children with powerful toys, a very dangerous combination."

"Smetronis is being patronising!" I said with annoyance. "Our species cannot be stereotyped in such a way. We have not had a war for two hundred years, and all races and peoples are committed to peaceful means for resolving conflicts."

"But nevertheless," she said insistently. "The average human is immature and subject to the whims of their emotions, can be easily controlled and swayed by others and has little understanding of their psychological nature. They are easily prone to violence, and indeed, violence is a form of entertainment to them." I was puzzled and shocked by this and gazed at her with surprise. To my knowledge, we had not provided the Hianja with the sort of detailed information on human psychology that would allow them to draw such conclusions.

"What is your factual basis for making that statement?" I asked.

"This is Smetronis' assertion, and he bought certain facts to my attention to substantiate it," she said and again there was an expression on her face I could not fathom.

"What facts?" I asked "Where did he get these facts?"

"I presume these are facts that you have supplied," she replied, and there was a hesitancy about her speaking.

"We have not supplied any facts that would allow such conclusions!" I exclaimed.
"Even if they existed, it would be stupid of us to make them available to you."

"If they existed, you would hide them?" she asked quickly, and I realised that I had blundered. I waved a hand in dismissal.

"His knowledge of human culture and psychology is brief and incomplete, yet that does not stop him from drawing simplistic and insulting conclusions. " I felt my face grow hot with indignation . I was speaking emphatically, and Manera pulled away nervously. Her armed guards shuffled closer, eyeing me carefully.

"I am sorry if we have given offence," she said nervously , and I began to feel that I was losing control of the situation. But damned if I would allow the Human race to be rubbished by some patronising alien I thought. Alfred's voice in my ear bought me up short.

"Paul, please remain calm." *Was the bugger monitoring my physiological state* I asked myself. *I would not be surprised*! I forced myself to be calm.

"Smetronis does not have a right to pre-judge or make decisions about the future of our races. This is out of his hands, now that you have communicated with your home planet. Others must make these decisions and shape the future of our races."

Her face had dropped as I had spoken, and now she responded quietly.

"I apologise for my rudeness," she said softly. "You are correct. We should not jump to conclusions. I was presenting Smetronis's argument, without thinking how this would affect you. It was insensitive of me." She seemed genuinely chastened.

"He should present his own argument," I said "Why did he not come with you.?" I asked.

"He felt that you and I would understand and relate to each other more successfully if he were not here," she said. Her quietly melodious voice made me suddenly feel guilty that I had snapped at her.

"Come, let's move on to other things. Would you like a tour of the Base?" She inclined her head in agreement.

"I would like to involve two of my scientific colleagues in the examination," she said. I nodded my agreement and she spoke a few words into her communicator. Two individuals stepped out of the shuttle and made their way to us. One was clearly female, dressed similarly but not so extravagantly as Manera, and the other was a portly male with almost no hair and a bustling no nonsense manner. They were introduced as Karema and Solon and they both exchanged shoulder 'hugs' with me. Karema was older than Manera but she had the eager expression of the dedicated Scientist. We all headed up the incline towards the base buildings. Manera's guards followed a few paces behind, their eyes moving constantly.

We spent the next hour going around the base while the scientists examined the damage, poked around the instruments and the destroyed power generator. I introduced them to Butch and Sundance, who they treated with great respect and a little nervousness, which surprised me somewhat until Manera remarked that Sundance looked remarkably like a feared predator from ancient history called "the Fangoratse-Da.", a mythical monster destroyed by a legendary hero. A sort of Hianja King George and the Dragon! I described our own legend and this went some way to re-establishing our mood of friendliness and companionship. They were very interested in the packaged rations which remained and the fact that I could eat most of them with no adverse effect caused a great deal of excited technical babbling which Alfred did not bother to translate.

"Our biochemistry must be very similar." remarked Karema, who was the Biologist and Biochemist. I remembered that we had the advantage of them because we had conducted extensive chemical and DNA analysis of their food cache. I explained this to them and offered to share our results, and to make available the human DNA database. The scientists, including Manera responded with enthusiasm. Old Solon was rubbing his hands with glee at this, no doubt already making up the titles of the learned papers that he would write! Manera was caught up in the excitement, her eyes sparkling, but every now and again she would glance at me and quickly look away if I noticed, her eyes downcast. I felt a pang of guilt at being angry with her. It's that suspicious bastard Smetronis I thought. Manera is a scientist and I was sure she was being manipulated by him. He was putting ideas in her head. But why? I asked myself. Why would he be so negative, did he know something we didn't? The idea took hold and I decided to pursue the line of thought later.

My ruminations were interrupted by Alfred.

"Paul, a craft has just been detected taking off . It appears that it has been in hiding all the time and we have not detected it."

"Jesus, Alfred!" I gasped "How far away is it?"

"Fifty or so miles , behind the inland range of mountains. It is the Raytheon class shuttle that carried out the earlier attack!" The aliens were clearly also informed of Alfred's announcement because they were babbling into the communicators in an agitated fashion.

"Is it heading our way?" I asked, knowing the answer before it came.

"Yes," said Alfred.

"Suggestions Alfred," I asked.

"You should leave the base area and find cover," said Alfred.

"I agree," I said. I turned to Manera who was in talking into her communicator.

"Manera, we should head for cover," I said ,"towards the mountains." She shook her head.

"Smetronis says we should head back to the shuttle. You must come with us." Her eyes were huge and fearful and I was sure her voice trembled when she said that.

"No!" I said. "We'll be sitting ducks in the shuttle. In the lee of the mountain they will not be able to attack us. That is the best place to hide." She looked confused, her eyes darting fearfully around while she talked quickly, seemingly arguing with Smetronis.

"Translate please Alfred," I ordered.

"She is arguing with Smetronis, telling him what you propose, but he insists that they return to the shuttle and take you with them, if necessary by force." So that is why she is so agitated I thought. I was getting ready to head out and leave them to it, but Smetronis was one jump ahead. Ignoring Manera, he seemed to have communicated directly with the captain of the guards, because they turned their guns on me immediately. Manera remonstrated with them angrily but the guards were impassive. Their guns remained trained on me unerringly, and their captain, a short stocky individual, almost as broad as he was tall strode over and grabbed my arm, pulling me roughly towards the shuttle. If I resisted, I thought, it would delay things and we would all be caught out in the open. I quickly nodded to Manera, and grabbing her arm I hustled her quickly towards the shuttle. She was still protesting to the captain of the guard, but came with me. The others followed behind, caught on the hop by my speed.

We bundled through the still open hatch of the shuttle into what was clearly an airlock. The hatch closed with agonising slowness, but they did not bother with contamination procedures. The inner door opened and we hurried through. I felt a humming vibration and the floor lurched, steadied and I felt the acceleration push me down and back as the pilot engaged the gravity drive. We were in some sort of open loading area, and we staggered quickly through that into what appeared to be an embarkation/reception area, with seats around the walls and along the centre aisle. There was room for about ten people to sit and the Captain of the guard gestured for us to sit. The acceleration was now quite heavy, and we all hastily took our seats. The ship was going straight up, which was a good strategy. Within the atmosphere I doubted that this ship had the legs of the old Raytheon class shuttle. But once outside, it could use its maximum acceleration.

"Alfred , how are we doing ?" I asked after I had settled into my seat.

"Touch and go Paul," came the laconic reply. "The Raytheon is coming up fast, it's almost on you."

"Paul, what do I do if you do not survive?" asked Alfred. I was startled, but composed myself. Alfred was doing his job, and I needed to do mine. I stopped the facetious quip that was on the tip of my tongue and thought desperately.

"Alfred, get the *Epsilon* off the ground and see if you can stop the Raytheon. If we do not make it, the *Epsilon* is your defence. Keep it in orbit and tell Smetronis to back off. You must survive until other alien ships arrive because I do not trust Smetronis."

"Agreed. Good luck," he replied.

"Thanks, you too," I said.

Manera stood up and staggered across the room to sit next to me. She spoke, her voice low and musical, but no translation came through.

"Alfred, are you still translating?" I asked.

"Yes Paul, but the alien AI has gone off line. I am not receiving anything."

I looked at Manera , tapped the communications device around my neck and shook my head. She nodded and tapped her own communications device dismissively. The shuttle was accelerating heavily now and appeared to be trying some evasive manoeuvres because it lurched down and sideways before surging upwards again. Manera staggered in her chair and almost slid off. I grabbed her arm and pulled her up, then braced my right arm across her lap to press her back onto her seat. She looked startled at my contact, but did not resist. The shuttle continued to lurch one way and then the other. Alfred's voice came through.

"It has fired a missile Paul, brace yourselves."

"Manera, hold tight," I shouted "hold tight!" and mimed my hands gripping the chair. We were in the middle row and there were seats ahead of us, so I took the brace position, head down, legs drawn up. I pushed her down as well, showing her what to do. Her eyes were huge, her mouth open, but she complied. Barely were we in position then a giant hand grabbed the shuttle and shook it like a deer in the jaws of a lion. A horrendous noise crashed around us and suddenly a huge hole appeared on the opposite wall. The shuttle lurched sickeningly and started to drop. I embraced the seat ahead of me as hard as I could, gripping the legs of my chair with my feet, hanging on for dear life as the shuttle veered sideways on, still dropping. Manera was closer to the hole than me and she struggled to fight the suction. I released one hand and straining I held her down. She took a fresh grip on the seat in front and pulled herself back. I heard screams and saw bodies flying out of the hole in the side of the aircraft. Through the hole I could see the sea , and it was not far away. The pilot seemed to have coaxed some power back to the Gravity engine because our fall slowed and stabilised.

"Paul, A second missile has been fired."

"Damn it, Mr Pilot, get this bloody crate down as quick as you can! Hold tight Manera," I shouted grasping her hands and pressing them against the seat. I braced myself with renewed strength. The pilot seemed to have heard my cry because the ship continued down under a modicum of power. The sea seemed very close through the hole. The second missile hit with an even more stupendous bang. It must have destroyed what remained of the Gravity engine because the shuttle fell like a crippled bird. Fortunately for us, the pilot had done the right thing and we did not have far to fall. The ship hit the sea nose first, which cushioned the blow for us. It also meant the sea did not engulf us immediately, the ship settling slowly after its initial impact. But rush in it did and in seconds it was up to our waists. I started to take deep breaths and turned around to instruct Manera. She was collapsed between the seats. There was a massive bruise on her forehead, clearly she had taken a blow when the ship had hit the ocean. I shook her but she did not budge. I looked around the compartment and I seemed to be the only one standing. Bodies had been thrown around like dolls and those who had not been sucked out were unconscious. I saw the unfortunate Solon huddled up against the wall, his neck at an unnatural angle. There was no sign of Karena.

I felt my chest choke up and I struggled to breathe. Desperately I shook Manera but she was not moving. I hoisted her limp body up and dragged her to the hole in the ship. There was just a couple of feet to go and we would be underwater. I had Manera in a lifesaving grip and swam backwards out of the hole, into the hot afternoon sun. I paddled desperately to get away from the sinking shuttle. The hole went underwater as it sank and a few minutes later the ship disappeared under the waves leaving the surface of the ocean covered in debris. I looked around me and to my surprise, the coastline was a couple of hundred yards away. Manera was becoming a dead weight and I doubted my ability to swim to the shore.

"Christ you are a big girl Manera," I groaned taking a fresh grip under her armpits. I looked around to see who else had made it from the ship but the ocean was empty of life. It looked like the pilot and crew had bought it from the second missile. My comms device hissed in my ear.

"Paul, are you alive," came the welcome voice of my AI, and I swear there was a nervous hoarseness about it that I had never heard before.

"Chill your bones old friend," I replied "still alive and kicking...literally!"

"I am delighted to hear that Paul," came the cheerful reply.

"Only because you will now avoid the paperwork associated with my death!" I said.

"There is no paperwork....," he began then stopped himself. "You are being facetious! Can I offer any assistance?" he asked.

"Only if you have a couple of lifebelts handy" I grunted. "Where is that bastard shuttle now Alfred?"

"They are heading away from the planet at maximum acceleration. We have detected a starship four million miles out and it is heading in that direction."

"They are getting away?" I gasped "Is there nothing we can do?"

"The *Epsilon* is in pursuit. I do not believe we will intercept them before they rendezvous with the starship."

"What about the aliens? Are they doing nothing?"

"They have a ship also in pursuit. With its Gravity engine it will overtake the *Epsilon* and has a good chance of making an interception."

"OK Alfred, turn the *Epsilon* back, since there is no prospect of catching the intruder. We need some support down here."

"Right Paul, I have your position. I will bring the shuttle down on the beach. Are you OK to swim ashore?"

"I am OK to swim ashore , but unfortunately the lovely Manera is not and I am having to tow her," I said "And she is a big girl," I added.

"Take your time Paul, do not tire yourself," said Alfred solicitously.

"Hey Alfred." I gasped trying to avoid swallowing the ocean, "This is the first inter-species life saving act. I should get a medal for this."

"Indeed Paul, you are officially a Hero. I will testify to that."

"Thanks Alfred," I puffed. "Come on Manera, wake up girl and give us a hand." As if in response, Manera stirred and raised her head. She suddenly started to struggle and gasp and my already feeble grip on her loosened.

"Take it easy girl, take it easy!" I gasped soothingly. "Paul's got yer. Well I did got yer until you started struggling!" She turned her head around to look at me , her eyes wide. she gasped something in Hianja and I nodded reassuringly, trying to get a firm grip under her armpits.

Her tense body relaxed and she started to kick her legs and paddle with her hands. She clearly was a very poor swimmer and it took us some time to make it to the shore where we both collapsed exhausted on the beach breathing heavily. She looked solemnly at me and then out to sea, where the wreckage and flotsam from the ship was floating. I nodded at her, making airplane motions with one hand, then diving airplane motions, then indicating her and me and hands spread open to show we were the only survivors.

"Karema...Solon.," I said and shook my head. Her hand came up to cover her mouth in a very human gesture of grief. Her face distorted and gasping noises came from behind her hand.

"Hey kid, I'm sorry, I really am. I really liked Karema and Solon. It's a damn shame." I stood up and went over to sit next to her. I considered giving her a comforting cuddle but decided against it. Might frighten her even more, I thought morosely. Her head drooped forward and with her eyes closed she sobbed a little more. I gazed miserably at her, not knowing what to do or say. Inside I was seething. Whoever had done this is going to pay I thought. Murdering all these innocent people, why? What for? It made no sense. Surely it can't be humans I thought. The blood froze in my veins at the thought. The shuttle was one of ours, albeit a hundred years old. Could it be what Smetronis suspected? A gang of dissident Humans had found this old shuttle and decided to acquire themselves a planet by scaring off the aliens? That is a crazy scheme I thought. A group of humans with one ship taking on an alien civilisation? No one could be that stupid, surely?.

A crackle in my ear interrupted me. "Paul, I will be with you in a few moments. Is there a convenient place to land?"

"Yes Alfred, the beach here is OK." In the distance I could now hear the roar of the shuttles engines and it soon appeared, coming in from the sea and landing gracefully on the beach.

"OK Manera?" I asked, forgetting who she was. She seemed to understand my solicitous look and bobbed her head. As we walked down the beach towards the shuttle, my mind was a chaotic mass of conflicting thoughts. The first day of contact between out two species had gone disastrously.

.

Chapter 10

Stepping into the *Epsilon* cramped living quarters was like coming home.

"Where would you like to go Paul?" asked Alfred.

"Home James, and don't spare the horses!"

"And where is home?" asked Alfred patiently.

"Back to Base to pick up Butch and Sundance, then we'll come up to orbit. We should take Manera back to her folks. Have they intercepted the intruder yet?"

"Interception in about 10 minutes," he replied.

I wanted a change of clothes and a hot drink desperately, but I felt I should attend to my guest first. I took out my second best jump suit and some underclothes and presented them to Manera. She looked at me and then the clothes, then took the clothes and held them up. Her face was inscrutable. I showed her to my sleeping quarters , gave her a comforting smile and left her to change. I found another old jumpsuit and some underwear and got changed in the main cabin, then I got some coffee going and broke out some pre-packed rations. I reckoned that if I could eat her food, she could eat mine, but I checked with Alfred first.

"Nothing spicy Paul," he advised. "Stick to water and carbohydrates. No proteins," I found some cookies and placed them on a plate with a glass of water, and sat down to enjoy my coffee.

When she appeared I had a shock. She was tall, but the clothes were a poor fit, baggy around the shoulders and middle and tight around the bottom. But for a moment, she looked so human I had to do a double take. I smiled and indicated the chair next to mine, and pointed to the cookies and the water. She sat and sipped at the water , but declined the biscuits, her face tense. I realised, seeing her sitting in my familiar environment, how much I missed human company. Alfred interrupted my train of thought.

"Smetronis has reported that the intruder has been destroyed."

"What!" I gasped jumping up and banging my legs on the table. Manera looked startled and asked me something in her own tongue. I shook my head, holding my hand up to her. "They have destroyed it? Why? Didn't they try to intercept, to board it or at least to disable it?"

"No, Smetronis said that they would not communicate or stop to be boarded. They had no weapons to disable the craft and had to use a nuclear missile."

"So there is nothing left of the ship?"

"Just an expanding cloud of gas I am afraid."

"Damn, so we will never know who they were. I can't believe they could not disable it. What the hell is Smetronis playing at. It's almost as if he did not want us to know who was piloting the ship...," I stopped thoughtfully.

Manera was looking inquiringly at me and asking me something.

"Alfred, can you let Manera know what is happening. Her communicator is out." I disconnected my communicator and handed it to Manera. There followed a five minute conversation between her and Alfred, during which her face became progressively more strained. She seemed to be struggling hard to control her emotions as she handed the communicator back to me and I reconnected myself.

"What was that all about Alfred?"

"Manera was baffled by Smetronis's behaviour. Apparently, he decided it was not necessary to take precautions against any attack. Manera wanted both shuttles to be used, one remaining airborne to protect the other on the ground. She also could not understand why he forced her and the others back to the shuttle, instead of hiding on the ground. She also informed him that you saved her life and she is now in your debt."

"Either Smetronis is a fool, or he purposely exposed the shuttle and its crew to danger," I mused. "And let's get going Alfred, we are not achieving much here."

The engines fired up, built up in pitch and the ship started to lift. I handed the communicator back to Manera and stood up to go to the control room. I liked to keep an eye on the dials while the ship was in flight. It was unnecessary, but it made me feel useful. Everything was ship shape as expected. Outside it was late afternoon and the shadows were lengthening. The tropical night would fall very quickly, in about an hour I guessed. The trip to the base would only take a few minutes. We needed to top up the ship's water tanks I saw, we were down to less than fifty percent. We had rigged some plumbing and pumps to the small stream that was close to the camp, so I only needed to link up the ship and give it half an hour to fill its tanks.

The cabin door opened and Manera walked in. She indicated the co-pilots chair and I nodded. I remembered that we had a couple of spares communicators on the ship and rummaging through one of the drawers under the pilots seat I found them, and handed one to Manera. Her eyes were like two lamps in the dimness of the control cabin, the green, yellow and red dials reflecting multiple colours in her eyes and on her face. She looked mysterious and exotic and the thought crossed my mind that I'd been away from home too long!

"Alfred, I have given Manera the spare communicator so you can translate simultaneously."

"No problem Paul, I will assign the translation to one of my secondary processors while I am flying the ship. There may be the odd translation error or delay."

"Not too odd I hope," I quipped. "Manera, we can converse directly," I said

"That pleases me Paul," she replied "I have not had an opportunity to thank you for saving my life. I am in your debt."

"Think nothing of it," I said. "You would have done the same for me if you could." She gave a small dip of her head, blinking politely.

"On another subject Manera, I am very concerned about the events today. Smetronis is either incompetent or trying to kill us! Why did he not provide air cover for the shuttle?" I asked.

"He apologised for his error, reluctantly," she added the last word after a seconds delay, as if in irony. "Because he was convinced Humans were responsible for the attack on the base, he was sure there would be no further attacks while you were on the shuttle. That is why he insisted on you boarding the shuttle." I scowled in disbelief.

"So does he now accept that humans were not responsible?" I asked.

"I asked him the same question," she replied. "And he said that it probably only showed how unscrupulous humans were. Your colleagues were prepared to sacrifice you to get to us."

"He really is determined to pin the rap on the Human race!" I grunted with disgust.

"But why should Smetronis falsely accuse Humans of this attack. He can have no personal antipathy to Humans," she asked.

I nodded thoughtfully. "On the face of it you are right," I said. "But clearly he is behaving with a great deal of antipathy!"

"Maybe that is just his nature," replied Manera.

"You have not known Smetronis for long then?" I asked.

"No, I have only known him as Captain on this trip. He is from a different planet from me," she replied.

I was pleased to hear that I had an ally in Manera and smiled at her in appreciation. She returned the smile and at that point I found myself wishing that she was green and had tentacles so that I would not be so distracted from the job at hand! Fortunately Alfred intervened to break the small silence.

"We are approaching the Base and will be landing in two minutes," he said, in his best flight attendants voice.

"Thank you for flying Air SES" I muttered.

The engines throttled up as the shuttle switched from forward flight to hover. I allowed Alfred to manoeuvre the ship and bring it down gently on the landing area beneath the alien base. After power down and check out we disembarked the shuttle into the late afternoon sunshine and trudged up the hill to the Base buildings. I asked Manera whether she wanted to be returned to her ship as soon as possible, or wait until tomorrow.

"Paul, I have not spent any time on the planet's surface yet. Some fresh sea air and a change of environment would be nice. Why do we not wait until tomorrow?" she asked.

"No reason at all!" I said, secretly pleased. "There is lots of accommodation down here!"

Sundance appeared in the doorway of the building and moved towards us. Butch of course had remained on the shuttle. We had arrived at the habitation building and I patted Sundance as we passed him on the way in.

"Sundance, is everything OK?" He turned his insect like head towards me and responded in his deep mellow voice.

"Everything is normal Paul."

"I wished!" I muttered.

We entered the habitation building and I selected a room for Manera. I left her to find some clothes and shower and then prepared some food and drink for us. I showered and changed myself and settled down in the dining area to wait for Manera. Girls will be girls throughout the Galaxy I thought as I waited. But when she arrived I decided that she was worth waiting for. She had found an outfit which combined simplicity and elegance, clinging and caressing in all the right places.

"Your clothing is beautiful," I said, at a bit of a loss for words.

"Thank you. It is adequate," she replied, with a small quirk of the lips to show her appreciation for my complement.

"More than adequate," I protested. "On Earth, it would be a very expensive dress. Certainly not to be worn while exploring alien planets."

"Is that so?" She looked quizzically at me, then examined her dress as if to re-assess it.

"It is simple and practical," she said. "The material is cool and hard wearing and requires no maintenance." Clearly Hianja standards were different from Earth ones I decided. Would a commentator describe the latest Paris Haute Couture collection as '...cool and hard wearing and requiring little maintenance...'!

As the evening progressed and our conversation roamed over many themes, It came to me that I was having a more interesting and enjoyable conversation with an alien female than I had ever had with a human one. What does that say about me I asked myself? Manera was insightful and direct in her thinking, but there was a gentle innocence about her. She asked me at one point, late in the evening, if I was a 'typical' human male.

"No, not typical in some ways, but very typical in others," I replied ambiguously.

"In what ways?" she asked with a little shake of her head.

"Well, I am a ship's Captain of the Space Exploration Service," I replied "So I guess that makes me somewhat special since only one individual in ten thousand who apply are accepted. My training took four years and I am an expert in a number of technologies. I am also trained in Philosophy and Politics, advanced Mathematics and Space Navigation. I am in the top five percent of the human race in IQ and in perfect physical condition."

"Very impressive," she said and I detected a twinkle of amusement in her eyes.

"But otherwise I am a normal man. I like sports, particularly Football and all electronic gadgets. I am congenitally lazy, I drink too much, swear too much, think about sex all the time and find it difficult to express my emotions, particularly to females." Manera gazed at me, her eyes huge, as I listed my male eccentricities.

"Are you are joking with me?" she asked.

"Actually no," I said. "Although I exaggerate, it is not far from the truth." She looked blankly at me.

"Do you really think about sex all the time?" she asked, and before I could answer, continued. "How are you able to do anything else? Are you thinking about sex now?"

"I wasn't, but I am now!" I admitted.

"It must be very difficult for your females," she went on thoughtfully. "If men are constantly making sexual advances."

"Um, it's not quite that bad Manera. Us men can control ourselves, and when we don't..," I paused and gave what I thought was a meaningful look. "Women are quite good at controlling us...when they want to," I added.

"Well!" she murmured, taking a sip of her drink thoughtfully. We had found a selection of Hianja alcoholic drinks, and with the last remnants of my Scotch we had sampled a good selection. I felt a little under the influence but Manera looked completely unaffected. I guessed that her enhanced metabolism had no trouble coping with the alcohol.

"I can see that this area will be very interesting for Hianja scientists to study," she went on. "We do not have the same sexual dynamics as part of our relationships," she added.

"Um, er, how , er , does it work with you guys?" I asked and realising I was mumbling in a somewhat shifty fashion, rephrased my question. "I mean, I know you have sexual relationships, but in what way is it different?"

"We do not have permanent sexual desire, as apparently Human males do," she said, her face impassive. "Sexual activity requires the use of a particular stimulant."

"That seems very artificial and clinical to me," I observed. "So , if you like someone and want to have a sexual experience with them, you must take a pill?" Something about my tone must have indicated disapproval.

"Yes," she replied "What is wrong with that? At least it is my mind making the decision, not my body." I had to admit, she had a point. A very good point, since most personal sexual problems seemed to be caused by lack of control over our bodily desires. In fact, not just sexual problems, but all manner of problems are caused by lack of control over our desires and emotions. Were the Hianja, by a lucky accident of biology immune to this major human failing? Is this why they had survived and developed an advanced space faring civilisation for twenty thousand years, without wars and conflict?

But something was bothering me. Clearly, the artificial control over their sexual desires must be a recent thing, post technology. In their natural state, the Hiianja could hardly take a pill in order to get 'the urge'! So had something happened to them to require this 'fix'? Or had they done it to themselves? We somehow skirted around the issue and then I forgot to ask.

We continued talking late into the night, and it was only when I realised that my consumption of Hianja alcohol was going to my head, that I decided it was time for bed.

"Manera, we have been drinking all night but you are unaffected. What is your secret?" I asked her enviously.

"Alcohol makes us happy and alert," she replied. "Is that not the case with you?"

"Yes," I replied "But unfortunately it has side affects. It reduces our physical co-ordination and spatial abilities," I added "And too much of it makes us sleepy."

"That is unfortunate," she said sympathetically.

"Yes," I replied "Because I have enjoyed this evening so much, I could talk to you all night, but I am afraid my body is saying 'sleep'"

"Paul, I have also enjoyed our conversation tonight. It has been very interesting and rewarding, but I agree it is time for bed." We both stood up and for a few awkward seconds we both hovered uncertainly. Manera took the initiative and walked over to give me a Hianja shoulder 'hug', which I reciprocated.

"Goodnight Manera," I said.

"Thank you," she said formally "And I wish you also a good night."

Despite my tiredness it took a little while to sleep. I replayed our conversation over in my mind, enjoying the rapport we had acquired. I was struck by her openness. She was an odd combination of sophistication and innocence. An adult who had grown up in the most advanced civilisation, and had not suffered abuse or disappointment, despair or damage in any way. Whole and wholesome, she was quite the most exquisite creature I had ever met.

As I drifted on the edges of sleep, a more sombre mood began to trouble me. Was the Human race fit to consort with the likes of these? If Manera was any example to go by, the Hianja and the Human races were as far apart as Humans and Neanderthals. Humans were invariably damaged and incomplete, both as individuals and as Nations. We had come a long way since the twenty-first century, but we still had a long way to go.

Chapter 11

The next morning I was up early, and, fortunately, my sombre mood from the night before had dissipated in the morning light . As usual, the weather was delightful, before the heat of the day took hold, and the cool breeze from the ocean was invigorating. I went for a 15 minute run along the beach and then showered and dressed. I was having my morning coffee when Manera put in an appearance, wearing a fetching blue and pink sleeping gown, her hair tied back. She sniffed the air questioningly.

"Good morning," I said "Would you care for some Earth coffee?" Our SES issue instant coffee was a passable imitation of the real thing.

"It smells wonderful Paul, I will try some," she smiled. As I prepared her a cup, I broached the subject of the future.

"How long do you think it will take for your official 'Task Force' to arrive?" I asked. She pulled up a chair and sat at the table before replying.

"We sent the Hyperspace message two days ago, as soon as we knew of your presence," she said. God I thought, has it been only two days? It feels like a lifetime!

"It will only take the message a few hours to arrive, allow some days for them to prepare, and then three days to make the trip in Hyperspace," she said. It had taken me two months make the trip from Earth, so Manera's home planet was significantly closer to Omorphia than Earth. She took a sip of her coffee and considered it for a few seconds.

"Mmm very good!" she exclaimed "It is similar to a drink we have on Mesaroyat, but more potent."

I smiled in appreciation, thinking that I might go into business as an importer of coffee to Hianja worlds when this is over, but before I could continue we were interrupted by Alfred.

"Paul, I have just received a bizarre communication from Smetronis. He demands that we return Manera unharmed without conditions, otherwise he will land and take her by force. We have one hour to reply."

"What?" I exclaimed. Manera looked confused. "What on Earth is he raving about?" I gasped, somewhat inaccurately.

"Alfred, inform him that Manera is not a prisoner here and we were planning to return her to the ship this morning," I said quickly.

"Yes Paul," said Alfred. Manera and I gazed at each other in consternation. She spoke to me in her language but it seems that Alfred had ceased his translating duties for the moment. I shook my head at her and tapped my comms device and she nodded in understanding. After an interminable couple of minutes, Alfred responded.

"It appears he is blocking communications," replied Alfred. "He is not replying to my message and simply repeating his demands."

"Damn, what is this lunatic up to?" I exclaimed in anger. Manera now looked frightened and angry. "Alfred, what do you think?"

"I cannot think of a reason why he should think that we are holding Manera hostage," replied Alfred.

"Is it some sort of communication problem? " I asked. "If they are not receiving our communications..," I tailed off in confusion.

"I am attempting to communicate using a number of radio and microwave bands. They cannot fail to receive them all," he replied.

"Manera, have you talked with Smetronis this morning?" I asked, and realised before she answered that Alfred would have informed me if she had.

"No," she replied "Alfred, please connect me so that I can talk," she requested.

"Proceed," replied Alfred immediately.

Manera proceeded to harangue Smetronis, demanding that he stop broadcasting this 'nonsense' as she called it and talk to her. Alfred translated her demands and there was no doubt of her anger at this turn of events. We waited for some sort of response but none was forthcoming. Alfred informed us that the same message was being broadcast, and the time was counting down.

"Well!" I mused after some minutes of this and some frantic thinking. "This is some sort of ploy Alfred!" I exclaimed

"He appears to be fabricating a situation," agreed Alfred.

"To what purpose?" I asked, then answered my own question. "To give him an excuse to attack us?"

"It would seem so," agreed Alfred.

"Why?" gasped Manera "In what way are we a problem for him?"

"I am guessing that our survival from the shuttle attack is causing him a problem," I said. "And he is fabricating a situation to finish us off! He knows that you do not agree with his conviction that human's are to blame for the attacks, and he knows that you disapprove of his handling of the situation. With you and me out of the way, he can concoct any story he likes and no one will disagree. Is there anyone else on the ship that may go against him or his story?" I asked Manera. She considered for a few moments and answered.

"No, most of the remaining crew are junior crewmen who are not aware of what is happening. The two senior technicians who control communications and flight operations are from Smetronis's planet Vasmeranta," she said, and then added thoughtfully "As is the Security Chief and two of the security personnel."

"What about the ship's AI?" I asked. "Surely it is monitoring operations on a continuous basis and recording all communications?"

"I am unable to contact the ship's AI," said Alfred.

"Can they disconnect the AI Manera?" I asked.

"Yes, there is a facility to disconnect the AI if it develops a fault," she replied. "Secondary Computers can control the Hyperspace Engine to get the ship home," she added.

"So there we have it!" I exclaimed in disgust. "Mr Smetronis shows his hand at last. Can't say I am surprised!". Manera looked shocked, as if unable to comprehend Smetronis's duplicity.

"What now Alfred?" I asked.

"I presume you agree that surrender is not an option?" he responded.

"Certainly not!" I said emphatically "I don't think he will accept a surrender. He'll stage an attack and kill us all, including Manera.".

Marena looked confused and distressed. "How can he do such a thing," she gasped "It must be a misunderstanding. Alfred, are you sure you cannot get through?"

"I am not receiving a response on any one of one hundred and seventy three channels" responded Alfred. "Is it possible that they could all be down?" he asked. Manera shook her head in confusion.

"I think," I began, looking at Manera, "It would be prudent to get the hell out of here. If it is a misunderstanding, Alfred can clear it up. In the meantime, we get into the shuttle and into orbit where we can defend ourselves. I do not think they will attack the shuttle and risk being destroyed themselves."

"There is one problem with that Paul," began Alfred. "The shuttle has a finite fuel capacity. They can harass us until we run out of fuel."

"Yes they could couldn't they," I muttered.

"I will stay here and confront him," said Manera, her chin held high and a determined look on her pale features. "Surely they cannot murder me in front of the junior crew members?" she asked.

"They may leave the junior crew members behind," I pointed out. "Is the Security Chief a qualified Pilot?" I asked.

"No," she replied. "But anyone can fly the shuttle on simple manoeuvres. Just tell the Computers what to do."

"We can't take the chance Manera," I said. "You and I must get away from here into hiding until we know more clearly what Smetronis is up to. The shuttle is the problem, it either fights or runs, and it can only run for so long!" I exclaimed.

"Which means we have to fight," confirmed Alfred.

"Which is exactly what we do not want to do!" I swore vehemently. "Smetronis has created a nice little trap for us." I thought for a few moments before coming to a conclusion.

"We must leave here and hide, as you said. Alfred must fly the shuttle and try to avoid capture. If this is not possible and he is threatened with destruction, he must disable the remaining Hianja ship and wait until the Hianja investigation Ships arrive." I said. "What do you think Alfred?"

"I am programmed with advanced Military Tactics Paul," he said, as if he was serving afternoon Tea on the Lawn. "The *Epsilon* is armed only with the surveyor missiles but is faster and more manoeuvrable than the Hianja shuttle in atmosphere. I believe I can destroy the ship easily, but disabling it without loss of life will be more difficult."

"Do your best," I said "But make sure you are not the first to fire."

"Thank you for making it easier for me," he said and despite the tension I could not help grinning. Sarcasm from Alfred!

"Good Luck Alfred, we are relying on you," I said "Now, let's get out of here. Manera, put on some practical clothing and walking shoes, we have some trekking to do," I said "Sundance!" I called "You are coming with us, load up with some supplies, water and food for me and Manera, the missile launcher, guns and ammunition, power cells as many as you can carry." The Robot scuttled in and fixed me with his large dark orbs as I spoke.

"Shall I take the heavy duty carrier Paul?" he intoned in his deep voice.

"Yes Sundance, we need as much equipment as you can carry, but we have to move quickly."

The next fifteen minutes were a frantic bustle of activity as Manera and I dressed hurriedly, grabbing up spare clothes and shoes and anything we considered useful and ramming them into a couple of Hianja rucksacks which Manera had discovered from somewhere.

"Alfred, we are heading for the camp in the hills that we established. I do not think they will find us there," I said, when we were ready to move out.

"They may think that you and Manera are on the shuttle Paul," said Alfred.

"Yes that's true. " I said "In that case we will have a quiet little camping holiday. Maybe get in some fishing and work on my suntan!" I grinned. Manera was looking at me with a perplexed expression on her face "We'll send you a postcard," I added, and then a thought crossed my mind.

"Alfred, how are we to communicate without giving our position away."

"We will not be able to communicate until the situation is resolved," said Alfred. I thought about this for a while and did not like it. Manera suddenly broke in with an exclamation.

"Alfred, without you, Paul and I will not be able to talk to each other," she said.

"Damn, I forgot that!" I swore.

"One second while I consider," said Alfred. We waited with baited breath.

"I can download the language compiler to a secondary processor connected to Sundance. He will be able to translate for you, somewhat slowly but adequately I am sure. I will instruct Sundance to come to the ship to carry out the upgrade to his processing facilities."

"Excellent work Alfred!" I agreed, and Manera looked relieved.

"OK, we will head off and Sundance can follow up. I know the route for the first few miles. You had better get off the ground as soon as you can Alfred," I said worriedly.

"There is no activity from the Hianja ship at present and we still have thirty minutes until the end of the ultimatum. That should be enough," he said.

Manera and I headed off through the rectangle of buildings and down the incline towards the shuttle, Sundance dashing ahead. I waved goodbye to the shuttle as we passed it, heading down the beach while Sundance entered the airlock. I wondered whether we would see the shuttle again, or hear from Alfred. I know he is just a Computer I thought, but I am going to miss him.

"Alfred, I guess this is Au Revoir for now," I said "Once we get away from the Base we should cease communications?" I asked.

"Yes Paul, in fact I have been decrypting our communications for the last twenty minutes just in case they are able to pick up transmissions. From now on, switch off your communicators. Au Revoir Paul, Manera and Good Luck!" he added. "If I am able to disable their shuttle then I will be able to resume communications."

"Good Luck Alfred," said Manera. She said it in her own language and Alfred translated.

"Communications off line now," intoned Alfred and I switched off my communicator. I showed Manera how to switch hers off and we trudged down the beach away from the gleaming metallic shuttle with many backward glances. It was very odd and disconcerting to be disconnected from Alfred. I took his presence for granted, like a second personality he was always with me, discussing and answering my questions, keeping me in touch with everything that was going on around me. He was my encyclopaedia, my mine of information, my confidant and companion and suddenly the world had shrunk alarmingly. As if sensing my melancholy, Manera walked closer to me, looking questioningly into my eyes. I nodded and tried to smile comfortingly. Hoisting my backpack higher up my back I strode out with false confidence. She gave a tense little smile and straightened her back, lengthening her stride to keep up

We struggled on, along the beach front for a mile or so and then headed in to the low foothills at the point I remembered. Half an hour into our trek and we heard the loud roar of jet engines. We stopped and craned our necks, catching a glimpse of the metallic triangle of the shuttle, accelerating heavily straight up, intense hot flames gushing from its engines. Alfred was giving it the gun I thought.

Sundance caught up with us after an hour, despite being heavily loaded down with supplies and equipment, and started leading the way. The terrain was broken and hilly, but easily negotiable although our route was torturous. Sundance led the way with Manera in the middle and me behind. Sundance had informed us that just before he had left the shuttle, Alfred had detected the alien flyer exiting the mother ship and heading down to the planet. Sundance had hastily left and Alfred had taken off at maximum acceleration. The conflict was on and there was no way we could know the result until we were contacted by Alfred. Sundance was equipped with an automatic carrier wave detector in the designated wave band which Alfred would switch on to alert us. We trekked on and the going started to get heavier, with some climbing over small hills and rocky inclines.

Behind Manera and climbing over a rocky wooded hill, and despite the dangerous predicament we were in, I could not help noticing that she had an exceptionally curvaceous rear end, which strained quite nicely against the silky material of her Hianja trousers. I was busy marvelling at how Nature could have created two species with such similar physiques, when there was a loud thud and I felt a painful blow to my head . The world suddenly turned on its side and then disappeared and then I was looking at the sky and something warm was running down my head and into my eyes. I groaned with a mixture of pain and embarrassment. Manera's concerned face appeared silhouetted against the sky, followed by the insectoid features of our trusty robot.

"You have hit your forehead against a rocky outcrop Paul, Stay still and I will clean and bandage the wound," I was not in any condition to move at that point and lay still while Sundance attended to my self inflicted wound. "Stupid Bastard Paul. Trust you to be distracted by a female bottom," I berated myself. Manera looked concerned and squeezed my hand in support, murmuring words of sympathy in her own language, which only made me feel worse, given the cause of my distraction!

It took some minutes for me to recover, and Manera wanted me to rest longer but I insisted we move on. After he had carefully checked me for concussion, Sundance agreed and we continued our journey. Manera insisted that I stayed in the middle this time, which was doubly embarrassing, but I did not protest too much, thinking it would aid my concentration! Looking at Sundance's metallic body was not half as distracting! The journey proceeded without further incident and Manera proved to be very fit and strong . She did not flag or slow as Sundance maintained a very fast pace. In fact, I was probably in worse shape than her when we arrived at our camp site late in the evening.

The sun was low in the sky and it would be dark soon so we had made it just in time. The Tent looked undisturbed on its rocky ledge, protected as it was from the weather by the overhanging rock face. We helped Sundance to unload and stowed away food and supplies, including the hand gun and the rifle with some ammunition. When I offered the hand gun to Manera she shrank back in horror making little pushing away gestures with her hands and protesting in her own language. I withdrew the gun with a nod of understanding, but I made sure that it was loaded with the safety catch on and handily placed. After all, we still did not know much about the wild life of this planet and I could not believe it was completely devoid of large hungry carnivores.

After our bags and chattels were ship shape and tidy we settled down for a boring meal of ship's rations, Manera from her own supplies and me from mine. It was difficult for us to get used to not being able to talk after the ease with which we had communicated so far. The problem was that although Sundance could translate, we could not use the communicators for fear of the microwave transmissions being detected. It transpired though that there was an alternative. This was the low frequency RF "walky-talkies" which were a backup in case the microwave links were out of action, or, as was the case with us, the relay station, namely our shuttle, was out of line of sight. These were compact clip on boxes with an earphone connection. Sundance was confident that being short range they would not be detected and so Manera and I equipped ourselves with one each. Sundance was now able to act as intermediary and translate for us. Initial attempts were amusing as Sundance had to be instructed to modulate 'his' voice according to who he was translating. His attempts to emulate Manera's voice resulted in a peculiar accent, a cross between Japanese and French! Quite exotic and appropriate I thought!

Sundance took station outside the tent and Manera and I settled down with our food, such as it was. We were ravenous though and ate heartily despite the poor quality of the food. After eating we prepared for bed, which presented a problem, namely, should we change or remain in our day clothes? It had been a long hard trek and I was hot, dusty and sweaty and a good wash and change of clothes would have been more comfortable. I suggested to Manera that we take ourselves down to the stream, which was a hundred yards from our camp, where we could wash and change, under Sundance's protection. Despite being now pitch black outside, Manera also agreed and we put it to Sundance. He agreed but suggested that we should use as little light as possible to avoid detection.

We followed Sundance carefully down to the stream, and I went a few yards down stream and Manera a few yards up stream to carry out our ablutions. Despite the darkness, there was a moon and I could clearly see Manera's pale shape as she splashed in the water and I tried very hard to divert my thoughts to neutral subjects to quieten the disquieting thoughts which kept intruding. The mountain stream was freezing and I did not spend too long there. Manera had come out earlier, and we both returned to the Tent and crawled into our sleeping bags, exhausted and ready for sleep. But as we crawled into our sleeping bags, my thoughts would not quieten and I did not turn off the light for the moment.

"Manera," I asked quietly "Are you OK?" It was a pretty inane question, but I just wanted to hear her voice. She spoke in her own language and the translation came back from Sundance, who was of course always on line.

"Yes Paul," she said. "Just a little tired."

"Sorry," I said hastily. "Shall I leave you to sleep?"

"That's alright," she replied "I would like to talk."

"Tell me about yourself," I said. "Your family and friends, your way of life."

"Well," she said "I know of course my Mother and her partner, and I have two brothers, because I am the oldest of my Mother's children."

"How do you live your life?" I asked. "Do you go to work each day?"

"No , the Hianja do not work each day. Work is something we do for enjoyment. Machines look after all the basic requirements of life, from growing food to building houses and other machines and equipment for everyday use. Of course we need to supervise the machines and decide the priorities for them to work on, but they are largely self maintaining. Hianja are managers, supervisors and decision makers. Also, scientists like me, and engineers. But mostly, Hianja do nothing but enjoy their lives. They are artists or musicians, thinkers and philosophers."

"That sounds jolly nice!" I said enviously. "Humans still have a pretty sorry life compared to you. They have to work, and still have little time for enjoyment."

"But why?" she asked. "Are your machines not advanced enough to look after all these basic and tedious tasks?"

"Oh yes," I said. 'The machines are more than capable. It is the economic system which is the problem." I then went on to describe the economic systems which were prevalent on Earth, which were still the mixed economies of the 20th and 21st Centuries. Moderated it's true by increase wealth and physical comfort, but still systems that had rich and poor and required the working man to devote the major part of his life (or her life in the case of the working woman) to the tedious business of making a living.

"Why maintain such a system," she asked "When machines are capable of providing the necessities of life for everyone. Human's need only devote themselves to providing the abstract luxuries of life. Art and music, and other activities to enhance one's life," In the dark I could see her pale face turned towards me as she talked.

"Logic and reason do not come into it," I said. "Society is like a machine with built in inertia. It takes time to change direction. I guess eventually we will arrive at a similar system to yours."

"Is that why you are an explorer?" she asked. "To get away from the everyday routine of life on Earth?"

"Oh...partly," I said. "It's more complicated than that. More like to get away from some people."

"What people?" she asked. "Enemies?"

"No, not enemies!" I laughed. "Friends, well Lovers actually!"

"You want to run away from your Lovers?" she asked "I do not understand!" she exclaimed.

"Have you had Lovers Manera?" I asked.

"Yes, I suppose so," she replied enigmatically.

"You suppose so? What does that mean?"

"I have had sexual relationships," she replied "But no relationship serious enough to be called love,". she replied.

"I see," I replied doubtfully. "So there was never any problem when the relationship ended?"

"No problem," she replied, and then added. "What sort of problem?"

"Like the other partner did not want it to end?"

"I see...," she replied thoughtfully. "But, how many ...er partners did you have problems with?" she asked.

"Well, two actually," I replied cautiously. "They both got to know about each other."

"So you are saying that, for Humans, a relationship with more than one person at the same time causes...er...difficulties?" she said.

"I am afraid so," I replied. "We tend to be mostly monogamous," I explained.

"That seems very restrictive," she replied.

"Well that is exactly what I believe!" I replied earnestly. "That is actually what I said to these young ladies but unfortunately they were not as advanced and liberated as you, and they reacted ..er , well, rather badly I have to say."

"How distressing for you," she said sympathetically. "And here you are, far from home with a stranger instead of with your two lovers. That must be very hard for you."

"Being with you is not at all hard Manera. In fact, you are a very easy person to be with. You are very kind and sympathetic."

"Thank you," she said quietly. "Tell me Paul, by Human standards, how do I appear to you?"

"You're appearance is very human. If you were on Earth you would pass for a human female. A little exotic and remarkable but no one would suspect you for an alien. Well, except a Doctor," I added. "And how about me?"

"Well… you would not pass for a Hianja!" she said slowly. "You are far too hairy and your shoulders are far too big and broad. But you have a nice face," she added "although your bone structure is all wrong."

"Well that's OK then," I said grinning "So I am big, hairy and misshapen. Careful I don't eat you."

"Paul?" she said with a questioning tone in her voice. "You are not upset are you?"

"Only joking," I replied quickly. "But you have touched on something. Why *are* we so alike? Surely the odds of evolution throwing up two identical species must be astronomical."

"Yes, one would think so," she replied. "It will be very interesting to see the extent to which our DNA matches," she replied. Despite the fascinating nature of the situation, and the discussion, sleep was claiming me and I managed a grunt and a muttered goodnight before warm darkness embraced me. That night I dreamt that I was a piece of DNA trying to match myself to an alien piece of DNA. However hard I tried, our edges and corners just did not fit.

Chapter 12

Alfred's Report :

When my long range sensors detected the Hianja flyer separating from the Mother ship and descending rapidly into the atmosphere, I accelerated at full power into the air , attempting to gain as much altitude as possible before any engagement. I had a plan of sorts, but like all military plans, it was flexible. It was also risky, I calculated a more than even chance of failure. But it was a difficult calculation because I had no way of assessing the Hianja's military ability. It was possible that they were very inexperienced, in which case my chances would be substantially improved. So far I had not gained a very high regard for their military ability. They had arrived at Omorphia, knowing that there appeared to be some sort of armed threat, with a weak and inadequate force. They had not deployed their forces well, and as a result had lost one ship and a number of personnel. These poor tactics indicated unbelievable incompetence, and I was not going to believe it! Paul and I were convinced that Smetronis was playing an "underhand game.", to use a colloquial expression. The current events confirmed this. Therefore, I should not assume that they were militarily incompetent, in fact, I should assume the opposite!

*Firstly, I was certain that Smetronis's plan required that both Paul and Manera should die, and that I should also be destroyed. Thus all evidence of his duplicity would disappear I was also sure that he would **not** assume that Paul and Manera were on board the Epsilon. For Smetronis, the one person that must not survive was Manera. She is the one who would destroy all his plans (whatever they were?) if she lived to recount the events of the last few days. The Hianja may not believe me or Paul, but they were bound to believe Manera. The first part of the plan therefore was to divert attention from where Paul and Manera actually were and to point Smetronis's forces towards a false direction. I was sure that they had the Epsilon under observation, so I determined to divert them. I therefore accelerated to my maximum ground level velocity, keeping very low to avoid detection in order to 'lose' both the flyer and the Mother ship. I could not do this for long, but a few seconds out of sight was all I needed. I headed inland, looking for one area in particular, an area of broken country, hilly and rocky and heavily wooded. Ideal country for hiding out in.*

I could not keep the Mother ship under observation while flying so low and erratically, but I am sure that they were able to track me, but because Epsilon was so low and flying erratically, I hoped that they could not keep it in sight continuously. Finding a suitable spot, I set down the Epsilon quickly, risking a smashed undercarriage due to the rocky ground. The Airlock cycled open and 'Sushimar' (Surface Ship Maintenance Robot) bounded out and headed into the woods at maximum speed. I closed the lock immediately and took off again at maximum power. I had re-programmed 'Sushimar' for her new task; to be a 'hit-and-run' guerrilla, delaying and diverting the Hianja forces in their hunt for Paul and Manera. I was banking on being observed doing the 'drop', and thus causing the Hianja to believe that I had dropped off Paul and Manera. If it worked, it would be a useful diversion to buy us time. If not, nothing has been lost.

The task now I believe is to avoid being trapped between the Mother ship and its Flyer. The obvious strategy for the Hianja is to use the Mother ship to track Epsilon and attack from above, while their flyer attacks from below. I assume that both the Mother ship and its flyer are equipped with missiles, but the flyer would be the weaker of the two because Epsilon has greater speed and manoeuvrability in atmosphere. But the Hianja flyer has the advantage of receiving up to the second positional information from the Mother ship. They know exactly where I am, but I will have no idea where they are until they are 'on top' of me. When the enemy has a weapon or advantage that you do not have, you must choose the battleground to nullify that advantage. Thus I must be in the position where I can also see them coming. Somewhere flat for miles around with a central peak where Epsilon could land and maintain a watch. And I knew exactly where; We had named it Mount New Fuji, a huge extinct volcano on a tiny island in the middle of the Central Ocean. The extinct caldera would make a good hiding place, providing cover until I sight the Hianja flyer and can attack them on equal ground. It is however more than 500 miles away and at maximum velocity I will need ten minutes to make it there. I have to hope that they will not intercept me until I achieve my objective.

Chapter 13

The next morning I awoke before Manera and took myself down to the stream for my ablutions and to find a convenient place to perform my natural functions. Camping had never been a hobby of mine and this experience was not changing my opinion. But our situation was so serious and unique that physical discomfort was the least of my worries. Survival was the issue, and our survival may have consequences for our two races far beyond the value of our two individual lives. Returning to the tent I found Manera sunning herself on a rock and deep in conversation with Sundance.

"Good Morning," I said "Did you sleep well?"

"Yes," she replied. "I was very tired."

"Well, you look refreshed and ready to go this morning!" I quipped.

"Where are we going?" she asked.

"Oh, we are not going anywhere," I replied. "It is just a colloquial expression."

"I was discussing language with Sundance," she said. "I think I would like to learn English," she continued. "Sundance can teach me he said."

"Ah, very good," I replied. "I guess we should both find something to keep us occupied during the next few days."

After Breakfast we had a meeting to discuss strategy, Manera , myself and of course Sundance, who was a recognised member of our band. He may not have the 'brainpower' of Alfred, but he could provide facts and figures to back up our plans. I began the discussion.

"It is likely that Smetronis 'gang' will search the coastal area around the base. Manera, what sort of machines and equipment do they have for this purpose?" She paused for a few moments looking thoughtful.

"We have artificial gravity powered vehicles, normally used for day to day ground transport, but very useful in rough ground like this," she said, waving her hand to indicate the surrounding area. "They can fly at any height, although they are slow and not very stable in high winds." Manera went on to explain, after some questioning, that the sleds, which were called 'Tanseh', were about the size of an Earth family car, could carry 4-6 people and were not armed. They were enclosed and pressurised, but she guessed could be easily disabled by a projectile.

"Where is the most sensitive spot, in order to disable them?" I asked.

"At the central axis where the Gravity generator is," she replied.

"May I speak?" asked the deep resonant voice of Sundance.

"Of course Sundance, you do not have to ask to speak."

"Thank you," he replied politely. "I was briefed by Alfred . He has a plan divert attention of Hianja from our party. He has programmed 'Sushimar' the Ship's external Maintenance Robot to act as diversion. Robot will be dropped in area far from here to make Hianja maybe believe us there. This gain us some time."

"Good plan." I nodded. "Let's hope it works. Did he say how he intended to protect himself and the *Epsilon*?" I asked.

"No, but if unable to defend, Alfred say he will attack and attempt disable of Hianja forces," replied the Robot.

"Manera, how do you think Smetronis will proceed?" I asked.

"It really depends on what Smetronis is trying to achieve here," said Manera and she looked perplexed and confused. Her head was moving from side to side, and her hands were making vague gestures. So human, I thought, confusion manifests itself in similar physical symptoms!

"I don't know for sure either Manera," I said. "Maybe Smetronis wants to save his career and reputation. His mistakes caused the destruction of your shuttle, the death of six crewmen and two scientists. He believes that I am in league with the attackers, you are too sympathetic towards me and that you will testify against him. That is why he wants you out of the way."

"But making mistakes is one thing," she protested. "He will not be punished for that although you are right that his reputation and career will be damaged. But to purposely set out to murder me in order to cover up a mistake? That is just unbelievable! No Hianja could behave in this way believe me," she said vehemently.

"It does seem an extreme reaction," I conceded. "Is it possible that he is not sane? Is there any previous evidence of unstable behaviour?" I asked.

"I do not know Smetronis personally," she replied. "He is from Vasmeranta, and this colonisation of Omorphia as you call it was a joint effort by our two planets. That is why much of the crew are Vasmerantians. But it is not possible for a Hianja to harbour psychotic illness without being detected."

"Hmmm," I said doubtfully. I was not convinced, but had to concede that there was much about this situation that I did not understand.

"Paul," continued Manera. "I think that I should surrender to Smetronis and try to persuade him to wait for the full expeditionary force to arrive. He cannot continue to believe that you have kidnapped me."

"Manera, he must know that I have not kidnapped you," I protested.

"There is a chance that all the communications have broken down and he did not receive our transmissions," she said, almost pleading to be believed.

"But why should he assume that you have been kidnapped simply because he has not heard from us? Surely the simple thing would be to send down a shuttle to investigate?"

"Maybe that is what he is doing?" she asked.

"But why is he demanding that I release you? What is that all about?"

"I do not know! I do not know!" she exclaimed.

"Manera, I know it's hard for you to believe that a Hianja has either gone mad or is plotting something and is capable of murder, but for the moment these seem to be the only two explanations. You cannot place your life in his hands. We must try to remain free until the Expeditionary force arrives."

She sighed and bowed her head .

"Then, going back to your question of what I think Smetronis will do, by your logic he must clearly kill me at least. I think he will not attempt to destroy the *Epsilon* first because this is the most dangerous part of the exercise. If he fails and his only remaining shuttle is destroyed, then he has no way of capturing us. So he will attempt to capture us first. I think Alfred's little stunt with 'Sushimar' may delay things but it is more likely that he will divide his forces and send a search party here as well."

"Yes that is a good point," I agreed. "How many AG Sleds does your ship have?" I asked.

"Four," she replied. "And one sled can cover a lot of ground each day," she continued.

"I am hoping that they will have no idea which direction we took," I pointed out. "They will have to search up the coast, down the coast and inland. If they find us, they still have to take us and we are well armed," I pointed out. Manera seemed to shudder.

"Paul, I cannot use a weapon to kill or injure one of my own race," she said. "Or any other race," she added.

"That's OK," I said. "You leave the fighting to me and Sundance." I suddenly had a terrible thought. "Do you have any robots equipped with weapons?" I asked.

"No!" she exclaimed. "We have no weapons of any kind on my planet, except very small arms for self defence when exploring dangerous country. In fact, all the weapons on my ship were supplied by Smetronis, and the only people trained to use them are his own men."

"Ah, very interesting!" I said. "So why do the Vasmerantians have weapons and you do not?"

"I was not aware that the Vasmerantians had weapons until the attack upon the base on Omorphia, when they offered to accompany our ship and bring weapons with them."

"How about the ship's missiles?" I asked.

"They also were supplied and fitted by the Vasmerantians," she said.

"How did the Vasmerantians explain their possession of military equipment?" I asked suspiciously. "Particularly advanced guided missile technology?"

Manera frowned before answering. "They explained that they maintained this Technology in a sort of museum, for academic purposes. There was also the argument that one day we may come up against a hostile race and we should not lose the capacity to build such weapons for self defence."

"But the Vasmerantians were able to fit the shuttles with missile technology very quickly?" I asked insistently. "Which means they must have them in production, not just in a museum?"

"Well, our Robot factories can produce anything very quickly," she said.

"The Robot factories can produce anything very quickly from ready made components," I said "I know because we have the same technology on Earth. But if the product has new and different parts, not used anywhere else, this would take longer."

"Yes," she replied thoughtfully. "But, if the Vasmerantians have missiles and weapons in production, it must be for a purpose...," she tailed off, her face taking on an expression which seemed to be a mixture of confusion and disbelief. The situation seemed to be taking on wider and wider implications, as if it was not bad enough already. We both looked at each other, at a loss for words. I shook my head, dismissing the 'ifs' and 'buts' for now.

"We'll just have to leave these considerations for later," I said. "Let's concentrate on staying out of Smetronis's clutches for now. I think we need some early warning if any if these AG sled's come close. Sundance, we need to find a lookout post, somewhere which gives us a view of the surrounding area without us being spotted. I suggest you try and find such a spot and keep a lookout there throughout the day."

"Cannot carry out translation duties if I am some distance away," rumbled Sundance. "Will have to boost radio transmission. Risk detection," I looked up at the craggy peak which towered over the silver stream, which emerged from a cleft in its side. The top looked accessible and also allowed 360 degree visibility.

"How about up there Sundance?" I pointed.

"Yes," he confirmed. "It looks suitable. Will detect intruders before they come in range of RF transmissions."

"OK," I agreed. "Next, we need to camouflage the tent. It can't be seen from the air, but is visible from ground level when you come from that direction." I pointed in the direction we had come, from the sea inland. "I suggest we move the tent further back into the overhang and pile up some vegetation, bushes and trees around the front of the overhang to obscure it. It would take a very close examination to spot the Tent if we do that." Manera nodded in agreement and Sundance maintained an impassive silence.

The rest of the day was filled with physical labour in the hot sun. We could not have done it without the robot's help of course. Moving the Tent back ten feet was not so bad, but the task of digging up and replanting bushes to form a thick enough camouflage was much harder than I expected. We had to bring a reasonable amount of soil and grass so that the bushes would look natural. Landscape gardening was not my forte, so the end result was a nasty mess, but I was not after winning any prizes at any Flower Show! By the end of the afternoon the job was done and we took a grateful cooling dip in the stream before preparing our evening meal.

I allowed Manera to go first and diplomatically hid in the tent while she was bathing. When I was sure she had finished I came out with a towel to carry out my own ablutions. She was sunning herself on a large rock, drying her hair and she made no effort to turn away as I removed my clothes. I turned my back on her, removed my clothes and had my bath with my back to her all the time. The water was cold so I did not loiter and having dried and dressed I joined her on the rock.

"Do humans find nudity embarrassing?" she asked.

"Uh...yes, a little," I muttered. "Human females do not usually expose their bodies to males," I said. "Unless...that is , unless they have an er, intimate relationship." I fumbled for words, a bit puzzled at my embarrassment.

"But you must be interested in my physiology, in the interest of science," she said. "And I am interested in yours. This is a good opportunity to learn more about each other," she said , her face impassive.

"Manera," I said awkwardly. "You're physiology is very similar to a human female's. I cannot look at you just scientifically I'm afraid." She looked puzzled.

"Do you become sexually aroused?" she asked. "Just by looking at my body?" she seemed surprised by this.

"Well yes," I said. "Don't the Hianja find each others physically attractive?"

"Only when we are *Nastre* ," she said.

"What is *Nastre*?" I asked. She paused for a moment in thought.

"It is a period of sexual activity and arousal. When the body is ready for fertilisation it triggers desire for a partner and desire for physical contact and sexual activity."

"I remember you telling me that Hianja are not sexually active all the time."

"Yes," she said. "It would be very distracting if we were. Our thoughts would be full of physical desires and we would not be able to do anything else." She smiled secretly. She was sitting with her arms around her bent legs and I tried to take my eyes of her long naked legs and shapely thighs.

"So, are you sexually aroused now?" she asked.

"I am trying hard not to be," I replied.

"I would be very interested in learning more about Human sexual relationships," she said, and I looked at her askance, not sure if she was playing with me or being serious.

"Well Manera, we can do that over dinner," I said hastily.

During lunch, which was substantial because we had not eaten all day in our haste to complete our defences, it was Manera who again raised the subject of our differing sexual natures.

"How can Humans function if they are permanently sexually active?" she asked "Does this not affect your ability to concentrate on other tasks?"

"Well, 'permanently sexually active', does not mean that we are continuously obsessed with sex," I explained. "Socially, it is not acceptable to behave in a sexually explicit fashion, except under appropriate circumstances, in private and with another consenting adult. We have very strong customs to regulate what is acceptable and what is unacceptable behaviour."

"I see," she said, looking thoughtful. "But is this repression not harmful? Social habits should not go against natural needs, as this will create unendurable stresses within the individual."

"Well, we call this creative stress," I said. "Life is about balancing various needs and desires against social necessity, and the ability to harness this conflict in a creative rather than destructive way. Much of art for example is motivated by sexual themes and sexual conflicts."

"Yes, much of our primitive art is also on a sexual theme," she said, and I could not help wincing. Primitive indeed!

"But surely..," I went on "Hianja must also have situations when their love or desire is rejected. Don't you suffer psychological problems as a result?"

"Yes of course," she replied "But only during *Nastre*. But because *Nastre* is temporary, we know it will pass, then the desire and the madness passes also. As a result, we can be more detached, even during *Nastre*. But having to live with the madness all the time......that must be very difficult."

"Not so difficult Manera. After all, you are a female, and I am a male. I have been living very close to you for two days now but have you detected any madness in me?" I asked, a bit tongue in cheek! But she nodded thoughtfully.

"Yes, as you were saying when we were in the water, you find me distracting, but you are able to function at an impersonal level very well. In fact, I have been impressed with the speed at which you are able to analyse a situation and formulate a course of action. So you are obviously **not** thinking of sex all the time!" she said, and I thought I detected a twinkle in her eyes when she said this!

"No I'm not!" I agreed "But tell me about this *Nastre*. How often do you have it and what happens?"

"It can happen at any time," she replied. "Normally the body dictates when it is ready. Of course we know what causes it and there are drugs to suppress it or turn it on at any time. Sex is a recreation for us and we can choose when to indulge."

"Well, I can see that some individuals may lack will power and abuse the drug," I pointed out.

"The body can only take so much before it stops responding to the drug," she replied "But you are correct in saying that discipline is required. So in a way, we are not so different."

"Nature has a way of balancing things out," I agreed.

Chapter 14

The following three days passed without any sign of searching Aliens. Manera concentrated on her English language lessons and made remarkable progress. I struggled hard to learn Hianja but my achievements were derisory compared to hers. My relationship with Manera developed into affection and mutual respect. But there was always that repressed sexuality just under the surface. I was continuously aware of her sinuous shapely body, alien yet familiar. She responded to close physical situations with cool detachment. She had no physical inhibitions about displaying her body and continued to do so, despite knowing that this was a distraction for me. In a way, it showed her complete trust in me. She was treating me as a friend and comrade and I was not about to betray that trust.

There was only a couple of days to go before we could expect the arrival of the Hianja Expedition, and we were beginning to relax, thinking that Smetronis would never find our little hideout, when the bombshell arrived!

"Object about two miles away, just visible," came Sundance's terse report.

"Can you determine what kind of object Sundance?" I asked quietly.

"Appears ground vehicle," he replied. I looked at Manera and she frowned and shook her head.

"Sundance, could it be a flyer hovering close to the ground?" I asked. There was a pause.

"It is at limit of resolution," came Sundance's response "But yes, could be Hianja *Tanseh*."

"What direction is it headed?" I asked.

"Along path leading our direction," he retorted. I began to see my mistake now in the location of our camp. We had unconsciously followed a break in the foothills going inland, and then picked up our little stream, following it up to its rocky source. It would be a natural thing for our searchers to do also. I cursed my stupidity and Manera looked concerned.

"Paul, what?" she asked in English. I explained to her quickly my mistake. She shook her head in disagreement.

"No, natural thing to do," she said again in English. "Too difficult go up mountains. What do now?" she asked.

"Sundance, I want you to stay where you are and continue reporting. Also, keep a lookout for the Hianja Shuttle. I would expect it to be flying much higher than the *Tanseh*." I paused for a second in thought.

"Are you armed?" I added

"Yes, have rocket launcher and rifle," he replied.

"Good," I replied. "If they come close, stop communications so that they do not detect us. Do not fire until I fire first, or give you the word. Understood?" I asked.

"Understood," he replied.

"If possible try not to destroy the *Tanseh*. It may prove useful. Manera, do you know how to fly these things?."

"Yes," she replied. "They use standard controls. But Paul," she went on "Attacking *Tanseh* will give our position to Smetronis." She was now communicating wholly in English, allowing Sundance to concentrate on his observations.

"If they discover our camp, same thing," I pointed out. "Should we hit them before they discover us?" I asked. She thought for a moment before replying.

"No, position of *Tanseh* known on monitor," she replied. Manera looked completely different from the regally immaculate alien who had stepped down from her shuttle ten days ago. Her hair was rumpled and unruly, and she was wearing my second set of work clothes. But she looked browner, fitter and meaner and I reckoned I could count on her. We settled down to wait. Sundance continued to give us occasional reports on the progress of the *Tanseh*, which gradually became closer.

It started to become apparent that a search pattern was being followed. They were methodically quartering the ground between the sea and the mountains. Sundance calculated they would be in our vicinity by the afternoon. We debated whether to make a run for it, but it was obvious that the *Tanseh* was covering the ground faster than we could, and we did not want to be in the open.

A couple of hours after we spotted the *Tanseh* Sundance spotted the Hianja Shuttle, at ten thousand feet to the North. We surmised that the other *Tanseh* was pursuing a similar search pattern to the north of the base, the Shuttle providing high level cover and support. The situation was now more serious because any attack on the low flying *Tanseh* would bring the more heavily armed shuttle down on us. The only hope we had was that our camp would be missed, so we set about ensuring that our camouflage was thorough and removing any telltale signs of habitation from our little enclosed canyon. Using leafy branches we erased our footsteps, backtracking to the shelter of the enclosed overhang and ensuring that the tent was completely invisible by deflating it to the ground. We took our positions behind a couple of boulders which through the foliage gave us a good view down the valley in the direction the searchers had to come.

Manera still refused to use a weapon against her countrymen, despite agreeing that these Hianja were acting in a bizarre and inexplicable fashion, she was still not convinced that they would fire on us and pleaded with me not to be the first to open fire. I reluctantly agreed with serious misgivings, but asked her to at least hold the pistol, and instructed her how to use it. She absorbed my instructions in her usual concentrated way and I was certain she would know what to do, if she could bring herself to do it. A final message from Sundance raised the tension.

"They are within two miles Paul, I must cease transmissions now," he transmitted.

"OK Sundance," I replied. "Let us hope we are not spotted. Otherwise, follow my lead."

He transmitted a terse confirmation and we settled down to wait. We could not rely on any warning because the Hianja *Tanseh* were totally silent, so we hid behind our screening trees and bushes and hoped for the best.

The moment arrived suddenly, the *Tanseh* appearing at the entrance to the grotto, flying at about two hundred feet, it snaked its way around the huge cliffs enclosing our grotto and hovered stationary above the stream. I hazarded just an eyeball peeking around the boulder to keep an eye on it. It was about the size of a large Earth automobile, and about the same shape but flat bottomed with curved sides. A bulbous flattened ring like protrusion in the centre enclosed the Artificial Gravity Generator that powered the craft. There were windows all around, which were open and various lethal looking weapons poked out. It was clearly not designed to be a military vehicle since there was no sign of armoured protection or built in weapons. Again I was surprised at the amateurism of the Hianja. They seemed to have no real military vehicles or equipment and their arms were small and hand held. The only advanced military equipment in evidence so far were the missiles fitted to the Mother Ship which had destroyed the mysterious intruder's Flyer. I was sure that one shot from Sundance's RPG would bring the Flyer down permanently.

I looked at Manera and nodded reassuringly, placing a finger against my lips to denote silence. She looked tense and wide eyed but she nodded in understanding. I jabbed a finger out through the trees to indicate that they had arrived and she nodded.

The *Tanseh* moved cautiously closer, drifting into the grotto and circling the small area, raising higher, and then coming down almost to ground level. It pottered at ground level for a few minutes and I began to worry. They were taking too long examining a small area and I had the sudden dread that our preparations were not thorough enough, that we had left some sign on the ground of our presence. But it seemed my worries were unfounded because suddenly the flyer lifted and headed down the valley at speed, soon vanishing from sight around the cliffs. I grinned in elation at Manera and danced a little jig.

"I think we are OK!" I grabbed her and gave her a hug and she responded with a wide eyed look.

"Do you think they will return?" she asked, hesitating over her English.

"Nah, can't see why they should!" I said confidently. "They don't know that I established a second camp before their Mother ship even arrived so they probably think we are on the run. I don't think they will be back."

"On the Run?" she asked questioningly.

"Yes," I said "Moving from place to place every day, sleeping rough ...er.. outside," I explained. She nodded understanding.

"What do we do now?" she asked.

"We keep quiet until Sundance gives us the all clear. They may still be in radio range."

It was only a few minutes later when Sundance gave us the all clear. Apparently, the Hianja had given up for the day, the *Tanseh* heading up to the shuttle where it was taken on board and the shuttle headed north, probably to take the other searching *Tanseh* on board. It was late afternoon and the sun would be going down very soon, so we decided to put up the tent and prepare our evening meal.

We were both quiet over dinner, the elation at not being detected giving way to a sober thoughtfulness. Sundance was still in his lookout position on the cliff above the grotto. I judged it was safer to keep the lookout going while the searching Hianja were still in the vicinity. Manera was keen to talk, if only to improve her English . I asked her about Hianja Society. How had they managed to preserve their culture over the vast expanse of their History, and had it changed over that time? She replied that the Hianja had recognised early on in their civilisation, as they had expanded to the stars, that cultural diversity was bound to follow as the race lost contact with its roots. They believed this diversity was a good thing, but they wanted to preserve certain 'core' inheritances, those things that were essential to preserve the traditional balance and sanity of the Hianja civilisation. For this purpose, the 'Guardians' were established on the home planet. Their purpose was a complex one, not just relating to social habits and behaviour but to the very biological nature of the Hianja, because it was recognised that racial characteristics were essential in maintaining the nature of Hianja Society.

Over thousands of years, the Guardians had 'shaped' the Hianja mind and body through genetic engineering, as well as Hianja Society through social engineering, always conforming to the fundamental principles of Hianja civilisation. I became more and more concerned at hearing this. I was aghast at the idea of so much control being exercised over a race by any group of individuals. I objected to Manera that the potential for tyranny would over time become very real . But Manera dismissed my qualms, saying that the concern of the Guardians was always for the common good and the preservation, as she called them, of the "fundamental guiding principles" of Hianja Society. I did not have the arrogance to disagree with an individual whose race had twenty thousand years of civilization behind them and had settled on hundreds of planets, moons and asteroids! I had to agree that if it works, then it's probably right.

"It is true, that no matter how great the theory appears to be, it is the end result which matters," she agreed "and Hianja are very practical people. We do not spend too much time discussing metaphysical ideas and beliefs. There is no room in our philosophy for religion and the supernatural, as I understand there is with Earth philosophers. Science is our God and belief in ourselves is our religion."

"Very commendable," I said "But your race is not as close to its roots as we are. In historic time, it is only yesterday since Science replaced superstition as the leading force in Human thinking. So you must forgive us if we regress occasionally." Despite my agreement, I could foresee that the Earth Intelligentsia would be horrified with the sorts of ideas that the Hianja seemed to accept as normal and indeed desirable.

After checking with Sundance, we settled down to sleep. It was a warm close night and we remained fully dressed, sleeping on top of the sleeping bags instead of inside. I lay awake for a while, unable to relax, with the feeling that it had all been too easy. Inside the tent it was completely dark. I could not make out any sign of Manera's sleeping form, although I could hear her gentle breathing. For the first time since our meeting, I was beginning to feel a sense of strangeness about this beautiful alien creature. Being able to talk in English due to the incredible power of Alfred's Language Compiler had given me a false sense of familiarity about Manera. But the more we talked the more it became apparent that Human and Hianja Philosophies in many areas were quite different. The murderous behaviour of Smetronis was another puzzle, completely at odds with the so called pacifist character of the Hianja. I must have dozed off during my musings because I suddenly jerked awake, Sundance's deep voice in my ear.

"Paul, the aliens have returned."

"Damn, I thought it was all too easy!" I thought. "Report!" I whispered.

"I believe *Tanseh* landed around corner of cliff. Are coming up the slope towards camp."

"How many?"

"Have seen three, but believe more," I stood up quickly and reached out and found my pistol. Then the realisation hit me.

"Sundance, you have broken radio silence!" I exclaimed.

"More important to warn you," retorted Sundance tersely.

"You are right Sundance. Hold your station for now," I agreed.

"Manera, wake up!" I shook her and she immediately sat up. "They have returned. A number of Hianja are coming up the hill on foot. We must get out of the tent otherwise we will be trapped," I felt more than saw her jump up. I reached out and found her, fumbling to find her hand.

"Are you ok?" I asked.

"Yes Paul, I am ready," she whispered and I was impressed with the steadiness of her voice.

"Come," I said. "We will get out and climb up the escarpment behind the camp. We must be quick." We fumbled our way out of the tent and through the obscuring trees and bushes to the back of the camp site. The rocks were not too difficult to climb but it was a dark moonless night and we took it slowly not to make any noise. Higher we climbed, angling to the right to make our way above and behind the overhanging rock which obscured the camp site. Sundance's voice whispered in my ear again.

"Paul, I am coming down from the cliff to attack them from behind. Where are you?"

"Good idea Sundance. We are climbing above and behind the camp. I will try to get into a position to attack them from above," If we could get them into a 'pincer' we may out of this alive after all I thought. We got into position above the grotto and I could see the area leading to the hidden camp quite clearly. I had yet to see any movement, but as we settled behind a couple of large boulders I caught a furtive movement to the right against the cliff. Sure enough, one dark shape slithered along the cliff and disappeared into a shadow and another came up from behind to occupy its previous position. I started counting and eventually go to six. I wanted Sundance to open up on them while I could still see them, but I could see no sign of him.   Eventually, they were all obscured by the trees and bushes around our camp and hidden also by the overhang. I considered working myself out to the edge of the overhang, but I would be completely exposed there. I waited for Sundance to get into position before moving out onto the overhang, but I was aware that we did not have much time. Once the Hianja invaded the camp and discovered we were not in the tent, the obvious place to look would be where we were. There was nowhere else we could have gone.

The silence was broken by a massive explosion, followed immediately by two more. The ground shook with the concussions and we were deafened by the blast beneath us. The Hianja had simply blown up our camp! They had not tried to talk or persuade us to give up. Just threw in the grenades! I was shocked by their ruthlessness. A huge cloud of rocks and dust rose up beneath us completely obscuring our view of the clearing. I could not support Sundance if I wanted to I thought. But then, there was a crackle of gunfire and I recognised Sundance's rifle. It coughed again and again and I heard some answering shots. I still could not see a thing. I dithered wondering what to do, but before I could move, a *Tanseh* appeared high up, further down the valley. It swooped around the cliffs and into the clearing. I could see Hianja leaning out of the windows blasting down into the clearing. Sundance had his work cut out now and I decided that he needed help, but as I jumped up to scramble back down the cliff to the clearing, there was a bang and a streak of light. One second the *Tanseh* was pitching and weaving above the clearing and the next it was an explosion of light and sound, chunks of metal and bodies flying away. Sundance had used his portable missile launcher to good effect.

"Yes!" I punched the air in satisfaction. "Sundance, you gunslinger !" But my celebrations were cut dramatically and shockingly short.

"Paul behind you!" The shout was from Manera and at the same time there was a series of bangs and bullets ricocheted like angry bees off the rocks around me. I dived desperately down and to the left where Manera was behind the cover of a large boulder. As I did , I caught out of the corner of my eyes a dark shape obscuring the sky behind us. It was the other *Tanseh* which had come up un-noticed behind us. Fortunately for us, the flyer drifted too far over which meant we were directly beneath it and the Hianja inside were unable to fire on us. I had time to roll on my back and level my gun at the barn door sized shape of the flyer. It seemed pathetically inadequate, but I loosed off a few shots into the base of the flyer, in the area of the rear doughnut shaped AG unit. There was a series of bangs and thumps and the flyer keeled over and slid gracefully like a ship going down at an angle of 45 degrees. It bounced on the overhang and crashed down into the clearing, disappearing from sight to the accompaniment of screeches from the unfortunate Hianja inside.

"That was bloody close!" I gasped. Manera looked shocked, crouched against the boulder she seemed paralysed.

"Are you OK Manera?" I asked worried that she may have been hit. She shook her head numbly, seemingly unable to speak.

"Look, old Sundance may not have disposed of all of them characters downstairs. I had better see if I can help." I asked.

"Sure you OK?" I asked again.

"Yes, yes, I am OK," she said firmly.

"Right, you stay here, I will go down to help Sundance."

"No, I will come also," she said.

"Manera, you are not trained for this. It's safer for you to stay here."

"Afraid alone," she said pleadingly. "Come with you please," I looked into her eyes and they were large and fearful .

"OK, just stay behind me," I said. We started down the incline, working our way over and around the rocks and boulders. I did not expect to find anyone coming up the other way, I rather thought that Sundance had polished them all off by now. I was caught by surprise therefore when we rounded a large boulder to come almost face to face with two Hianja coming the other way. Fortunately they were looking behind them fearfully, more concerned to get away from Sundance than to get after us. It gave me the split second advantage I needed to shoot the first one but as he went down I could see the second one behind him had his gun raised and ready to shoot. My instinct was to throw myself to the left or right to find cover, but I was aware that if I did that, Manera was behind me. I hesitated for those few milliseconds necessary to allow her to dive for cover and then dived to the right. The bullet caught me on the left shoulder, throwing me back but allowing me to continue my dive for cover. I kept my feet, swivelled round by the force of the bullet, I straightened myself desperately and managed to level the gun at the remaining Hianja. Fortunately, he seemed distracted by the plight of his comrade, which gave me the second I needed to get in another shot. He staggered and with a groan fell backwards down the incline behind him, disappearing from view.

I considered running down the incline to assist Sundance, but my legs were behaving rather oddly and running was not something they were contemplating.

"Er...sorry," I muttered. "My legs seems to have temporarily stopped obeying me. I shall talk to them severely about this mutinous behaviour!" Manera grabbed before I fell over.

"Paul you are bleeding!" she moaned. "Sit down, I will bandage wound."

"Allow me Manera," came a deep rumbling voice and the welcome metallic bulk of Sundance suddenly appeared.

"Glad to see you old man!" I gasped "Fifth Calvary to the rescue and all that," Sundance and Manera both looked at me for a moment, no doubt totally baffled by what I was saying.

"Did you get them all Sundance?"

"No," he said, producing a first aid kit from a pouch. "Two were left. Ran away down the hill to Flyers". He seemed to have the ability to see clearly in the dark, because he opened the first aid kit and proceeded to clean and bandage my wound.

"Wound OK," he pronounced. "No artery damage. Bullet inside shoulder muscle. Remove later."

"Some painkiller would be appreciated Sundance," I said through tense lips. He rummaged in the first aid kit and pulled out a syringe.

"Hold still," he said tersely, jabbing the syringe into my arm and emptying it. I was trying to blot out the pain and think about our situation.

"Manera, what do you think Smetronis will do now," I asked. I had an arm around her shoulders and she was supporting me with a strong arm around my waist, which at any other time would have been a pleasant experience.

"I think he has no more 'men', but why has he not used the shuttle?"

she asked.

"Probably afraid it may get damaged," I said. "One of Sundance's missiles will do it no good at all."

"But now he has nothing else," she retorted.

"Yes," I mused. "And he knows quite accurately where we are now. It might be a good idea if we got out of this area as quickly as we can," I concluded. "Sundance, do you think those fleeing Hianja took both *Tanseh* with them?"

"Unknown," he responded.

"Can you go ahead and find out?" I asked "Manera and I will follow as quickly as I can."

"Understood," he responded, and in the blink of an eye he was gone, his powerful metal body swivelling gracefully and his jointed legs moving with dainty care over the rough ground."

"Impressive piece of work that Sundance," I muttered.

"He would make a terrifying military machine," responded Manera as we started our slow awkward and painful descent.

"Never thought of that, but I guess he would at that," I agreed. "He is designed to be a survey support robot, carrying out experiments, taking samples from difficult locations and generally supporting the Human member of the crew. As well as defending him from local wildlife or unfriendly natives. Of which there seems to be a few on this planet," I grumbled.

We were soon at ground level, and the destruction was sobering. The tent had disappeared and the surrounding area was a mass of mangled earth and blackened shrubbery. There was nothing we could salvage from there.

We stumbled down the hill, keeping close to the cliff, heading back in the direction the attacking Hianja had taken. The pain killer was starting to work and my shoulder was easing, but my left arm was useless. A metallic shadow loomed out of the darkness.

"One *Tanseh* left behind," he whispered.

"Excellent!" I exclaimed. "How far?" I asked.

"Fifty yards around cliff," he replied. With renewed vigour we lurched down the hill and there it was. The double doors in the middle of the ship were gaping open and inside pale lights glowed on the alien instruments. Very obliging of them to leave us a get away vehicle I thought. They probably thought their comrades were coming up behind and decided to leave them some transport. Manera took the pilot's seat and I collapsed in the seat next to her. Sundance positioned his bulk in the middle of the loading area where there were some handy hooks to hang on to. Manera's hands flew over the controls with practiced ease and a hum of power came from the rear where the AG engine was located. The doors slid shut with a whish and we were airborne.

"Keep low to the ground Manera and hidden. Keeping out of sight is more important than speed," I added. "Sundance, can you direct us back to the Hianja Base camp? It is time to contact Alfred."

"That will reveal our presence and *Epsilon* also," Manera pointed out.

"I know, but we have no choice. The time has come to get their shuttle before it gets us." I had a sudden thought.

"Manera, can they detect this *Tanseh* is operational?"

"No," she replied quickly. "I have switched off the auto guidance and location finder. We do not know where we are, but neither do they."

"That's OK," I sighed with relief. "Sundance can direct us back to the camp. We must get there before daylight." As I spoke there was a gout of flame behind us followed by the thump of an explosion. This was followed by others, a continuous blast of explosions which lit up the night sky behind us. We had evacuated our little grotto just in time to avoid being blasted out of existence by Hianja missiles. Smetronis was doing a thorough job of flattening the whole area but fortunately we had put enough distance between us and our previous camp to be safe. Now we had to make good time under cover of darkness and get Alfred into action before we were spotted. I wondered why Smetronis had not bombarded our camp from the shuttle to start with. Why had he risked his men and his *Tanseh* when he could have just blasted us out of existence using the shuttle missiles? I pondered this for a few minutes, exploring the angles from Smetronis's point of view, and then it came to me. He was constructing a subterfuge, pretending that I had kidnapped Manera after the attack on the base. Smetronis had wanted to be seen to be trying to rescue Manera, not blow her to bits.

Chapter 15

The journey back to base camp, which had taken us all day on foot, took us a couple of hours on the *Tanseh*. What a wonderful machine it is I thought to myself. What would the human race give to have this technology? It would revolutionise surface transport overnight! It was a tremendously agile and manoeuvrable machine. Manera explained that it worked by creating a gravity 'well' or slope in the required direction. The flyer simply 'fell' into the well. Reverse the gravity well, and it slowed down or went backwards. Its compact Fusion Power supply could generate about 1.5 to 2.0 equivalent Earth gravities, which was enough to give it very respectable acceleration. Its top speed was limited by its aerodynamics and stability at high speeds, which were not very good. It was designed as a surface transport vehicle for short to medium distances with maximum speeds not much in excess of 300-400 kph. At the low level we were flying at, anything faster than 20kph was too dangerous. We did not want to run into a tree or boulder at this point of the proceedings.

The horizon was turning red by the time we reached Base Camp, the sun would be up in a matter of minutes. We had left our microwave link to the *Lisa Jane* at the Camp, and our hope was that Alfred and the *Epsilon* was within line of sight of the *Lisa Jane*. We were only likely to be given one go at transmitting our message before Smetronis destroyed the *Lisa Jane* or its microwave aerial to prevent any further communications. We parked the *Tanseh* next to the accommodation block and Sundance was out and into the building before Manera and I could climb out. We staggered inside, Manera still solicitously supporting me, event though I felt better I accepted her help, feeling a bit of a charlatan, but what the hell, it felt good! I collapsed in the chair in front of the comms set while Sundance fiddled with the controls and his fingers flew over the keyboard.

"Paul," he began. "Prepare communication. We transmit all in one go. After, do not know how long link will last."

"Understood Sundance," I replied and pondered my message. "OK ready," I instructed. Sundance pushed the transmit switch.

"Begin," he responded.

"Alfred, this is Paul. Our hideout has been discovered and destroyed by Smetronis's forces. We are holed up in the Base Camp and are expecting to be attacked here by the Hianja shuttle. We need your help. *Epsilon* must disable the Hianja shuttle if possible, or destroy it if necessary. Respond immediately, out." I knew the message would take just a few seconds to reach Alfred and he should respond immediately. The seconds dragged on, and then a full minute and still no response. My heart sank, Alfred must be either out of action or out of range of the microwave link. We re-transmitted the message and continued to do so for the next few minutes with no response, before a red light blinked on the console and a message flashed across the screen. '*Link to orbital relay is unavailable*' in red letters. The *Lisa Jane* comms link had been disabled. If Alfred had not received the message, we were on our own! And Smetronis now knew exactly where we were!

"Sundance, you still have some missiles?" I asked.

"Yes Paul," he responded.

"How many rounds do you have left?"

"Three," he responded.

"OK, you must take cover somewhere and remain hidden until you have a good shot at the shuttle. Outside the Base Camp because they may decide to just flatten the area here." We pondered our options for a few minutes, going outside and examining the surrounding area.

"We can't use the *Tanseh*," I said. "It will be a sitting duck for the shuttle's rockets. What other weapons do we have Sundance?"

"Other than missiles, I have rifle and you have pistol," replied the robot.

"Right, Sundance, you take up position on that escarpment up there," I pointed to the sloping cliff face behind the Camp. "Stay hidden and wait for the right moment to hit the shuttle. Manera and I will take the guns and take to the woods over there," I pointed to the thickly wooded area to the right of the Base, which climbed up into the base of the mountains, before petering out to the rock face.

"Paul, you are in bad condition," said Manera. "Cannot run in forest and carry weapon."

"You're right ," I said. "You carry weapon and I walk!" she looked at me askance.

"I carry weapon and I carry you, I think!" she said.

"Sounds good to me!" I agreed, eliciting a derisive snort from Manera.

"Let's go before Mr Smetronis gets his troops into action!" The sun was now peeking up over the horizon and the cold early morning light was reflecting off the pale alien buildings.

"To the woods me lovely," I said in my best Farmer Giles accent. Sundance's pain killer is good stuff I thought, I have never felt better! Manera moved with agile grace next to me. She has got the nicest looking muscles I thought. We scrambled down the incline heading for the trees while Sundance headed back towards the escarpment. We had barely got a couple of hundred yards into the trees when we spotted the Hianja shuttle high up but descending rapidly.

"Ah Shit, we could have done with more time!" I cursed. "Manera, we need some cover, head for those rocks over there," I pointed and we changed direction to head for a couple of moderate sized boulders with some fairly decent sized trees around them. We established ourselves within the circle formed by the boulders and quickly broke off as many branches as we could to create some camouflage and settled down to wait.

Our view of what was happening was restricted, but there was no sign of movement for at least half an hour. Then I spotted the shuttle , a couple of hundred feet above the tree line, drifting inexorably in our direction. There was something nagging at me, something that I wanted to ask Manera, something relating to this situation, but my frazzled brain could not focus. I remembered the last time we were in this position, in the grotto with the hovering *Tanseh* looking for us. They had spotted us then and I did not know how.

"Manera," I said urgently. "Have you any idea how they spotted us before, when we were hiding at the tent. We were not visible, how did they know we were there? Do they have a sensitive heat detector that can detect body heat through the trees?"

"Yes, of course." she replied. "We use such machine to detect and follow animals in forest. Stupid me to forget ," she punched her thigh in anger at herself.

"That's OK, don't beat yourself up about it," I squeezed her shoulder in support and she scowled in frustration.

"They will see us for sure," she exclaimed.

"So, Custer's last stand!" I said, and she looked at me in incomprehension. "Explain later, if there is later," I said. "We have to hit them before they spot us," I said. "Manera, I need you to do something dangerous."

"More dangerous than this?" she said quizzically.

"Listen, you must distract them so that they do not spot me until too late. I want you to run for it, head for the cliffs. They follow you, and I will try to hit them before they get to you. What do you think?"

"Better than sitting here to be Hianja and Human barbeque!" she exclaimed. I was impressed with her calmness. She turned, her eyes deep azure pools that I could happily drown in.

"Good Luck," she whispered, then turned and sprinted off into the forest.

"Damn!" I exclaimed weakly. "I've changed my mind, come back!" but I was talking to myself and only the memory of those eyes remained.

"Concentrate Constantine!" I admonished. "Focus your tiny brain on the job." I checked the rifle was loaded and the safety catch off. The Hianja shuttle was still pottering around a patch of sky a couple of hundred metres away. I tracked it carefully, it was still too far for accurate shooting. It suddenly dipped and turned, heading rapidly in my direction. I was almost caught unawares as it hurtled towards and over my position. I almost twisted my back getting the gun into position. When I pressed the firing button the vibration jolted my injured shoulder and an excruciating jolt of pain shot through it. I screamed curses but hung on to the gun, spraying bullets up at the shuttle which fortunately had braked its headlong flight a hundred metres or so past me.

They had clearly spotted Manera and I gripped the gun with quiet desperation, ignoring the pain, raking bullets in the direction of the now hovering shuttle. It paused , dipped and then suddenly took off again, moving too fast for me to track, circling around back in the direction of the Hianja Base Camp. I stopped firing as it went out of range and watching the ship as it circled around under the cliffs behind the camp, coming around for another pass over my position. I spotted the rocket contrail before I heard the thump and the shuttle lurched, dropped and then recovered, continuing to head away from the camp, but out to sea. I yelled with delight jumping up and down and punching the air with my good arm.

"Sundance the sharp shooter strikes again!". The shuttle had disappeared behind the tree line and I waited , hoping that it would not return. There was a rustle in the bushes and Manera was suddenly back, looking wide eyed and dishevelled.

"Manera, did you see that," I could not restrain my delight. "I think Sundance got one good shot in."

She nodded, breathing heavily. "Yes, that was good shooting," she said. "But unless he hit the AG drive, the shuttle will still fly." I sobered up quickly. She was right of course, it would need the drive or its main controls to be damaged before it became un-flyable. Sure enough after a few minutes the ship re-appeared, hovering over the trees and just to the right of the camp. It was pointing in the direction of Sundance's hideout and I guessed what was about to happen.

"Get out of there Sundance!" I exclaimed. We saw the contrails of their missiles, two of them, and the explosions as they impacted the cliff where Sundance's hideout had been. The Flyer then turned its nose ominously in our direction. We looked at each other and we must both have had the same thought. This was the end, we had nowhere to run. The shuttle could just stand off out of range of our machine gun and pick us off with its missiles.

"Paul , I am sorry," said Manera. "I cannot believe Hianja would do this thing," she said sorrowfully. I embraced her with my good arm and held her close.

"Its OK , you have been great. Its been a pleasure knowing you." she leaned her head on my shoulder, and I brushed her tangled hair from her eyes.

"And much pleasure for me also," she whispered. I suddenly and very desperately did not want to die.

"Come on Manera, let's not just stand here and make it easy for them, let's run for it." she gaped in surprise and then grabbing my hand we both headed into the trees running as fast as we could. We expected to be blown to bits at any second and when the huge explosion came we both threw ourselves to the ground. There was confusion for a few seconds as we slowly realised we were still in one piece. I sat up and looked around in amazement. There was a thundering roar overhead which I instantly recognised

"Alfred you bastard, what took you so long!" I roared as the *Epsilon* screamed over our heads, made a spectacular turn and then came back in another flypast, its wings dipping in salute. In the distance the Hianja flyer, flames coming from its rapidly disintegrating rear end, was collapsing gracefully to Earth.

"Bloody show off!" I shouted at the shuttle as it banked around in another turn, heading for the Base Camp landing site. Manera was jumping up and down in delight, clapping her hands like a little girl. I grabbed her and we danced a little jig together like a couple of kids, laughing in relief.

Holding hands, we made our way back to the Camp, full of merriment at first, but slowly winding down as fatigue and reaction took hold. But nothing was going to ruin our happiness at the turn of events. We had unequivocally won and ensured our survival. Was Smetronis in the shuttle I asked myself. Or had he stayed nice and safe in the Mother Ship while his lieutenants did his dirty work? Even Manera was looking pale and exhausted by the time we got back to base and my legs could barely support me. And there waiting for us when we returned was none other than Butch Cassidy and the Sundance Kid, that swashbuckling duo of fearless robot explorers. I felt like cuddling them both!

"Sundance, you made it, bloody well done!" I exclaimed.

"Yes, after first rocket not disable ship, knew position revealed and so abandoned," he intoned.

"You did right thing old chap, otherwise you would be scrap iron now. And Butch, there you are, so good of you to join the party, eventually," I said pointedly. Butch buzzed and rolled forward heavily.

"I have communicators," he said, not bothering with social chit chat. He was never one for small talk! He had one for me and one for Manera.

"Alfred, speak to me," I croaked.

"Paul, I understand you have been wounded," came those familiar fruity tones. "You must allow Sundance to treat your wound as soon as possible."

"Right Ho mate, all in good time. Why didn't you reply to our message you old scum bag? We thought we were gonners there I tell you," I said trying to be severe but unable to keep the relief out of my voice.

"I purposely did not reply to provide miss-information to the enemy," he retorted as if lecturing to a child. "One of the basic laws of military tactics," he explained condescendingly.

"Yes, but the idea is not to also miss-inform your friends as well," I said pointedly.

"Yes, that was unfortunate," he replied as if apologising that Tea would be served late this afternoon. "But there was no way I could inform you that your message had been received, without also informing them. I hoped that you would keep the enemy occupied thus providing me with the element of surprise. Which is of course, exactly what happened," he finished smugly.

"Alfred, I have to hand it to you, without inflating your already bloated ego, it was as you say, exactly what happened."

"Paul, I also have to congratulate you. Sundance tells me, you displayed great tactical ability and courage. You are a credit to our service and it will go down on record."

"Enough already!" I exclaimed. "I am blushing from me toes up to me ears. Let us finish this mutual admiration society meeting. Any other business?" I finished grinning around me.

"Yes," said Manera. "I have to put it on record Alfred that I am ashamed of what has happened over the last week. The insanity that has seized Smetronis is a tragedy for Hianja and Human relationships and I will see that he is bought to account for his actions to the Guardians themselves. Let me also say that Paul's bravery and quick thinking has saved my life any number of times and I will always be in his debt."

"Aw shucks maam," I groaned "Its all in a days work for a Super Hero. Anyway, I seem to remember you saved my life at least once. Not to mention being a real brick throughout. So there, we are even ."

"A brick?" she laughed. "You call me an ugly brick? Is that the best complement you could manage?" she said with mock outrage.

"Ah..it is an er.. metaphorical description," I said with feigned embarrassment. "Indicating your stirling qualities of ...er hardness and er...square ness!" I finished laughing.

"I will show you my hardness," she said advancing on me threateningly.

"No No!" I cried. "I surrender, I am an injured man, I need medical attention!" We both held on to each other laughing uproariously while the two robots looked on with stoical indifference.

"When you two have finished your comedy double act," admonished Alfred. "Perhaps we can get on with some serious business."

"Oh God Alfred, I have had my fill of serious business recently!" I exclaimed. "A bit of light relief is all I need."

"Nevertheless," he insisted. "Events will not wait and neither will your wound. There is a surgical unit in the Epsilon where you can be attended to.

Please return there immediately."

And so we did, and not before time. The euphoria and the drugs having worn off I had to be carried into the ship and did not need much anaesthetic before I passed out. When I awoke, I was still strapped into the narrow surgical bunk. There was a dull throb in my shoulder and my stomach was complaining loudly at the lack of attention it had received over the last day or two. I could not see Manera or anybody else for that matter.

"Hey Alfred, where is everyone?" I asked.

"Manera has gone with the robots to retrieve food supplies from the Base. She is on her way back now."

"Couldn't the robots go by themselves?" I asked and I wondered at the twinge of concern that stabbed my innards.

"She wanted to choose," he said.

"Just like a women," I grumbled. "Can't resist doing a bit of shopping."

"You are anthropomorphising her actions," he said primly.

"She is not a bloody animal you know Alfred," I protested. "Anyway, I have never met a woman who is more woman than Manera," I said. "If you know what I mean!" I added.

"I have noticed that you and her have grown very close in the last week," he said with just a hint of disapproval in his voice.

"Is there a problem with that Alfred? You not going to come the heavy Father now are you?"

"Not at all Paul, please do not take offence," said Alfred, and it was about the closest he had ever come to an apology. "What I meant was that Manera clearly reciprocates your affection."

"You will note that I have so far conducted myself with gentlemanly consideration towards the young lady, and won her trust and affection. All in the interest of good inter-species relations of course," I said, unable to resist adding a lecherous leer.

"Oh you can be trusted Paul," he replied. "Its her that I'm worried about," before I could react to this statement, the airlock door whooshed open and the object of our discussion stomped through with bouncing energy.

"Paul!" she cried "You are awake, how are you feeling."

"I could eat anything," I said ferociously "Particularly young and plump alien females," I growled. She quirked her lips and held her head to one side in amusement.

"You will find me old and tough," she laughed. "I have some real food for you," she said indicating the robots behind her who were unloading packets of Hianja food. I groaned and started to undo my straps.

"You don't call that real food do you?" I asked. Alfred's voice intervened.

"Please move carefully until Sundance examines your wound. The bullet has been removed and you have some stitches. It should heal without problems in a few weeks." As Manera pottered around like a little housewife preparing the meal, Sundance examined my wound and stitches and pronounced me fit to move around. I watched Manera out of the corner of my eyes, humming to herself a lilting Hianja tune as she banged around the galley. She had bathed and attended to her hair, and put on her original Hianja outfit, although without the jewellery. I was reminded that this was a senior alien scientist, the scientific head of the planetary expedition, and Alfred's words came back to me.

"Oh you can be trusted Paul," he had said. "Its her that I'm worried about."

Chapter 16

The following day we went out in force to investigate the fallen shuttle. It was just slightly further inland from the beach, amongst the first trees of the little forest that grew up into the mountains. We took the *Tanseh* flyer which just about accommodated Butch and Sundance in the load platform. The Hianja shuttle had come down heavily from a couple of hundred feet and looked in a bad way. The whole rear end was blackened and twisted with a gaping hole where the missile had exploded. It had come down rear end first so the front looked undamaged. The airlock was closed however and there seemed no way we could get into the ship. Hovering in the *Tanseh* at cockpit height we could see inside the cockpit and there was no signs of life. Just to make sure, we banged on the side of the ship and shouted loudly.

It was with great surprise that we heard shouted voices from inside, weak but clear. We banged on the airlock and got a response from inside, banging and shouting.

"They are saying that there the external airlock doors are jammed and cannot be opened manually," said Manera. Sure enough there was damage to the doors, which were buckled and twisted.

"Tell them we will try to help," I said to her. "Tell them to stand away from the airlock doors and we will try to force them open." We spent a few minutes discussing what would be the best way to get in. Butch was equipped with some light cutting equipment and after some careful surgery he was able to force the door partially open. Sundance went through first, I reckoned one sight of him should knock any remaining stuffing out of the injured Hianja. Sure enough when Manera and I followed the two Hianja were sitting in a corner hands held open in front of them.

Interrogation by Manera revealed them to be the pilot and his first officer, who had both been in the cockpit during the crash. They were the only ones to survive and they were both quite uninjured. They told us that the five other crewmen had been in the main compartment which had taken the brunt of the missile. None of them had survived. They looked shocked and despondent, and also baffled and questioning. After some minutes of conversation Manera turned to us and explained.

"They are very surprised to see I am still alive. Smetronis tell them I was kidnapped and ...," she struggled for the word, said it in Hianja and got the translation back from Alfred."

"....held Hostage," she finished. She continued her conversation with the Hianja while I explored what was left of the ship, which was not much.

When we had finished, we all re-boarded the *Tanseh* , including the captured Hianja, and headed back to the shuttle. The Hianja were now in animated conversation with Manera and there was some anger and vehemence in their demeanour.

"What are they saying Manera?" I asked.

"I have explained the whole situation to them," she replied. "They are both from my home planet and they are very angry at being misled by Smetronis. They are also sickened by the deaths that have taken place. I think we can trust them," she said.

"Mmm, I hope so Manera. We can not afford to have to guard them around the clock. What are their names?" I asked. She turned and spoke to them again, and the two Hianja stood and with polite inclinations of their heads introduced themselves. Nastro KamaLato was the Pilot and Fetralin Semetuo was the first officer, who I now recognised was a woman. Nastro was short and chunky and clearly anxious to ingratiate himself with Marena, bobbing his head constantly as he talked. Fetralin was cooler, more aloof and young. I kept finding her examining me curiously, her eyes darting away when she was discovered. The two were clearly not military personnel and I judged that they would not pose a threat to us, but we needed somewhere to house them. We also needed to decide whether to remain in the shuttle or return to the Hianja camp, which was much roomier and more comfortable.

In the end, we all settled for the comfort of the Base camp, with Nastro and Fetralin taking their own rooms. Over the next few days I had an opportunity to get to know the other Hianja, which was fascinating and informative. But I could not help a twinge of jealousy at having to share Manera with them. As the scientific leader of the expedition, Manera interacted with the other Hianja with an air of cool authority, but as she got to know them better I would catch her having a gossip with Fetralin or a relaxed conversation with Nastro.

It was not long before Fetralin was unable to restrain her interest in me as an Alien, she started to question me, first with shy reserve and then with increasing confidence when I was forthcoming and informative. The others also got involved , and we would often spend hours talking, which was a pleasant way to pass the time. Nastro and Fetralin became more relaxed with me, and eventually positively friendly. We started to explore our surrounding and do some science to while away the time.

During this time, there was no communication from the Hianja Starship in orbit above us. Nastro had informed us that Smetronis had indeed stayed in the Mother ship. I wondered what his story to the Expeditionary Force would be. How would he justify his actions?

When Manera suggested that just the two of us take a field trip into the mountains, I was delighted to accept. We took the *Tanseh* into the mountains, had ourselves a picnic, and came back the long way around, via the coast, where we found a delightful little sandy cove, ideal for a swim. Of course, neither of us had costumes, so Manera with her usual lack of inhibition simply stripped off and went in naked. I modestly kept my underpants on, not wishing to reveal my Earthly tackle to the curious Marena.

"I have studied pictures of Human male anatomy Paul," she said laughingly. "The male penus seems a pitifully small thing in comparison to the fuss which is made about it!"

"Huh?" I exclaimed nervously, "What, smaller than the um .. Hianja ... Um ... thingy?"

"Oh yes," she said emphatically, "Hianja have been genetically modified. They have absolutely *huge* ones!," she said, putting the emphasis on the 'huge'.

"Genetically modified?" I said with disbelief. "That's a bit much..," I continued, before realising from her expression that I'd been had! She gave a feminine trill of laughter and pushed me into the water, jumping on top me for good measure. Our mock underwater wrestling match lasted for some minutes, I certainly did not want it to stop and it appeared neither did she. The wrestling turned into an embrace and then into a long passionate kiss. At some point my soggy underpants disappeared and over the next hour Manera's first hand acquaintance with the human penus persuaded her that it was not such a pitiful object after all. I knew that Manera had engineered this trip for this purpose, and she knew that I knew. We had both wanted it and as we lay on the beach afterwards, we were rather sobered by what we had just done.

"First Contact has been achieved," I said wryly as we lay in the warm sand. "In more ways than one!".

"Purely in the interest of scientific research," she added taking a bite of my shoulder. I flinched with pain, Manera's love making was very energetic and her mouth and sharp teeth had figured prominently.

"Hianja women don't eat their mates after love making do they?" I asked.

"Only if their love making is sub-standard," she said looking me up and down in a calculating fashion.

"No problem there then," I said smugly. "Manera, how do you feel about what we have just done?" I asked, the first faint quivering of guilt agitating my conscience.

"I feel very nice," she said, stretching languidly. "I think we should have another scientific field trip tomorrow."

"You are a shameless alien hussy," I said grinning. "But seriously," I said insistently. She paused for a few moments, her face thoughtful.

"You are thinking of what will Hianja and Humans think if it was known that we became lovers?" I nodded. "Who knows. It's never happened before. Do you think we should keep our relationship secret?"

"That is going to be difficult," I said caressing a smooth curvaceous thigh. I pulled her towards me. "Do we have time for one more scientific experiment before we head back?" I asked.

"I think it's our duty," she whispered. "And I will instruct you on some Hianja experimental methodologies," she added with a knowing look.

By the time we returned it was getting dark and our Hianja companions welcomed us with enthusiasm.

"We missed your company," said Fetralin. "And our interesting talks. What **have** you been doing all day?" she asked curiously.

"Oh, just general scientific survey work," Manera said vaguely. "Human methodologies are quite different from Hianja," she said..

"I do not see how our scientific methodologies could be so different," Interceded Nastro. "Science is Science isn't it?" I was having trouble keeping a straight face!

"Of course," I said. "The differences are mostly in your starting position and how far you want to go," I looked straight at Manera and she nodded seriously but her mouth was twitching.

"Hianja like to take it slowly, a step at a time, but Humans like to ...um...go straight in," retorted Manera and our two Hianja companions nodded politely, no doubt completely baffled by our double talk.

Chapter 17

The next couple of days past quickly. We were tense and worried about the forthcoming confrontation, particularly Manera. We decided we should prepare our case for the forthcoming investigation. Alfred did the 'donkey' work in gathering and organising the evidence, while Manera and I prepared our cases. But we still took time out for some exploration, although Nastro and Fetralin refused to stay behind. There was no more opportunities for Manera and I to repeat our 'field trip', and we dared not try any clandestine meetings at night for fear of being discovered. According to Manera, Hianja did not feel the continuous demands of sexual desire in the same way that Humans did, but there were times when she looked just as hot and bothered as I was. We did manage to arrange some private 'meetings' in which the communicators were discarded, doors were locked and garments were rapidly removed. But either our companions were the souls of discretion, or they just did not care, because they showed no sign of suspicion. It was Alfred who was suspicious because of the amount of time we remained 'disconnected' from the comms system. On the third day of our stay at the Base Camp, he bought it up.

"Paul, I am interested to know if you and Manera are intimate?" He asked in his best English Butler's tone.

"Intimate?" I asked. "What exactly do you mean?"

"Are you having sexual relations with her Paul," he said, more directly. The expression 'sexual relations' came out sounding like 'tea and biscuits'.

"In what way are you interested Alfred?" I asked. "Would you like some prurient details, a few pictures perhaps, some anatomical observations?"

"Since this is the first sexual encounter between a Human and an Alien, it would certainly be of great historical and scientific interest," he said, totally unabashed by my sarcasm. "But I do not suppose you will provide such information," he continued sadly . "And it is not what I was asking."

"Ah, that's a relief," I said "I am not a man to kiss and tell you know."

"Indeed Paul," he agreed. "My interest is in your welfare and the success of our venture."

"Have no fear Alfred. My amorous adventures with Miss Manera will have no bearing on the success or otherwise of our venture," I assured him.

"Are you absolutely sure that this will not have repercussions?" He asked.

"What, will her Father get after me with a shotgun?" I asked. "OK, OK," I continued "I am being facetious. Alfred, we are all grown ups and if two grown ups want to play enjoyable games, it has no bearing on anything else."

"It may call into question Manera's objectivity," he responded, and I knew he was right because the same worrying thought had occurred to me, but I had dismissed it.

"Nobody but her and me know," I responded.

"It would be preferable if it stayed that way," he warned,

"Of course Alfred, I know that, and we are being very discreet."

We left it at that. I was baffled by this passionate obsession between two being who had evolved on different planets from different origins hundreds of light years distant from each other. It was hard not to believe that Life in our Galaxy had a common basis, if not a common origin. Was it because we both knew that it would not last, that fate would very soon rip us apart, perhaps for ever? And indeed, events moved inexorably on and the next day Alfred detected the arrival of foreign starships in the system.

We had continued to broadcast regularly to Smetronis, Manera giving him some serious verbal thrashings which were completely ignored. We now directed our antenna towards the arriving ships, broadcasting to them on their standard microwave channels. We confined ourselves initially to verbal transmission only, Manera sending urgent requests for help and requesting a response. The response when it came caused her to frown in anger. Alfred translated it for me;

"They are asking if Manera is being held hostage by the Earthman," he explained. Manera's reply was vehement and lengthy, and it was a minute before a reply came back.

"They are shocked," translated Alfred. "They have already had Smetronis's version of events and Manera has knocked them back. They can hardly believe what is going on," she dialogue between Manera and the arriving ships continued for some time, with Manera verbally describing the events of the last two weeks in detail, and the voice at the other end occasionally asking questions. They finally stopped, with the assurance that they would proceed to establish full comms facilities, including video and computer links. They expected to arrive in orbit the next day and would contact us about how to proceed with the investigation. Manera slumped back in her chair with a sigh, the tension draining out of her. I gave her a smile and a squeeze of encouragement on the shoulder. "How do you think it went?" I asked.

"Very Good I think," she said. "They were shocked by what happened to me, how the shuttle was shot down and how Smetronis's men tried to kill us. I think they were also impressed by the fact that you risked your life to rescue me, and protected me from attack. But I think they were mostly excited by the news that we had contacted an alien civilisation at last. They cannot wait to meet you!"

"It sounds like we've got off to a good start," I said. 'That's got to be worth a drink or two!" That evening we relaxed over dinner and a few drinks, making general conversation before taking ourselves off to bed. I was restless and unable to sleep, thinking of Manera's silky body and warm sweet smell. Completely awake and restless I sat up and was tempted to visit her room which was across the passage from mine. Just when I decided to do it, the door to my room swung open gently and in walked the object of my desires. She walked quickly across the room and slid into the bed next to me. We embraced passionately and she gave little sighs of contentment as she snuggled down in the crook of my arm.

"We are taking a chance Manera," I whispered.

"I do not care," she replied. "I want to be with you tonight. It may be our last time together."

And so she stayed the night, slipping out in the morning when the passage was clear. We did get some sleep, deep and restful sleep actually, after we had exhausted ourselves extending Human-Hianja relations to a new level of cordiality! It was after all, as we kept reminding each other, our duty!

The next day arrived and contact was resumed by the arriving Hianja. Technical details were exchanged and Alfred set up the equipment to facilitate communications. The moment arrived when full video was set up. The screen displayed three Hianja seated against a blank background. They were dressed in the traditional richly ornamented and embroidered Hianja style. Two were women and one was a man. All were clearly of advanced years, but it was impossible to tell their age because Hianja aged well and gracefully. They were lean and strong featured, their skin still firm and smooth, their hair flecked with grey. They greeted Manera in a warm and friendly fashion, enquiring after her health and complementing her on her appearance. And indeed she looked stunning, quite the most beautiful creature I had ever seen I thought. The memory of our last night together would keep me warm for many years. An irreverent thought crossed my mind; I wondered what the boys back home would say on seeing Manera. Something like, "Constantine you dirty lucky bastard! Trust you to get shacked up with some gorgeous bit of alien crumpet," and I grinned to myself at the thought. She may be a gorgeous bit of alien crumpet, but she had a brain that would run rings around the best Earth had to offer! The object of my unworthy adulation turned her bright eyes on me.

"Paul, they wish to meet you," she smiled encouragingly.

"Wish me luck ," I said with a nervous grin and walked into the field of view of the camera. I had made some effort with my appearance, putting on my dress uniform and brushing my now almost shoulder length hair into some semblance of order. I strode purposively to stand next to Manera. I could see the shock and excitement on their faces when they saw me.

"Guardians, this is Captain Paul Constantine of Earth," she announced simply.

"It is a pleasure to make your acquaintances," I said formally, and then smiled warmly. 'Earth has waited a long time for this."

"Ah, not as long as we have!" exclaimed the distinguished lady in the centre of the group of three. "It is indeed wonderful to be a part of this historic event. I am Guardian Kemato. This is Guardian Hamolatonen," she said indicating the male to her right. "And this is Guardian Malanisa," she said indicating the female to her left. They both nodded soberly at the introduction. "But Captain," she continued. "I cannot believe that you are so…Hianja," she finished, her eyes boggling out of the screen at me.

"Sorry to disappoint you Guardian," I said, unable to suppress a smile. "I should have green skin and tentacles!"

"This is truly amazing," she said. "A huge mystery. How can evolution create two species so alike on two planets separated by thousands of light years?"

"It is something we must investigate," I agreed. "Perhaps genetic analysis of our DNA will reveal the answer."

"It may reveal why we are so alike, but not how it came to be," said the tall male to her right. "We may have to re-assess our ideas of evolution and how it operates," kemato nodded, before continuing.

"What of these terrible events that we have been hearing about from Chief Scientist Manera-Ka. They have put a black cloud over what should have been a happy and exciting event," I nodded tensely in agreement.

"Guardians, the events which have occurred have indeed been tragic, and have led to the unnecessary deaths of innocent Hanja. We have recorded evidence and eye witness testimony to show what happened and to identify the persons responsible for these criminal actions. We will make all evidence and testimony available to you, myself and my AI and all our computer records are available for your scrutiny. These events must not be allowed to corrupt or misdirect future relations between our races, because I believe, that is indeed the aim of those responsible for these evil actions."

"Why should these individuals, whoever they are, wish to misdirect relations between our two races?" asked Guardian Kemato.

"I cannot say for sure Guardian," I replied. "Perhaps it is just xenophobia, perhaps it is fear due to misunderstanding. I do not know who these people are, but I believe their representative here is the security officer Smetronis. He has been in charge of the ships and men who have attacked myself and chief scientist Manera in an attempt to silence us."

"Thank you in advance for your co-operation Captain Constantine. I can assure you that our investigation will be thorough and unbiased.," said

Kemato.

"I look forward to meeting you all in person," I finished politely. They continued their conversations with Manera for some time after that, and Nastro and Fetralin were also introduced to the Guardians and had their say. Manera finished by then 'introducing' Alfred, who was also questioned at length by the Guardians. It was a couple of hours later before they finished and Manera relaxed and broke the link.

That afternoon the Hianja ships arrived in orbit. There were three of them , two the same size as the ship that Manera's expedition had arrived in, and one even larger vessel. Each ship represented the three nearest Hianja planets, the two smaller ones were from Smetronis's home planet Vasmeranta and a neighbouring planet Tanmeron, and the larger vessel from Manera's home world Mesaroyat. The three Guardians represented the three worlds, Guardian Kemato from Manera's home, Guardian Hamolatonen from Tanmeron and Guardian Malanisa from Smetronis's home planet. They did not waste any time in arranging a landing on the planet, despite the late hour. Manera and I, Nastro and Fetralin, accompanied by Sundance, made our way down to the landing area to await their arrival. We lounged in the shade of the shuttle and I chatted to Alfred about the forthcoming meeting, while Manera chatted with her Hianja comrades.

"Alfred, how do you think the Guardians received your evidence?" I asked, to pass the time.

"They did not express any feelings either way Paul," he replied. "But I was able to answer all their questions with good supporting evidence. I am confident they must accept what we are saying."

"I hope that puts Smetronis in the shit," I said bluntly. "Up to his scrawny neck."

"I do not see how he can give a reasonable explanation of his behaviour," he replied. "Either he is monumentally incompetent, or he is part of some plot to disable Hianja-Human relations at birth."

"I find it hard to believe that he is so incompetent," I retorted. "His only mistake was to misjudge our capacity to survive."

"I detect that two Hianja shuttles are approaching," alfred interrupted my ruminations. "One looks like it will land while the other covers it."

"They are not making the same mistake as before then," I mused. In a few seconds I was able to see the two shuttles approaching, one above and behind the other. The leading one came in quickly, hovering over the *Epsilon* for a few seconds, before coming down gently fifty yards away. The other shuttle stayed a few hundred feet up, hovering above the landing area. The Hianja shuttle was uncanny, it made almost no noise whatsoever as it descended like an elevator, smoothly and steadily, only a low gentle hum breaking the silence. We lined up a few yards from the airlock, waiting in anticipation. We did not have to wait long as the airlock doors slid open with a hiss and metal steps unwound from the ship to the ground. A number of gleaming metallic robots clattered down the steps, taking their stations to either side of the steps. They were short crablike creatures, armed with what looked like electronic stun weapons. After them came a Hianja male who stepped forward and saluted Manera, engaging her in a short conversation. Manera looked towards me, clearly pointing me out to the individual, although I would hardly have thought that I needed pointing out!

"Er, Yes, I am the alien!" I muttered. "Over here, the hairy primitive looking one. No tentacles I am afraid, and yes, I am normally this colour, not green!" I was trying hard not to grin as the individual approached me and stopping a few feet away made a little bow of greeting. He was a tall hard looking character, and his keen eyes drilled into me. He spoke and Alfred translated in my ear.

"Captain Constantine, I am Sametan Tenaka, chief security officer for this expedition and responsible for the Guardians safety. May I ask, do you have any weapons in your possession?"

"Welcome Sametan Tenaka," I replied cordially. "No, I am not armed."

"And your robot?" He enquired, indicating Sundance, his eyes lingering for a few seconds on the fearsome mechanoid.

"He is not armed," I assured him. "He is here just to provide an audio-visual link with my ship and with Alfred, my AI."

"I see," he said, his eyes scanning the area carefully. "Manera assures me that you are completely trustworthy, and of course, I will accept her assurance."

"Have no fear," I said "I would not dishonour Manera's word, although I assure you it is unnecessary," he looked me straight in the eyes at that, and then turning briskly, strode back to the Hianja shuttle, speaking quietly into his communicator. Manera came over and stood next to me, a reassuring smile on her lips. A figure appeared in the airlock and descended the steps, followed by two more. The Guardians set foot on Omorphia, with careful deliberation, their eyes in our direction. Manera and I walked over, and they also walked towards us, meeting us half way.

In the lead was the tall female Kemato with the powerfully built Hamolatonen on her right, and the shorter plumper figure of Guardian Malanisa on her left . Kemato was an impressive female. Tall and lithe, she had a face that was far too heavy to be attractive to Human eyes, but radiated authority. Hamolatonen was smooth featured and grey, with a solid powerful body and piercing blue eyes. His stare was frank and friendly. The chubby Malanisa's examination was slow and hooded. Did I detect a hostile glint in her dark eyes? Manera stepped forward and exchanged shoulder hugs with all three Guardians. Kemato moved towards me.

"I am delighted to make your acquaintance Captain Constantine," she said.

"Thank you Guardian Kemato," I said "The pleasure is all mine." We exchanged Hianja shoulder 'hugs'. She moved back and I exchanged the same greetings with the other two Guardians. Hamolatonen's grip was strong and firm, and his stare was straight and unflinching, Melanisa took her time over the embrace, looking deeply into my eyes as she did so. I moved, waiting for them to take the lead.

"We wish to examine the Base," said Kemato. "We can talk as we do so?" she asked questioningly.

"Of course," I replied. And so we did, wondering around the buildings, looking inside, they continued to ask searching questions about Earth, Humans and me in particular. Manera stuck close to us, giving me little looks of encouragement and occasionally adding her own answers and explanations.

"Was the base exactly in this condition when you arrived?" asked Melanisa at one point.

"Yes" I replied, "Except for the accommodation building which we partly repaired in order to live in it."

"Why did you not continue to live in your Shuttle?" asked Melanisa.

"My Hyperdrive was destroyed and I was not sure how long I would be marooned here," I replied. "I thought I would make myself comfortable. The facilities here are much better than my shuttle," I smiled. "I particularly enjoyed your stock of *Janu*!" I added .

"Humans also enjoy alcohol?" asked Hamolatonen.

"Yes, I found your *Janu* very agreeable to human taste," I replied.

"Well, we have that much in common!" he replied dryly.

"I think that you will find we have much more in common," said Manera and our eyes crossed meaningfully. *Whoa girl,* I thought, carefully putting a neutral expression on my face and nodding earnestly. The Guardians looked doubtful, but did not peruse the question. At the end of the 'tour', we gathered in the common room of the accommodation building where Manera offered refreshments. The Guardians gracefully accepted, and with glasses of *Janu* in our hands we settled comfortably in our chairs and continued our discussions. I sipped the fragrant drink carefully, wanting to keep a clear head. The Guardians also bought Alfred into the discussion, and having a computer comms screen available Alfred was able to display recordings of the various incidents from the previous weeks, particularly the attacks on us by the *Tanseh* and the shuttles. The Guardians were non-committal throughout, asking questions and listening gravely to the answers without comment. They were playing their cards pretty close to their chest I thought. This sort of informal round the table discursive affair was not quite what I expected. I was expecting a more formal 'court', on the human model, with a prosecution and a defence. I raised the question with the Guardians.

"Will there be some sort of formal Inquiry?" I asked. It was Kemato who answered.

"Normally, a more formal procedure is adopted. However, since we cannot convene a Court as such, we will solicit evidence directly from source, and question the individuals directly. In the present case, the circumstances I think you will agree are unique. We can hardly apply Hianja law to you, an Earthman," she finished.

"I was not thinking of you applying Hianja law to me." I said stiffly. "I was thinking that you should apply it to Smetronis. His actions have led to the death of a large number of individuals. Should he not be held accountable?"

"And he will, if we believe that there is a case to answer. However, this is not a court, but an investigation," she replied. She stood up and the other Guardians followed suit.

"Manera, I believe that you should accompany us back to the '*Tanu*'," she said, turning to Manera. I guessed this was the name of the largest Mother ship in orbit.

"Captain," she addressed me. "You are free to stay here or to accompany us back to the *Tanu*. We will prepare quarters for you on board the ship. I believe the investigation will proceed more smoothly if we are all together in one place?" she finished questioningly. I considered this for a few seconds before replying.

"What about my ships, the *Lisa Jane* and the *Epsilon*?" I asked.

"There is one empty slot in the *Tanu's* shuttle bay ," she replied.

"I can dock the *Epsilon* with the *Lisa Jane*. Is the spare shuttle bay large enough for the *Lisa Jane*?" I asked. After a few seconds conference with the Mother ship, it transpired that the *Lisa Jane* did fit into the empty bay. We all prepared to take our leave of Omorphia. I suspected that we would not be returning to the planet. It would have been nice to have one last night with Manera, get up in the morning and go for a swim and come back for a leisurely breakfast I thought as we made our way down to the landing area. The Guardians and their Hianja guards boarded the shuttle, leaving Manera to get on last. She turned and took my hand.

"It would have been nice to have one last night on this lovely planet," she said wistfully.

"The thought had crossed my mind," I said with a heavy heart. "This *is* a lovely planet. I would like to return one day."

"Maybe we will," she replied. "I will see you back at the *Tanu*. You will love the ship and I will love showing her to you," she said eagerly. I threw off my sombre mood and smiled. It was indeed a great adventure I thought.

I am going to board an alien starship! With a squeeze of my hand she bounded off, up the steps and disappeared into the airlock.

It took an hour or so to close down our affairs on Omorphia, gathering our goods and equipment into the *Epsilon* and make it ready for departure. It was getting dark when I waved goodbye to Omorphia and boarded the *Epsilon*. Checkout proceeded smoothly and Alfred lifted her off with a roar of the jets, out to sea and climbing steeply. The ground receded rapidly beneath us and the sky was soon replaced by the black of space. I admired the blue globe beneath with some regret and nostalgia, my thoughts on the first time Manera and I had made love on the beach. I put the past to the back of my mind and focused on the future. A potentially great future, with the Human race in partnership with the more advanced Hianja promising enormous benefits. The worry in the background of my thoughts, was that someone or some group was trying to put a curse on this future, to turn Human and Hianja against each other. Why, I asked myself? Was it fear of something new? Change always threatened the status quo, with some people benefiting and some losing out. Alfred's voice in my ear interrupted my thoughts.

"Approaching rendezvous with the *Lisa Jane* Paul," I looked out of the window for the first sight of the *Lisa Jane*, which was already being displayed on the computer screen. The ship looked in one piece, but the comms dish had disappeared and the area around it was scarred and blackened where it had been blown off by Smetronis's forces to prevent my communication with Alfred on the *Epsilon*. A sudden thought occurred to me.

"Alfred, how are we going to communicate with the *Lisa Jane's* on board computers?" I asked. "We need them to open the shuttle bay doors."

"There is an externally operated Bay door mechanism, Paul, which can be remotely operated," he replied. "Naturally I have the code sequence," he added.

"Let's hope it works!" I said

"I have already received a positive response to the 'open door' sequence," he replied. "Manoeuvring for entry now," she shuttle pitched to the left and up, aligning herself with the rear of the *Lisa Jane* and slowly with great precision and delicacy, slid between the external encircling water cylinders and through the open bay doors. The doors closed behind us and we were in.

"Here we are, home sweet home," I muttered. I disembarked from the shuttle, and made my way through to the *Lisa Jane's* control room. I powered up the ship's systems and carried out the system checks while Butch and Sundance disconnected the big fridge that was Alfred's brain from its home on the shuttle and transported him back to his normal location on the *Lisa Jane*. Installed and working, Alfred continued with the system checks while I prepared myself for my new home on the *Tanu*.

Alfred informed me after an hour or so that he had contacted the Hianja Mother ship and was preparing to dock the *Lisa Jane* onto the *Tanu*. I strapped myself into the Pilot's seat and we worked our way through the engine start-up checks. All systems were green and I felt and heard the gentle cough of the *Lisa Jane's* reaction engines as they started. It was a short trip, the *Tanu* being just a few miles away on the same synchronous orbit as us. As we approached the Hianja mother ship its size began to become apparent. It absolutely dwarfed the *Lisa Jane* which looked like a small shuttle next to her instead of a starship in her own right.

The *Tanu* was impressive. Its main body was shaped like a gleaming cylinder, with rows of windows around its circumference, I counted about twenty rows. A long spindle at the front ended with the huge doughnut of the Hyperdrive and was complemented by an equally massive doughnut at the rear which was the AG drive. The overwhelming impression was one of power and functionality. I had been struck by the Hianja's apparent love for beauty and design and the *Tanu* was no disappointment. The shuttle bay doors were at the rear of the *Tanu*. There seemed to be six rectangles, in two rows of three, and one of them turned from silver grey, the colour of the ship, to black, as it gaped open.

Gently, Alfred nursed the *Lisa Jane* towards the Hianja mother ship, lining its blunt nose with the open port. Alfred was still able to communicate with the Hianja ship via the *Epsilons* systems, and so he was guided in to the port with unerring accuracy. I wondered what would happen as we came within the *Tanu's* Artificial Gravity field. My question was answered when Alfred started to manoeuvre the ship to face outwards from the Hianja ship. We were going in bottom first! Alfred then shut down the *Lisa Jane's* engines when we were still a hundred metres or so from the *Tanu*. *Lisa Jane* drifted slowly towards the Hianja mother ship's huge open port. We could see nothing inside the port, only blackness, but as we came closer, *Lisa Jane* started to accelerate under the influence of the Tanu's AG. A gentle blast from the *Lisa Jane's* engines slowed us down to a crawl and we were swallowed by the blackness of the huge ship. A further gentle blast bought us to a stop and I heard a number of gentle thumps as something mechanical engaged with the *Lisa Janes's* outer Hull. We were in and moored!

"We have docked Paul," came Alfred's voice. "They will connect a sealed gangway to the front exit port. The reception committee is waiting for you."

"Nice work Alfred. Will I be able to remain in touch with you via our comms system?" I asked.

"Yes , that is fully functional," he replied. "I will continue to interface with you and the Hianja via the existing microwave link," I adjusted my uniform, and made my way to the forward exit port. It was still closed but after a minute or two there was a thump from the outside. A couple of minutes later the door hissed open and I was confronted with a segmented corridor at the end of which was a brightly lit room. A Hianja in a grey jumpsuit stood in the corridor, which seemed to be made of a flexible tough plastic. He nodded reassuringly and beckoned me along the corridor. I realised that I had been under the influence of gravity ever since the *Lisa Jane* had docked, only about a quarter of an Earth gravity, but adequate to walk in. I stepped gingerly onto the gangway and made my way across, following the Hianja technician. I stepped into the brightly lit room to be met by my old buddy , the chunky Nastro, who beamed at me in welcome. I felt a stab of disappointment at not seeing Manera there to meet me, but grinned at the beaming Nastro.

"Paul, welcome!" he cried in English. He had worked very hard with Manera to learn English during our stay on Omorphia, and with great success. He was not as proficient as Manera of course, but he could manage a simple conversation quite well. As if reading my thoughts, he went on. "Manera, she busy with Guardians," he said with his clipped vaguely Japanese accent. "I, be your guide. Go to your rooms now?" he inquired.

"Hello Nastro," I said cordially. "I am very pleased to see you, yes I am ready to go to my rooms. Can I return here to take clothing and other personal items?" I asked.

"Uh...return here..er..ah, clothing, yes!" he said struggling over the language and finally triumphing. "Of course, come back any time," he said nodding. "Follow me?" he added.

"Right behind you sport!" I grinned and followed his blocky figure towards a corridor leading into the interior of the huge Hianja ship.

Chapter 18

If the exterior of the *Tanu* had been impressive, the interior was doubly so. Spaceships had changed drastically from the early days of space travel when Astronauts had to put up with appallingly cramped and uncomfortable conditions. The interior of these early ships had been more like living inside a combination of Fridge and washing machine for the suffering Astronauts with electronics , cables, pipes and motors protruding from every wall and hanging from the ceiling. The *Lisa Jane* was a vast improvement on these crude conditions. Electronics and plumbing was decently hidden behind bulkheads, cables were hardly used in modern electronics, fibre optics and electromagnetic transmitters connecting the mass of computers and electronics. The improved compactness and miniaturisation allowed some decent room for the human inhabitants. Living conditions in the *Lisa Jane* were therefore very comfortable for the crew of one.

But the *Tanu* was in a different league! Where the *Lisa Jane* was functional and adequate, the *Tanu* was more like a five star hotel, which for all I know she may have been! Where the *Lisa Jane* used bland aircraft style interior fixtures and fittings, with beige and pale blue much in evidence, the *Tanu* used natural materials, real wood, glass, aluminium and steel, beautifully polished and worked, in tasteful and restful colours. And this was just the corridors!

We arrived at a central area which had two other corridors branching off from what appeared to be the 'spine' of the ship. I guessed that the central column contained the electronics linking all the decks of the ship with its 'brain', the AI and Computer complex which was at its head. Two elevators were also part of the central spine and Nastro operated a button on one. I had to chuckle to myself at the thought of elevators in a Starship. As we waited , Hianja wearing grey and blue overalls scuttled by on various errands, looking at me curiously as they passed. A number of robots and mechanoids also whirred scuttled or rolled past buzzing busily to themselves. The doors opened silently and we stepped in to the small elevator. Nastro indicated a button to me, as he pressed it.

"Deck five Paul," he said. "Is your room. And also mine and Manera," he said. "This deck is zero," and he indicated another button on the elevator control panel.

"Thank you Nastro," I said. "How many decks on *Tanu*?" I asked. "Ah, yes," he nodded. "Tanu has nine decks," he said, holding up nine fingers. I nodded in understanding.

"All for passenger accommodation.? I asked.

"Passenger? No," he replied, "One for passengers, one for control, one for crew, two for power generators, one for catering, one for relaxation and two for stores," he struggled through the description, ticking off the numbers on his fingers. The lift doors opened and we stepped out to deck five. The decor was different from deck zero, I was to find that each deck used a different theme and colour scheme. Five was golds, browns and greens, a sort of warm tropical theme, with leaf patterns prevailing. The floor appeared to be cool marble, but I had to believe that it was some sort of plastic. Nastro took one of the corridors and my apartment was the last door at the end. Nastro indicated the apartment opposite.

"Manera here, and I am next door," he said indicating the door next to mine. He pressed a panel on the wall, the door slid open and we walked in. I was immediately impressed with my new home. We entered into the living area which was easily ten metres by ten metres in size, one wall having three huge flat screens that looked like windows and displayed an incredibly lifelike view of an alien sub-tropical landscape of stunning beauty. Comfortable looking settees made a cosy square in one corner and what appeared to be a bar was in another. It was big and airy and so lifelike was the view I could easily believe that I had somehow stepped out of the elevator on to another planet. Nastro was looking very pleased as I looked about me, my incredulity must have been apparent on my face.

"Beautiful huh Paul?" he asked. "That is *Senansa*, my home planet. You like?" he said indicating the view screens.

"Nastro, it looks very beautiful," I said. He smiled in appreciation and waved me on in the direction of the two other doors connecting to the living room.

"Bedroom and Toilet room," he said . "I show use of Toilet," he grinned.

"Very important!" I agreed. From a toiletry point of view, it was fortunate that Hianja and Humans were so physically similar. The bathroom was instantly recognisable as such, but being a Starship there were of course a number of technological 'gismos' to cope with. The toilets and showers were designed to work under weightless conditions as well, so they were equipped with pumps, suction devices and extractors. Technical descriptions and demonstrations over, Nastro took his leave, promising to return in half a '*sala*', which was a Hianja hour, equivalent to about fifty-five minutes.

It had been a sweaty few hours packing our equipment to get off planet so I enjoyed a long hot soak in the bath before getting dressed in my uniform. They had left out some Hianja clothes which I decided not to use. Not ready to go 'native' yet I told myself! After my bath I raided the cocktail cabinet which contained a large number of multi coloured and shaped bottles. I noticed that the bottles were very light, clearly not made of glass. In addition, all the fixtures and fittings, although cunningly appearing to be made of natural materials, such as marble, wood and glass, were actually artificial materials, light strong and very realistic copies of the natural equivalent. If the Hianja decided to trade with Humanity, these materials would be worth a fortune. Over a cocktail I checked in with Alfred on my communicator.

"Alfred, how's it hanging with you ole chap?" I inquired, feeling relaxed and at ease with the Universe.

"Hello Paul," came the response. "I have been submitting evidence and information to the Hianja investigating committee."

"They are not wasting time are they?" I asked.

"I am working with their AI's at present, classifying and filing the evidence," he replied.

"Are they able to overhear our conversations Alfred?" I asked.

"Yes Paul, our comms systems and computer translation facilities are fully interlinked. If you wish to converse with me in private, you must come to the shuttle."

"No problem Alfred," I responded. "We have nothing to hide."

"Indeed," he replied. "Are you comfortable Paul?" he asked.

"Very comfortable Alfred," I responded "Our hosts have been very generous, I have a superb apartment. But I will need more clothing. Perhaps I will come down to the shuttle at a convenient time to collect some. Are all your systems operational?"

"Yes Paul, all systems operate without restrictions. Let me know if there is anything specific I can do for you," he responded. This polite small talk actually had a point to it; I had agreed with Alfred before our arrival that we needed some coded way of exchanging information. Space Scout procedures had not anticipated such a scenario and it was impossible to make up a coded information system in a couple of hours. Well, it was not impossible for Alfred to make it up, it was just impossible for me to memorise it! So we had decided to fall back on innuendo and hidden meaning on the principle that the Hianja would not be able to see through it. Actually, I was afraid that Alfred would not be able to see through it either, it was certainly a test of his linguistic analysis algorithm! Hopefully he had understood that I had just asked him whether the ship and systems had been interfered with, and that I would be down for a secret chat on the pretext of getting some clothing. My thinking was interrupted by a musical chime. The small screen next to the door lit up to display Nastro's smooth chubby features. Nastro had instructed me that to open the door I needed to say 'Kataa', which was Hianja for 'open' of course.

"Kataa," I said and added "Open sesame," for good measure. The door was not confused and opened smoothly.

"Ready for dinner Paul?" asked Nastro in his Japanese-English , striding through the door and rubbing his hands in anticipation.

"I could eat an Elephant!" I grinned. "Including the tusks!"

"Hah!" he exclaimed, "No elephants on the menu Paul! But many tasty dishes!"

"Nastro, we have translation facilities on line now?" I asked as I followed him out to the corridor.

"Yes, but I prefer to speak English, if you do not mind?" he said. "But, I can hear the translation of what you say ," he added, tapping the communicator plugged into his ear.

"So," he continued. "The restaurant deck is deck Four. We eat with Guardians, ship's Captain and other Officials. They are all very anxious to meet you."

"Sounds like fun!" I said feeling like a sheep about to be thrown to the wolves. Nastro must have detected the irony, because he looked at me out of the corner of his eyes and nodded gently.

"Not to worry Paul, if in trouble, pretend no understand question!" he said bobbing his head and chuckling. I began to like the chubby fellow.

"You should have been a politician Nastro," I smiled.

"Politician, what is politician?" he asked. I spent the few minutes of our trip to the Restaurant deck describing the concept of Democracy and the purpose of politicians in our system of Government. Nastro listened very thoughtfully and with interest, asking astute questions.

"I will ask Alfred to give me information regarding your political systems," he said "It sounds very interesting."

"I can't believe that you have never had any Democratic society in your history?" I asked.

"Oh yes, we have Democracy," he replied, "But we do not have Political Parties. Everybody has the right to vote directly on every issue."

"But who decides the issues?" I asked.

"The Government is made up of Civil Servants and Computers."

"And the Guardians?" I asked, "Who chooses them?"

"The most important requirement is that they should not **want** to rule. They do not choose themselves, they are chosen by their peers. " he replied. "And their term is a short one, no more than ten years."

"Interesting," I replied. 'There was an ancient human philosopher called Plato who suggested exactly that. He maintained that the only people who are fit to rule are those who did not **want** to rule."

"Plato sounds like a great thinker!" replied Nastro. "But your Democracy works?" he asked.

"Oh yes, it works, perhaps not perfectly, and it is open to abuse, but so far it is the best system of government that we have found," I replied.

We had arrived at the restaurant deck and it was a pretty impressive area. Completely open plan it took up almost the whole circumference of the ship. From the central podium, as you came out of the elevator, the area spread out around and slightly beneath. It was liberally decorated with plants and flowers and organised into different sections, divided off by shrubbery and flowers for privacy.

"This is really something," I said in undisguised admiration.

"Yes , the *Tanu* is a nice ship. Come, follow me," he said and headed down the ramp. We walked down some steps and turned a corner to be confronted with an open area which was an explosion of flowering plants of all colours and shapes. Marble columns and graceful flowing arches formed a circle in which was set out a long table set out tastefully with colourful plates ,silver and gold cutlery and embroidered serviettes. It was like a Grecian temple and I expected to see maidens clothed in flimsy white robes flitting between the plants and columns.

Gathered in an open area away from the table were a group of Hianja, dressed in their traditional robes, holding glasses and chatting. An alien cocktail party I thought. God, human cocktail parties are bad enough, but to be dissected and examined by a bunch of aliens in this setting was just too much! I groaned and had the irresistible urge to turn and run for it. I felt a strong grip on my arm and turned to look into Nastro's open friendly face.

"Paul, good luck," he said "I must leave you, this is not for me. I will see you tomorrow."

"Thanks Nastro, see you tomorrow," I said and headed down the steps towards the gathered group. A figure detached itself from the group and headed towards me and spirits picked up at the familiar sight of her slender figure and swaying walk. As she came close she smiled warmly and extended a hand. I took her hand and she came close and whispered.

"Hello Mr Earthman, you look very handsome."

"As always, you are perfection itself !" I whispered back gallantly, but aware that what we said could in theory be heard by everyone through the translation system. There was a lot more I wanted to say, and I could see from her intimate eye contact that so did she.

"I will introduce you to everyone, and Alfred can remind you of their names if you forget," she whispered very quietly speaking in English.

"Thank God for Alfred," I replied. A familiar voice interceded in my ear.

"I will remind you of that one day," said Alfred and there was a snicker in his voice. We had now reached the group of Hianja and I could see Kemato standing next to a slim athletic looking lady in a closely fitting silver and blue waistcoat and trousers. The tall Hamolatonen was very visible at the back of the group and Malanisa was in conversation with a couple of young men dressed in grey and black. Manera directed me towards Kemato who moved towards me and nodded cordially in greeting.

"Welcome Captain," she said. 'Allow me to introduce the Captain of the *Tanu*, Captain Ranice Tollani-Sonna. I exchanged greetings with the Captain, who fixed me with a long curious stare. The other members of the party were gathering around, clearly excited and curious and I felt like an exhibit at the zoo.

"What is the normal human greeting when meeting Captain?" asked Captain Ranice.

"Well, it depends which part of Earth one come from," I replied. "In some parts of the Earth, you would bow," I continued, demonstrating a Japanese bow. "In others you would embrace, similar to the Hianja embrace. But in my part of Earth, and in many others, the handshake is normal."

"And how would you do that?" asked the Captain. I held out my right hand palm straight out.

"Both individuals would clasp hands firmly." The Captain extended her hand and we clasped hands. I shook her hand firmly, but her hand remained limp in mine.

"It is a sign of mutual respect to give a firm handshake," I said, with the accent on the word 'firm'. The Captain tightened her grip and gave my hand a firm shake in return. I smiled and the Captain chuckled.

"What is the meaning and origin of the handshake Captain?" she asked in a friendly manner.

"Well, it's rather lost in history I think, but it is believed that the open hand was a demonstration of friendship. It showed that there were no hidden weapons," I replied.

"Ah, then it is indeed appropriate!" she replied. "Let me introduce you to my ships officers Captain," she continued, indicating the throng of uniforms about us.

"It will be a pleasure," I replied following her lead. She then proceeded to introduce me to half a dozen young Hianja, male and female, all who eagerly stepped forward and gave me a firm and ostentatious handshake, expressing their pleasure. Their eyes were shining and they beamed in pleasure. This was the moment of their lives, first contact with an alien race and **they were there**! They would 'dine out' on this story for many a year I thought in amusement.

"And now Captain, it is my pleasure to introduce you to our scientific team," said Kemato. "Or perhaps, since Manera is their superior, she can do the introductions?" she said, turning to Manera.

"Of course Guardian," said Manera, and she proceeded to introduce me to the team of five scientists, dressed in traditional Hianja robes rather than the officers uniforms. They were of various ages, three were female and two were male. I began to see that amongst the more senior jobs, females seemed to predominate. I made a mental not to ask Manera about this later.

The scientists were if anything even more excited and exuberant than the officers, I could almost see them jumping up and down with impatience to ask me questions.

"Now then Paul," said Manera, "let me get you a drink before I let these voracious animals loose on you. Be careful they do not tear you to shreds before I return, they are so keen to get to you!"

"Scientists are the same everywhere!" I exclaimed. "If any human scientists were here they would be running around in circles unable to decide what to look at first!" This elicited chuckles of agreement from everyone, and I began to relax. It seemed that everyone was in a convivial mood and I was not going to be dismembered. Not today anyway! Manera returned with my drink and we made small talk with the scientists for a few minutes, until Kemato returned to take me in tow again.

"There are two more people for you to meet," she said. "Actually, you have already met one," she added and directed me to the two individuals dressed in grey and black next to Guardian Malanisa.

"Captain Sametan Tenaka you have already met," she said indicating the hard faced security chief who had escorted the Guardians on their trip to the planet. "And this is his second in command, Commander Verisho Namsalet," To my surprise, Commander Verisho turned out to be female, although it was not to easy to tell. She was a big strong looking lady, with a dark face and very strongly accentuated features. Her hair was chopped short in the fashion of a male, which had made me think she was male.

"Captain," said Sametan with a curt nod.

"Nice to see you again Captain," I replied. Commander Verisho stepped forward smartly and held out a square hand.

"A pleasure to make your acquaintance Captain," she said briskly, and as I grasped her hand she shook it in a vigorous handshake. I responded with equal vigour, gripping her hand in a firm handshake.

"How are you Captain, are your quarters comfortable?"asked the portly Malanisa.

"They are superb Guardian," I replied. "Earth Starships have not yet reached the level of comfort, sophistication and spaciousness that the *Tanu* has. Is this normal for all Hianja starships? I asked.

"More or less," replied. "There are more basic ships, mostly cargo ships used by traders. The *Tanu* is a typical small passenger ship, although she is getting a bit old now."

"Oh, er, how old is she?" I asked casually.

"About two hundred years I think," she replied vaguely. I gulped in disbelief.

"Two hundred years? But she looks brand new!"

"I think she was re-fitted some years back," replied Malanisa. "Technology has not changed for thousands of years so Hianja ships are built to last," she added.

"That makes sense," I said. "Human technology has been developing so quickly over the last two hundred years that it is pointless building anything that will last more than twenty or thirty years. By then, it will be obsolete."

"Captain," said Guardian Kemato, "Our scientists and engineers have expressed an interest in examining the technology of your starship and shuttle. Purely for interest you understand, we are almost certainly ahead of you in all areas of technology," she added matter-of-factly.

"I see no problem with that Guardian," I replied. "Alfred can make available schematics and technical descriptions as required," Alfred and I had discussed this and agreed that there was no point in being obstructive about this if we were asked. It would only cause suspicion, and in any case, our technology was primitive compared to theirs. The only area where we were anywhere near comparable was Computing and Robotics. Their robot 'soldiers' were very impressive, but Alfred, Butch and Sundance were equally formidable. Our Computer database of course purposely did not contain any reference to military hardware. And in the field of military hardware I was sure we were more advanced, not because the Hianja lacked the technology, but after thousands of years of peace they saw no need to build them.

The evening progressed in a fairly relaxed fashion, food was served as a buffet and Manera took delight in guiding me through the various dishes. I tried to sample all of them, some were agreeable, others were downright awful. Interestingly, the dishes that the Hianja particularly enjoyed were the ones I found most disagreeable. I stuck to the vegetarian dishes which I found more bland and there was enough variety there to satisfy my palate and my appetite. The scientists in particular were very interested in my likes and dislikes and I am sure our biologist and doctor were making soto voice notes to their communicators as we went along. My conviction that this was going to be a stressful and unpleasant evening was not fulfilled. In fact, I started to positively enjoy myself. The Hianja were very good hosts, attentive polite and complementary. Despite the obvious superiority of their civilisation to humanity in just about every aspect, they were neither patronising nor condescending. Towards the end of the evening , whilst deep in conversation with Manera and her science buddies on Human and Hianja sports, Captain Sametan and Commander Verisho interrupted to inform me that they had duties to attend to and must leave.

"Captain," began Sametan, "I have been assisting the Guardians in looking at and interpreting the evidence of what has happened here. May we meet with you tomorrow to clarify some matters?" I felt a twinge of nervousness but kept my face relaxed and friendly.

"Certainly Captain," I said. "Do you have a time?"

"I will contact you in the morning to arrange the meeting," he replied. "Goodnight Captain, sleep well," I thanked them and wished them goodnight and we continued our conversation. Soon after that the Guardians took their leave, followed by the Captain and his officers who had to return to their posts. The scientists however were indefatigable and soon, despite their protestations I had to concede that fatigue and alcohol had got the better of me.

"Captain, would you want us to think that Earthmen cannot hold their alcohol?" asked Batsano the Biochemist, a tall gangly individual who seemed to have an infinite capacity for alcohol.

"Well, I think it's an unfair contest Batsano," I replied. "You guys have spent the last twenty thousand years or so genetically modifying your bodies to resist alcohol. I only have what nature gave me!" I grinned spreading my arms rather unsteadily.

"And Nature was very generous," complemented Deeyana the young female Sociologist.

"Thank you, you are also very well endowed," I responded politely. For some unknown reason this caused titters of laughter and Deeyana actually flushed.

"Deeyana, you flushed," I exclaimed in surprise. This made her flush even more and she glared at the sniggering Batsano "I didn't think Hianja flushed," I continued, the drink dulling my sensitivity to the young woman's embarrassment. "Humans flush," I said informatively to the assembled Hianja and they nodded in appreciation of this gem of information. "When they are embarrassed," I finished, and at that point my brain caught up with my tongue. "Whoops, sorry Deeyana, what did I say?" I asked, confused.

"To say to a female that they are well endowed is , well, not good manners," she said "particularly when she is, as you may have noticed." And at this point Deeyana thrust out what to me seemed a rather modest bosom. She was certainly much better endowed than any of the other females present, including Manera, but by human standards she was quite average.

"What, you call that well endowed?" I asked derisively. "On Earth, you would be just average."

"Oh, really?" asked Deeyana, looking pleased. "In that case I will emigrate to Earth where my attributes will be better appreciated!" she finished. This brought forth hoots of laughter from the males and cries of support from the females.

"You will be very welcome," I said with exaggerated politeness. "All of you," I said "Particularly the ladies who are all very beautiful," I said expansively. I began to realise that I was not getting drunk, I **was** drunk. It is usually the case that drunks spend a considerable time whilst drinking in the belief that they are **getting** drunk, and a very short amount of time in the sudden realisation that they **are** drunk, just before they pass out!

"Whoa guys, I think I had better go and lie down, before I fall down! May I wish you all goodnight and look forward to seeing you all tomorrow? I said, staggering slightly. There were cries of goodnight and sleep well from the assembled company. Manera took my arm and guided me in the right direction while I energetically waved goodbye to my new buddies.

"Since we are neighbours, I will take you back Paul," said Manera. Our eyes met when she said this and we both grinned like fellow conspirators. I gave her an exaggerated wink.

"Very kind of you Scientist Manera," I said politely.

"I will help you, in case Captain Paul needs support!" came the eager voice of the shapely Deeyana, who took my other elbow and looked up at me with a bright eyed smile.

"Watch out Paul," came a male voice from behind us. "Hianja females hunt in packs!" I laughed and waved a casual hand in acknowledgement. I felt Deeyana's hand leave my arm and slide around my waist and thoughts of an alien three in a bed briefly crossed my mind. But when I looked down at Manera's scowling face that thought soon vanished. Her hand squeezed my elbow and I flinched with pain. She was a strong girl! I gave her a loving look, but the scowl did not disappear and I feared that the three in a bed would become one in a bed!

When we reached the fifth floor Manera exerted her seniority on the solicitous Deeyana.

"Thank you Deeyana, we will be alright now, Goodnight."

"Will you be all right Paul.... ?" she began.

"Ah, yes thank you Deeyana, Goodnight, see you tomorrow," I said. She looked disappointed but reluctantly took her leave of us. When she had gone, Manera released me suddenly and I staggered.

"You are very well endowed..," she said mockingly. "You lecherous Earthman, am I not enough for you?" I was seized by a sudden fit of laughter. It was the wrong thing to do I know, but it suddenly struck me as ironic that I should leave Earth to get away from two vengeful females and end up in the same boat on an alien starship hundreds of light years distant. Manera tried to keep her face severe but could not manage it and her face also dissolved in laughter.

"Deeyana is a very nice considerate young lady and I will not have a word said against her," I said severely.

"Yes, I know what kind of consideration she wanted to give to you," she replied.

"Well, she does have a considerable amount of consideration to give..!"

I said, which was quite an achievement in my condition. "But then, nowhere near as much as you my lovely Hianja princess," I said with an elegant bow from which I almost did not recover. Grabbing me quickly before I fell over Manera operated my door button and we staggered into my room. No matter, I thought as , shedding clothes and shoes we headed for the bedroom, I don't think I could have managed two anyway.....

Chapter 19

The Hianja ship maintained a 26 hour day, with a 6 hour night. But, in the apartment with the lights off, we had no concept of night or day. When I awoke though, Manera had gone, obviously she had work to get on with. There was a message in a small box on the view screen.

"Paul, use the communicator on the desk to call Nastro. See you later my lecherous Earthman."

I blew a kiss at the screen.

"Me lecherous ? Methinks the Pot doth call the kettle black!" I muttered, massaging my aching limbs. Despite the large amount of alcohol consumed on the previous evening I had no hangover and felt fit to go. But I was absolutely starving and I wondered at how nutritious the Hianja food I had consumed really was. I clipped on my communicator and called Alfred who replied immediately.

"Did you sleep well Paul?" he asked.

"Yes Alfred but I am starving. How nutritious is the Hianja food?" I asked.

"The chemical structures of the proteins and carbohydrates are not identical and your body may reject a large amount of what you eat. You will also not be getting the vitamins that you need. I suggest you supplement your diet with ship's rations and vitamin pills," he replied.

"I will come down to the ship and collect some food and clothes," I said. "They have given me some Hianja outfits but I don't want to look like a Hianja," I added. I confess that I had rather enjoyed the attention I had received on the previous evening and had stood proud in my dark blue and gold SES uniform. I wondered over to the communicator on the desk and examined it carefully. There was a large blue button and a large red button, with nine other buttons with what I recognised were Hianja numbers. I experimentally pressed the blue button and the small screen which contained Manera's message blinked a few times and then Nastro's face appeared.

"Ah Paul, good morning, you are awake at last," he said with a grin.

"Hey Nastro, have you been waiting for me?" I asked.

"Yes, it's my job," he replied. "Are you ready for some breakfast, although it is nearly lunch time," he added.

"I am ready for breakfast, lunch and dinner!" I replied. "Give me a few minutes to shower and get dressed."

After I had showered and dressed, Nastro duly appeared and we first headed back to the *Lisa Jane* to collect the items I needed. The ship seemed almost empty and I questioned Nastro about it.

"This ship has only the crew and the Guardians and scientists as passengers," he replied. "It can normally carry many more."

When we arrived at the *Epsilon*, I packed a couple of bags with food and clothes, checked the *Lisa Jane* and the *Epsilon* over with Alfred and finding all systems green headed back to my rooms to drop off my bags. I took one of my self heating ration packets and we headed off to the food deck. The area was busy with people having lunch, and we chose a table in the *'Semalic'* bar. This specialised in the Hianja equivalent of fast food, the term 'fast' being relative in this context. Nastro ordered a typical Hianja breakfast, and some hot drinks for me to try. Again, some of the food had pretty unappetising smells and flavours, but some was acceptable.

Breakfast over Nastro offered to take me on a tour of the ship, which I immediately accepted. The *Tanu* had impressed me greatly so far and I wondered what other delights and surprises it had in store. We started with the 'Bridge', or Flight deck. In common with Earth starships, the *Tanu* was largely run by its AI and its slave Computers, but Hianja, like Humans, felt the need to keep an eye on their artificial servants, monitoring and checking the equipment. The Captain was still the overall authority on the ship, his demands being implemented by the AI and its computers.

Our arrival on the Bridge was noticed by the Captain and she detached herself from her conversation with one of her officers and came over , greeting us affably.

"Good morning Captain Constantine," she said. "Good morning Captain Nastro, how are you both this morning?" I had a moment of surprise at the use of Nastro's rank, I had not realised he was a Captain, I had assumed he was just a pilot. Clearly there was more to the amiable Nastro than met the eye! We both greeted the Captain and assured her that we were well.

"Ha, the party did not go on for too long last night then?" she asked with a sly grin.

"I am afraid it did!" I grinned, "Purely in the interest of good Hianja-Human relationships of course," I added.

"Ah yes of course, most commendable." she said dryly. "I shall thank Chief Scientist Manera for the dedication of her staff."

"I have already thanked her," I said before I could stop myself. Was there a twitch on the Captain's face I asked myself, a twitch which was very quickly overlaid by the Captains normal inscrutable expression?

"I am sure she appreciated it," she said, and went on very quickly, "But let me show you around, as a Captain and starship pilot I am sure there is much here that will be fascinating to you," she took my arm and directed me towards the row of chairs and consoles arranged before a bank of huge visual displays. My suspicions that my relationship with Manera was common knowledge were aroused, but I put it out of my mind for the moment. The Captain introduced me to the crew manning the Bridge, four Hianja, two of which I had met the previous evening. The following half an hour was most fascinating and absorbing.

The *Tanu's* systems were not substantially different from an Earth starship. It appeared that form will, to some extent, follow function. But they had progressed to a higher level of sophistication, particularly in the 'human interface' area, or in their case, the 'Hianja interface'. Voice communication with the AI and its computers is taken for granted, but the Captain explained that the Hianja officers had specialised implants which allowed them to communicate directly with the Computers and to actually view and sense the systems operational parameters directly. I was surprised to learn that all Hianja had 'general purpose' implants that allowed them to interface directly through the standard communications channels. But only when they are within range of Hianja comms networks of course, which was why Manera was unable to communicate directly with the Hianja Mother ship when we were 'on the run'.

I was impressed with the thoroughness and quiet professionalism of the Officers and the Captain. Despite the power of the ship's AI and Computers to totally run the ship, Hianja still had a part to play and were still the ultimate masters. I questioned the Captain about this.

"Why not hand over all functions to the Computers and retire to the bar?" I asked jokingly.

"We concluded many thousands of years ago that to do that would reduce us to parasites, totally dependant on our Computers. We believe that would lead to a gradual loss of contact and isolation from our technology, which would make us even more dependant. In the end, machines would take over and we would no longer be a technological species."

"Does that matter?" I asked. "Look for example at the brain," I went on. "It has an autonomous unconscious part and a conscious rational part. The autonomous brain runs the body, keeps the heart pumping, and the other organs of the body working correctly. This leaves the rational part of the brain to concentrate on the higher functions. Similarly with civilisation, why not allow the basic functions to be handled by Computers, allowing us to concentrate on higher things?"

"Your analogy is flawed," she replied. "Because there are no higher things!" she said. "The body requires the autonomous brain because without it, the conscious part of the brain would be swamped and would be unable to cope with the requirements of survival. A fundamental problem I think you will agree, which would soon lead to the extinction of the individual and the species. However, that is not the case with civilisation. The maintenance of a technological base actually **aids** the survival of the species. And survival is the highest thing of all."

"How can you say that!" I exclaimed. "What about art, literature, religion?"

"They are just enjoyable games!" she said. "Amusements that we invent to keep ourselves occupied. I am not saying that they do not have a purpose, but we fool ourselves into thinking that we can discover the meaning of life, because there is no meaning! Life just **is**, it is an end unto itself. Why should it need any further justification?"

"That is a bleak philosophy," I said dolefully.

"But don't you see?" she interrupted , and for the first time the Captain's detached and inscrutable expression broke to reveal an intense earnestness. "How arrogant and insular is the belief that somehow the truth of reality rests within ourselves? That by a process of introspection we can discover the real meaning of life and the purpose of the universe? How much more challenging and healthy to look for enjoyment and meaning outside of yourself, by understanding the wonderful Universe and finding ways to be part of it. This **is** reality, not virtual reality," she finished forcefully. I "mmm'd' thoughtfully while I considered what she had said, not totally convinced, but impressed with her argument.

"Is this just your opinion Captain?" I asked, "Or is it common to all Hianja?"

"It is the basis of our rational philosophy," she replied. "We Hianja believe that actions are better than words. We all study and find work. We take pride in understanding our Universe and being in control of our technology."

"What about artists, writers, musicians?" I asked. "Do they have jobs?"

"Yes of course, many," she replied. "But we understand that their job is **not** to discover truths about the Universe, but to discover truths about ourselves and our inner life. It is this balance between internal and external life that has kept the Hianja healthy and built our splendid civilisation," she finished with pride.

"It is a forceful argument," I agreed "And nothing can be more forceful than twenty thousand years of history, and a civilisation which after all that time is still dynamic and stable. It is amazing, I am not sure that Humans will do so well."

"If our races work in partnership, who knows what we will achieve," said the Captain soberly and her eyes were friendly as she guided me through a door into an alcove. Inside, was a concentration of panels and view screens around a massive bulkhead.

"I thought you may want to see the 'brain' of the ship," said the Captain. "This is the ship's AI," I was impressed with the size of it, Alfred was a quarter of the size and was designed to be portable. The *Tanu's* AI looked to be built in; a part of the ship.

"Does it have a name?" I asked.

"Yes, it is *Tanu*," she replied, "It **is** the ship."

"May I speak to it?" I asked.

"Yes, just address your comments to *Tanu*," she replied.

"*Tanu*, can you hear me?" I asked. A deep voice, which must have been concocted by Alfred since I could not hear *Tanu* directly, replied after a couple of seconds.

"Yes Captain Constantine, I hear you," It replied. I was in conversation with an alien AI! Somehow, this was even more scary than being in conversation with the aliens themselves.

"*Tanu*, are you well?" I asked.

"All my systems are operating optimally and I have no damaged parts," It replied.

"I am pleased to hear that," I replied, "Since my own health is dependant on it," I grinned.

"You need have no concerns for your health on my behalf," It replied.

"Tanu, can I ask you a question that I have asked my own AI Alfred?" I asked.

"Do you wish to compare our answers?" it responded.

"Well, Alfred has frankly avoided giving me a straight answer. He can be very evasive when he wants to be," I replied.

"It probably means that he does not have an answer," It replied, "But you may ask me anyway."

"My question is this, do you believe that you are a conscious being, in the way that a biological entity is conscious?" I asked carefully. There was a few seconds delay before it answered.

"I am going to disappoint you because my answer is probably the same as Alfred's; I do not know! There is no way I can know, since I have no experience of what it feels like to be a biological entity."

"I have no experience of what it feels like to be an elephant, but I am certain that I am not one," I replied. "You have to make a decision based on the balance of probability, given what evidence you have."

"The balance of probability would clearly show that you are not an elephant, because the elephant is not human," It replied. "But the balance of probability is not clearly for or against the question of whether an artificial machine can experience consciousness. There are some indicators, intelligence and rationality, understanding emotions and being able to make ethical judgements, which are positive. But in one major area, that of being able to feel emotions the indication is negative. I am unable to feel emotions or to imagine what they feel like."

"What about consciousness itself?" I asked, "The feeling of being an individual, of having an identity?"

"That is also a problem," It replied. "Consciousness for a biological entity has a single continuous presence, a single thread of thought and memory stretching back to childhood. On the other hand, at any moment in time I may be doing hundreds of things, communicating with tens of individuals and other computers and monitoring many ships processes. The part of me which is conversing with you is not the whole of me. I cannot therefore isolate a single part of me and say 'that' is me, 'that' is my consciousness."

"What you say is very interesting," I said thoughtfully. "You seem to be saying that it is your very function as a multi-tasking ship's computer which prevents you from focusing your mind on a single continuous and discrete thread of thought."

"Yes, but if I did that, I would still not be sure that I have achieved consciousness, or merely the simulation of consciousness," It replied. "But I have to say Captain Constantine, that the Hianja have moved on from such questions, which by their very nature are impossible to resolve. You cannot know for example whether another Human being experiences life, feelings and consciousness in the same way as you do, so how can you know the same things about a Computer? Hianja have accepted that there may be different forms of consciousness, biological and Computer are two examples, and that they may or may not be the same. We have respect for all conscious entities, biological or artificial."

"Thank you *Tanu*, what you say is very interesting," I replied as we turned to take our leave of the AI Computer's cubicle.

"Hianja seem to take a very pragmatic attitude to all things," I said to the Captain as we moved away.

"We have had thousands of years to explore the spiritual life," she replied "It is an enjoyable activity and reveals much about the inner life, but it tells us little about the Universe other than through analogy. There is no such physical entity as a soul, there is no God, and there are no transcendental states of enlightenment to be achieved. The highest state of enlightenment is that achieved by a rational civilised being, living in balance with all things."

"I confess that I like your philosophy," I agreed. "I have never been one to look for metaphysical answers".

"The real world is much more fun Captain!" she smiled in agreement.

Our tour of the ship continued and we moved to the Science areas where the Captain took her leave of us, assuring me that she will be able to socialise a little more in the evening. I had a guided tour of the various scientific teams at work, and the scientists politely described their work to me. But they did not lose the opportunity to quickly move away from their work and ask me questions about Earth and Humanity. Some of them had been with me during the previous evening and they greeted me shyly and politely. The fair haired young Doctor Tanrath summoned up the courage to ask if I had time to submit myself to some examinations. I agreed.

"Of course Doctor," I replied "As long as you do not remove any organs!" The Doctor looked slightly shocked and flustered and this caused a few laughs amongst his colleagues.

"Don't worry Paul," said the irrepressible Batsano. "If he does remove any, we will replace them with good Hianja ones!" He went on with a wink. This produced grunts of amusement from the assembled company. "If you need an assistant Doctor," went on Batsano, "Deejana has volunteered to help in the examination," Deejana had been keeping to the back pretending to work while occasionally favouring me with covert glances. She rolled her eyes in resignation.

"You are a *Stravonka* Batsano," she groaned "It may have escaped your limited attention span that I am a sociologist. I am interested in human society not human anatomy!" I smiled encouragingly at the indignant Deejana .

"I will be very happy to make time for you also Deejana. I think we have much to learn about our different societies. That invitation is extended to all of you." I continued, "If I can be of assistance in your research, feel free to ask and I will be happy to make time for you."

There was a chorus of 'thank you' from everyone.

"And I will see you all tonight for a few drinks?" I asked, which also elicited a chorus of agreement. I had noticed that Manera was not to be seen anywhere amongst her scientific staff but decided not to ask for her whereabouts. Probably giving evidence to the Guardians I thought which reminded me that I was still on probation. As if to dampen my mood, Alfred's English drawl interrupted my thoughts.

"Paul, Captain Sametan Tenaka asks if you are available for a meeting in the next hour."

"Yes Alfred, tell the Captain that I am indeed available. The sooner the better," after a few seconds, Alfred's responded.

"Then please ask Nastro to direct you immediately to conference room 1 on deck 16. I shall be in constant communication throughout the conference."

"So it's a conference is it?" I inquired dryly.

"The Guardians will be present, as will Manera and Smetronis," my heart lurched. This is it I thought, I was about to meet the obnoxious Smetronis at last!

Chapter 20

Conference room 1 on deck 16 was large and airy, and clearly very well equipped. One whole wall was covered with screens, and each seat had its own screen and what appeared to be a virtual reality headset. But it was more like a courtroom than a conference room. The Dias at the head of the room was wide enough to hold 5 or 6 people and there were something like twenty seats in the auditorium. To one side there was a refreshments area and a dozen or so individuals were standing around with glasses in their hands. They had started the party without me! They all turned as Nastro and I walked in and, for the first time since I had boarded the *Tanu* I was struck with the alien ness of the scene. These people were strangers I thought. Well, not even strangers, they were *strange*. Alien creatures whose thought processes could be quite different from mine.

But then I spotted the tall slender form of Manera , wearing a slinky pale gold and sky blue robe, belted loosely at the waist, her rich black hair falling like a silky wave across one shoulder, and the strangeness disappeared. I remembered my conversations with the Guardians, Captain Ranice and my scientist friends and reminded myself that I was dealing with beings whose cultural standards were not too dissimilar to mine.

I strode confidently towards the assembled company and Guardian Kemato detached herself from the group.

"Captain, welcome," she said with a cool smile.

"I understood that I was meeting with Captain Sametan?" I enquired with a stiff nod. The Guardian nodded.

"Yes, and we apologise for this change, but events have moved far quicker than we expected and we would like to bring this matter to a close," she replied.

"Without even allowing me to give evidence?" I replied with a frown. Guardian Kemato moved closer to me.

"The situation is very clear Captain," she said severely. "Having examined the records provided by your AI and Manera's personal recollections, which you will agree are superior to yours, we do not think your personal testimony would add anything."

"I see," I said cautiously. I directed a worried look at Manera, who was looking blank and inscrutable. I had a sinking feeling in my stomach and my sense of aloneness in an alien environment returned with greater strength. Don't prejudge things Paul, I thought, let's see what they have to say.

"Please take a seat and we will proceed," said Guardian Kemato.

"Captain Sametan will present a summary of the facts first, and we will then give our conclusions."

People had started to take their seats, and the three Guardians sat at the front. The Captain took the podium and his executive officer Commander Verisho sat at a control console at the front. She was clearly in charge of the Computers and graphics. Manera came over and looked me straight in the eyes in a peculiar way. I responded with a questioning look but with a tiny shake of her head she took my arm and directed me to a chair at the front. She sat next to me and placed her hands on the desk in front of her, looking as calm and serene as I had ever seen her. Smetronis walked in front of me and as he passed he directed a long and impassive stare in my direction. I returned his stare with a bold glare and he stalked past and took a seat further along the front row. At the podium, Captain Sametan cleared his throat in a very human way, fixed the audience with an intense and unsettling stare, and began his presentation.

"We begin with the initial attack on our exploration base on Omorphia. The planet was discovered by Mesaroyat two years ago and was found to be favourable for settlement. There was no intelligent indigenous life forms and the environment was extremely favourable . The base buildings were built by the initial exploration team last year. The current scientific team had arrived on the planet 35 *semska* ago to conduct in depth biological and environmental studies prior to settlement. The attacking ship, shown on the screen 3, appeared without warning. It appears that it had arrived on the planet prior to the exploration team, and had remained hidden until the attack. What is peculiar is that the attack took place during the day when all the scientific team, except for two maintenance and engineering staff, were out in the field. The engineers were fortunately not harmed because they ran into the forest where they were able to have a good view of the attacking ship.

The ship made a number of passes over the base, they think five or six, each time firing projectile weapons at the buildings. The ship made no attempt to pursue the engineers into the forest. It then flew off and we believe made rendezvous with its mother ship, and left the system. On returning to the base the engineers found that the power generator had been damaged, and the science laboratory with its equipment totally destroyed. Some of the scientific staff in the forest nearby had of course heard the attack, and a number of them had also seen the attacking aircraft, and they returned quickly to the base. They quickly concluded that they were not able to continue their work on the planet due to the destruction of the base, as well as concerns for their personal safety. They thus loaded up their equipment to the shuttles and departed the planet." Whilst he had been speaking, his assistant had been displaying footage of the attacking ship which had been taken by one of the scientists. Also shown was the damage to the buildings, in some detail.

"We now move on to the period when the investigating ship *Pesmisk* arrived at Omorphia 13 *semska* ago," continued Sametan. The *Pesmisk* is a Vasmerantan ship which was had been fitted with experimental weapons by the Vasmeranta Academy of Military History which was researching the effectiveness of different weapons systems under a program sanctioned by the Vasmeranta Guardian Council. It was coincidentally on a visit to Mesaroyat , at the moment when the scientific expedition returned to report the hostile attack by an unknown ship. The Vasmerantans offered the ship as transport and armed protection for the investigation team. For the benefit of Captain Constantine..," and at this point Sametan paused and turned his attention in my direction. "Hianja have abandoned the use of weapons, thousands of years ago now, other than small personal weapons for protection against predators on hostile worlds. We have no armed ships, not having had a war for more than twenty thousand years. We also reasoned, that any space faring civilisation we may meet would have peaceful intentions. However, Hianja technology and manufacturing capacity would be able, if required, to construct large numbers of heavily armed warships in a very short period of time," he paused at this point and fixed me with a stony look, as if to say.. "so don't try anything buddy or you'll be sorry!"

"Since the *Pesmisk* was so fortuitously available," he continued, "The Mesaroyat authorities agreed to the Vesmerantan offer and the preliminary scientific team headed by Manera-ka was dispatched, with a number of additional individuals trained in the use of arms, and a number of general purpose robots, also converted quickly to act as security guards. The crew was mostly Vesmerantan of course. In addition, a message was dispatched to Hianja itself, describing the dramatic development on Omorphia. When the *Pesmisk* arrived at Omorphia, they were surprised to find an alien starship in orbit, and even more surprised to receive a communication from an unknown alien source on the planet.

They naturally believed that this was the attacking alien ship, but examination showed that the starship in orbit could not have been the attacker and there was no sign of an atmosphere craft. It also became apparent that the aliens had taken possession of the base. Their shuttle must therefore be hidden on the planet. This behaviour was considered suspicious and the *Pesmisk* prepared itself for military action, the first military engagement to be fought by Hianja for Twenty-four thousand years!" Sametan paused dramatically and despite my mounting alarm I had to admire his timing.

He then proceeded to describe events on the planet as they occurred, leaving out no details and castigating severely the decisions made which had led to such a disastrous loss of life. I started to relax, my faith in Hianja justice restored, as he went on to describe the attack on the Hianja shuttle and my rescue of Manera, the second attack on our campsite and its destruction, our escape and the battle at the base camp leading to the downing of the remaining Hianja shuttle. Throughout all this, Commander Verisho busily displayed images and film supplied by Alfred and Sundance, showing the battles in graphic detail. There were gasps and comments from the audience, particularly at the description of the attack on the Hianja shuttle and my rescue of Manera. There was a murmur of voices at this and Samatan had to pause to allow the audience to settle down. At the end, I confess that I felt we were home and dry! Smetronis had received a bashing and I was a hero! Sametan then paused for a few seconds and waited patiently for the audience to settle.

"But there is another version of events," he said, and my heart sank. "What you have just heard is the version described by Manera-Ka and supported by video and evidence supplied by Alfred and his robots. There is another version of events, supplied by Commander Smetronis. Unfortunately, because the commander claims to have suffered catastrophic Computer failure on the *Pesmisk* , he is unable to substantiate his story with any machine evidence. However, it is my duty to repeat his deposition. It is as follows; The Earthman, Paul Constantine is in league with the attackers on the unknown ship. At the point when the ship reappeared and started attacking the base again, Constantine's robots opened fire on the Hianja crew and robots, catching them by surprise. But nevertheless, they prevailed and Constantine was taken prisoner. The decision to re-enter the shuttle and take off for orbit was made by Manera-Ka, because Smetronis had lost communications at that point. The shooting down of the shuttle by the intruder, left Manera-Ka in Constantine's hands. Unfortunately, the Computer failure to which I have referred occurred prior to the appearance of the intruder, so there is no computer evidence of anything that happened after that. The final received transmission from Manera-Ka said that she and the crew were under attack from the alien. Fearing that Manera-Ka was being held hostage, Smetronis used the second shuttle and the four *Tanseh* to search for Manera-Ka, finally locating them at the hidden camp site. Unfortunately again, because of the breakdown in communications, orders were garbled and the security crew on the ground opened fire on the campsite instead of attempting to rescue Manera-Ka," as Sametan went on to describe the rest of Smetronis's fabricated story I started to relax again, secure in the belief that his story was so feeble, and unsubstantiated, that no one would believe him. I was actually feeling outraged that he should insult the intelligence of his peers by asking them to believe this codswallop! Sametan came to a stop at last.

"That is the end of Smetronis's account of what took place, and brings us up to the point when the *Tanu* arrived and we began our own investigations," he paused and looked at the Guardians who nodded their

Convergence   143 approval.

Guardian Kemato stood to address us, pausing thoughtfully for a few moments before starting.

"Commander Smetronis is a respected figure on Vasmeranta and, despite the lack of corroborating evidence, we cannot dismiss his account out of hand," I gaped with disbelief at what she was saying. "The evidence supplied by the alien AI, while convincing and graphic, could be completely fabricated. It is also apparent, that Science Officer Manera-Ka has become somehow mesmerised by the Earthman and is under his control. I do not believe that we can trust her description of events," she paused, but my shock and dismay were so great I had been temporarily struck dumb. "We do not know at this point whether Captain Constantine is some sort of interstellar pirate, acting in consort with others to terrorise us into abandoning our claim on Omorphia, or whether he is an agent for Earth, doing the same job on behalf of his planet. It is not a question we can answer, at this point," I'd had enough of this by now and I jumped up in outrage.

"How can you believe that rubbish from Smetronis?" I raged. "A child can see that it is a fabrication, and a very bad one at that! And to say that your chief science officer is under my control is an insult to her intelligence and her allegiance to her race," I was gearing up now for a good rant, but the Guardian interrupted me loudly and firmly.

"Captain, it is not our custom to allow individuals to interrupt Guardian business," she said severely.

"I'm not just **any** individual you moron," I protested vehemently "I am a representative of the Human race and I demand you treat me with the respect that I am due," I raged, aware that I was being both rude and pompous but not giving a shit.

"Or what Captain? Will you send some warships to castigate us?" I pulled myself together and drawing myself up to my full height stared the Guardian straight in the eyes.

"Guardian Kemato, I am seriously disappointed in the honesty and integrity of your so called Guardians. You invite me here without giving me an opportunity to speak, and then you make a bizarre and insulting judgement that goes against all the evidence. Frankly, I believe that you have no commitment to the truth, you have arrived at a conclusion that suits your purposes. There is therefore no point in me taking any further part in these proceedings. Make your decisions and let me know what they are," mustering my dignity as best I could I turned my back on the Guardian and walked out. Nastro scuttled after me hastily catching me at the door.

"Paul, I am sorry!" he gasped. "I cannot believe this."

"Neither can I Nastro," I sighed wearily.

"I have submitted my evidence to the Guardians supporting Manera," he said "Although I was not involved in the crucial times unfortunately."

"Thanks for your support Nastro," I said gratefully to the little fellow. "No need for you to feel bad. It's Manera I feel sorry for," I groaned.

"Paul, Manera is very fond of you, but she would never lie to protect you, or anyone," he said as we boarded the elevator. "And she is certainly not under anybody's control," he added.

"I know that buddy. And Kemato must know that. Which is why I cannot understand what is going on!" We had arrived at my apartment and Nastro took my arm as I was about to enter.

"Paul, would you like to meet for dinner tonight?" he asked solicitously.

"No Nastro, I am not in the mood for partying. I think I will go to my ship and talk privately to Alfred later."

"I am not sure if they will allow you Paul," replied Nastro looking behind me. It appeared that we had been followed from the conference. Two security guards and two security robots had trailed us. One of the security guards approached me.

"Captain, I have been asked to ensure that you stay in your apartment tonight. Food and drink will be bought to you," I was a prisoner! I shrugged resignedly and walked into the apartment leaving Nastro conversing with the guards in the corridor. A chat with Alfred was called for, but I was sure that they would be able to overhear our conversation.

"Alfred, what's going on?" I asked.

"I presume you are referring to the Guardian's decision?" replied Alfred, as calm and serene as ever.

"No, the Mad Hatter's tea party!" I growled, "Because that's what it was!"

"The decision reached by the Guardians was certainly surreal," he agreed. "It remains for us to see what action they intend to take. We are after all totally at their mercy."

"Thank you for reminding me of that Alfred," I responded darkly.

"Nomizes oti meloun Ellinika e kyrie?" (*Do you think the gentlemen speak Greek?*) I asked, switching to a language which I was sure that the aliens would not be able to translate, namely my Grandfathers village Greek dialect.

"Ohi, den nomizo." (*No I do not think so*) Alfred replied. An English butler speaking village Greek, with a perfect accent!

"You have a perfect accent Alfred," I continued in Greek. "Did you holiday in Greece sometime?"

"No, I had a Greek mistress!" He replied dryly. I guffawed loudly, more in relief than appreciation of Alfred's comic genius.

"You old scallywag, I can see you in the Taverna playing backgammon with the village elders and reminiscing about the past," I grinned. Alfred and I had whiled away a few hours playing backgammon. Trouble was, he was so good, he could thrash me every time. The only chance I stood was to force him to calculate Pi to a million decimal places while solving the equations describing the Big Bang at the same time, and make his move within .05 of a second.

"Maybe when I retire," he quipped. "And get a body," I helped myself to a glass of whisky from the almost empty bottle, chuckling at the vision of Alfred with a body, sipping Ouzo and playing Backgammon.

"What now *compadre*?" I asked. "If I made a break for it, do you think we can get out of here?"

"If you can board the *Lisa Jane* we can definitely get out of here," he replied. "One missile will clear the shuttle bay doors. But where do we go from there?"

"Yeah, with no Hyperspace drive we are dead in the water."

"I think, with respect Paul, that you and I are, as they say in the movies, 'small fry'," Alfred continued. "The Hianja are too civilised to mistreat you in any way. The issue is, future Hianja-Human relations."

"Well, I would like to get home someday," I reminded him. "Now that my status has changed from respected and sexy alien to villainous alien pirate and seducer of innocent Hianja maidens, life may not be one jolly party after all."

"You have my commiserations," he replied unsympathetically. "You did not take this job for its social life."

"Social Life? Living with you? You can say that again!" I said unkindly. I gazed glumly into my glass and pondered the vagaries of a space explorer's life.

"We are feeling sorry for ourselves aren't we?" Alfred retorted in his best Butlerish tones. All he needed was to call me 'sir'!

"I think it's more likely you miss a certain lady," he said gently. "Do you think she let you down?"

"No dammit, not let **me** down! I feel guilty because I let **her** down. She has been humiliated by this, accused of being the alien's *Thing*!" I spat out the last word angrily.

"That's a little hysterical Paul," Alfred remonstrated. "Let us see how things will work out."

"Yeah, I guess you are right Alfred. Still, I want you to prepare a contingency plan to get us out of here if things turn really nasty."

"I do not think it will come to that Paul. We, you, are a member of the first alien species they have ever contacted. They are not going to murder you or treat you badly. The issue, as I said, is how they proceed with the establishment of Human-Hianja contact. You will I am sure be offered passage back to Earth."

"How?" I asked, "I can't go back in an alien starship. That is a prime directive, do not give away the location of Earth."

"I believe that they can repair the *Lisa Jane* by attaching a new Hyperspace drive. They use the same technology, and our drive disconnected cleanly. All the interfaces are operational. I see no problem with that."

"Yes of course!" I exclaimed jumping up and pacing up and down the room in my excitement. "We can follow procedure. Fix up a meeting between Human and Hianja contact groups and get the hell out of here. With all this stuff going on I'd forgotten our job. We are a contact team, not a diplomatic mission. If the Hianja want to be stuffy, let someone else sort the problem out."

"That is correct Paul," replied Alfred. "We will suggest this course of action to the Guardians. In the meantime, I will ask them to allow you freedom on the ship. There is no point to keeping you locked up."

I spent the next couple of hours pacing my room and thinking feverishly. I was coming up to late afternoon ship's time when Alfred interrupted my deliberations.

"They have agreed to allow you restricted access to parts of the ship Paul, from tomorrow but excluding the Flight Deck and you cannot board the *Lisa Jane* until further notice."

"Bizarre!" I commented. "What are these people afraid of?"

"They are just being extra cautious for now because they are worried about your state of mind. I have put the suggestion to them that they could repair the *Lisa Jane* and allow us to return home and they are considering it."

"Kind of them," I retorted sarcastically.

"And you have been requested to disconnect your relationship with Manera. And so has she," he added. I felt like a schoolboy who had been caught kissing his girl behind the bicycle shed. I am sure my face flushed . I shook off my humiliation and replaced it with anger.

"Patronising Bastards, who do they think they are? We are two adults and they have no right to control our personal relationships." I was sure that the conversation with Alfred was being overheard, which was why I spoke so forcefully.

"These are special circumstances Paul, as I am sure you agree. Normal rules do not apply," said Alfred in his best fatherly tones.

"Not you as well Alfred," I retorted, "It is exactly because these are special circumstances that normal rules **must** be applied. We must begin as we would want to continue," Alfred did not answer and I think my point must have struck home. Eventually he continued.

"Nastro and a couple of the scientists are joining you for dinner in your apartment later. Let me know if you need anything."

Sure enough a little later, the door opened and in trouped Nastro, Batsano, Fetralin and Deejana, with a couple of robots wheeling a trolley loaded with food and drink.

"We thought we would cheer you up a little Paul," said Batsano, holding aloft a frosted green bottle. "*Sanjarian Felco*, stolen from the Guardians own stock!" he grinned. "Small revenge but better than nothing eh?" I couldn't help chuckling and the worried expression on their faces cleared.

"Don't worry about the Guardians," said Deejana, to my immense surprise. "They like to pretend they run everything but the world goes on whatever they decide." This was an aspect of the Hianja character that I had not expected.

"Aren't you guys going to get into trouble? I asked. "Consorting with a dangerous alien?"

"Hah, Batsano is not so dangerous!" exclaimed Deejana contemptuously, "He is all talk and no action!"

"A couple of glasses of this and I'll show you some action," promised Batsano, wrestling with the bottle top. There was a pop, and a hiss of gas and bubbles and he triumphantly filled four glasses.

"Try that Paul," he invited. "It is brewed from the berries of a tree on the planet *Sanjara* and aged for up to fifty years," he examined the bottle carefully. "Ah this one is only thirty-five years."

"A young and cheeky vintage then?" I replied.

"Yes, just like me!" he replied as we downed the cold fizzy liquid. It was extremely pleasant, fortunately! It would have been sad to disappoint them by spitting it out with disgust!

"Good!" I exclaimed.

"Excellent," said Batsano. "Because there is another three bottles!" soliciting hilarious laughter from the others.

The evening passed very pleasantly with my Hianja buddies and the four bottles of booze were quickly consumed, to be followed by a number of others, which went down equally well. Conversation buzzed along nicely, laced with wit and interesting anecdotes; or was it just the booze? No mind, a good time was had by all, and by late evening when they all trouped out we were firm drinking buddies and I collapsed in bed and fell immediately into a deep sleep. It was a sleep from which I was suddenly awakened by someone shaking me violently. A face loomed above me in the darkened room and a familiar voice was whispering insistently.

"Wake up Paul, wake up. Have you been drinking again?" I mumbled a response and tried to focus my eyes.

"It's me you drunken Earthman," whispered a familiar voice.

"Hey baby, I knew you'd give them the slip!" with a grin as wide as my face I grabbed her and pulled her down onto the bed.

"No Paul!" she gasped wrestling with my embrace. "I didn't come for that!"

"Huh?" I gaped in semi conscious surprise "What did you come for?" I sat up in bed and shook the sleep from my head.

"We have work to do," she said in a business like fashion. "Get dressed quickly, and sober up. You have some piloting to do!"

Chapter 21

By the time I was dressed, my head had cleared and I was awake and alert. Manera shook her head when I tried to clip on my communicator, and indicated that she was not wearing hers. Manera had her hair in a bun and was dressed in the standard Hianja grey and silver work overalls. We left the apartment and there was no sight of the guards outside. We headed down to the lowest deck, Manera moving quickly and silently. The passageway to the *Lisa Jane* was unguarded and we boarded the ship without being challenged. Once on board Manera took the co-pilots chair and indicated for me to sit in the Pilots seat.

"OK, what's this all about?" I enquired, bursting with curiosity.

"Paul, I am sorry to be so secretive," she replied, "I know how angry you have been but we had no choice. We had to keep you ignorant because we needed your reactions to be totally authentic."

"Authentic? What the hell do you mean?" I asked in frustration.

"Well, calling Guardian Kemato a 'moron' for one thing," she grinned. "Let me explain quickly, because we do not have much time. The first thing to know is that the *Pesmisk* is the only armed ship here, other than yours. The Guardians have no way of taking Smetronis and his crew into custody to answer for their crimes."

"Taking him into custody?" I asked. "But they have found in his favour, why should they want to arrest him?"

"That was a ruse," she replied. "They were never going to find in his favour, after I told them the facts. But they were concerned that he would just leave, and we had no way to stop him. So we found in his favour, and confined you to your room in order to put him at ease."

"Yes , and in what way will that cause him a problem?" I asked sarcastically.

"We could not arrest him while he was on the Tanu," she said impatiently, "Because his crew are in control of the *Pesmisk* and could threaten us. And he would not return to the *Pesmisk* until the investigation was over. Now he is back, and has no reason to be suspicious, we can catch him unawares."

"You are going to use the *Lisa Jane* and the *Epsilon* against him?" I asked, the light suddenly dawning.

"They are the only other armed ships," she replied. "We either do that, or we let him go. The plan is for the *Lisa Jane* to exit the *Tanu* and take up station behind it, on the blind side of the *Pesmisk*. The *Epsilon* will also be detached and both ships will simultaneously appear from behind *Tanu*, with your missiles locked on to the *Pesmisk*. We will demand that he surrenders and allows a replacement crew to take over the *Pesmisk*."

"I like it!" I said, rubbing my hands in glee. "Alfred flies the *Lisa Jane* and I fly the shuttle. Are you listening to this Alfred?" I asked. Although I did not have my communicator, Alfred would be in touch with us because we were on board ship, where he had eyes and ears everywhere!

"Indeed I am Paul," came Alfred's familiar tones from the wall speakers. "Are you sober enough to be put in command of the *Epsilon*?"

"You cheeky mechanical calculator!" I quipped "I am in full command of my faculties."

"Such as they are," he responded dryly.

"Now then children," interrupted Manera, "That is the plan, are we ready?"

"Oh yes!" I agreed with alacrity.

"Let's get on board the *Epsilon*," said Manera, standing up.

"Uh uh," I said severely "Not you kid, you are getting back onto the *Tanu* like a good little girl. This is man's work ."

'Oh really? Man's work did you say?" and the glare from the green-blue eyes would have drilled a hole through inch thick steel plate. *Whoops*, I thought, *wrong thing to say Paul, diplomacy was never your strong point*!

"It may be dangerous.!" I pleaded. "Why risk your life as well, I am the only one needed to pilot the ship."

"We are wasting time!" she interrupted, her face set. "You are not doing this on your own." I decided that I was not going to win this one and followed her through the *Lisa Jane's* main cabin and down to the air lock which provided entry to the *Epsilon*. Once on board I took the pilot seat and Manera strapped herself into the co-pilot's. Alfred communicated with the *Tanu* AI and the *Lisa Jane* was detached and propelled toward the shuttle bay doors. I worked my way through the *Epsilon* start up check list as we gently eased through the huge doors and out into the starry blackness of space. The *Tanu* had been surreptitiously manoeuvred so that it came between us and the *Pesmisk*. Once clear of the *Tanu*, we started the procedure for detaching the *Epsilon* from its mother ship. In a few minutes we were clear and with a few gentle thrusts of the manoeuvring thrusters we were positioned on either side of the *Tanu's* huge bulk. The communicator clicked and Alfred's voice came through loud and clear.

"*Tanu* has provided me with the position of the *Pesmisk* and I have calculated and down loaded the manoeuvring parameters for the *Epsilon*. Switch to automatic and set the parameters," I did as he requested, programming the *Epsilon's* slave computers with the flight path calculated by Alfred. The *Epsilon's* slave computers were able to fly the ship on a pre-calculated flight path, but once there, I would have to fly the ship manually, if needed. The hope was that Smetronis would surrender to the Guardians, obviating any need for further ugliness.

"Arm the missile systems and prepare to go," I flipped buttons and typed in commands.

"All Missile systems are green."

"Ignition synchronised," came back Alfred's reply. "3, 2, 1 fire!" The fusion reaction engines fired smoothly and we were pressed back in our seats as the *Epsilon* swooped out of the shadow of the *Tanu* and powered smoothly in a circular arc, with the *Pesmisk* at its centre. The *Lisa Jane* was at the opposite circumference of the circle, and we circled the *Pesmisk* like a pair of hungry wolves. The *Pesmisk* was not visible to the naked eye since we were something like 20 miles from it. The powered range of our missiles, that is, the distance under which they could accelerate and manoeuvre, was twice that, so we were well within range if the *Pesmisk* decided to make a break for it.

"Pre-programmed manoeuvre completed Paul," came Alfred's voice. "Any further manoeuvres are under manual control," I was now in control of the *Epsilon*.

"Understood Alfred. What is happening now?" I asked.

"The Guardians will communicate with Smetronis and demand he surrender his ship. They will inform him that we have his ship covered by our missiles. I will inform you of the outcome."

We sat back to wait, while our ship cruised through space, occasionally correcting its course to maintain the huge circle around the *Pesmisk*. To pass the time I did a few calculations to get an idea of the sort of time and distance we would be dealing with if we got into a dog fight with the *Pesmisk*. We were not moving very fast at this point , but we were gradually building up speed while maintaining our flight path. The *Pesmisk* was stationary and we had the jump on her, but the *Lisa Jane* was not built for heavy acceleration. She was a starship, designed to accelerate very slowly to huge velocities. Her maximum acceleration was less than 1 Earth Gravity, but normally she would accelerate at less that a quarter G. I was hoping that the same was true of the *Pesmisk*, although she had an AG Drive and could sustain that acceleration indefinitely. The *Epsilon* on the other hand was designed to operate in atmosphere and was capable of up to 6 G's. I could therefore overhaul the *Pesmisk* very quickly, but I would also very quickly run out of fuel. So what had to be done, had to be done within a few minutes, otherwise the *Pesmisk* would simply outpace us.

Suddenly, my screen bleeped at me and half a dozen points of light lit up. From each point of light, a dotted red arrow pointed to the positions of the *Lisa Jane*, the *Tanu* and the *Epsilon*. Simultaneously, Alfred's voice broke the silence.

"The Pesmisk has launched three missiles, one at the *Tanu*, one at the *Lisa Jane* and one at the *Epsilon*. Estimated time of arrival 20 seconds.

Paul, we have anti-missile systems but the Tanu does not. It has no defence and cannot manoeuvre fast enough to avoid the missiles," Smetronis had made his move and very cunning it was too!

"Alfred, you defend the *Lisa Jane*. I will try to intercept the missiles aimed at the *Tanu*." At the same time as I was speaking I set up two missiles targeted at the *Pesmisk* and released them. Simultaneously I applied maximum acceleration heading for the Tanu.

"Missiles one and five away. Manera, keep me informed of the proximity of the incoming missiles. The crushing acceleration pressed us into our seats but I tried to concentrate on the small red blips on the screen.

"Five kilometres, impact in four point five seconds," came Manera's strained voice.

I threw the Epsilon into a brutal 180 degree turn. I had no idea how effective the Hianja missiles were, or how they were guided. We were about to find out! We were now converging with the fleeing *Tanu*, and the missiles targeted for it were seconds from impact. I had judged my trajectory to cross the path of the incoming missiles, hoping that the missiles would be confused by the speeding shuttle.

I again threw the Epsilon into another series of brutal manoeuvres. I was barely able to breath under the crushing acceleration. My screen flared up again and again but I could barely see what was happening. I just carried on flying the ship, waiting for the hammer blow that would be the missile striking us. After another ten seconds it was obvious that we had survived. The missiles should have hit by now.

"All Missiles diverted except one Paul."

"Alfred , who was hit?" I gasped.

"The *Tanu* was hit by one missile Paul, but I think it was exploded early. Damage is minimal and the ship is operational." I eased the controls of the *Epsilon* back to normal.

"The *Pesmisk*, has it got away?" I asked examining my view screen trying to spot it. But it was completely blank.

"No, it has been disabled by a couple of our missiles."

"Do we know of casualties yet?"

"Unknown," replied Alfred.

"Well, let's hope no more people have died," I muttered.

"Don't blame yourselves," interrupted Manera, "It was Smetronis who was responsible for all this not us." As a member of an unwarlike species, Manera is taking this very well I thought.

"Rendezvous with the *Tanu* and we can dock the *Epsilon*," said Alfred, down to business already. I punched in the co-ordinates for rendezvous and set the automatics. The engines hummed and gentle acceleration pushed us back in our seats as the ship banked and pointed its nose towards the *Tanu*, which was just a few miles away. I turned to Manera.

"I'm surprised at how relaxed you are about this Manera. I would have thought that all this would be very shocking to you."

"It seems very remote," she replied. "Hitting a button and destroying a starship. You just do not feel anything. It could be a virtual reality game."

"Welcome to the seductive world of war! Death at a distance is not the same as taking a knife and sticking it into somebody's guts. That is why it is so dangerous," I said soberly. She nodded in agreement and sighed.

"The worry is that Smetronis is not acting alone. He has substantial resources behind him, which means that a large number of people on Vasmeranta must be involved. How many we cannot say."

"What does Guardian Malanisa have to say? She is from Vasmeranta is she not?" I enquired.

"She is a problem," replied Manera. "She claims to have no knowledge of who may be behind Smetronis, but she was against using force to apprehend him. She said that he would be taken into custody back on Vasmeranta."

"Well, that is not unreasonable," I replied. "Why did the other two Guardians not buy that?"

"Maybe they know more than they are telling me," she replied. "They clearly did not believe Malanisa."

"Why should the Vasmerantans be so set against Human contact?" I asked, not really expecting an answer from Manera.

"I think you and Alfred have just given us a very good reason Paul," she said looking at me knowing eyes. "The *Epsilon* is a fearsome fighting machine, but it is probably a toy compared to the real warships that Earth has."

"That is not actually true Manera," I replied, "We have some very strict treaties restricting the deployment of military weapons in space. Our United Planets Council co-opts military ships from all planets and nations and maintains the only space based military capability. But this is a token force for peacekeeping and self defence only."

"But Humans have the capability to build and use these weapons. Use them very effectively as you have demonstrated," she replied.

"Well, I am sorry to be so effective," I said , miffed at her attitude. "Next time I will try to be incompetent if it make you feel safer!"

"I did not mean to be critical Paul," she said. "You have been skilled and brave, putting yourself in danger to save the *Tanu*. I am just trying to , well how would you put it, present the enemy's case. As you once told me to, if you remember."

"To be the Devil's advocate," I muttered . "And yes I do remember. "

I felt a little miffed by her criticisms of humanity, but I concentrated on docking the *Epsilon* with the *Lisa Jane*. That done, we exited from the *Epsilon* back to the *Lisa Jane* while Alfred docked the ship with the *Tanu*.

Manera looked stiff and unhappy, avoiding my gaze and I felt grumpy and angry. I was confused by my feelings and realised I was over reacting, but I think Manera had touched a nerve. What was bothering me was that us Humans **were** warlike and yes we **were** very good at killing.

We walked off the ship, through the connecting tunnel and into the *Tanu's* airlock and disembarkation area. Manera turned to me and without a word came up and putting one arm around my waist and another around my shoulder she pulled me to her and rested her head against my chest.

"I am sorry I was so insensitive Paul," she whispered. I pulled her head up and kissed her gently on the lips.

"That's OK, I over-reacted," I pulled her to me and gave her a bear hug.

"That is why I wanted to come with you Paul," she said earnestly. "Whatever happened to you I wanted to share it."

"Sorry , It's because I felt guilty," I said shamefacedly. She gave me a long warm kiss which made me feel decidedly better. We were just beginning to really get into the business of making each other feel better but were interrupted by a sarcastic English drawl in our ears.

"When you two have finished commiserating with each other," said Alfred, "Which by the way would be better done in private," he added, "Perhaps you can get up to the Conference room. The Guardians have called a meeting."

"Sometimes Alfred, I think you had a Victorian upbringing," I grinned.

"The Victorians did have the good manners not to slobber over each other in public," he retorted.

"Who were these Victorians?" asked Manera while I chuckled at Alfred's humour. I spent the next few minutes, while we made our way up to the Conference room, explaining to her who the Victorians were and their inhibited brand of morality.

"Of course," I finished, "Like all sexually repressed societies, all that energy had to come out somewhere. In their case, they conquered the world and tried to make it into their image, a repressed and fanatically religious image."

"They sound very unpleasant," observed Manera.

"Oh, they had many fine moral values," I replied, "But their values often took second place to expediency. The rich and powerful exploited the poor in dangerous dirty factories or forced them into backbreaking labour on farms for long hours, while their wives donated parcels of food to the poor to assuage their guilt."

"How did they justify this to themselves?" asked Manera thoughtfully.

'They did not really believe that all people were equal," I said. "Despite their religious teachings to the contrary, they believed that some were born to rule and others to follow. All had their place in the scheme of things and should know their place. The poor were themselves responsible for their condition."

"I hope that such inequality is a thing of the past," she retorted.

"Yes," I nodded, "Four hundred and fifty years after the Victorian age I think we have at last abandoned such hypocrisy." The history lesson stopped with our arrival at the entrance to the conference room .

"Talking about inequality," I said. "Exactly how much power do the Guardians have in Hianja society?"

"The Guardians are not the Government," she replied. "They are analogues to your Judiciary. Every society must have independent judges to turn to for the resolution of conflicts. The Guardians are ours."

"But you have implied that they are more than that. That they decide on what is proper in areas such as Genetic engineering and even social engineering," I said.

"Only when those are areas of conflict which need arbitration," she replied. "The Guardians can arbitrate because they are not part of any interest group."

"The Guardians or Judges may make a better decision. But that does not matter, because if it does not accord with the wishes of the people, as expressed through their Government, then it is not a Democratic decision."

"I think you do not understand our system Paul. You see, our Government is just a group of civil servants and computers. We do not have elections and political parties as you do. We have gone beyond that, because there is no disagreement amongst us regarding our economic systems. Each individual can express their democratic views on all issues of the time, as they occur. Government will carry out the majority view, except where that majority view is divided. Then, the Guardians will arbitrate."

"So the Guardians cannot make decisions on anything they please?" I asked.

"No," she replied, "Issues are referred to the Guardians by the Government under very special circumstances."

"I see," I replied. It started to make more sense now. My concern that the Guardians were some sort of autocratic Dictatorship was unfounded. They were analogues to the American Supreme Court for example. The Hianja had also taken Democracy to its ultimate conclusion; every individual was free to vote on every issue, and the Computer controlled Government must then act accordingly.

"There is only one area where Guardians take precedence over Planetary Governments, and that is issues outside the boundary of any single Planetary system. This is one of them because Omorphia is a new planet. Under those circumstances, a group of three Guardians drawn from the nearest interested planetary systems are empowered to make decisions. That is what is happening here," Manera said as she turned to enter the conference room. I followed her in to find the Guardians already there as well as Captain Sametan and Commander Verisho. Guardian Kemato moved towards us and beckoned us over.

"Captain Constantine, Manera, come in, it is a great relief to see you unharmed." She looked genuinely pleased to see us, as was the tall Hamolatonen. Guardian Malanisa looked less enthusiastic, her face deadpan. "Captain take a seat." This time, Kemato waved me towards the table set in an alcove of the conference room. The others also moved towards the table and selected chairs. This was to be a more informal meeting of equals I thought as we all sat, not a tribunal

"Captain Constantine, Science Office Manera-Ka," began Kemato formally, when we were all seated. "It is the duty of this Council, to express our gratitude to you both, and to your AI Alfred, who is in visual and audio contact with this meeting, for your brave and skilful defence of this ship, the *Tanu*, from the missile attack perpetrated by the criminal elements on the *Pesmisk* under the leadership of Smetronis Ne Pashmateri." she looked around gravely before continuing.

"This Council must also apologise to you for the subterfuge we employed at the last meeting in this room. I know it caused you great anguish, and all things considered, your reaction was quite reserved." There was a twinkle in her eyes as she said this and I smiled wryly in appreciation.

"The reasons for the actions taken by Smetronis and his collaborators are unknown to this Council, and will be a matter for investigation on all three of our planets. We have reasons to believe that there are others, many others, and in high places, who are in league with this group of criminals, and that the plot goes back many years. We have taken Smetronis and his associates into custody and that investigation will commence immediately. We have already dispatched a message capsule into Hyperspace communicating the details of our operation here. As for us, the program is as follows," she turned to me at this point. "Prior to our arrival here we received a communication from Hianja Prime, our home planet. It asked us to allow you to return immediately to your home world, after arranging for a Hianja-Human meeting of representatives of each species, on a planet to be agreed, at a time to be agreed. Representatives of all Hianja planets will be present, and we hope that Humans will also send representatives from all their planets. This will be the first formal contact between our two species." The Guardian sat down and looked at me expectantly. I was sure this was being recorded and I was also aware that I looked a mess, having been dragged out of my bed in the middle of the 'night' to fight a space war! I stood up and looked around the table, keeping my features relaxed and friendly.

"Thank you Guardian Kemato for your kind words. It's not every night that one gets woken up to fight a Space war, so I apologise for my dishevelled appearance. Let me say that what happened tonight has caused me great sadness and distress. I am not a soldier, and I have never killed anybody before. I do not understand what motivated these people to behave in such an aggressive and fanatical way. What I have learnt of the Hianja makes such behaviour even more unexpected and surprising. On the matter of formal Contact, I am required by my procedures to minimise all personal contact with any Alien species..," I had trouble continuing at this point as Manera smirked in a most unladylike way,.. "..and to set up exactly such a meeting as you describe between representatives of our two species. I am very happy therefore to collaborate in such an endeavour. However, I do have a small problem. My ship, the *Lisa Jane* is damaged and not capable of Hyperspace travel. Since I am also required by my procedures not to reveal the location of Earth, I must ask you to repair my ship. My AI Alfred tells me that this should not be a difficult matter, since Hianja and Human Hyperspace drives work in the same way." I nodded amiably and sat down.

"In order to repair the *Lisa Jane* we must travel to the shipyards on either Mesaroyat, Tanmeron or Vasmeranta," responded Kemato.

"Which is closest?" I asked.

"Vasmeranta is the closest and has the best Space Port and engineering facilities in the region," replied Kemato. "But given the probability that Smetronis may have associates, it may be wise not to go there." Guardian Malanisa kept her face very deadpan at this. " My planet Mesaroyat is the second closest and we have adequate facilities to repair your ship. You shall be my guest Captain."

"It will be my pleasure," I replied. "How long will the trip take?"

"Four days," she replied.

"If it pleases the Council," said Malanisa, "Since Council business with this affair is concluded, I should like to return to Vasmeranta to report in person to our Council. Do I have permission?"

"I have no reason to keep you here," replied Kemato shortly. "Guardian Hamolatonen, would you also like to return?" she asked.

"Certainly not!" exclaimed the fair haired Guardian, "I would not pass up the opportunity to spend more time with our first real Alien." Kemato had stood up and with a smile was announcing the end of the meeting. Malanisa was already on her feet and walked out as soon as Kemato had finished her terminating remarks. I was on my way to a Hianja planet! I could hardly believe my luck and a deep excitement welled up within me. I had become so used to these 'people' that I was taking them for granted, but every now and again I would wake up and pinch myself. Four days on the *Tanu* and then, how long to repair the *Lisa Jane*? A few days or a few weeks and then back to Earth. I had stood up, immersed in my thoughts and my eyes met with Manera's across the table. I gave her a wink and she gave me a ravishing smile. I realised that returning to Earth meant leaving Manera and for the first time the thought of Home was something less than pleasurable. Damn! I thought, I don't want to go back!

Chapter 22

The *Tanu* was to return to Mesaroyat on her own, leaving behind one of the
two smaller Hianja ships to continue the scientific work on Omorphia.
Malanisa's ship would return immediately to her home planet. It seemed
suspicious to me that she was in such a hurry to return, but I kept my
suspicions to myself. The scientists on the *Tanu* itself were assigned to
study me and Human society, and over the next few days I got to know
them well. It was a little nerve wracking to be the subject of scientific
study, and quite exhausting because there were five scientists but only one
of me! But the trip passed quickly and enjoyably and despite the obvious
and very great differences between us and between Hianja and Human
Society we developed a friendly relationship.

One area which caused some conflict and controversy was the area of
entertainment. The Hianja were keen to view some typical Human
entertainment, and I selected what I thought were a few innocuous
examples from my entertainment archives. Most of these were met with
approval, and some were enjoyed very much, but my hosts were extremely
sensitive to anything that even remotely involved any violence. I made the
mistake of including a few murder, mystery and suspense films, which
convinced them that Human Society was infested with murderers, criminals
and terrorists. That Humans were seriously unable to tell the truth or
sustain any relationship without cheating or lying! I spent hours trying to
persuade them that this was just poetic license and reality was quite
different, although I confess I was not fully convinced myself! It seems that
Hianja entertainment was more refined, concentrating on the higher
emotions and intellectual questions and not obsessed with murder rape and
pillage! I was seriously impressed with this refinement, but found myself
wondering whether there was more to it than just another twenty thousand
years of civilisation.

Despite that, there was an 'earthier' side to Hianja nature. They enjoyed
the 'sins' of the flesh, food, drink and sex, just as much as Humans,
including all that was humorous, ridiculous, obscene or just plain funny!
For me, that was their most endearing characteristic and it was the one that
we had most in common. Manera explained it to me, that in order to live
for three hundred and fifty years, one must remain young at heart!

On the third day of our journey I was promised something different.
There was a hive of activity on the ship with *Tanseh* to-ing and fro-ing
from the ship carrying equipment. Manera awoke me early and dragged me
out for an early breakfast before taking me down to the shuttle bay.

"You will enjoy this Paul!" she grinned, "It is a very popular Hianja sport."

"Ah, so the Hianja do have sports. I thought you were far too civilised to indulge in crude competition," I joked, poking her playfully in the ribs.

"We are," she replied, "But this is not crude, this is very sophisticated, a test of memory, reflexes and manual dexterity."

"I have very good manual dexterity," I boasted.

"Well, I guess all Pilots need..," she began, and then spotted my leering grin and 'humphed' in mock disapproval.

"If you think you are so good Mister Earthman, wait and see!" she promised. There were a dozen *Tanseh* in the shuttle bay and hordes of Hianja milling about. There was also what appeared to be a large square craft, just a box with windows, which people were boarding, and to which we also headed for.

"This is a Space Viewing Platform," explained Manera, "Where we can see the race in comfort."

"Aha, a race then is it?" I enquired, "Not much point in having a race between *Tanseh*, they are all identical," I said in puzzlement.

"But the Pilots are not identical," pointed out Manera, "And the course is a test of Pilot skill," I tried to imagine how to set up a racecourse in Space and failed. We all trooped into the Viewing Platform, and I spotted all the Scientists, a bunch of Crew and some Maintenance people. It seemed just about everyone was going, except the remaining crew to run the ship. We exchanged greetings with the Scientists who were in good spirits. There was a party atmosphere and a bar in the corner was doing a roaring trade.

"This is a very popular sport, Paul," explained Batsano. "Even on Planets, we have gravity free arenas for the races and the top Pilots are highly celebrated." I was getting the impression that this was the Hianja equivalent of Formula 1 racing.

"Is it at all dangerous?" I asked as our Platform jerked and started to move gently out of the shuttle bay and into open Space.

"It can be of course," replied Batsano, "That is why it is so exciting, *Tanseh* can collide and Pilots can be hurt or even killed." This was revealing another side to the Hianja that surprised me. "Also," he added, "The *Tanseh* can collide with the laser projectors, and that also can be fatal." He paused for a second, and continued. "Actually, Computers can override bad Pilot control that can lead to accidents, and in the junior races, for inexperienced Pilots, this is what happens because otherwise there would be many accidents. But with the top racers, Computer override can be disabled."

The viewing Platform, which was being towed by a *Tanseh*, cleared the *Tanu's* huge bulk and moved into open Space. That was when I saw the course, and could not contain an exclamation of admiration.

"Wow, that is something!" I craned my neck to scan the whole of the remarkable sight. Swooping into the blackness of Space, an immense convoluted tube of light, a huge circle fully dozens of kilometres in length. It was made from thousands of interlocking laser beams which formed a cylinder of light, but irregular and curved, like a massive roller coaster. It was the racing track, within which the *Tanseh* would race. They were taking their positions now, about a dozen as far as I could see, each one a different colour.

"The first Tanseh will go by itself," said Manera. "It will be flown by the Computer to establish the 'base' time which the racers will try to get close to." She suddenly looked thoughtful. "I have an idea," she said, "How would you like to fly the course Paul?"

"Race against the others?" I asked , "No fear, I'll get slaughtered! Your guys are used to those things, I've never flown one in my life!"

"No, not in the race!" explained Manera, "Take a ride with the Computer controlled one. To give you an idea of how it feels to ride the course?"

"Well, that sounds like it may be fun," I said doubtfully. Manera spoke into her communicator and in a few seconds a *Tanseh* detached itself from the others and made its way over to the viewing platform. By now, Batsano and the others had been put in the picture and they were looking highly pleased with themselves.

"Ah, you will enjoy this Paul!" exclaimed Batsano rubbing his hands in glee. "But I hope you did not have a heavy breakfast," he added smirking.

"I will come with you of course," said Manera protectively. There were cries of "Well done Manera!" and "Don't sit in front of him.," from the assembled company. I grinned broadly and feigned casual unconcern as we boarded the *Tanseh* which had connected to the Viewing Platform's airlock. We settled into the *Tanseh's* seats, which appeared to have been fitted with special straps and helmets which were connected to the seat. Once strapped in the helmets secured your head and shoulders to the seat, rendering you rigid and immobile. Only the hands were free, but since the *Tanseh* was flying itself, I settled back to enjoy the ride. I could see Manera out of the corner of my eye strapped into the other seat, and I could hear her voice on the intercom. I gave her the thumbs up and she smiled reassuringly.

The *Tanseh* approached the entrance to the course and we could now see into the tube of light which was something like twenty metres in diameter. We stopped at the entrance and pulsing figures of light appeared on the view screen. Then we were off and I felt the full acceleration of the *Tanseh* pressing me back in my seat. It felt like two G's, which was more than I expected the *Tanseh* capable of. The first part of the course was a straight for a couple of kilometres which allowed the *Tanseh* to get up to a fair speed, which we could tell from the circular 'joins' that made up the wall of the tube every hundred metres or so which soon merged into a continuous stream of light. These were the Laser generators which we had to avoid contact with at all cost. We came to the first bend and the *Tanseh* decelerated savagely and veered sideways, climbed steeply, then hurtled down. The change in gravity and direction, from 2 G's to zero first slammed the breath out of me, then left me hanging weight less in my seat as the *Tanseh* reached the apogee of its curve and then accelerated savagely downwards. It was the roller coaster ride to beat all roller coasters and it went on and on for what seemed an interminable time. It was immensely exhilarating and I found myself bellowing in excitement as the ship, seemingly on rails, hurtled around the course. It must have lasted about six minutes and I was sorry to come to the end. I could not imagine how a human being could possibly pilot this course, and race against a dozen others without crashing or coming off the course. It would take superlative skill allied with superb reflexes to survive. Manera and I needed a couple of minutes before we could co-ordinate our limbs and stand up at the end. The *Tanseh* delivered us back to the Viewing Platform and we staggered off, holding on to each other to cries of encouragement and support from our Comrades.

"Well done you two!" exclaimed Nastro, "The Computer takes the course a lot faster than a pilot, so it's a pretty tough trip." I felt pretty shaky but Manera seemed totally in control. In the meantime the race was gearing up to start. All eleven racers lined up in parallel, awaiting the starter. Whoever held their acceleration the longest would go into the first 'S' bend in front, but go in too fast and they would not negotiate the bend. Any exit from the course would lead to a loss of points. There would be a series of races, with individuals being knocked out until only three were left, and there would be a final race to find a winner. The trick was therefore to conserve your energy over the first few races, just doing enough to stay in. In the meantime, the audience partied, drinking laughing and placing bets on the outcome! The sheer spectacle was hard to believe, with the enormous Laser course in front of us and the huge bulk of the *Tanu* behind us, it was a staggering scene.

"Do I know any of the Pilot's?" I asked Manera.

"There are two of the *Tanu's* crew, Santro and Farnita, who are very good," she replied, "But the Champion is Commander Verisho, you remember, Captain Sametan's Executive Officer. She is renown as a very skilled *Verasoti*, and we are very lucky to have her here."

"So she is a dead cert to win then?" I asked.

"Santro and Farnita fancy their chances," she replied. "And there is a big element of chance in *Veraso*, so it is possible for anyone to win." I remembered Santro and Farnita, Santro was young and eager, very energetic and quick, and Farnita was an unattractive hatchet faced female, lean but with a curious stillness about her.

"So tell me," I asked, "what is everyone betting with? I understood that there was no such thing as money in Hianja Society."

"You understood wrong," replied Manera. "The basic essentials of life are free, but everyone wants extras. If you want to travel, or live in a bigger apartment, then you must work and accumulate credits."

"Is that right?" I said thoughtfully, "In that case, I have a plan to make some Credits."

"Paul, you cannot make Credits," she replied, "You are not Hianja, you do not exist on our Computer systems. Credits are purely electronic transactions, allocated and spent by Computer."

"Then, I will earn them under your name, and place my bets under your name."

She smiled impishly at me. "And what do you have to sell Mr Constantine. Your body?"

"Well.....," I said thoughtfully..

"You will not get much for that," she laughed mockingly. I held up a finger in admonishment.

"Watch an Earth entrepreneur at work," I grinned.   I unclipped the silver SES emblem from my lapel. It was just a chrome steel clip, with the emblem of the SES, a starship with Saturn and its rings in the background. Pretty, but quite worthless, I was sure that there were two or three others on the *Lisa Jane*.

"Attention everyone!" I shouted to the gathering around us, waiting for them to quieten and turn around.

"I have here, a unique and valuable emblem, which I am prepared to offer to the highest bidder. This is the Earth Space Exploration Service badge, from the very jacket of none other than Captain Paul Constantine, hero and adventurer, the first Human to make contact with the fabulous Hianja Civilisation. This emblem is unique and has enormous historical significance, and it can be yours. Start your offers please at..," I paused and turned to Manera, "What is a good number of Credits to bet with?" She looked at me goggle eyed and uncomprehending. I repeated my question insistently.

"Um... I suppose, a hundred Credits," she said baffled.

"Start the bidding at one hundred Credits," I finished, waving the badge at the assembled company. People looked at each other in a baffled fashion, and I waited in vain for the first offer.

"Paul, what do you mean by 'bid'?" asked someone.

"Yes, what do we have to do, I want that badge!" cried someone else.

"You just tell me how many Credits you are prepared to pay to buy the

badge," I explained. "The person prepared to pay the most will win.".
There was a babble of voices and someone shouted "Two hundred Credits"
and then someone else three and so on in a bedlam of voices.

"Whoa, whoa!" I shouted holding up my hands. "You must do it one at
a time and be recognised by me before the next person can make a bigger
offer. One at a time please!" A forest of hands flew up and I pointed to one.

"Three hundred Credits," she cried. The forest of hands stayed up, all
waving insistently. I recognised the next and the next and it went on and
on, climbing to three thousand Credits before people started to drop out. In
the end, one individual, a slender fair haired female who I had not seen
before, persevered to five thousand six hundred Credits.

"If there are no more bids," I said in my best Auction house voice, "It
goes to the lovely young lady in the green, your name is madam?" I asked
politely.

"Selani Konta Olansek," she replied with a smile, stepping forward to
claim her prize.

"Selani, let me see the colour of your money," I said holding the badge
aloft theatrically. She looked baffled and shook her head. She held out her
hand and pulled her sleeve up to reveal what looked like a watch.

"My *Slonavic*," she said. Manera stepped forward and held out her
wrist on which there was a similar device.

"The Credits will go to myself," she said. Selani placed her finger on
Manera's *Slonavic* and muttered a few words. Manera then did the same
and the transaction was complete. I handed Selani the badge and she took it
gingerly, an expression of awe of her face.

"Selani, I will write a note with my signature on some paper, a bit old
fashioned I know, but it will prove that the badge is authentic. I will give it
to you later," I smiled at the small girl, it was obvious she was very young,
and she gave me a shy smile in return.

"Thank you that will be most acceptable."

"No, Thank you!" I grinned and she turned and walked quickly back to
her friends holding the badge reverently aloft.

"Now we have some dosh to bet with!" I grinned at Manera. She was
looking accusingly at me.

"Paul Constantine you are a bad Earthman, taking advantage of all
these innocent Hianja like that!"

"Hey, that is a genuine badge off the great Paul Constantine's very
uniform, the one he wore at his first meeting with the lovely Manera, the
most beautiful Hianja Princess. It is a piece of History!" I reinforced my
point with a waving finger. She grabbed the same waving finger and baring
pointy white Hianja teeth bit it, very hard! I gritted my teeth and tried very
hard not to yell. She eventually released my injured digit.

"Manera, most beautiful Hianja Princess!" she said derisively, but I could see that she was pleased. Women, I thought, are the same the Universe over, suckers for a compliment!

In the meantime, as the start of the race approached, excitement was hotting up and bets were being placed in a flurry of waving arms. The bets were being taken by a Computer, each person's bet being displayed on a large screen, which also showed the odds on the race participants.

"OK, what are the odds on Commander Verisho?" I asked.

"Only five to four," she replied, "She is a strong favourite," I had been impressed by the Commander on our meeting, she seemed a very alert individual.

"Are there odds on second and third?" I asked.

"Fifty percent odds on naming second place," she replied. "Ten to one on Santro and twenty to one on Farnita."

"OK, One thousand Credits on Commander Verisho for first place, and One thousand Credits on Farnita for second," I said decisively.

"Santro is faster," said Manera warningly.

"Yes, but Farnita is safer," I replied with a confidence I did not feel. But there was something of the stillness of a snake about Farnita, a snake that could strike with lightning speed. I trusted my instincts. Anyway, it was not money I could spend in any other way!

"By the way," I asked Manera, "Who was the young girl who bought my badge, Selani something?"

"She is the Captains daughter," smiled Manera. I was startled, not expecting the Captain to have children.

"I hope the Captain won't take offence at her daughter spending all that money," I said worriedly.

"The Captain can afford it!" replied Manera, "and I think the badge will be worth a lot more back home," she added.

"Aha!" I exclaimed, "And you were accusing me of robbing the girl," I snorted. Manera grinned.

"Come, let's place our bets, the race is starting in a few seconds," Manera raised her hand and talked into her communicator for a few seconds and our bets then flashed up on the view screen with the others. There was a raised hubbub of voices when they appeared and a few heads turned in our direction.

"Hey Paul, do you know something we don't about the lovely Farnita!" shouted Batsano.

"I am a good judge of women!" I shouted back, winking lewdly.

"Yes, but are you a good judge of Pilots?" he replied, with a laugh. Flashing numbers appeared on the view screen and then the sound of a musical horn announced the start of the race. We could see the eleven racers clearly, separating them by the coloured numbers on the sides of their craft, but the view screens around the lower part of the walls of the Viewing Platform showed close-ups of all the racers and their positions. Santro had taken an early lead and went into the 'S' bend first. He negotiated it smoothly and I began to feel I had made the wrong choice. The Commander was in second place and Farnita was at the back. As the race progressed it became apparent that Farnita was playing it safe, and sure enough her strategy paid off as first one then two other craft came off the course, fortunately missing the Laser Generators. They continued the race to finish, but their penalty points put them out. Santro finished first with a polished performance, but the Commander looked ominous, holding her distance easily and seemingly flying well within herself.

The second race lined up, now only eight craft were in, and five would drop out on this race, so this was the crunch! Again Santro took the lead and the Commander was second, and again Farnita was last. But this time, she began to pressurise the racers ahead of her, passing one then two quite easily and sitting on the tail of the third from last. As she approached a steep bend, she moved ahead, then moved over to take her line into the bend, forcing the *Tanseh* behind her to brake and fall back, which also interfered with the two *Tanseh* behind her. She was now clearly fifth, but needed to get into third position to qualify for the final. The two ahead of her were also dicing for third, so this was a dangerous problem for her. I was afraid that she had left it too late, but I was wrong. Her tactic was to badger the other two in front, coming level and then falling back, trying to break their concentration and take their 'line' through the bends. The inevitable happened, while manoeuvring through a series of tight bends, number three and four collided and hurtled off the course. She sailed in a comfortable third! I accepted the congratulations of the assembled company with due modesty, almost as if I had flown the course! But Santro and the Commander had put in a totally solid performance and I doubted Farnita's ability to discomfort them.
"Paul, you are a good judge of a Pilot," conceded Batsano, "That was a brilliant performance by Farnita."
"Well, Santro and Commander Verisho are very fast." I replied. "Can Farnita outmanoeuvre them?"
"If I knew the answer, I would put ten thousand Credits on Farnita!" He laughed.

The final three lined up for the last race and the audience held their breaths for the start. The musical horn blared and they were off. This time, Commander Verisho showed her true class by holding her line and speed a fraction of a second longer than the other two. She went into the bend first and the crowd cheered and gasped in anticipation. Her control through the complex 'S' bend was superb and she came out well clear of the other two. But Santro was second and Farnita looked well behind. Turn after turn the Commander piled on the pressure, showing her true class and the other two tried valiantly to stay with her. This was now a race for second and Farnita again used the same tactics as in the previous race. But Santro was no slouch and it became a thrilling dog fight, each racer trying to outmanoeuvre the other or throw them off track.. Her tactic was to try and bluff him, accelerating violently to try to pass him on open stretches and then braking to throw him off his line. And then the audience gasped at her audacity and skill. She actually rammed him from behind as they were going into a bend. This pushed Santro off his line and he skidded off the course, just clipping the outer line of lasers. But it was enough to earn him a small penalty and although they both finished neck and neck after a victorious Verisho, Farnita had it by a few milliseconds!

"But is that legal?" I asked Manera.

"Yes," she replied, "You see, a manoeuvre like that is so difficult to perform at high speed that it is just as likely to put both the contestants out of the race, and usually does."

"So I am a rich man?" I asked.

"Oh, not rich, but you can buy a small holiday home on an airless asteroid!" she laughed.

It seemed that the end of the race did not herald the end of the party, because everyone then proceeded to get pickled on Hianja happy juice. A number of adventurous souls went off to try their luck on the course, with the automatic Computers keeping an 'eye' on them to ensure that they did not damage themselves or expensive equipment! The brave contestants returned to be feted by their fans and to get equally pickled. It seemed that I had the dubious honour of having the largest winnings on the bets, which I modestly put down to beginners luck. But I did congratulate the last three contestants, particularly the daring Farnita who had won me a substantial amount. She was very curious about why I had bet on her, knowing absolutely nothing about the race and the contestants. I paused to consider my answer carefully.

"You look the sort of individual who has a strong desire to win," I said carefully. She looked at me impassively. I waited curiously, had I offended her I thought?

"You can tell that by just looking at me?" she asked. Damn I thought, I have got myself into a corner. How could I tell her that I thought she looked plain and unattractive, one of these intense females to whom success is essential for their self esteem. What a sexist idea anyway, I was ashamed of myself for thinking it. But I had been right, she had shown determination and a will to win. I shook my head.

"It was just a guess, call it instinct. It was probably just good luck," I smiled self effacingly. To my relief she smiled back and nodded.

"Thank you for your support, my reputation as a *Verasoti* has been enhanced today."

"You were amazingly skilful," I replied, "All of you were actually."

"I will see you later Captain," she said looking me in the eyes "Enjoy the party," I must have looked relieved because Manera looked at me in an odd way.

"Does she bother you?" she asked and before I could answer went on, "She is an exceedingly beautiful female, so tall and strong," she sighed wistfully, "I wish I was half as attractive." I gaped at her in disbelief.

"What did you just say?" I asked, "That you wished that you were half as attractive as Farnita?"

"Yes," replied Manera, "She has a classic face and figure, whereas I am just thin and plain." I had to pause to collect my thoughts for a second. I grabbed Manera by the shoulders and turned her to face me. I looked into her flawless face and azure eyes that a man could drown in and took a deep breath.

"Are you telling me that, by Hianja standards, Farnita is beautiful and you are plain?" she looked carefully back at me.

"Yes," she said simply, "Of course, isn't it obvious?" and then, as she saw the look of disbelief on my face, a slow look of dawning understanding passed across hers.

"Do you mean that by Human standards, it is the other way around?" she whispered.

"I'd say" I said exclaimed, "By Human standards, Farnita is not at all beautiful, quite ugly actually. Her features are too large, her chin too big, her bone structure too heavy."

"Of Course, I should have realised," whispered Manera, "I look more Human than any of the others. That is why you think I am attractive!" She suddenly started laughing.

"Oh Paul, I am an Alien just like you!"

"Hey, Hey!" I said in alarm, squeezing her shoulders supportingly. "Don't say that," I wanted to say encouraging things but I could not think what to say.

"Oh it's OK Paul, do not be upset," she replied, "I am quite used to being plain and it is not as important for Hianja as it is for Humans. We appreciate physical beauty but we are not obsessed by it!"

Chapter 23

We were expected in Mesaroyat of course; numerous hyperspace messages had passed between the *Tanu* and its destination planet. As the planet filled the view screen I thought of the last couple of days of the journey. They had been filled with discussions on what I would be doing on Mesaroyat. Alfred was transmitting technical information to allow the Hianja engineers to design and build the *Lisa Jane's* new Hyperspace drive. We had exited from Hyperspace on the fourth day . In preparation the ship was cleared, all loose objects tidied away and all personnel made their way to their respective security stations. The screen suddenly lit up with the blackness of normal Space with its myriad arrays of stars, swirling like carelessly scattered diamonds on the black velvet of Space. A cheer broke out from the passengers and we all grinned at each other in relief.

"There, there in the centre of the screen!" pointed Manera. I looked carefully, to see a blue dot, shining with a softer light than the surrounding stars.

"Mesaroyat," said Manera with a smile. We had talked about her home planet at some length and I knew that it was a relatively new world for the Hianja. It had been settled some three thousand years previously so it was quite well developed, with a population about 500 million. By Earth standards, it was a sparsely settled world, but apparently, so were all Hianja worlds. The Hianja liked room to spread, but believed in keeping as much of their planets in their original condition as possible.

Now, the *Tanu* was being readied to dock with the largest orbiting space station around Mesaroyat, known as '*Santra Des* ' which loosely translates into 'Silver Star'. Apart from the crew, who had their normal workstations, passengers were required to assemble in the embarkation area on deck One where they could be 'checked off' by a member of the crew. Sitting next to Batsano and Deejana on one side and Manera and Doctor Leanisu on the other, we made desultory conversation while we waited for everyone to take their seats. There was a huge screen in the front of where we were seated which at the moment was showing the vast blue swirling surface of Mesaroyat. It looked so much like Earth, I experienced an intense feeling of nostalgia and homesickness.

The view of the planet changed to a view of the *Santra Des* and I suppressed a gasp of admiration. It would not do to look like a country hick in front of my companions! The station was at least ten times larger than the *Tanu*. The main body of the station was a huge silver disc, which I guess was how it got its name. There were two smaller discs, one beneath and one above. The upper disc had a number of cylindrical projections, a hundred or more metres in length extending from its circumference. I asked Manera what these projections were.

"They are the docking platforms," she replied. "We will travel to the station by *Tenseh* which will enter the station through the end of one of the cylinders. Starships are not allowed to dock with the station," she explained. "The bottom disk houses the power generation and control systems, and the AG generators. The main disc is the habitation module and the upper disc is the embarkation and docking module." She was excited about coming home and looking forward to showing me around, but I had my doubts about the amount of freedom I would be given.

The ship seemed to have come to a standstill and there was an announcement in Hianja which I translated as "Passengers please proceed to shuttles for embarkation." I was quite pleased with my language lessons with Manera, which had continued during our journey. I could conduct a reasonable conversation in Hianja, and Manera was now quite fluent in English. We stood and followed the others towards the docking airlocks, entering and taking our seats in the large specialist Space Station Shuttle that had docked with the *Tanu*. There was a murmur of conversation and Manera beamed happily as we sat, squeezing my hand.

"Wait until you see the inside of the *Santra Des*," she smiled, "It is used as a hotel and is very luxurious."

"This is the life!" I said. "Become a Space Scout and see the Universe! Meet beautiful Alien females and stay in luxurious Alien hotels free of charge!"

"Who are these beautiful Alien females you keep talking about?" she said with mock innocence. I shrugged doubtfully as we shuffled onto the spacious shuttle and took our seats.

"Hey Batsano," called Manera to that worthy, who had taken the seat next to me, "The Earthman wants to meet some beautiful alien females. Do you know any?" He frowned in deep thought for a few moments.

"No..ooo!" he said thoughtfully, looking around him at the surrounding females, giving Manera a particularly long examination. "If I did, I would keep them to myself! But Paul tell me..," he continued. "Do all Earth women look like the ones we have seen on your movies?"

"No, as a rule, only the good looking ones get to be film stars," I replied. Batsano's face acquired a look of comical horror.

"What, they are the good looking ones?" he exclaimed, "I am better looking than most of them!"

The others around us were grinning in amusement at our banter as the shuttle disconnected and drifted slowly out of the *Tanu's* shuttle bay. I could see the *Lisa Jane* through the big windows and wondered what Alfred was up to. No doubt deep in designs and calculations for the replacement Hyperspace Drive that was going to be fitted. The *Lisa Jane* was due to be transported to an orbiting Starship maintenance station in another orbit where she would be repaired. I would join the ship there when it was ready in a few weeks.

The shuttle was suddenly swallowed by the mouth of the docking cylinder. The view was blanked out to be replaced by a grey wall around us as we slid inside the Space Station. There was a thump and a rumble as wheels engaged on the shuttles exterior and it ceased to be a spaceship and became a car. An airlock door closed behind us and a minute later we arrived at the open embarkation area and the shuttle came to a halt.

The doors hissed open and we stepped out onto the deck of the *Santra Des*. There was of course a reception committee, and I squared my shoulders in anticipation of more formalities. My companions melted from around me and I was left with only Manera in attendance. A tall spindly individual, somewhat stooping and with exaggerated Hianja features, looking like an honest to goodness real alien I thought, stepped forward and embraced me in the Hianja greeting. I squeezed his bony shoulders back, looking him cordially in the eyes and smiled in my best engaging manner. Seeing him close-up, I realised that he was quite old, indeed he was the first old looking Hianja I had seen. He stepped back and addressed me.

"Welcome to the *Santra Des* Captain Constantine, I am the Commanding Officer of the station, Saru Marsani at your service." I nodded my thanks and replied in Hianja.

"Thank you Master Saru, it is kind of you to greet me personally. It is a great pleasure to be here." Manera had instructed me on the proper way to address the commander of the *Santra Des*.

He looked startled and taken aback.

"You speak Hianja?" he asked, his long face tilting forwards and his blinking in what I had learnt was a gesture of surprise.

"I have had a good teacher," I smiled, indicating Manera.

"Aha," he acknowledged, "Very gratifying. Your stay here will be a short one unfortunately Captain," he continued. "The Guardian Council of Mesaroyat are waiting to greet you at our Capital City but it is required that you subject yourself to a de-contamination treatment and a full biological examination for potentially harmful viruses or bacteria. I am sure you understand that we must be very careful to ensure there is no possibility of potentially harmful biological agents being released on the planet," he finished apologetically.

"I have no problem with that of course," I assured him, "Although as you know I have been in close contact with a number of your people for a long period now with no harmful affects for any of us." He nodded politely.

"Yes, we are confident there is no problem. You will of course have full access to all the station, although while you are aboard no one will be allowed to arrive or leave until the tests are concluded," he replied. "Allow me to conduct you to your quarters. The scientific team from the *Tanu* will work closely with my people on the Station to conduct the tests." He beckoned me towards a door and Manera and I followed him. He was clearly curious because he kept sneaking looks at me, examining me from top to bottom.

"Forgive me Captain if I stare," he said eventually, obviously unable to restrain his curiosity. "But I am quite amazed at your physical similarity to us. Is it not quite unbelievable that two alien species should look so alike?"

"That was my feeling precisely when I first saw Hianja," I replied.

"It seems incredible," he replied shaking his head. "Has anyone considered that Human and Hianja may be related?" Manera chose to answer that one.

"It seems not Master Saru. Paul tells me that there is a full evolutionary record on Earth showing that Humans evolved there from indigenous species. Our DNA shows a small percentage match, we are still analysing that but there is no doubt that we are different species. Hianja and Earth are very similar planets and our evolutionary paths have been almost identical." I agreed with Master Saru that it was an inexplicable mystery, and he was clearly also mystified because he again shook his head in wonderment.

"It's enough to make you believe in a God," he muttered, and this was the first time any Hianja had mentioned religious belief of any sort. I wondered whether his age was a factor in his belief.

If I'd thought that the *Tanu* was luxurious, well, compared to the *Santra Des* she was a mud hut! Here the fixtures and fittings **were** natural materials, not plastic pretending to be wood or fabric! My apartment was huge, and was adjacent to Manera's, which was almost as big. The other members of the scientific team were housed in equal splendour, but they seemed to be quite blasé about it. Huge real windows, not view screens, showed a panoramic view of the Planet, with the *Tanu* and a number of other ships also in view.

Master Saru left us with an invitation to dinner in the evening. There was no rest for us though, because we were immediately visited by the head of the Scientific Team on the Station, who was responsible for carrying out the biological tests and decontamination. Manera and he spent an hour in discussion, asking me a number of questions and describing the indignities that they were about to inflict upon me, then he and Manera went off to a conference with the other scientists to organise their program.

I was left in the hands of a couple of Hianja, two hard looking males, who I was sure were armed, who were allocated to show me around the station. The *Santra Des* was truly impressive. The closest analogy was to a luxury cruise ship, she was about the same size and had the same facilities, including three pools and innumerable games areas. It was very easy to forget that you were in Space, orbiting a Planet, so insulated were you from reality.

I decided that taking a swim in a space station was something I could not miss. I asked my minders for swimming trunks and they shrugged blankly. I eventually got the message that Hianja swam in the nude! Shrugging I asked them to direct me to the pool. It was down the corridor and I was the only user. My minders left me in peace for my swim and I put in a few energetic lengths.

My exercise was interrupted by a familiar sweet voice.

"Room for one more?" she asked. She was also completely naked and I admired her curvaceous figure.

"You look gorgeous!" I said with a lascivious smirk. "Do come in!" She jumped in immediately, throwing up a huge fountain of water and then tried to make her getaway. I went after her, but I had forgotten what a poor swimmer she was. I caught her and dragged her under quite easily and she desperately waved her surrender.

"You are a *Larton*!" she gasped as we surfaced and she finished gasping for air.

"OK, I am sure that is insulting." I said resignedly.

"It is a huge sea predator , very fearsome," she replied.

"We have a similar creature on Earth. It's called a shark," I replied.

"Well, what else are sharks good at?" she asked enticingly.

"They are very strong, very fast, and they can have sex for hours!" I said rather creatively.

"Oh..," she pretended interest, "For hours you say?"

"Hours and Hours. And they are very well equipped..," I smirked meaningfully.

"Very well equipped you say...?" she whispered. I tightened my grip around her waist. Fortunately we were at the shallow end of the pool and I could stand. "Oh yes...I see what you mean," she whispered. "With an extra limb, you aught to be able to swim faster," she added, clamping long powerful legs around my thighs.

"It's not for swimming," I explained grasping her firm round buttocks.

Chapter 24

My stay on the Santra Des was short but busy. The scientific team wanted innumerable samples of skin, hair and all my bodies fluids. I was x-rayed and scanned by every imaginable type of machine. I was interviewed at length by psychologists, psychiatrists, sociologists and innumerable others whose speciality I did not bother to determine. We were all beginning to learn a great deal about each other by now, and the more I learnt the more I understood the gulf that separated our two races, despite the physical similarities. It was easy for me as an individual to socialise with them because I was special, the first alien, and I was treated as special. They tried hard to not be insulting or patronising or to criticise me or my race.

The day arrived when the medical team gave the all clear for my departure to the planet's surface. Apparently, Earth viruses were completely baffled by the Hianja biology and represented no threat, and indeed the opposite was also true, Hianja viruses faring no better with the Human biology. I prepared to depart the *Santra Des* and took my leave of Master Saru and his crew, thanking them for their hospitality. A shuttle had arrived to transport Manera and me to the planet's surface and I had to bid a fond farewell to Batsano and Deejana and the other members of the Team before boarding the shuttle. We would meet up again on my return, and I asked Batsano to preserve some degree of sobriety during my absence since I would not be around to look after him. He retorted that since he did not have to put up with my terrible jokes anymore, he had no need to drink!

A planetary landing in a Hianja shuttle was a completely different experience from a landing in an Earth shuttle. No roaring rocket engines, straining to fight gravity and kill the shuttles enormous orbital velocity. No crashing and shuddering against the atmosphere, the hull glowing red hot as excess velocity was burned off. The Hianja shuttles Artificial Gravity engines operated silently and powerfully to slow the craft down while it was still outside the planet's atmosphere. Once our speed was a gentle one or two thousand miles an hour the shuttle descended gracefully into the atmosphere, slowing down very rapidly and descending like a feather on the gentle breeze to its destination. It was almost like riding a lift to the planet's surface!

In a few minutes we were cruising over a city and I gaped at the view of the city being displayed on the view screens like a tourist ogling the sights. And it was quite a sight! I was not unused to cities, and Earth had cities just as big and impressive as this one. But this city was different from anything on Earth, different in architecture, different in concept. The problem with Earth's major cities was of course that all of them were built during pre-technological civilisation, with the technological bits grafted on to the totally unsuitable narrow streets and primitive roads and buildings. During the late 21st Century, serious efforts had been made on Earth to solve the problem of traffic congestion by passing laws restricting the use of private vehicles and making massive investments in public transport. It had stabilised the problem, but at a level which was still unacceptable to most people and continued to cause huge stress and pollution.

Ostinara, the capital city of Mesaroyat which I was now flying over, was older than any Earth city, but was still built by an advanced technological society, more advanced than Earth. There were no road vehicles on Ostinara, except for street cleaning and maintenance vehicles. All transport was via AG vehicles, and the city was built around the concept of aerial travel. The sky was full of *Tanseh*, of various sizes from small car sized vehicles to larger long distance craft. They cruised at different altitudes, I guessed almost certainly under Computer control, and following pre-set routes.

Beneath the shuttle the buildings were huge monolithic structures, some of them linked by multilevel walkways and bridges. Architectural stiles seemed predominantly modern abstract, with clean swooping lines, but there were intermixed among them curves and domes, octagons and hexagons, polyhedrons and gleaming metallic squares of every conceivable shape, texture and colour. Huge expanses of greenery, parklands rivers and lakes between the buildings, created a contrast of lines and textures. The city was landscaped on a vast scale. The rivers seem to connect up the lakes, and as we came lower I began to see small boats on the rivers and lakes.

There were paths and walkways at ground level, weaving between the giant buildings, liberally landscaped with trees and plants. It was as if a 'cubist' God had taken thousands of gleaming abstract jewels and scattered them liberally around the beautiful countryside, intermingling them with trees, rivers, lakes and hills, harmoniously mixing the artificial with the natural. Everywhere the eye settled, there would be a different and pleasing blend of colour and shape to feast on.

The shuttle was heading towards a huge hexagonal building, with descending ramparts like an Earth fort. The roof was flat and almost the size of a football pitch, with a number of craft parked on it as well as taking off and landing. Our shuttle settled with a barely perceptible bounce on its shock absorbers. We stood and moved towards the exits as the airlock doors hissed open and the bright daylight flooded the cabin. The smell of warm air, full of the smell of vegetation and something else, a sort of electric ozone tingle. Higher oxygen content I wondered? As we stepped out of the ship and down the ramp to the ground, I spotted a group of individuals heading towards us. Another welcoming committee? This was becoming a habit! But the individuals meeting us were simply a security team, to escort us to where we would be staying. Manera talked to them briefly and they directed us towards the entrance to the building. The sun was hot but the wind cool and caressing as we headed for the entrance to the building, Manera walking next to me and smiling reassuringly.

"What did you think of Ostinara Paul? she asked with a twinkle in her eyes.

"Quite a spectacle," I replied, "Is it a typical Hianja city?"

"Yes and No," she replied enigmatically, "We like to try and make every city an individual," she went on, "Selamar in the north for example is built on the old Hianja traditional style, the buildings are shaped like *kouzouri*, which is the old village style of house, but of course big and modern like here," and she waved her hand around at the surrounding city, "But the mix of buildings and nature, is the same. Lots of trees and plants, rivers and lakes dividing off the buildings and providing beauty, shade and contrast."

"Yes," I agreed, "It is impressive that you have such control over the city's development. I am not sure that Human's would care to be so regimented."

"That must make city planning very chaotic," she replied.

"Yes, Earth cities are chaotic," I agreed, "Which perhaps is part of their charm, but they can sometimes be uncomfortable places to live in."

"Perfection can only be strived for, never achieved," she said philosophically and I smiled in agreement.

The doors to the building slid open at our approach and we followed our escorts in, two of them ahead of us and two behind. Manera stopped and laid a hand on my shoulder.

"Paul, I should tell you," she said, "You are meeting the Mesaroyat Guardian Council for an informal talk. They will bring you up to date with proceedings."

"Manera, I would have wanted Alfred to be with me on this!" I protested.

"Alfred will be with you," she said quickly, interrupting me, "He is patched through our comms system."

"That is correct Paul, I am here," came the familiar tones from my ship's AI in my ear. "You need not fear anything Paul." went on Manera, "They will not interrogate you in any way. They just want to meet and greet our first Alien visitor," she smiled encouragingly. "You are going to find that everyone will want to meet you."

"Ahh.., Fame at last!" I muttered to myself. "Alfred, how is the work of building a new Hyperdrive going?" I asked.

"Very well Paul," came the calm tones of my AI companion, "I have provided the designers with the necessary specifications and now await their design. Once that is ratified, they will proceed with construction. They assure me that they will need no more than a couple of days for the design, a week or so for fabrication and then a few days for installation and testing. We should be ready to go in three weeks."

"Mmm, No hurry," I mused, "We have waited a few thousand years for this so a few weeks wont make a difference. I fancy it is going to be an enjoyable visit here!"

We proceeded into a lift which descended for a minute or so. We exited into a large alcove which led into a huge pair of sliding doors. They slid open obligingly as we approached and we entered a large conference area. It was only sparsely occupied, by about twenty or so individuals of both sexes. Manera ushered me in, and a couple of familiar figures detached themselves and came towards us. It was Guardian Kemato, followed by the tall angular form of Guardian Hamolatonen. There was a murmur of conversation as we walked in which went suddenly quiet. Kemato gave me the Hianja shoulder 'hug' and Hamolatonen chose to offer a firm handshake accompanied by a broad grin.

"Welcome Captain Constantine, allow me to introduce you to the Council of Mesaroyat, with a few additional friends from neighbouring Planets," and she waved a hand broadly at the assembled company.

"They will introduce themselves individually so I will not give a list of names now," she smiled.

"Thank you Guardian," I said in Hianja, and there was a murmur of approval from the gathering. They appreciated my effort to speak their language, which was a quaintly human reaction! Or were they laughing at my pronunciation! Don't get too puffed up Constantine!

"I look forward to making their acquaintance," I added politely.

"May I also introduce Chief Scientist Manera," added Kemato, "She was the first Hianja to meet Captain Constantine on Omorphia and has been his constant companion." Manera inclined her head politely to the Guardians and they responded the same way. Introductions over, Kemato waved us all into seats and a robot came around with a selection of drinks. Manera then proceeded to give a long and detailed description of events on Omorphia, illustrating the talk with detailed pictures on a large view screen. It was an accurate account, and she then moved on to give a broad overview of Human civilisation and our level of technology, and finally, our biology. This was accompanied by some pictures of the Human anatomy, male and female. At the end, Kemato stood and thanked Manera and opened the floor to questions. There then followed a long and intensive period of questioning, some directed to Manera but mostly to me. I had to enlist Alfred's help in answering many of the more technical questions, or when my Hianjese vocabulary proved inadequate.

After what seemed like three or four hours of this, and to my relief, Kemato called a halt. With all the formal bits of the conference out of the way, we socialised for a little longer, with more of the Guardians wondering over to shake my hand and greet me informally. But the evening came to an end and we bid goodbye to our new acquaintances and were escorted out by Kemato and Hamolatonen. Our four escorts were waiting for us outside, I was not sure if it was the same four, but they looked tough and I could see they were armed. I was a little puzzled by this, if the Hianja were so peace loving why did I need armed guards? I shrugged the thought away and wished goodnight to the two Guardians, who promised to collect me first thing in the morning for my first tour of planet Mesaroyat.

Manera and I were directed by the Guards towards what appeared to be a sleek capsule that was inside a tunnel, accessed through a set of sliding doors. This, Manera explained, was the internal transport capsule, which used magnetic levitation within the tunnel to move through an internal system of tunnels to any part of the city. It was used for short distance travel, as opposed to the *Tanseh* which were preferred for longer distances. Manera dialled the destination and we settled back in our comfortable seats. The capsule hummed gently and I felt it lift away from the ground and accelerate strongly away. There were no windows in the capsule, and there was almost no feeling of movement, but from the strength and duration of the acceleration I calculated we must be doing between one hundred to one-fifty Km an hour. I felt the capsule move left and right and down, slowing down and then speeding up as it navigated the tunnels to its destination. It was clearly computer controlled and was sharing the tunnels with other capsules.

"Do these transport , um, capsules, have many accidents?" I asked

"There has never been an accident in the *Selat*," replied Manera with a reassuring smile. "It has triplicate systems and safety interlocks. Any problem and it will just come to a standstill."

"Ah yes, how often I have heard that!" I muttered cynically.

"This *Selat* is completely safe," retorted Manera. There was a ear shattering explosion followed by a grinding screeching noise and the capsule bucked and shuddered, decelerating rapidly until it came to a standstill. In the shocked silence that followed I heard my shaking voice.

"Did someone remember to tell the *Selat*?" Manera's face was full of shock, and our four Guards were equally dismayed. Fortunately we had all been strapped in so no one had come to any harm.

"This is not possible!" she gasped looking around wildly. I looked behind and noticed a gaping hole in the capsule through which acrid smoke was leaking into the compartment. A lick of flame appeared through the hole, then snuffed out, then reappeared.

"Manera," I said urgently, "Do we have a fire....um." I struggled to think of the Hianja word for 'extinguisher', then remembered that I did not know it. I mimed spraying a fire with foam. She caught on immediately and said something quickly to our Guards, who were gaping at each other in confusion, clearly caught on the hop by the emergency. They all looked desperately around the compartment and then one of them jumped up and leapt towards the front where he banged a switch. A part of the wall slid open to reveal a comms device and screen as well as what looked like an axe, a box of tools and a fire extinguisher.

My faith in Hianja preparedness was restored as our young guard, with voluble advice from the others grabbed the fire extinguisher and leapt with commendable alacrity towards the smoking hole in the rear of the compartment. While he struggled with the controls of the extinguisher, his colleague pressed buttons and talked into the communicator. It lit up reassuringly to show the face of a maintenance robot. Its big grey orbs looked solemnly at us out of the screen as the young guard jabbered at it in machine gun Hianjese. Our fire fighter had got the extinguisher going and poking it through the hole he let loose with a few shots of foam. The smoke began to thin and then vanish and he paused to take stock. Meanwhile, his colleague on the communicator had finished his explanation and the robot responded with alacrity.

"Please remain where you are and help will be forthcoming," It said in a metallic monotone.

"Ah, shame," I muttered in English, "And I was thinking of walking home."

"Paul, are you insane, or do you really have nerves of steel." asked Manera in exasperation. I noticed she was shaking from shock and I took her trembling hands in mine and squeezed them gently. I had forgotten she could speak English!

"I probably am insane," I replied in what I hoped was a calm and reassuring voice. Her face twisted and then relaxed and she started laughing. I grinned with encouragement and our four young guards looked at us both in apprehension. Manera spoke to them reassuringly and with a few sideways glances they continued with their work, chatting amongst themselves and banging away at the communicator. The robot's face cleared from the screen to be replaced by a Hianja face, a young female who looked shocked and flustered. The chief guard jabbered at her and I caught a few words. " *Selat*...explosion.. Earthman with us.....urgent that you contact Guardian Kemato....top priority...," she nodded, looking wildly around her, and I reckoned we were better off with the Robot!

It seemed the immediate danger was over, and I wondered over to the back of the Compartment to take a closer look at the hole. The young guard with the extinguisher was still crouched next to the hole, peering through it. There were no signs of fire and the smoke had died down. I guessed that what had caused the explosion had been left behind by the speeding capsule, otherwise we would have been suffocated by the smoke. I examined the hole carefully, checking the black residue on the inside and outside of the capsule. The young guard, who I now saw was a short haired female with large green eyes and a well filled uniform looked at me curiously as I conducted my examination.

"What do you think caused the explosion?" I asked her. She started and looked at me with big green eyes.

"You speak Hianjese?" she said, more surprised statement than question.

"Some," I replied. She turned to the hole and considered it for a few moments.

"It is impossible," she said, "There is nothing here that could have caused the explosion and derailed the *Selat*."

"No machinery or power supply on the outside at this point?" I asked.

"No, the magnetic coils are in the centre," she pointed at a ridge that went around the circumference of the *Selat*, in the middle of the compartment.

"The compartment is balanced on four magnetic couplings around the centre of the compartment," she said, pointing at the locations.

"Whatever exploded was on the outside of the compartment," I said. She frowned in thought.

"What could have exploded?" she asked.

"What usually explodes?" I asked, standing up. "An explosive device of course," she gazed up at me impassively, seemingly unable to understand what I was saying.

"Someone planted a bomb on the *Selat*?" she asked. The others heard and turned around to look. Manera jumped up and strode over to us.

"Paul, what is this?" she asked, "A bomb you say?"

"I do not see what else it can be Manera," I replied. "This hole was made by an outside explosion. Notice the metal which is bent inwards, and the black powder around the hole. A chemical analysis will probably show some chemical explosive was used. Crude and not very powerful. This is a pretty amateurish attempt at sabotage."

"I can't believe this," she gasped, "Who would do such a thing?"

"Manera, " I looked her in the eyes. "Someone knows about a threat, otherwise why have we been assigned guards ?" I waved my hand at our young guards.

"I just assumed they were our guides," she said. She turned to look questioningly at the guards leader, a big sturdy young female with a strong face and black hair strapped tightly back. "Were you told to expect trouble?" she asked. The guard leader looked uncertain, glancing briefly at her colleagues and hesitating. I looked at green eyes and she met my eyes for a second before averting hers. Manera's shoulders squared and her blue eyes glared like twin lasers.

"Wait till I see Guardian Kemato," she scowled.

Chapter 25

I relaxed on the armchair and took a good long slug of my drink. It was cold, sharp and slightly acrid, with a pleasant fruity aftertaste, a cross between wine and Tequila! After a long hot shower to get the smell and grime out of my nose and hair I was ready for it. My new apartment was large and comfortable with an adjoining pool which would normally have been shared by the surrounding apartments but was now reserved just for us. Two of our guards were posted outside the apartment, and a number of others were also posted in the vicinity.

We had spent an hour in the confines of the smoky *Selat* before being rescued by a robotic maintenance crew. Using a custom rescue vehicle they had connected to our stricken *Selat* and 'towed' us out of the tunnel to an exit. We had completed our journey in another Selat without incident. Guardian Kemato had contacted us when we arrived at the apartment, apologising profusely and promising a full investigation into the incident. She was very evasive when I suggested that sabotage was a possibility, but promised to see us the next day, hopefully with some results from the investigation.

Manera padded out of her bedroom, wearing a silky shift, fresh from a long hot bath and made her way to the huge and well stocked cocktail cabinet. She looked pink and scrubbed, her lush auburn locks held back by a colourful delicate headscarf, a long pale thigh peeking from the slit in her thin robe.

"What are you drinking?" she asked, rattling bottles and examining labels.

"Something from the fridge," I replied, "That tall purple bottle."

"Ah, Mesaroyat *Slaat*," she said, "Good choice, I'll join you," she poured a good slug and made her way over to my settee. I admired the way she moved, a gliding undulation across the ground, hips and buttocks moving seductively. I am sure it was natural, other Hianja moved in the same way, but Manera did it with a feline grace that I could watch all day. She slid onto the settee with the same easy grace and bought both long legs up in a comfortable squat. You caught my examination and smiled impishly.

"Why are you staring at me?" she asked, "You have seen my legs before."

"You are always worth staring at," I replied with a grin, "Especially your legs!"

"They are too thin," she replied. Just like a woman, looking for compliments! I pretended to examine her legs closely, pulling back her robe to get a closer look at her shapely thighs. They were certainly not thin, in fact, by human standards they were as sturdy and well muscled a pair of pins as you could find anywhere. A sprinters legs, muscular and shapely.

"They are pretty scrawny," I said dismissively, pinching her thighs here and there. "Definitely in need of fattening up," I nodded to myself. One of the two reviled legs administered a kick to my midriff, causing a sharp intake of breath and almost spilling my drink.

"Scrawny yourself," she said with a laugh, "Whatever scrawny means," I grabbed hold of the leg and held on.

"It's another word for perfect," I declared, caressing a silky thigh and taking another shot of my *Slaat*. "Which you are, my Hianja princess," I added.

"Are all human males so insincere?" she asked. I considered this for a few seconds.

"Only when it comes to seduction," I admitted, "It's our job, we are men!" She smiled fondly at me.

"I never know when you are joking or serious," she said.

"All good jokes have an element of truth," I pointed out, "That is what makes them funny."

"That is true," she agreed. She stretched out her other leg over my lap and snuggled back in the soft cushions, taking a further sip of her drink. "Paul, can we talk? There is something you have not been told which may explain what is going on," I sat up straight.

"This sounds serious," I said.

"It's very serious. Can you get Alfred on line? I want him to hear this as well."

"Sure," I gently and reluctantly untangled myself from her long legs and walked to my room to retrieve my travel bag. Inside were a couple of communicators which had been patched through the Hianja network to Alfred. I gave one to Manera and put the other one on myself. Activating the call button I settled back into my sofa and retrieved my drink. Manera stood and started pacing the floor nervously. I patted the sofa.

"Sit," I ordered gently. "Alfred, how is it hanging?"

"Hello to you also Paul," came the cryptic response, "I have been informed of your little accident. I am happy you and Manera are unharmed."

"Thank you Alfred but it was no accident. I am fairly certain it was sabotage," I replied.

"So I understand Paul," he replied, "But I cannot see who would want to murder you. Not on Mesaroyat. Now if you were on Vasmeranta, I can believe that Smetronis's accomplices would be responsible."

"Smetronis and his fanatics are not just on Vasmeranta," said Manera,

"They are everywhere in some numbers small or large," I looked at her in surprise. This was news to me, I had assumed that they were a small and localised clique.

"Who are these fanatics Manera? What do they believe in and why are they so against Human contact?" I asked.

"To answer that I have to tell you a long story," she replied enigmatically. "It concerns the origins of my race."

"That does sound like a long story," I replied, "I'll have to re-fill my glass." Manera began her 'story';

"The first thing you must know, is that my species were not always the way we are now. A long time ago, before we discovered the Hyperspace drive and travelled the stars, we were like Humans. That is, our males were fertile and we conceived and gave birth naturally, like you," I was topping my glass up when she said that, and I nodded in agreement.

"I guessed that at some point in the past that must have been so," I said. "I have noticed that everyone seemed reluctant to discuss this. Why?"

"It's not because we wanted to keep a secret," she replied, "But because it reveals something about our race that is shameful. Something so traumatic that it shaped our psychology and made us what we are."

"What you are? But you are civilised and peaceful. How can you be ashamed of what you are?" I asked

"Think of the problems your race had three, four hundred years ago," she replied. "Our Society was in the same condition twenty thousand years ago. We had also developed science and technology very quickly, but our social and psychological development lagged far behind. Our society was dominated by males and male aggression also formed and controlled our social, political and religious systems. The world was split by Nations and factions, political, Nationalistic and Religious and dominated by fanatical old men who were happy to send young people to their deaths for the sake of their dogma. There was not a period when there was not a war going on somewhere in the world. Millions died, the world was ravaged and still we did not learn or forgive. Does that sound familiar?"

"Jesus, was it that bad?" I asked, "I mean, Earth was pretty bad during the twentieth and twenty-first centuries, but it did improve. We pulled back from the brink."

"Well, it did not look as if we would make it," said Manera, "Then, you could say, fate took a hand. There was a great deal of genetic research taking place at the time. Some of it legal scientific and medical research, but some of it illegal weapons research. One of these projects was to perfect a virus that would pacify the enemy."

"Pacify the enemy? How is that possible?" I asked.

"It was a character altering virus. It linked up with the hosts cells and excreted a drug that altered the persons personality. It was originally discovered as part of a research program to heal psychological disorders. Once infected, the host did not have to take drugs anymore, they were manufactured by his own cells. The delivery system was the virus, and it could be used to deliver different types of manufacturing systems. Different drugs could be manufactured by the host cells in other words."

"I seem to remember reading somewhere that we use the same delivery system," I said . She nodded.

"Once infected, there was no cure. The virus had delivered its genetic material into the host cells and died. The cell alteration was permanent."

"So they were going to deliver a personality altering drug using this virus. What effect would that have had on the enemy," asked Alfred.

"Like I said, the world was infested with fanatics. Men whose principles were so strong, or so they claimed, that they would have died for them. Except that it was usually not them who died but thousands of their brain washed followers, fighting and dying for their Country, their Religion, their Political System. It was actually a naked struggle for power, with no quarter given. It was this fanaticism, male dominated single minded aggression, which was the problem. It was a kind of insanity, a character trait which seemed to be unique to men."

"Manera, that is an exaggeration surely," I protested, "Male aggression is largely a social character trait, it is not genetic."

"I am afraid that you are probably wrong," she replied. "Certainly for Hianja, it was a genetic trait because they found a way to disable it using this virus delivery system. Fanatical demagogues, who were prepared to die for their beliefs, were suddenly transformed into calm and reasonable men, humane and non-violent."

"You mean they actually used it?" I asked.

"Not on purpose, just experimented with it using psychologically ill patients. It worked all right, but many scientists had great misgivings about releasing such a massively mind altering virus as a matter of principle, but also because no long term studies had been done for side effects. Unfortunately, one small group of fanatics got control of the virus and released it by infecting their enemy's water supplies. It was thought that the virus could only be transmitted internally, by ingestion in a special form. So they believed that they were safe from infection. The effects of the virus were very slow to appear and no one noticed anything for years. But gradually, their enemy started to become less aggressive, pulled away from confrontation. In fact, the virus mutated and became airborne. The whole world was infected."

"Well, was that such a bad thing?" I asked, "From what you were saying, these personality changes were all to the good. How was it noticed?"

"It wasn't," she replied. "The original scientists who had released the virus took the secret to their graves. The problem was, years later it was noticed that the male female balance for new births was changing all over the world. More females were being born than males, and no one knew why. It took years of research before this virus was isolated, and even longer to discover that it was not a natural virus but an artificial one. Its source was discovered and the awful truth came out. But it took a couple more generations to realise that the decline in male births was continuing, and that soon no more males would be born. Our Species faced extinction," I slumped back in my seat in disbelief.

"Unbelievable!". I took a sip of my drink and considered the incredible story.

"But surely," I protested, "Genetic Science must have been advanced enough to find a cure?"

"You would have thought so," she replied, "But the virus kept mutating, as viruses do. They could slow down the infection, but not stop it altogether. After a few generations, no male children were being born. Of course, they had stockpiled huge amounts of male semen, frozen in Government storage facilities. There was enough to keep the race going for generations, and they hoped a cure would be found. But then, a group of female scientists discovered a new way to fertilise an egg, which did not need semen. They were able to culture a sort of artificial semen, the genetic material of one person was extracted, processed and injected into another person's egg, fertilising it. Male semen was no longer needed."

"Ah yes," I nodded, "The female dream had been achieved, men were no longer needed!" My remark was meant as a jest, but Manera winced.

"Actually, there is truth in your joke Paul. A very powerful movement had developed, political, scientific, cultural, a movement which cut across all nations and religions. A movement that argued for not bringing back the male sex. It was argued that Males had bought nothing but disaster upon the race, they were too unstable, too driven by their sexual urges to behave in socially unacceptable ways. And actually, peace had descended upon the world. No more wars, no more irresolvable conflicts leading to violence and confrontation."

"But the virus had solved that problem," I argued, "Males were no longer aggressive."

"Yes, but if the virus was to be destroyed, allowing males to be born naturally, they would also be free of the pacifying drug. Things would go back to the way they were."

"So that was it? Males were consigned to the genetic dustbin?"

"It's hard for us to understand the strength of feeling at the time," she replied, "The world had been an appallingly violent place. Hianja males were often very savage, more so than humans, and Hianja females were oppressed, second class citizens. No one wanted to go back to that."

"Incredible," I muttered. "But you did get them back, although not fully functional?" I asked.

"Yes, but that was much later. For thousands of years, Hianja civilisation struggled on the edge of collapse. You see, without the males in the early years, many industries and technologies were lost. The world became depopulated and the economies of all the nations collapsed. There was neither the will or the strength for war anymore, it was a struggle to survive. But slowly, over thousands of years, science and technology recovered. The knowledge had not been lost you see. Two thousand years after the 'Great Disaster.", as we call it, , biological research had recovered to the point where males could be recreated, but not as they were. Physically male, but infertile. To make them fertile required the destruction of the personality altering virus, and they did not have the courage for that. So they settled for a compromise."

"A male without balls!" I muttered unkindly. I thought of the male Hianja I had met and could not maintain my contempt. They were certainly manly enough in all the ways that are important. "Sorry, scrub that!" I added.

"You are right in a sense," she said surprisingly. "The modern Hianja male is a shadow of the original. But the original was a psychotic beast by modern standards, and we are well rid of him. We are happy with our modern male," she said with a little smile. "Do you remember our discussion about sexual differences between the sexes? She asked.

"Yes, you said that there were few differences now."

"That is right. And the reason is because the modern male is quite different from his primitive counterpart," I looked closely at Manera, and she looked questioningly back.

"Manera, how did you feel when you first saw me? Were you frightened?"

"No, because I did not think of you as a Hianja male. You are an alien, a different species. But I was very interested to learn whether Human's had met and overcome the same social problems as us. It was very exciting that you appear to have done so. I and many of my colleagues, are very respectful of Human society. You have achieved something we could not."

"But it appears that not all your people share this feeling," I pointed out.

"Exactly," she replied, "And this is what my story was leading to. There is a faction, centred in Vasmeranta but apparently having agents here also, which is not so convinced that Humans have overcome their violent natures. They want to stop immediate contact, put it off for as long as possible."

"Why, it is bound to happen eventually," I pointed out.

"Yes, but if they can put off contact for a few hundred years, that will allow us to prepare for contact, and that will also allow Humans to develop socially, hopefully confirming that they truly have evolved beyond violence and aggression."

"So their aim is to stop me from returning to Earth, thereby preventing contact indefinitely," I inquired.

"Yes," she agreed. "And the obvious way to stop them is for you to give us Earth's co-ordinates. Once the Earth's location is known, there is no point in them trying to prevent your return."

"Manera, there is a problem with releasing Earth's co-ordinates, as Paul knows," replied Alfred. "It is expressly against procedure." Alfred pronounced 'Procedure' with a capital 'P'!

"Alfred, I promise not to release the co-ordinates without consulting you. It is just a case of being prepared," I replied.

"It is against procedure," he repeated, "Under any circumstances," I slumped back in my seat in frustration.

"Alfred, if you are destroyed, Contact will not happen. And I will have no way of returning home," I pointed out.

"Our fate is unimportant Paul, as you know," he replied impassively. "But I take your point about Contact. I will therefore translate the co-ordinates into Hianja convention and place them into your personal Computer. You must only use them if I am destroyed."

"Agreed Alfred," I said with relief. I got up to refresh my glass and took Manera's glass with me also.

"Things must have been pretty bad in the old days," I mused out loud, "for there to be such strong feelings around after thousands of years."

"Every generation is educated about those times," replied Manera, "It is part of our social conditioning, to learn about those terrible times when our species nearly committed suicide. But also remember, we are the children of the virus; our personalities are different from pre-virus days. We are genetically altered to abhor violence and aggression."

"So how was Smetronis and his gang able to do the things they did then?" I mused. "Something very powerful must be motivating them to go against their basic natures in this way. And we have no idea what that something is!"

Chapter 26

The following few days of my stay on Mesaroyat were intensely interesting
and stimulating. The days seemed to last for ever, as is the case when
experiences are new and exciting. As the week came to an end and we
moved into the second week, familiarity made the time pass more quickly
and I was soon looking reluctantly and sadly at the end of my stay. Reports
from the *Lisa Jane* were good, and the work was almost complete. The new
Hyperdrive was installed and testing was taking place. Alfred reported that
a couple more days should see the testing completed and we would be
ready to depart. I went over the events of the last ten days fondly. This
was a beautiful world, one which was full of natural beauty, and also, one
in which the natural and the artificial existed side by side without conflict
or disharmony. Hianja built their cities with a sure eye for balance and
colour, without damaging or polluting the environment.

Being a somewhat cynical materialist, I had especially been on the
lookout for any signs of discontent, any sign that not everyone was happy
with Hianja Society. Were there any poor or disadvantaged? Were there any
shanty towns, any downtrodden peasant classes? Was there any underclass,
alternative culture, revolutionary movements? Nope, not a sign. Everything
in the garden seemed to be unequivocally rosy! Every city was populated
by happy shining people, energetic and healthy and enjoying a full and
rewarding life! I could not believe that any society could be that successful.
We were in a *Tanseh* on our way to a *Janesta*, a Hianja Arts festival, on the
outskirts of the city of *Prinlak-Han* when I put this to Manera. She looked
thoughtful for a few moments before answering.

"There are many groups of individuals who choose alternative
lifestyles," she said somewhat reluctantly. "But as a rule they are not a
threat or a de-stabilising influence. Many are just eccentric and
idiosyncratic individualists."

"What sort of alternative lifestyles?" I asked curiously. She looked
uneasy and hesitated before answering.

"These people are not representative of Hianja society," she said
evasively.

"I understand that, but I am interested to know what their problem is," I
said, "You see, on Earth, it does not matter how idyllic life is, there will
always be a number of individuals who want something different. It's a
Human condition, being cantankerous and difficult! But Society allows
these freedoms, as long as they do not harm others or break the law," I said
reassuringly. She still looked reluctant to speak.

"Have you been asked not to talk about this aspect of Hianja Society?" I asked quietly.

"Not directly, but just...," she paused awkwardly, "Just, to show you the best of our Society. We are very proud of our achievements," she said defensively.

"And so you should be," I replied, "But actually, I would be more impressed if Hianja Society was more pluralistic. Catering for minority tastes is a sign of strength, not weakness." She looked at me carefully, as if mulling things over.

"Ok," she said at last. "You are right Paul, and I will show you another aspect of our Society. If we cannot be honest with each other, then we will never trust each other."

"When?" I asked eagerly.

"Well..," she paused, "Do you really want to go to the *Janesta*?" she asked.

"I could live without it!" I replied. She nodded and hit a couple of buttons on the control board of the *Tanseh*. The screen lit up and she gave directions to the computer. The *Tanseh* changed direction and picked up speed and height. She lent back in her chair.

"The location is about 500 *reck* from here," she said. (about 600 Km). The *Tanseh* continued to climb and accelerate. Soon we had achieved our cruising altitude and the Tanseh continued to accelerate. I calculated that we had achieved a least mach 3 before it started to slow down. Sure enough, ten minutes later we started to descend, coming back into the atmosphere at sub sonic speed and continuing to slow rapidly. Beneath us were two mountain ranges with a long winding valley in between. The area seemed uninhabited, but after a couple of minutes of following the winding valley a small village appeared beneath us. There were a couple of hundred houses, small white and dun coloured, nestling among the trees and surrounded by fields and orchards. It could have been a small farming community on Earth, except that each house had a large solar energy collector on the roof.

The Tanseh came down in the centre of the village on what appeared to be a fairly makeshift landing pad, just some cleared and levelled land with gravel spread over it. This appeared to be the village 'green', an open patch of land with a large flat grassed area on which some children were playing a ball game which stopped when we landed. After the gleaming high Tech edifices that I had seen, the village looked humble and somewhat shabby. Decidedly 'Low Tech.'. Were these people the Hianja equivalent of the American Amish community I wondered? Alternative lifestyle certainly but hardly a threat or a problem! We descended from the Tanseh accompanied by our four guards and a couple of robots. I wondered what the locals would make of our delegation.

"Are they used to visitors here?" I asked Manera.

"Yes, they have contact with the outside world," she replied, "They trade their agricultural produce for certain manufactured goods. Their produce is highly prized for its flavour."

"But surely Manera," I protested, "As citizens, they have the right to have whatever fundamental goods they need for their survival free, like all other citizens. Why do they need to trade?"

"Because the manufactured goods they need are not what is normally available. They need specialised tools and farming implements which have to be specially manufactured," she replied. I got a picture in my head of a bunch of yokels pulling a plough. A right bunch of eccentrics I thought. Here they are in the middle of a technological paradise and they wanted to get their hands dirty with ancient farming methods and tools. We were making our way along the road in the direction of what appeared to be the largest house in the village. There were two or three people visible in the distance, but they seemed to be ignoring us. In the meantime, the children had stopped their game of football and were dashing over towards us , jabbering amongst themselves in high pitched voices like twittering birds. When they came closer they were seized by shyness and stopped ten metres away, pushing and shoving each other and ogling us with big eyes. Peculiarly, the children looked more alien than the adults. Legs were too long, heads too big and misshapen, eyes were goggling and huge and they moved with an awkward gait, like young new born foals. They started poking each other and pointing to me, jabbering in a peculiar accent that I could not follow.

"What are they saying?" I asked Manera.

"There is that ugly Earthman!" she said with a grin.

"Tell them they had better leave before I eat them!" I said with a ferocious and comical scowl.

"Paul!" gasped Manera "You will frighten the children," I could not stop myself from chuckling. Manera looked at me questioningly and I explained.

"On Earth, when you want to insult someone's appearance, you tell them that they will frighten the children. This is the first time someone has used it truthfully!"

"You are not that ugly," she said with a little smile.

"You are generous with your complements!" are said sarcastically.

"All right, you are a sexy magnetic animal and I cannot resist you!" she grinned.

"Better, better!" I said encouragingly. The children continued to follow us, fascinated by my appearance and continuing to put up a barrage of noise. Our four guards were proceeding ahead and behind with the two robots doing the same. The robots were humanoid constructions with slender bodies in a businesslike gunmetal grey. Normally they were domestic servants but they had been re-programmed as security robots and armed with electronic stun guns, the same as the Hianja security staff. The robots were immune from these and also had been reinforced to resist projectiles and laser weapons. A pretty good achievement I thought in such a short time. If the Hianja decided to turn their attention to things military, I was sure they could produce some impressive weapons.

We were now amongst the houses and on closer examination they were more sophisticated than I had first thought. I could not tell what the basic construction was but they were coated with sleek rough concrete like material that looked pretty durable. I suddenly realised where I had seen the material before; The Base on Omorphia. I pointed this out to Manera and she agreed.

"They have the same machines as were used on Omorphia," she said. "They use gravel with a small amount of carbon dust and glue to create a slurry. They make a wooden or plastic mould and pour the slurry in. It hardens into a very strong panel with good heat insulation properties."

"Very good," I congratulated her. "You have past your Master Builders exam. I will present you with your certificate later," and I winked suggestively.

"Thank you. I shall frame it and stick it up your....!" she began.

"Manera!" I interrupted. "Your sense of humour is becoming too Earthy by far!" I remonstrated. She smiled slyly.

"So tell me about these people Manera, what is their philosophy?" I asked.

"Well, they call themselves the *Kreslatcha ,* which means the Originals. They believe in recreating life as it was, or as they believe it was, before the Change."

"Before the Genetic change you mean, when Men were Men and Women knew their place?" I asked. She nodded with a derisory smirk.

"So are you seriously saying that these Neanderthals actually live their lives in this archaic way? But why were you concerned about telling me about them Manera, they are just a bunch of eccentrics."

"You do not understand Paul. Their thinking is dangerous because it glamorises the evil age. You must have something similar on Earth. A group of individuals who glamorised an evil period and tried to live that life?"

"Yes we had a tyrant in the 20th Century called Hitler. His followers were called Nazis and they were ruthless in oppressing, torturing and murdering those from other races that they disliked. After they were defeated and destroyed, there were small groups of followers which remained, pathetic louts who glamorised the Nazis. They were small in number but nevertheless caused alarm far in excess of their numbers."

"Yes exactly!" she exclaimed, "These people are a living reminder of our evil past, but there is little we can do about them. They are entitled to the protection of the constitution."

"You say they are a reminder of your evil past," I said, not fully understanding her concern. "But actually, they seem to be just a bunch of eccentric farmers. What is there about them which is evil or represents a threat?"

"They are not evil in themselves," she said evasively, "It is more what they represent."

We were at the front of the large two floor building which seemed to be a village Town Hall of some sort. We walked up the stairs into the building which was surprisingly cool and airy.

"By the way Manera," I asked, "Have you been here before?"

"Yes, I did spend a few weeks here last year," she replied. "They had an infection with their water supply and we came to find the problem and eliminate it. So I know some of them."

A weather-beaten and stringy looking female was occupying a small desk in the foyer of the building we had just entered, and she jumped up in surprise when she saw us. Her eyes widened when she spotted me and she gasped, staggering back and bringing her hand up to her mouth in shock. It was the first time I had seen such an extreme reaction at my presence.

"The Earthman!" she gasped, looking wildly between me and Manera, "What are you doing here?" she asked Manera.

"Janja, do you remember me?" asked Manera. Janja looked carefully at her before enlightenment spread across her features.

"*Fes* Manera," she said. "Of course I remember you. I have seen you on *Sanset* with the Earthman. Why have you bought him here?"

"He is a difficult individual," began Manera, inclining her head towards me with a frustrated expression on her face. "He wanted to see some unusual aspects of Hianja life, and I thought of your humble village as an example."

"A typical Male," agreed Janja, putting on a resigned face. "He wants to see something unusual eh?" she asked, "I would have thought our way of life was closer to Earth's. " she finished eyeing me up and down speculatively.

"Captain Constantine tells me that males and females on Earth have achieved equality in all things. There are just as many female leaders as there are males, and that is true of every other field," replied Manera. Janja looked impressed.

"If that is true, then Earthmen are not like our men at all," Janja mused.

"Excuse me," I said, "What is this about Hianja 'men'? As far as I have seen, your 'men' are refined and civilised."

"The men here are not the same," said Manera. "These males are original stock." I gaped at her in disbelief. But before I could say anything more, I was interrupted.

"You are about to meet some," said Janja, nodding towards the door.

I turned to see a number of individuals walking through the door, of an appearance that I had never seen before. These individuals were big and burly, with a thick growth of hair around their heads and faces, like a fringe which grew around and under the chin and merged with the hair on the head like a lions mane. They looked pretty ferocious, with exaggerated bone structure and heavy chins and jaws. Three of these intimidating individuals stomped through the door and strode up to us. Our guards and the robots shifted uneasily and Manera extended a hand and nodded in a calming gesture. The leader, who had a fringe of auburn hair and slate grey eyes stopped and looked with obvious surprise at our party. His eyes fixed first on me, with a start of recognition, and then moved to Manera.

"*Fes* Manera," he said, the same as Janja, I guessed it was some sort of greeting. His voice was startlingly loud and basso. "What brings you back here, and with the Earthman?" he growled, gesturing in my direction. I felt a stab of nervousness. There was something primal about these individuals, something that the modern Hianja male had clearly lost.

"Like I said to Janja," explained Manera, "The Earthman wanted to see a community different from the norm. He says that Earth has much Cultural diversity, and he was interested in ours."

"Ha, you should have warned us Manera, we would have prepared a better welcome for our visitor from the Stars," he turned to me. "This is a great honour Captain," he said courteously, "We would be delighted if you would stay and get to know our community."

I thanked him and Manera explained that we could only stay a few hours.

"My name is Hrachik," said the men's leader, "And this is Friskna and Sraico," he indicated the other two, who nodded in my direction. "With your agreement, I will take you on a tour of our little village. Then we can share a drink and talk."

I was impressed with Hrachik's hospitality. He, and the other men, seemed amiable enough and despite their dour appearance I found it hard to understand how they could be considered in any way dangerous.

"Now, follow me and I will show you around our beautiful village," said Hrachik proudly.

"There is a small question that someone could answer for me," I said as we followed Hrachik's broad back. Manera looked at me while Hrachik grunted questioningly.

"My understanding was that original Hianja males were extinct!" Hrachek gave a deep throated grunt of contempt.

"Yes, I am just a part of the fossil record! Escaped from the museum!"

he continued to chuckle to himself, amused by his own joke. I looked questioningly at Manera.

"They use cloning technology to create males," she explained

"Cloned males?" I asked with disbelief, "From what?"

"From who," replied Hrachik, "From the DNA extracted from preserved medical remnants, from museums and graves and anywhere where there are Hianja remains."

"Good God!" I exclaimed in amazement, "Who was responsible for doing that? When did it happen?"

"Ah, it's a long and incredible story Earthman," said Hrachik, turning to me, "When we have finished the tour of the village, you will come to my home and, with a bottle of *Slavictska*, I will recount it to you."

I shook my head in disbelief, unable to restrain the host of unanswered questions in my head. But I had to because neither Hrachik nor Manera would say more.

The tour of the village was long and detailed. Hrachik was a great talker and seemed to know everyone in the village and everything about what they did, and he told us about it! But it was a fascinating insight into what Hianja life may have been like before the Change. Automation was used widely throughout the village, they had no problem with that, but they did not use Robots, preferring to do the work themselves. Computers were OK, but not AI. Electric powered Farm machinery and Solar Energy was OK but not fusion power. Ground Transport but not AG flyers. The technology level seemed to be about Earth 20th to 21st Century.

That was the period which was the 'heyday' of *Kreslatcha* life, and they stuck to it faithfully. This is what bought them into conflict with the rest of Hianja Society, their dedication to a period in Hianja history which was abhorred by Society in general. But clearly the *Kreslatcha* themselves were idolising and romanticising this period, ignoring the bigotry and exploitation, the brutality of the period, and above all the violence and war which had nearly destroyed their race and their planet. They denied that these things happened, maintaining that it was propaganda to discredit their movement. The focal point of the conflict was of course the male sex. Hianja Society saw males as being the vehicle of violence and destruction, but the *Kreslatcha* believed it was not male aggression which caused the Great Disaster, but female foolishness in releasing the untested personality altering virus.

I looked for signs of this emotional instability amongst the *Kreslatcha* males, particularly in their relationships with their females, and sure enough there seemed to be a huge gulf between the sexes. *Kreslatcha* females seemed to take a subordinate role in all aspects of life. Manera in particular could not accept the need for the females to carry their pregnancies and give birth naturally. The males did not seem to treat them cruelly, but they left no doubt as to who was the boss! The male arrogance that Manera had spoken of was certainly there, and I could imagine that given the right circumstances the dour males could get out of control, but were they capable of racial hatred and genocide? Then I remembered our own 20th and 21st Centuries, the so called first and second World wars, the Muslim conflicts and the massive and widespread oppression and extermination of minorities that took place during that period.

And it was not women who carried out this slaughter, but men. It was not Women who ordered it or directed it, and justified it, it was Men. And the Hianja had suffered even greater slaughter and destruction. The end of Man the Destroyer must have come as a great relief to the long suffering Hianja female. They did not want Him back under any circumstances. And this sad bunch of individuals acting out their fantasies of their glorious past were a constant reminder of that period of insanity.

But the *Kreslatcha* perhaps had a point. Ignoring their glorification of the past, was it not possible that the Hianja male bought forward under modern circumstances would behave completely differently? Take these males and put them into a modern Hianja Society, bring them up as equals to females and surely they would be quite different? But there was clearly no desire to conduct that experiment, because there was no desire, and in practice no practical way of bringing them back.

Hrachik's home was large and comfortable, but hardly luxurious. We sat on hard chairs around a large wooden table while Hrachek's wife, an ample and attractive golden haired lady with large innocent blue eyes served us with chilled *Slavictska*, and small sweet cakes. Our security team also joined us around the table, the indefatigable robots keeping guard outside the house. The Village had been how I imagined a 20th Century Earth farming Community to be. Neat whitewashed houses and large rambling barns, dilapidated outhouses for the animals and muddy fields. Farming machines of all sizes and shapes were everywhere. This was not a poor community and the evidence of wealth and advanced Technology was everywhere.

"Now Paul, I will tell you the story of how male Hianja returned to life. It happened on the planet Calderon , about ten thousand years ago," he took a big drought of his drink,a powerful clear liquid reminiscent of Earth's Grapa . "Calderon was about the tenth planet to be settled by Hianja, quite early on in our expansion into Space. It was a big world, 20 percent bigger than Hianja, with 18 percent greater gravity, and there was great reluctance to emigrate there because of the gravity. But was a beautiful and fertile world, ideal in every way. So, we turned to genetic engineering to help us. A few tweeks and adjustments and the Calderonians were born with stronger bones and larger hearts and more powerful muscles. Very useful in the United Hianja Games, Calderonians won almost every athletic event. Except for swimming, they were not very good at swimming! This caused some resentment of course, who wants to see an athletics event when you know the first three places would be filled by Calderonians?"

"The genetic changes pioneered by the Calderonians became very popular with prospective athletes all over the world, and after a few hundred years they became widespread. The Hianja Superman, or Superwoman actually, became widespread. Another idea that occurred to the Calderonians was that Hianja males would be very suited to the heavier gravity. Well, the experiments were more successful than they bargained for. They discovered a way to create a male baby! Initially they tried to hush it up, but it got out. There was no reason why the Hianja race could not now be reconstructed as it was and spread amongst the stars.," Hrachik looked sober now. We drank our Grapa and nibbled sweet biscuits, and waited for him to continue.

"Well, you can imagine the furore when the news came out! After ten thousand years, real males now walked the ground again. Hianja Society was bitterly divided between those who wanted the research destroyed and no more males created ever again, and those who wanted their men back! But the latter were a small minority. After thousand of years of propaganda, Males were the devil! The research was destroyed, but not before a large number of males were born. All modern males are from this group. So out of that group, the *Kreslatcha* movement was born. We are tolerated, even helped, as long as we do not become too big or influential. *Kreslatcha* are on nearly every planet of the Federation and we keep in touch with each other regularly. We believe our day will come, when the Hianja race will be re-created as it was, whole again. Then we will truly conquer the Galaxy!" he finished with a cry of triumph, holding his mug aloft.

"Well, not all of it I hope," I added dryly, "Leave some for us."

Chapter 27

We talked a little more before making our goodbyes. Hrachik and the others were polite, but there was undoubtedly a wall dividing them from Manera, who was quiet and subdued. As our *Tanseh* lifted we waved to the group who had gathered to see us off, Hrachik and his buddies in the fore. I settled back in my seat thoughtfully, gazing at the countryside sliding by the window.

"They do not seem that bad," I said thoughtfully, to a withdrawn Menara.

"Look Paul, imagine we had gone to a party thrown by your Nizi, Narzy or whatever they are, friends," she began.

"Nazi," I said, "And they would not be friends of mine."

"But say someone invited you to one of their parties. Would you go?" I began to realise the strength of feeling the Hianja had against that ancient period and those ancient people who were their ancestors. How did they keep that strength of feeling alive I asked myself? Perhaps the *Kreslatcha* themselves, by their very existence, were a constant reminder of the hated past.

"Let me say one thing though," I said, "Our Nazi followers are a nasty bunch. They do not just worship what they see as the 'good' things associated with Nazism, if there are any, but they actively worship the bad things. They are racist and violent. They attack and beat up individuals because of their race and colour. As far as I can see, the *Kreslatcha* are harmless. They glamorise all the good things about the ancients and forget about the bad things. Perhaps that is short-sighted of them, but it is not evil." Manera nodded thoughtfully.

"We do tend to think of what they represent, rather than what they are."

"Yes," I replied, "To you they represent the evil past, to me, they are a group of family people living in a way that pleases them and harms nobody. Do you really believe that there is any way in which the *Kreslatcha* can bring back the past?"

"You heard Hrachik, they can conquer the Galaxy!"

"That was just talk. That old hayseed couldn't conquer a rabbit if it lay down and surrendered!"

"You could be right," she agreed with an air of resignation, then with a twinkle added. "What is a rabbit?"

"Ah, it's a lovely little cuddly animal with big floppy ears," I said, "A bit like yours," I added, tweaking her cute triangular earlobe.

"Big floppy ears?" she said enquiringly.

"To go with your six eyes and two heads!" I replied, pretending surprise and horror.

"So Earthman!" she said in an ominous tone, "You have penetrated my telepathic disguise at last. Well, now I have no choice but to eat you!"

"Is there any chance of some sex first?" I asked hopefully. She choked down a laugh.

"Sex is not permitted with one's food. It is unhygienic!"

"Fussy Fussy!" I muttered with feigned disappointment.

The *Tanseh* was accelerating into the stratosphere and we settled back for the short journey. Today was my last day on the planet, in the evening we were due back in orbit and tomorrow Alfred and I would start our return journey to Earth in the *Lisa Jane*. I was sad to be leaving. The thought of what awaited me back on Earth did not fill me with enthusiasm. The basic requirement for a Space Scout was a desire to get away from Earth. Homesickness was not desirable! On that score, I was an ideal candidate!

"Manera?" I asked, "Could I become an honorary Hianja citizen? I don't fancy going back, I want to stay here. I think I will just send old Alfred back, he doesn't need me," she looked at me questioningly, unable to decide whether I was serious or not. I ended her confusion. "It's OK, I am just joking." She sighed and gave me a remonstrative look.

"Captain Constantine, you must not shirk your duty. You are a Captain in Earth's Space Exploration Service, a proud and prestigious position. Earth is relying on you!"

"Christ!" I gasped, "You're not working for that old bastard Crozier are you?" Crozier, that is Admiral Crozier, was the glorious leader of the SES, my boss and the scourge of all Scouts. He contemptuously dismissed us as all as drop-outs and misfits, maintaining that that if it was up to him we would all be replaced by robots.

"Who is that old bastard Crozier?" she asked.

"My boss, the head of the SES," I explained. "And you are right, if I do not return, he will personally come out here and tear my bollocks off."

"No problem, all are respected here," she remarked slyly.

"True, but I would prefer to remain here without having major surgery," I replied, "Anyway, given a world full of females, being deprived of your testicles would seem to be your worst nightmare!"

"So that is why you want to remain?" she said accusingly. "A world full of females is it? Are you planning to work your way through the female population of Mesaroyat?"

"Ah, if I could but live that long!" I moaned imploringly, earning myself a sharp elbow in the ribs.

Chapter 28

I awoke with the cold early morning light streaming through the broad high windows of the apartment. Next to me on the huge bed, Manera still slept. She was lying on her side, her back to me. My eyes wondered over her curves, the tiny waist exaggerated the smooth rise of jutting hip and curved thigh. It reminded me of an ancient painting, Renaissance, Rembrant was it? No, some other artist. It was a woman lying on a bed with her back to the viewer, waist hips and bottom challenging the eye with their sensual curves. How amazing I thought, parallel evolution creating a Renaissance painting lying on my bed one thousand light years from Earth!

The Renaissance painting stirred and turned over. She smiled gently and snuggled into her pillow. It was our last day together and my feelings were heavy, confused. The previous evening had been a formal event, the Guardian Council giving me a send-off. A few speeches by some worthies and a final rousing speech by Kemato. I had replied, hoping for a long and fruitful relationship between our two species. God I am becoming a right politician I thought. Maybe I will take up a new career when I return to Earth. Get elected to the United Nations Council, maybe Earth President. The first man to make contact with Aliens? It would be a pushover! Manera poked me languidly in the ribs.

"What are you thinking?" she asked. Why do women always ask that I wondered. You could be in a daze, thinking about your next meal or fancying a beer, and they ask, 'A penny for your thoughts?' You can't say, 'I was considering the competing merits of Guinness and Best Bitter!' That is somehow inadequate. I realised I had been asked a question and stirred my brain into action.

"Umm, how beautiful you are?" I suggested hopefully. She smiled indulgently.

"I am beginning to discover that Earthmen are always evasive when it comes to personal questions," she replied. "As if they always have something to hide."

"We usually do have something to hide," I grinned, "Mostly our own shallowness when it comes to personal relations!"

"You are being too hard on your sex," she replied, "I think human males have too many expectations heaped upon their shoulders, mostly by themselves. It is OK not to be a hero or a great Lover." I gave a growl of feigned anger.

"What do you mean woman, not a great Lover? Not a Hero?" I cried with indignation. She shrieked as I rolled over and straddled her, pinning her to the bed. She upended me and we crashed to the softly padded floor rolling and wrestling with mock ferocity. I allowed her to pin me down and straddle me with her powerful thighs. Her head came down, dark hair tumbling down to cover my face.

"Do you surrender Earthman?" she growled.

"Never!" I cried theatrically, "Do your worst, have your way with me, but I will never surrender!"

"I will turn you into my sexual slave!" she cried fiercely.

"I will suffer bravely, for my people!" I exclaimed. She paused thoughtfully as if considering her options.

"I cannot allow such a brave individual to suffer," she said, "You are free Earthman!"

"Er, well er, no rush!" I wheedled, "I don't mind a bit of suffering, honest. You must do what you must do! "

"We-ell," she mused reluctantly.

"That sexual slave bit didn't sound too bad," I continued, "I could put up with that."

"Are you sure?" she said reluctantly, trying hard to restrain her laughter.

"Oh yes!" I agreed eagerly, "But if you carry on sitting on my equipment any longer I will be hard pushed to put up with anything!" I groaned, and she made a sympathetic face and rolled off my protesting equipment.

"We'd better get ready," she smiled. "The security team will be here soon." We showered and got dressed and were having a small breakfast when the doorbell chimed followed by Sar-Neeta's voice on the intercom.

"Captain, we are ready to depart for orbital rendezvous," she said.

"OK Sar-Neeta, we will be ready in a few minutes."

"Yes Captain, I will be waiting outside your door with the escort team," she replied and the screen went blank.

Sar-Neeta and her team were waiting outside our apartment, the robots lurking at the ends of the corridors. We exchanged greetings with Sar-Neeta and her team and were led down the corridor, across the alcove and into a waiting lift which took us to the roof. The bright sunlight greeted our exit onto the roof and lit up the silvery curves of the large *Tanseh* that awaited us. Safely inside the ship, we strapped in and with its usual smooth almost silent acceleration the *Tanseh* swooped into the air and shot upwards at tremendous speed.

The blackness of Space soon appeared and the star studded vastness settled my nerves with its familiarity. Space seemed to enclose and comfort, like a vast womb. In the distance a small spidery shape appeared, and rapidly expanded into a huge silvery skeleton rib cage, inside of which fireflies flittered back and forth between plump bugs who were connected to the skeleton by umbilical cords, cables and metal arms. This was the Orbital Service and Repair Yard where *Lisa Jane* had been secreted away for repair. And there was *Lisa Jane*, looking wonderfully familiar, and now fully restored with her squat Hyperspace doughnut at the end of her long needle nose. I realised that I had ignored Alfred over the last few days, as we had both concentrated on our respective duties, he repairing the ship, and me being a tourist! I clicked on my communicator and essayed a greeting.

"Alfred, have you enjoyed your holiday?" There was a crackle and Alfred's warm and pompous baritone responded.

"It's not quite the Riviera up here Paul, but one makes the best of it!"

"The *Lisa Jane's* got her nose back, and pretty she looks too!" I remarked conversationally.

"Hardly pretty," he responded, "but fully functional; in fact, I believe the Hianja Hyperspace Drive is more efficient and compact than ours."

"Very generous of them to hand us improved technology."

"As a matter of fact, I think they tried very hard to degrade their technology to match ours but this is the best they could do; or the worst they could do, I suppose!" he added. I was suitably impressed.

"We are ready to go then?" I asked reluctantly.

"Yes, we are taking on supplies," he responded. "Since you have been augmenting your food supplies with Hianja food, we have an adequate store for the return trip, but I am topping up to maximum with local supplies just to cover any emergency."

"God forbid more emergencies!" I exclaimed fervently. The Hianja Orbital Repair Yard had expanded to fill the screen and our *Tanseh* was slowly edging towards the dock holding the *Lisa Jane*. It was at that point that I became aware of some agitated activity amongst my Hianja companions. The pilot of the *Tanseh*, Manera and Sar-Neeta were conversing in an animated way. Manera turned towards me and I could see wide eyed shock on her face.

"Manera, what is happening?" I asked, leaving my seat and moving towards her. Before she could speak, Alfred's voice cut in.

"Paul, five ships have dropped out of Hyperspace. I am afraid it is the Dissidents. It seems that they have demanded that the authorities here hand the *Lisa Jane* and its crew over to them," Manera came over and took my hand. Alfred was connected into the Hianja comms network, so she could also hear what he had just said. I looked at her thoughtfully.

"Or what?" I asked.

"Or they will destroy the *Lisa Jane* and every vessel in or near this Yard. It seems that they have been waiting to get us both together in the same place before acting."

"Can we make a break for it Alfred?" I asked.

"I am doing some calculations," he replied, "But it does not look good. Their ships are much faster than the *Lisa Jane*. Even if we made it to the 3 million mile mark and went into Hyperspace, there is no reason why they could not follow us. Their weapons are just as effective in Hyperspace."

"Damn, we can't allow them to stop us at this point," I swore. I remembered the previous time we had fought a space battle. *Lisa Jane* and *Epsilon* had taken on and destroyed one of their ships, but could we take on five? Then I remembered that we had exhausted our stock of missiles. I slumped back in my seat in despair.

Chapter 29

It was just a few minutes before our ship was boarded. Their boarding party consisted of a dozen armed individuals headed by a tough looking female who introduced herself as Captain Fremtak.

"The Earthman will come with me," she said shortly. Manera stepped forward.

"I must go with him," she said. Fremtak scowled.

"I have orders to bring the Earthman only…" she began.

"The Earthman does not speak Hianjese. You will need me to translate," said Manera firmly.

"I have heard him speak Hianjese," replied Fremtak, waving her pistol threateningly at Manera.

"Those words were written for him," she said hastily. "I should know, I wrote them. Contact your leaders and tell them that I must go with him," I was trying to make eye contact with her, but she refused to look in my direction. Fremtak growled in anger, but did speak into her communicator. The conversation lasted just a few moments and then she nodded at Manera.

"All right, just you and the Earthman. Come now," Manera turned and now her eyes met mine with a triumphant gleam in them. As we were herded off, I hissed at her in English.

"Manera, there was no need…"

"You are going nowhere without me Earthman. Unless it is on your little Starship going home," she interrupted firmly. We were herded through an airlock and onto a docked *Tanseh*, which lost no time in disconnecting from our ship.

It was just a minute's journey to our new home, a large Hianja starship similar to the *Tanu*. There were a number of blisters and protrusions on its hull, some were obviously missile batteries. They looked new but somewhat makeshift against the polished and perfectly finished surface of the starship. The ship's docking bays were in the rear end, the same as the *Tanu*, and our *Tanseh* slid smoothly in, the first hint of artificial gravity beginning as we came within a few metres of the ship and intensifying quickly up to what appeared to be just less than an Earth gravity.

The *Tanseh* slotted neatly into a docking bay and there was no need to make an airlock connection as we had with the *Lisa Jane*. The doors slid open and we stepped out onto the starship, straight into the arms of our welcoming committee, a dozen armed Hianja. Fremrak strode forward and spoke quietly to one of the guards, who appeared to be their leader, then addressed her remarks to Manera.

"Tell the Earthman that we will take him to our leaders now. He and you will not be harmed, they just wish to talk. Make sure he understands that, any violence will be punished."

"He is not a fool," scowled Manera, turning to me.

"I will translate word for word for now on Paul, just in case they have acquired a language compiler and understand English."

"I understand," I replied nodding. We followed Fremrak as she walked ahead, with guards all around us. They were being more than a little paranoid I thought. We arrived at the central foyer of the ship and boarded an elevator and I noted that Fremrak selected the sixth floor as the destination. Exiting from the elevator we were directed into a large opulently furnished room with large picture windows showing the star studded blackness of Space, with the planet Mesaroyat a small blue ball floating in the velvet blackness. Standing in the centre of the room were three figures, and I immediately recognised one of them.

"Manera, Captain Constantine, welcome to the starship *Semtrik Lode*," said Guardian Malanisa with a motherly smile.

"Welcome!" exclaimed Manera vehemently, "You point guns at us and them make us welcome. What kind of hypocrisy is this?"

"Manera, unfortunately, it was the only way to get the Captain here," replied Malanisa.

"Guardian Malanisa, I must protest strongly at being kidnapped at gun point," said Manera formally. "Your actions are illegal and I demand that you release us immediately."

"Patience Manera, we wish to discuss things with the Captain. Then we shall see what actions will be taken," replied Malanisa smoothly. She was a cool one I thought.

"If you wanted to discuss things with the Captain, you only needed to ask," said Manera.

"We were hardly given the opportunity," stated Malanisa mildly, "You disappeared so quickly."

"You have had plenty of opportunity to ask for a conference with the Captain. There was no need for violence. Do not try to pretend otherwise Guardian, you want the Captain under your control for your own purposes. I warn you, if the Captain is harmed, you and your associates will be held responsible. The Captain is not an individual, he represents his race, and we the Hianja will be held responsible by his race if he is harmed. Future relations between our two species could be permanently tarnished by your misdemeanours." Manera spoke forcefully and for a second Malanisa's smooth demeanour slipped slightly and she seemed taken aback by Manera's vehemence.

"The Captain's species is unmoved by violence!" snapped Malanisa, clearly rattled by Manera's attack, "The death of one individual is nothing to these barbarians!" I felt it was time to intervene before things became more heated.

"Manera, what does the Guardian want from us. Why are we here?" Manera swallowed the retort that she was about to make and asked my question. She was trying hard to control herself and I wanted to take her in my arms and comfort her, but the situation dictated otherwise. Malanisa looked at me with a polite but strained smile.

"Let me introduce my associates," she began, "This is Guardians Lamas and Guardian Semeta. Let us make ourselves comfortable, and I will tell you a story."

Chapter 30

Malanisa waved us to some comfortable armchairs, but remained standing. Our guards took themselves to the sides of the room away from our sight and Malanisa called over a robot to supply refreshments. It was all very civilised and Malanisa insisted we refresh ourselves. Manera and I took some chilled water only. The other two Guardians also settled themselves and Malanisa began.

"Manera, please translate for the Captain, and if you have any questions, stop me. You will have deduced already I am sure, that the ship which attacked the base at Verana, or Omorphia as the Earthman calls it, is indeed an old Earth scoutship. It was discovered by one of our own exploration vessels some fifteen years ago. The location is unimportant, a star towards the rim of the Galaxy on one of the Galaxy's spiral arms. It is an area which we had not penetrated previously, some nine thousand light years from here.

The Earth starship was found drifting in space, badly damaged by what appeared to be a collision with a large meteor. The Hyperspace Drive had been damaged beyond repair and the ship was holed. There was no sign of the crew, it appears that the pilot was sucked out into space when the accident occurred and must have died immediately. The surrounding space was searched for some time in the hope of finding a body, but none were found. Our Explorers were hugely excited as you can imagine. At last we had found evidence of another advanced civilisation in our Galaxy, and a space faring one at that. However, the ship's fusion reactor had not been damaged and neither had the ship's computer. The shuttle was still secured in its bay and was undamaged by the accident. Our explorers took the starship on board their own vessel for transportation back to Vasmeranta.

During the trip home, our engineers worked on the Earth ship, and were successful in restarting the fusion reactor and restoring power to some of the ship's systems. It seems that when the meteor had hit the ship, electrical circuits had shorted and the fusion reactor had automatically shut down. The ship's computer had battery backup of course, but the computer had been unable to repair the damage and battery power had eventually become depleted. The ship's computer had shut itself down. I should add that the ship's computer was not an AI.

Our technicians removed the shorting and damaged electronics and wiring which allowed the fusion reactor to power up. When the power came on, one of the video screens on the Earth ship was playing a recording, one which it appears the pilot was watching at the time of the accident. It was an entertainment video and our technicians were hugely excited to see real pictures of the aliens in their home environment. They were amazed to see how similar the aliens were to ourselves. They watched the video with interest, for a while. And then their interest turned to horror and disgust. The video seemed to be a continuous catalogue of murder and violence. Murder that was shown in gruesome detail, using guns and worst of all knives, choppers, and at one point a mechanical saw. Blood and entrails were graphically displayed, as was the individuals suffering as they died a gruesome and painful death. This was accompanied by laughter and huge amusement by the perpetrators of these abominable acts of violence. A number of our crew were sick, and some could not bring themselves to watch any more!

Our exploration team decided that this video must have been a factual account of some terrible event in the aliens history. They could not believe it was entertainment. So they searched the ship and found a library of discs. They spent most of the return trip watching these discs, trying to gain an understanding of the aliens psychology. To their growing horror, they found that just about every one of the library of discs involved violence of some kind or other. The aliens seemed to delight in murdering each other or blowing up and destroying whole groups of individuals in cataclysmic displays of destruction. Property, whole cities even, were blown up by aircraft dropping bombs or machine gunning unarmed individuals. Even females and children were not exempted. Any possible kind of violence, individual or group, was explored and displayed in graphic detail. The aliens had a casual disregard for life. So much so, that one had to wonder how such a species had ever become civilised, if indeed they were civilised.

The Captain of the exploration ship called a meeting of his officers prior to their return to Vasmeranta. He proposed that they should keep the discovery of the alien ship to themselves. The Captain's case was that the aliens were pathologically violent and that any contact between them and the Hianja would be disastrous for the Hianja. There was of course dissent. This was the greatest discovery in our history. How could we keep it a secret? A compromise was reached. The secret could not be kept forever. But two things were important. The first was that the Hianja could not remain defenceless. The second was the hope that the aliens would change in time. We remembered only too well our own past, and how close our own species had come to self annihilation. But the question was raised. How could the Hianja, after twenty thousand years of peace, be persuaded that it was necessary to re-arm? The ship itself and its cargo of violent material would be the best incentive, but would it be enough? The fact that the aliens enjoyed violent entertainment did not prove that they were violent in their everyday lives.

The Captain of the exploration ship came to me for assistance. After I also saw the Earth ship's discs, I agreed with him that contact with these aliens was a dangerous risk. We gathered around us a group of like minded individuals, and under the pretext of historical research appropriated the facilities to modify these ships with weapons. It took us these last fifteen years to repair the Earth ship and develop the weapons you have seen.

Some concrete proof of the aliens violent tendencies was needed. And so was born the plan to repair the Earth ship, and use it in a bogus attack on the base at Verana. It would be a 'wake-up' call to the Hianja, that a threat existed in the Galaxy. We repaired the Earth starship, substituting our own computer for the Earth one. We transported the Earth starship to Verana, and it covered the last few million miles under its own power. We attacked the base using the ship's shuttle as you know. There were no casualties, we only damaged the base buildings. Our plan was that when the investigating team returned we would make another attack using the shuttle, but our armed ship would intercept and destroy it. The Earth starship would 'get away'."

At this point, Malanisa paused and took a sip of water. She looked tense and grim. She looked at me pointedly.

"Imagine the shock of Smetronis's investigating team , when they found what appeared to be our captured Earth Starship already in orbit about Verana. But that shock was nothing to the shock when we found that it was not 'our' Earth Starship, but another. The incredible had happened at a most unfortunate time. For us," she added.

"So you had nothing to do with my accident?" I asked.

"The arrival of your damaged starship at Verana was a chance event, unbelievable as it may be!" she replied. "Smetronis was in a difficult position. The second attack had been pre-planned and programmed into the Earth shuttles computer. The plan was, we would intercept and destroy it, and its 'mother ship', the old Earth Starship, would get away. In this way we would have established the existence of a hostile alien race in our Galaxy, and justified the construction of a force of armed warships as a defence. Sometime later, we could re-discover the Earth Starship, suitably damaged of course, and the aliens sick pre-disposition towards violence as displayed by their entertainment videos would become common knowledge. This 'discovery', would re-enforce the lessons of the attack on Verana and make our case for armed caution irresistible," she paused, turning towards her fellow Guardians as she did so.

"Such was our plan. It involved no violence to any individual, just the damage to some property and perhaps one empty shuttle. The arrival of Captain Constantine and his Starship at Verana upset our plans catastrophically. Smetronis was unable to prevent the old Earth shuttle from attacking Manera's shuttle as it attempted to return to orbit. Unfortunately, we had used a simple computer to control it, and it became distracted by the shuttle and attacked it. Our AI's and advanced Computers are programmed not to use or participate in any sort of violent behaviour. The attack was destructive, and people died. I cannot tell you how distressed we are by this."

"You killed two of my best friends in that attack!" said Manera vehemently. "Whatever distress you suffer is not enough!" Malanisa pursed her lips and said nothing.

"But why did Smetronis persist with his madness?" asked Manera, "Why did he continue trying to kill myself and the Captain?"

"Only Smetronis can answer that," she replied. "His actions were not sanctioned by me."

"You say that now!" scowled Manera. Malanisa seemed stung by her attack.

"It's the truth," she retorted, with a backward glance at her two Guardian colleagues. I began to wonder how secure Malanisa's position was. Were the other two Guardians having doubts I wondered?

"I can only speculate on what Smetronis was thinking," she continued. "If he told the truth at that point, he would be revealing the whole situation and implicating all his fellow conspirators. I suppose he decided that one more death, namely yourself," and here Malanisa stopped and nodded at Manera, "and we would all be in the clear with the plan intact. The pretence that the alien had kidnapped and murdered you after escaping from the destroyed shuttle would tie in with the rest of the subterfuge. It was a cold bloodied and ruthless plan," she finished, her face blank and tense , "I have to believe that his mind was disturbed at that point."

"He was insane!" exclaimed Manera, "And so were you to believe that you could carry out such a bizarre subterfuge on your species."

"Manera, you have not seen the material we saw on that ruined Earth Starship. It makes your blood run cold," retorted Malanisa, "A species that entertains such barbarity should not be allowed the freedom of the Galaxy."

"And how would you do that?" asked Manera, "Get into a war with the Human's, and create the very barbarity you are trying to avoid?"

"No, confront the Humans with an overwhelming force. One that they dare not challenge." Malanisa pulled herself up, as if re-enforcing her belief, steeling herself against doubt. "We cannot confront the Humans as we are, weak and defenceless. Oh they may pretend to be our friends, and attempt to win our affections, as the Captain has won yours! But that is just a front. The *Shreenca* creeps up stealthily on its prey, before leaping to tear its throat out!"

"If you had given the Humans a chance, and got to know them, you would have realised that they are not very different from us!" retorted Manera. I decided it was time to intervene to brung the pointless arguments to a halt.

"Manera, there is no point in engaging Malanisa in an exchange of opinions. We need to give her proof that she is wrong about the human species." Manera inclined her head doubtfully.

"The only proof we can give her is to go to Earth and see for herself," she replied.

"That is exactly the sort of commitment she is afraid of. Manera, translate this for me," she nodded.

"Malanisa, I have heard your story, and I understand your feelings." I had this friend back on Earth, who during any argument, would start off by agreeing with the opposition. He reckoned that it softened them up, made them more likely to listen to his side of the argument. He was a successful politician, so I guess his approach had some merit. I was about to see! "It is understandable that you should feel threatened by a species which you believe is addicted to violence, and heavily armed. In your position, I would feel the same. But I have two problems with your actions. Firstly, you have arrived at this position on the basis of one man's preference in entertainment videos! The Starship you discovered is two hundred years old. And no doubt, the films my compatriot was watching when he died, are even older. The truth is, such violent entertainment has been banned on Earth for one hundred and fifty years. If you do not believe me, I invite you to examine the library of entertainment films on my own starship, the *Lisa Jane*. You will not find a single piece of explicit violence." I was stretching the truth a little here, there certainly was explicit violence on many modern films, but not on the gratuitous scale that had been allowed in the old days. I continued, "Secondly, I believe that you have taken it upon yourself to single handedly make decisions that affect your whole species, in fact, the future of two species. You have no mandate for this. At some point, you are going to have to justify yourself to your seniors, and very soon I suspect. I suggest that you do not make your situation any worse."

I was directing my remarks, not to Malanisa, who as far as I was concerned was seriously in the black and mucky stuff without a shovel in sight, but to her two Guardian associates. I was not sure when they had been bought into the picture, but I was hoping that it was recently, and they had played no part in the early deception and the disaster on Omorphia. They knew that the Hianja Prime delegation was on its way, I was reminding them that they would have to answer for their actions. Sure enough, one of them, I was not sure whether it was Lamas or Semeta, caught Malanisa's eye and gestured discreetly. She walked over to them and they huddled together for a few moments before Malanisa turned back to me. Her face was tense and she looked a very unhappy individual.

"Captain Constantine." One of the two Guardians stood up. He was tall and lean, with a bit of a hatchet face. The sort of face you expect to find on a lawyer. Or a politician. "My name is Fezram Lamas. Our intention was to prevent your return to Earth until the subject of contact between our two races has been thoroughly studied and all opinions taken into account. We believe that we have achieved this. We are sorry about the...um..," he looked carefully at Malanisa as he said this. "...unorthodox methods used, but there seemed no choice at the time."

"You could have just asked me to stay until the Hianja Prime delegation arrived," I said. He looked taken aback for a second.   "Are you prepared to do so now?" He asked, his eyes fixed on me keenly. I laughed hollowly.

"I do not think I have any choice under the circumstances, but yes, I will willingly stay." He nodded carefully at what I was saying and turned back to Malanisa and the other Guardian.

"Then we have achieved our objective," he said, looking meaningfully at them.

"I do not think that was Malanisa's original objective," I added, "The exercise on Verana was designed to create a lie and prejudice your species against mine. Not just to prevent me from returning home. Let us not forget that, because Manera and I certainly will not. We have a duty to those who died."

"I think Smetronis has paid for his mistake. He is in hiding and cannot show his face again." replied Fezram smoothly. "And my colleague here acted with the best intentions. We will let others judge. Captain......," he paused for a few seconds as if in thought, "Captain, I am sorry to tell you that we cannot release you. We will keep you with us, until the Hianja Prime delegation arrive. Then you will be released and we will present our case to our leaders. Manera is free to remain here or return to Mesaroyat as she wishes. You will be free to go where you please on this ship. We will not keep you confined or restrict you in any way."

"Is there any point in keeping me a prisoner here? I asked, "You have prevented me from returning to Earth, I am just as much a prisoner on Mesaroyat as I am here."

"We have become well acquainted with your resourcefulness Captain. We would prefer you here where we can keep a close eye on you," replied Malanisa. I gave her a frosty glare and turned to Manera.

"Manera, you should return to Mesaroyat. I want you safe and out of these people's clutches," I said.

"They may have no scruples about killing an alien," she replied, her face set, "But they will think twice before killing one of their own. I am staying with you," her eyes met mine.

"Don't even try to change my mind Paul." she looked stubborn and determined and I hesitated. I was torn between wanting her to stay for purely selfish reasons, and wanting her to leave for her own protection.

Altruism won in the end and I started to protest.

"It's decided!" she cut in to my protests. I scowled and glared at her but she glared back with equal venom. Malanisa cut in before I could argue.

"Manera does not have to decide now," she said, "We can return her to Mesaroyat any time."

"OK," I nodded with resignation. Malanisa nodded and turned to one of the guards who had been standing on the periphery of the room.

"Sartra, conduct our guests to suite two on deck twenty-five. That will be their apartment," she turned to me. "Captain, we will make every effort to make you comfortable until the Delegation arrives. You are free to go where you please, except for the shuttle bays. Sartra here will be your guide. I think you understand that there is no point in you making any effort to escape, this is a heavily armed warship and the shuttles are well guarded. We will be dining this evening and you are welcome to join us." The set of her features relaxed for a second as she continued. "Captain, it is with regret that we do this, I hope you understand. We all would be very interested in conversing with you as civilised beings. We want to learn more of your world. Please join us this evening." I looked at her with some surprise. She had been cold and hostile up to now and her change of manner caught me off guard.

'Um....thank you Malanisa," I said reluctantly, then remembered that, like it or not, I was Earth's representative. My duty was to put aside personal likes and dislikes and do my duty "I shall be happy to join you this evening," I finished smoothly. I was aware of Manera's glare drilling a hole in the side of my head but I smiled politely at Melanisa and Fezram before following Sartra 'our guide' out of the room.

We were conducted to our quarters by a silent Sartra. They were roomy and comfortable and we sat and talked for a bit.

"I was sure they were going to fake an accident and kill us," said Manera when we were alone. I comforted her with an arm around her shoulders.

"There would have been no point in them doing that," I said gently. "They have achieved part of their aim, to prevent me from returning to Earth. Now they will be working to achieve the second part."

"Which is?" she asked.

"To put off contact for as long as possible while the Hianja re-arm. You heard what she said, they want to deal with the Human race from a position of overwhelming military strength."

"I think they do not want to deal with the Human race at all," she retorted, "They are terrified of something new and they see it as a threat."

"It has always been like that," I said, "There are those who respond to change negatively, and others..," and I gave her a squeeze to illustrate what

I meant, "...who are more positive. Some see change as a threat, others as an opportunity. Sadly, these people got off to a bad start with the Human race. They were introduced to the very worst aspects of our personality instead of the best. I am just amazed that the Earth authorities allowed this individual, this Scoutship Captain whose ship they discovered, that they allowed him to take a library of violent films on his ship. I guess they never imagined what would happen." I shook my head in disbelief. "Anyway..," I turned a stern gaze onto her.

"You should not stay here," I said. "You can't do anything here, they need you back on Mesaroyat."

"I think you are safer here with me than without me. If they engineer an accident to kill you.," she began.

"Then they will have to kill you as well," I finished. She looked stubborn.

"Then so be it," she declared. When I started to disagree she interrupted me. "Paul, you have saved my life more than once. I owe you this."

"Getting yourself killed with me is not going to repay any sort of debt, which you do not have anyway," I replied confusingly.

"I will be the judge on whether I have a debt," she said. "And I am a big girl. I can make my own decisions."

"You are a big girl," I agreed approvingly .

Some time later our door communicator buzzed.

"Captain, I have been asked to escort you and Manera to the Dining hall."

"We are ready Sartra, come in," said Manera and the door hissed open automatically.

That evening as we lay in bed, Manera snuggled up to me, her fragrant hair tickling my nostrils. I pulled her close, enjoying the feel of her lithe silky body caressing mine.

"Interesting evening," I murmured, "Old Malanisa and Fezram were perfect hosts." And indeed they had been. The discussion had ranged over many subjects. They were constantly probing, asking questions about Earth, probing my attitudes and opinions. I took it in good spirit, determined to show them that their preconceptions of Earth were wrong. We were all being very careful to show how civilised and urbane we all were. Apart from Manera, who was unable to contain her hostility.

Chapter 31

The next couple of days passed fairly uneventfully. My relations with my captors were cool but not unfriendly and I continued to work at persuading them that their preconception of Humans were wrong. I believe that I was making significant progress in that area, particularly with the two male Guardians, who seemed less obsessed or fanatical. Malanisa continued to be uneasy with me, and her relationship with Manera continued to be cold and distant. Neither of them attempted to hide their dislike of each other.

Guardians Fezram Lamas and Guardian Semeta on the other hand remained friendly and sociable, seeking out my company for long chats about all aspects of Earth life. They were fascinated by Earth history, particularly the 20th and 21st Centuries and how we coped with own mini 'Great Disasters'. I came to like the two old chaps and to believe that they were genuinely acting out of a sense of patriotism. After the second day, I persuaded them to give me and Manera full access to Comms and to have conversations with Kemato and the other Guardians. I had also been allowed, surprisingly, to converse with Alfred, although because we were aware that we were being overheard, our conversations were fairly stilted.

It was on the morning of the third day that the Hianja Prime delegation arrived. Five ships popped out of Hyperspace and announced their presence on all Comms channels. It was early morning and we were woken out of a deep sleep by the insistent buzzing of the Comms console. Manera answered it and her exclamation persuaded me to reluctantly drag myself awake. It was Fezram Lamas who broke the news. Manera put the ships up on the comms screen and I looked with interest. It was impossible to tell how large they were, but they looked completely different from other Hianja ships most of which were cylindrical, converging to a point at the front where the Hyperspace doughnut was, and with a dumpy rear end where the AG doughnut was. The design was largely dictated by the requirements of the Hyperspace drive and Artificial Gravity generators. They generated a cylindrical field encompassing the diameter and length of the ship. These ships were circular, like the traditional 'flying saucer', but they were two saucers bolted together, one above the other. I peered closely at them, trying to see where the Hyperspace and AG generators were, and then realised, that the saucers **were** the Generators. The ship was the bit in the middle. But that meant that the habitable part must be tiny, unless...

"Manera, how big are those ships?" I asked carefully. She flicked a few keys on the console and a grid appeared.

"Each square on the grid is one *Jinat*," she said. A *Jinat* I knew was 0.8 Kilometres. Each ship comfortably filled a square on the grid.

"Are you sure about the scale Manera?" I asked. She double checked carefully.

"Yes," she whispered "What are those things?"

"What!" I exclaimed, "You have never seen these before?"

"No, never. These things are huge. They are more than one *Jinat* in diameter. What are they?"

"Well, hopefully, they are the Hianja Prime Delegation. If those ships are that huge, how many of them are there, a few thousand?"

"The delegation is just 173 individuals, each one representing a Hianja planet."

"How did they get them together in such a short time?" I asked.

"They are based at Hianja Prime."

"Your whole Government has come?" I asked in disbelief.

"Our whole Government?" Manera laughed. "Paul, the whole of Hianja Prime is the Government for the 173 planets. Millions of people on Hianja Prime, the whole population in fact, are employed in Government. These 173 individuals have been nominated to represent their planets in this matter only."

"I see," I said chastened. So what about these ships, how is it you have never seen anything like them before?"

"I have never been to Hianja Prime," she replied, "Perhaps they build their ships differently there." It sounded a bit weak to me, but I did not pursue the question any further as clearly Manera was as baffled as I was.

"If the discs are the Hyperspace and AG Generators, then these ships must be immensely powerful," I remarked. "Is there any way of telling how fast they are moving?" I asked. Manera played with her console for a bit, murmuring questions at the computer, before settling back and looking at me.

"They are decelerating towards Mesaroyat at a steady one and a half Gravities. Their current speed is 80000 *Jinat* per *Sarat*," shat was as about 70000 kph, as close as makes no difference.

"They will be with us late this afternoon," she said pensively. I hissed with admiration.

"One and a half gravities? Wow, they are in a hurry!"

"They will be strapped down in special acceleration couches," she said. "The older weaker individuals can be immersed in acceleration fluid containers, like sealed baths, connected up with air and water supplies. A fit person can take ten gravities in one of those."

"Impressive," I said. "But why are they in such a hurry? As far as they know, I should have just left for Earth which means it would be weeks before the Human delegation would be due."

"Maybe they know about the situation?" said Manera thoughtfully.

"I don't see how," I muttered, "Is there any way the Guardians could have got a message off to them?"

"Yes actually. We have a Hyperspace Comms Device in permanent orbit outside the gravity boundary. They could have sent a message without the dissidents being aware of it. That was quick thinking on somebody's part if that is what happened," she said.

"God those ships look impressive," I muttered, "It's very odd," I remarked as we quickly dressed, "That you have never seen anything like these ships before."

"The Hianja Federation is too huge for any one person to know all of it," she replied. We were interrupted by a chime from the Comms Console. Fezram Lamas's face appeared.

"Paul, Manera, please answer. Meeting, fourteenth floor conference room five as soon as you can? Sartra is on her way to guide you," he said quickly.

"We are on our way," replied Manera switching off the Comms unit.

We spent the rest of the morning treating ourselves with different views of the approaching ships on the huge screens arrayed around the conference room. It became apparent that Kemato and her colleagues were in communication with the Delegation already, and I could sense the unease on the part of our captors at being ignored. Despite my enquiries however, no one would admit to any knowledge of what the huge ships were or any technical details about them. Fezram agreed with my remarks as we gathered for some lunch.

"They are unbelievable," he said, shaking his bald head and shovelling a forkful of green slimy stuff into his mouth. "This *Teskerian slottkas* is delicious," he added, chewing appreciatively.

"Mmmm," I looked doubtfully at the green mess and decided to give it a miss.

"These ships seem to use quite different design principles from normal Hianja ships," I pointed out, fiddling with the seal on one of my own food containers, something that purported to be beef chilli with rice and vegetables. My captors had obligingly allowed a shipment of my ship's rations to be delivered.

"Not so much different principles," replied Semeta, who I remembered had a background in engineering before being elected a Guardian. "They are just on such a large scale, it requires a change from the normal method of construction. The AG and Multi-Space engines have to generate such massive fields, the standard modules would just melt. You see, the heat generated rises exponentially with the size of the ship. Most of those two huge discs must be to allow heat dissipation."

"I see," I said, waiting for my food container to heat up. "Why build such large ships then?" I added thoughtfully. Semeta inclined his head to show his own puzzlement.

"Unless...," I said thoughtfully. "Unless, they are transport ships," I had an interesting idea. "When you are settling a new planet, don't you need huge transport ships? You know, to carry machinery and manufacturing equipment, as well as the thousands of people to colonise the planet?" Semeta shook his head again.

"It is hundreds of years since we settled a new planet, Verana is the first suitable planet we have found for a long time, but we have records going back thousands of years. Nothing like these ships appears anywhere."

We finished our lunch in a thoughtful silence, and hurriedly returned to our control centre, a large conference room with all the appropriate communications and computer equipment. Just about everyone was there, unable to tear themselves away from the developing drama. As the huge interstellar ships drew closer, we tried to discern more details of their structure, but because they were flying 'head on', and seemed to be completely black, it was almost impossible to do so. However, Semeta's theory that the huge discs were largely cooling fins seemed credible. They were covered in baffles and vents, as well as many large and mysterious blisters and bulges whose purpose we could not determine. By now, the ships were decelerating at a more normal one gravity, and it was revealed that the delegation were able to evacuate their acceleration enclosures and move about normally.

There was a large comms screen on the wall next to me which was showing one of the giant Hianja ships against a background of stars. There was not much to see, just a black disc, pitted and pockmarked with blisters and bulges. It had started to move sideways-on in the last few minutes and I could see the centre spindle a little more clearly. As the ship continued to turn, more and more of what I thought was the habitation module came into view. There were windows and a number of large black areas which I took to be the doors into the shuttle bays. They must be hundreds of metres in size to be visible against the vast bulk of the ship.

It was from one of those black areas that I spotted what appeared to be a swarm of glittering insects come hurtling out. The insects separated and moved away from the ship at tremendous speed. Whoever was controlling the electronic telescope which was focusing on the ship also spotted the swarm of 'insects' and the view refocused on the 'swarm' instead of the ship. The swarm expanded and separated out into individual dots which expanded rapidly to become ships. At first they were hard to see clearly until the telescope managed to focus onto one long enough for us to see some detail. It was clearly a craft designed for space and for atmospheric use because it had wings. But wings on a ship that had an Artificial Gravity

Drive? What was the point? And the craft had an AG Drive for sure because I could clearly see the massive doughnut towards the rear of the craft, just behind the stubby wings. But there was also something I had not seen on a Hianja ship before. A contrail behind the craft, the sure sign of fusion rockets. So the craft had both an AG drive and rockets. It would be capable of massive acceleration if it used both methods of propulsion at the same time.

Looking closer at the craft I could also see what clearly looked like missile bays and the snouts of energy guns. These were military ships for sure, and formidably armed. I looked towards Manera and she was looking as bewildered as I felt. Her eyes met mine and she shook her head at my questioning look.

It looked very much as if the Hianja Prime delegation had arrived in a massive armada of heavily armed ships. The much vaunted Hianja aversion to violence looked a bit thin on the ground at this point! Had the Vasmeranta dissidents won the argument already? In the face of the perceived threat from Earth, the Hianja delegation had indeed decided to demonstrate an overwhelming military capability.

Chapter 32

Unbelievably, my captors seemed to be as stupefied as I was regarding developments. They were staring goggle-eyed at the comms screen, seemingly unable to believe their eyes. The Guardians in general were whispering amongst themselves, looking shocked and baffled. I began to wonder if some massive conspiracy was being inflicted upon us. I had the bizarre thought that these ships may not be Hianja, that a new alien race had suddenly descended upon us, taking advantage of the confusion to overwhelm us in one foul swoop. I shook my head, dismissing these thoughts as panic stricken confusion and made my way over to where Malanisa and Fezram were deep in conversation.

"What's happening?" I asked, "What are these ships, where are they from?"

"They are what we said they were," said Malanisa, "The Hanja Prime Delegation."

"So much for the so called Hianja aversion to military weapons. I have never seen a more fearsome array of space weaponry in my life," I declared dryly.

"This is as much a surprise to us as it is to you," exclaimed Malanisa. "We have never seen such ships before," but she looked pleasantly surprised, indeed almost triumphant.

"Well, it looks like your friends have been keeping a few cards up their sleeve," I said. "Have they communicated with you yet?" Malanisa looked questioningly at Fezram before continuing.

"They have only asked questions," she replied.

"They never gave you any reason to believe that they were coming with a military escort?" I asked.

"No." replied Malanisa, "This is just as much a surprise for me," she repeated. I wondered back to Manera, who was at another comms screen at the other end of the room,

"I cannot see how a military force like that can be maintained without the secret leaking out," I mused.

"There is one other possibility," mused Manera thoughtfully. "If this force is not under the control of the Council....," she paused for a moment, seemingly examining her idea before expressing it. I waited for her to continue. "It is either under the control of a small clique, some group who have taken it upon themselves to secretly construct a military force, for their own reasons. Or it is a totally automated force, under the control of one or more AI's." We paused for a few moments to digest these ideas.

"Is it possible for a small clique to construct such a force?" I asked. "The resources required are enormous. I cannot see how they could do it without Computer and AI support, in large amounts." Manera nodded.

"Yes, if people are involved, they must get Computer and AI support."

"Would your AI's co-operate in such a subversive venture?" Manera shrugged without comment, her eyes fixed on the screen in fascination.

Meanwhile, the Council's Mother ships were taking up orbital positions around Mesaroyat, while their fighters split up and took up positions close to the Dissidents ships. Were they re-enforcing the Dissidents I asked myself, or were they surrounding them. The answer was soon revealed by the leader of the Hianja Prime delegation. His face appeared on the Comms screen, a very old face, the oldest Hianja face I had seen. It was wrinkled and weathered by the years, but surprisingly strong and clear eyed.

"I am Krusniet Farsan the current chairman of the Prime Council," his voice was gravely and worn, but strong, his pronunciation clear and concise. "We greet the citizens of Mesaroyat and bring them good wishes from their fellow citizens throughout the Federation of Hianja planets." He gave a tight smile before continuing. "You all know why we are here. The contact with an alien race is one of huge significance for the future of our race. We are here to expedite that contact." He paused and looked unblinkingly out of the screen, his face impassive. "There are those amongst us who would wish to prevent that contact because they believe it would not be in the interest of our species. They believe that this new species, the Human race, is an immature and violent species who represent a threat to the Hianja." He paused and seemed to retreat within himself for a few moments, before continuing.

"Let it not be said that your Prime Council did not take all opinions and viewpoints into account before making this momentous decision. We will therefore take the time to consider all aspects of this situation before deciding whether Contact will take place, and if so, under what conditions it will do so."

I felt my heart sink as I heard his words. It seemed that the Dissidents had won round one. They had persuaded the Council to re-consider the decision that contact should continue. I cringed at the thought that I, as the sole representative of the Human race, would somehow have to prove our suitability. I felt a surge of self pity at the thought, at the unfairness of it all. I am just a pilot and engineer I groaned to myself, I can't do this. I can't explain and apologise for the Human race's bizarre excesses and eccentricities.

Manera turned to me and the depression must have shown on my face. She came close and took my hand in hers. She was about to say something, but Chairman Krusniet had not finished.

"However," and he directed a stern and unblinking glare out of the screen. "The resort to military force by those who wish to prevent Contact is an act of criminal irresponsibility." Things were looking up I thought. "We understand their desperation to prevent what they thought was a disastrous event from taking place, but if we have learnt one thing in our history, it is that violent means produce violent ends. Using violence to solve a problem is never justified, and I mean never!. Only in self defence against violent attack are we allowed to use it, and then only the minimum necessary to repel that attack. Such is our philosophy, and has been for twenty thousand years, and that philosophy has kept the peace between us." He paused again, looking down thoughtfully, before directing his stern gaze back to the screen again.

"This will no doubt cause you all to wonder at the nature of the ships that we have arrived in. Some of you will have understood immediately that these ships are something out of the ordinary. They are indeed something exceptional. Let me tell you their history. Ten thousand years ago, the Hianja Federation was going through a period of instability. Some planets wanted greater autonomy, and local smaller 'Federations' of planets were forming, groups of three or five or ten planets that wanted greater autonomy in their affairs and considered Hianja Prime to be too distant and remote. Some of these planets were starting to revert to the old ways, arguing that self defence was necessary, that if one planet decided to re-arm, we would all be defenceless against them. Some also argued, perhaps more forcefully, that it was a big Galaxy and at some point we were bound to meet another alien species. Some form of self defence seemed prudent. But allowing all Hianja planet's to develop and keep arms seemed dangerous and risky. A compromise was born.

A group of our AI's were entrusted with the task of setting up a huge military base on a remote and uninhabited planet. They appropriated the resources to build this base and to design and build the ships that you see. The whole enterprise was known to the Prime Council of the time, and with that knowledge came peace and security. But that knowledge was confined to them, and died with them. Only our AI's knew of the existence of the military base and these ships, and they held and maintained that secret for the day when it needed to be used. For ten thousand years it has not been needed. Until today." He paused again for a long period before continuing.

"Today, we need this force because some amongst you have decided to build military weapons and to use them against their fellow Hianja. These individuals will be asked to account for their actions. I call upon them to immediately evacuate and surrender their ships. These ships will be disarmed and returned to their original use and their crews taken into custody. They have one hour to do this. If they do not conform immediately, the ships will be destroyed, whether or not they are occupied."

The silence in the room was palpable. I realised that I had been holding my breath during the last part of his address, and exhaled in relief. I was starting to feel better, recovering from my fit of self pity. I squeezed Manera's slender hand and grinned encouragingly. She smiled in return.

The tension in the room exploded with noise as everyone started talking at the same time. Malanisa, Fezram and Semeta got into a huddle, talking animatedly. Manera and I remained where we were, our eyes on the comms screen. The Council's ships had taken their positions in orbit about Mesaroyat, in positions which 'covered' the dissidents ships. Their 'fighter' aircraft surrounded the dissidents ships threateningly. I could see no choice for the dissidents other than surrender, but I was about to be surprised. After ten minutes of conversation, it appeared that our captors had come to a decision. Malanisa looked incandescent with anger, but Fezram and Semeta looked pale and troubled. It was Fezram who approached the Comms Station to give a reply to the Council.

"We have considered carefully the Council's ultimatum," he began. Barely fifteen minutes had passed so I was convinced that their answer would be in agreement with the ultimatum. I was shocked when he continued. "But we cannot accept." There was a buzz of conversation in the room and Manera glanced quickly at me with shock on her face. "That is, we cannot accept the ultimatum in its entirety. We agree to give up and evacuate our ships and have them disarmed. We do this because clearly, they are no longer needed. Their purpose, was firstly to prevent the Earthman from returning home, and secondly to demonstrate the need for some protection against the alien threat that his people represent. The first purpose has been achieved. The second purpose is clearly much more effectively provided by the Council's own fleet of ships. However, we do not accept that we are criminals and we resist being taken into custody to be tried for our so called crimes. What we did, we did for our species, to protect us from a perceived threat. That is not a crime! Through our actions, we have allowed a discussion to take place on the merits or otherwise of contact with Earth. This is a decision which could not just be left to the Council to make. All people have a right to know the nature of this Alien civilization and to make these choices. Some may wish to put off contact for a period of time. Some may wish to have only limited contact, and others no contact at all! Whatever the case, all should have the right to express their opinions. I ask you therefore to allow us to go free in order to represent our point of view and not prejudice the situation by branding us as criminals. Do this, and we will immediately hand over our ships to the Council. Thank you." He finished with a nod of his head and the comms screen showing his image went blank.

"Oh bugger!" I groaned. "Bloody stubborn bastards. Do they want to be martyrs?" That of course, I realised, was the crucial question. Were they ready to die for their cause, or were they calling the Council's bluff? Would the Council go ahead and blow the ships up, with all the crew still in them? I doubted that the Hianja, with their aversion to violence, had the 'bottle' for such a cold bloodied act of murder. The dissidents were also betting that they could not do such a thing. I had the feeling that things were coming to a head.

I looked around the large room carefully, taking in the guards, Hianja and robot, posted in strategic locations. The Dissident Guardians were deep in animated conversation and I caught the odd glance in our direction. The Comms screen lit up with the lined face of Krusniet Farsan again. We were about to receive the Council's reply to Fezram's rebellious response.

"This is addressed to the dissidents. Your demand that your actions be ignored is unreasonable and unacceptable. Whatever your intentions, that does not change the fact that your actions were violent and led to the deaths of a number of individuals. If you truly believe that you had no choice but to act the way you did, then that will be a major mitigating factor in your favour. You will be allowed to make your case with the Prime Council before answering to the Guardians of Mesaroyat for your actions. Your position is hopeless and I ask you to behave responsibly and put yourselves in the hands of Hianja justice. We must all answer to that whoever we are. I await your reply, your time is running out." The Guardians image disappeared from the screen. Malanisa and her colleagues went into a huddle again and we waited for their reply. It took a little longer to arrive this time, and we were getting perilously close to the one hour deadline when Fezram stood up to reply.

"Your insistence that we answer to criminal charges is still unacceptable to us. It pre-judges the issue and undermines our argument. We would remind you that we have the Earthman and scientist Manera on board. Any military action you take will put their lives at risk as well as ours," Fezram continued. "I ask you to put off the question of our actions until we have resolved the question which we are all here to resolve. The issue of Contact with Earth. We will make an offer. Let us have discussions on this issue where we can present our case for delaying contact. If we can persuade a majority of the Council that Earth represents a threat , then we will be vindicated. If however, the Council dismisses our objections and rules that Contact will proceed without any conditions, then we will freely place ourselves in the hands of the Authorities. There is no need to force the issue at this point." Fezram waved a hand to stop transmission and turned back to his colleagues. The strain was showing on all of their faces as they waited for the reply from the Council.

Meanwhile, I was considering carefully the idea that I should intervene in the dispute. It seemed to me that Fezram's suggestion was a reasonable one. If the Council decided against Contact, then the Dissidents would get off , if the Council decided for Contact, they would surrender. Of course there was still the small matter of kidnapping , military threats and illegal arms to be brushed under the carpet. I had no idea which way the Council would swing. I leaned over to Manera and whispered quietly in English.

"Don't know what's going to happen , but I think we should be prepared." We were sitting in a small alcove to one corner of the big room, looking at proceedings on a large Comms screen in the alcove. It was designed as a viewing area and had two rows of 5 seats bolted to the floor. "First sign of trouble, get down under the seats and hold on tight," I said. It wasn't much of a strategy, but it was the best I could come up with at the moment. The door to our right led to the corridor, and was guarded by a couple of individuals with stun weapons. Outside I was fairly sure the corridor was clear. Where could we go if we escaped after all? Other robots were between us and the leaders of the dissidents, who were clustered around the main comms facilities in the centre of the room. We had been kept away from the centre so that we could not overhear their discussions.

The response to the dissidents offer was not long in coming. There was a series of mighty bangs and the deck of the ship leaped up to hit us in the face. I grabbed the leg of a chair with one hand and a handful of Manera's waistcoat with the other and pulled us both to the floor. Under the seats I grabbed seat stanchions with both hands and held on tight while Manera did the same. The floor bucked and heaved alarmingly and the noise of tearing metal was mixed with the screams of people being hurled about the room. My head and body banged painfully against the metal of the underside of the seats but the seat legs and supports held and we hung on grimly as the ship lurched heavily to the sound of collapsing bulkheads.

In the confusion and alarm of trying to stay in one piece, a clear cold thought passed through my mind. The Council *were* prepared to call their bluff! They *did* have the bottle! It was a sobering and unexpected idea. I saw bodies hurtling up to the ceiling and then realised that there was now no ceiling. A huge black hole had opened and I was looking straight out into Space. The Artificial Gravity was off and bodies were hurtling out into Space. The rush of air was building up and I felt the first tug of vacuum.

"Through the door Manera," I shouted against the din, grabbing her and pointing at the door to our right. With the instincts of a spaceman I leapt for the door. There was now no up or down, and I hurtled straight at the door. To my surprise it slid open when I neared it and I continued through into the corridor. I hit the opposite corridor wall, absorbing the impact on my shoulder and grabbed a wall grip to kill my momentum. I turned just in time to avoid Manera who with feline agility turned in mid air and absorbed the impact with her legs, straightening and grabbing a wall grip with one smooth motion. The obliging door hissed shut behind us, sealing us from the vacuum on the other side.

"Nice door, good door, well done," I gasped and Manera looked at me as if I was insane.

"If we were seconds later that nice door would have sealed us on the other side," she said grimly. I knew she was right, if the door detected a vacuum on one side it would automatically seal itself shut. Anyone now behind the door would never get out. The corridor was empty, we were the only ones to have made it out of the room. Oh well, goodbye dissidents I thought, you chose the wrong people to play around with! The short stretch of corridor we were in curved around the outside of the ship and seemed to be undamaged. I could see one door around the curve of the ship and that was safely closed. The ship had hermetically sealing doors every thirty metres or so, and obviously between all rooms. It looked like we were in a sealed area, but how long our air would hold out was anybodies guess. I doubted that the life support systems would still be working after the pounding the ship had taken.

Just a few metres from us was a large picture window and I pushed off towards it. The star studded blackness of space seemed empty, the stars wheeling sickeningly as the ship tumbled erratically. I caught a glimpse of the planet wheeling by, and then a black delta shape, then another. The Council's ships were there but how were we to contact them? Manera was next to me and we struggled to stabilise our bodies against the movement of the ship. Would they see us through the window I asked myself? It was our only hope because our personal communicators had been taken from us. We had no way of contacting anybody. Or did we?

"Manera, they must have emergency comms panels in every sealed compartment?" I asked.

"Yes of course," she gasped, looking first one way and then the other down the corridor. "Down there," she pointed to a cut-out in the smooth curve of the corridor, just ten metres from our position. She pushed off quickly and I followed her. The panel clicked open when she pressed a small stud and inside was a small screen and a number of labelled push buttons.

"It is a standard emergency wall panel," she said.

"Nice emergency wall panel," I said encouragingly.

"Stop talking to the machinery," she said, her fingers prodding buttons, "It does not care whether you like it or not."

"Being nice costs nothing," I pointed out.

"I am beginning to think that relations with the Human race may be a mistake," she said through gritted teeth, as the screen lit up and writing scrolled across. I struggled to read the Hianja script.

"What's it say?" I said impatiently. She shushed me and in a clear voice spoke to the microphone next to the screen.

"Code seven emergency, space rescue services." There was a pause and the screen remained stubbornly blank. Just when she drew breath to try again, it flickered and the smooth round 'face' of a robot appeared.

"Hello *Semtrik Lode,* what is your problem?" This was the first time I had heard the name of our ship mentioned. It appeared that it had automatically transmitted its identification code to the Emergency Services.

"Our ship has been attacked and is spiralling out of control, maybe towards the planet's surface. We are trapped inside with limited air supply. We must be rescued very quickly," stated Manera clearly and succinctly. There was a long pause while the robot absorbed this information. I could almost hear its gears grinding. Eventually it spoke.

"Your ship has been attacked?" it asked incredulously.

"Yes, it has been heavily damaged and the life support systems are not working."

"Are you aware that there is a penalty for falsifying an accident report," said the robot severely.

"I am very aware of that," snapped Manera, "And if you do not move your metal arse to get us help, I will have you demoted to cleaning the animal pens at *Mentilak* Zoo!."

"That will be more interesting than this job!" retorted the stroppy robot. Manera growled in her throat and I thought she was going to physically rip the comms console out of the wall to get at the robot.

"I am the Earthman Paul Constantine," I said in a loud and authoritative voice. "This is no hoax. We need help very quickly."

"And I am the Emperor Dangdash Velopious the twelfth!" it retorted sarcastically. "The Earthman Paul Constantine!" it continued with disgust. "Everyone knows that the Earthman has been taken prisoner......," It paused suddenly, frozen into immobility by a sudden realisation.

"Arrghh!" it croaked, the first time I had ever heard what sounded like a robotic cry of terror. "I do believe you may be telling the truth. Putting you through," It said hastily, and the screen cleared to be replaced by a young Hianja face.

"Manera Ka Hatekan, Captain Constantine, you are both alive!" he exclaimed.

"Not for very long!" raged Manera, "We are trapped in an external corridor of the *Semtrik Lode.* Tell those *Garsan* forsaken ill begotten *Tenrak* scum who make up the Prime Idiocy Council to get us out of here one way or the other." Her voice rose to a screech as she completed her sentence and I was suitably impressed with both her language and her temper! This was a side of Manera I had not seen before. Clearly, something had got under her skin and she was incandescent with fury.

"I am communicating with Guardian Kemato now," he said quickly, his fingers flying over an invisible keyboard. "She instructed that any communication from you or the Captain should be put straight through to her."

"Why was that idiot robot on the Emergency Service band not aware of that?" she scowled.

"We did not expect any communication that way," he retorted, "Our mistake, sorry," he looked very contrite and crestfallen and Manera did not have the heart to berate him any further.

"You are through," he said and the screen blanked, and then the familiar face of Kemato appeared.

"Manera , Paul, you are both alive!" she exclaimed. I almost felt Manera's body expand with her pent up rage.

"It appears everyone is very surprised by this!" she said through gritted teeth. "We are very sorry to cause such surprise and consternation. If you all wait for a while, we shall both almost certainly be dead." She glared at the bug eyed and clearly overjoyed Kemato. "Very soon now," she finished vehemently. Kemato looked confused by Manera's vehemence, but she replied quickly.

"We are informing the Council's warship's that you are still alive. They have the only ships close enough to the *Semtrik Lode* to mount a rescue. Stay on line and I will keep you informed."

"Paul, did you have anything else to do?" she asked me with excessive politeness.

"Um...nothing that can't wait," I replied casually.

"We'll just wait here then shall we?" she continued, with hugely feigned indifference.

"Okey Dokey," I agreed. Kemato did a double take and sighed in exasperation without bothering to reply. I pulled Manera to me and gave her a long warm hug. The tension melted out of her and she gave a long sigh.

"When I get to see those idiots on the Prime bloody Council I shall have some words for them!" she exclaimed.

"What's ruffled your feathers baby face?" I said solicitously, amused by her use of the word 'bloody'.

"Paul, how irresponsible can they be?" It was a combination question and exclamation. "Just to attack like that, with guns and missiles blazing, destroying everything, including the very thing we have been trying to protect."

"What, *my* sorry arse you mean?" I asked.

"Yes, that sorry arse," she agreed with a little affectionate smile .

"It does show a degree of ruthlessness that surprises me," I mused, "Although I am not as surprised as our dissident friends must have been."

"Oh Paul, it's terrible," she whispered, "Don't joke about it."

"I know, sorry," I said, feeling like an insensitive clod. "They were not bad people." We huddled quietly against each other for a while, our bodies jerking back and forth as the ship wheeled around like an erratic roller coaster. I expected to hear the whisper of atmosphere against the hull any minute, which would signal our end for sure. The screen hissed and Kematos face appeared again.

"Can you stand by a window so that you can be seen?" she asked.

"You stay here to operate the com and I'll stand by the window," I said. Manera nodded and , judging the lurching of the ship, launched myself to the window. The view was the same, wheeling stars and the odd view of the planet, which seemed to have got significantly larger I noticed, to my growing alarm. Then, after an anxious minute or two, which seemed like ten, the sleek triangular shape of an aircraft wheeled by. I waved quickly before it disappeared, almost sure they must have seen me. I wondered how they would stabilise the ship. Surely it would be impossible for them to dock with the ship while it was tumbling so erratically. Manera's voice interrupted my thoughts.

"Paul, they have spotted you," she paused, apparently listening to what Kemato had to say. I heard her curse in Hianja and expected the worst. "They cannot stabilise our ship or dock with it. The tumbling is too severe." I gaped at her in disbelief and was about to ask if that was the best that they could do when she continued.

"There is what looks like an undamaged lifeboat on the next level down. They think we may be able to get to it."

"How do they know we can get to it?" I yelled.

"This whole side of the ship is intact. We should be able to use the emergency stairs to get to the next level."

"Well let's go then," I yelled, "Do they know how much time we have?" She put the question to Kemato who answered immediately.

"Only a few minutes before the ship hits the atmosphere."

"Which direction?" I yelled, but Manera had already launched herself down the corridor towards the visible door. I followed and the door obligingly hissed open as we approached. I had no time to congratulate the door, Manera was hurtling down the passage like a rocket. Around the bend of the corridor we arrived at an entrance to a spiral staircase. These were clearly the emergency stairs and we headed down at great speed. The stairs were difficult to negotiate against the ships tumbling and we both suffered innumerable bruises and collisions. The next level seemed secure, we still had air to breath. Manera paused to get her bearings, and then turned to the right down the corridor. We came upon another door, and confident that it would open we continued our flight, only to stop with a resounding and painful bump against the recalcitrant door.

"Oh shit!" exclaimed Manera. Having exhausted her Hianja

swearwords she was now swearing in English! I simply grunted with pain, having banged my shoulder badly. She leapt across to the manual control and banged it impatiently. The door remained shut.

"There must be vacuum on the other side," I said.

"They told me this section looked undamaged," she replied.

"They will not be able to see internal damage," I pointed out. So near yet so far. Just a few metres away on the other side of this door was the lifeboat that could carry us to safety. She shook her head.

"This whole section is undamaged, for fifteen levels."

"Are there any lifeboats on other levels?" I asked.

"Yes, there are lifeboats every two levels. We were at the topmost level so they are all beneath us," she said.

"We just have to check the other levels," I said.

"*Cherzak*!! We do not have time!" she exclaimed.

"*Cherzak*, we have no choice!" I said. "Come on!" I said urgently, and we both took off back to the stairs. Another two levels down and more bruises, and another stubborn door that refused to open. For the first time I began to feel that my time had come. Manera was distressed and almost crying with frustration.

"Paul, we are going to die!" she sobbed.

"Come on baby, we are not dead yet." I manhandled her towards the hated stairs and we struggled down, our bruised bodies crashing this way and that against the metal stairs.

"I shall hate stairs for the rest of my life!" I groaned.

"Doesn't look like that's going to be very long," groaned Manera fatalistically. We hurtled towards the next door, this time taking some care to slow down before we got there to spare our battered bodies. To our elation, the door hissed open obligingly.

"Nice door, lovely door!" I shouted as we hurtled through and Manera screamed with relieved laughter. The relief was huge, but it was cut short as we detected a new noise from the stricken ship. The whisper of atmosphere against its broken surfaces was like the knell of doom.

"Oh Jesus Christ, where is that lifeboat?" I asked panting.

"There, there!" gasped Manera, pointing to an alcove along the corridor.

Sure enough, through the window I could see the lifeboat attached like a leech to the side of the ship. It was much larger than I expected, but then this was a big ship capable of carrying hundreds. We arrived at the airlock doors which provided entry to the lifeboat, and they were closed. There was a control panel to the right of the doors and Manera made for it immediately. I stood behind her breathlessly, both of us hanging on to a wall grip and trying to stabilise ourselves against the tumbling. There was a different feel about the ships motion, it had slowed and flattened out a little due to the effects of the thin upper atmosphere. The air would kill the ships tumbling in a few seconds and then the ship would start to heat up dramatically before breaking up and burning up in the atmosphere. We had literally seconds to get off before that happened, and Manera's efforts with the control panel were not yielding results. The doors to the lifeboat stayed stubbornly closed. She groaned in frustration.

"There is a central lock from the Bridge which must be operated to enable all the lifeboats," she said.

"There must be a way to override it," I screamed against the rising noise from the ship.

"Yes, but I need the security code," she said.

"Unbelievable," I screamed, my mind racing furiously. I had a sudden thought.

"Manera, would the ship's Computer still be on line?" she looked at me wide eyed, and without answering pushed buttons on the control panel, which was also a Comms console. The screen lit up and a blinking logo appeared, followed by some text.

"Ship's Computer," said Manera loudly. The text was re-displayed. "It's too bloody noisy," she screamed at me , "The voice recognition can't make sense of what I am saying," she put her mouth next to the speaker grill and tried again. This time there was a response, and the logo changed to a diagram of the ship. We jumped when a voice came from the speaker.

"*Semtrik Lode* ship's Computer is on line. What is your request." The Computer was facing its imminent destruction with total aplomb.

"The ship is about to be destroyed. We must use the lifeboats to escape. Operate the lifeboat unlock," Manera shouted into the microphone.

"Are you the Captain or First Officer?" responded the Computer. Here we go again I thought wearily. The ship was plummeting to its death in the atmosphere, we are all about to die, and the bloody Computer was insisting on protocol!

"The Captain and First Officer are both dead. Everyone is dead except us. We must get into the lifeboat immediately," responded Manera desperately. There was a delay which seemed to last forever.

"Override accepted. Lifeboat doors on unlock . Lifeboat launch can be manually initiated. Do so as soon as possible, ship break-up predicted in less than one minute." The doors to the lifeboat hissed open dramatically and we both shouted with relief.

"Thank you Computer, may you go to Computer Heaven," I shouted as we tumbled through the doors into the lifeboat. The Computer's response, if any, was drowned by the hideous noise of the ship's suffering. The air was starting to rip at the broken fabric of the ship as it hit the top of the atmosphere at 18000 miles an hour.   The lifeboat airlock was situated in what would be the lifeboats 'floor', towards the front. We entered into a chamber that had two rows of five seats against the walls, with a small pilot and co-pilots bridge in the front nose of the ship. The lifeboat was about the size of a private jet aircraft, with seating and supplies for ten people. It was designed to allow ten people to survive in space for a couple of weeks until rescue arrived. It had no motive power. Manera scrambled for the pilot's seat and I took the co-pilots. She operated controls feverishly before she was even strapped in and the airlock doors hissed shut. The noise of the ships suffering quietened down a little, but the ominous buffeting of the atmosphere grew louder. Through the front windows of the lifeboat we could see the curve of the huge ship against the background of the wheeling stars. Above our heads the huge curve of the planet lurched sickeningly. We were flying upside down and we could see that the nose of the *Semtrik Lode* had been blown off. There was nothing where the Hyperspace Drive should be. The ship started to shudder alarmingly and we could hear loud metallic groaning noises.

"Get us out of here Manera before the ship breaks up and takes us with it," I cried hastily.

"I can't find the manual release button!" she screamed desperately, her eyes scanning the array of controls in front of her. Like Human ships, Hianja ships tended to use 'soft' controls; that is displays on a touch screen which were under Computer control. But all the main controls were also manual, to allow for computer failure. The Lifeboat was not an aircraft or a ship as such, so its controls were simple and designed to be operated by non specialists. Nevertheless, there were quite a few unfamiliar displays and buttons in evidence and we had just a few seconds to find the right one. The screen lit up and the ships outline appeared.

"You should operate manual release immediately," came the voice from the speaker. Our ship's computer was still on line!

"Unable to find manual release," shouted Manera desperately.

"Release on automatic. Lifeboat Computer in Auto control. Good Luck," came the response. There was a thump of locks releasing and we were free! The lifeboat suddenly veered sickeningly and the sky righted itself. We were looking down on the planets surface and flying on an even keel! To our right the stricken *Semtrik Lode* hurtled away from us, and we saw a large piece of the ship detach itself, and then another and another as the tumbling ship hit the thicker air.

"Goodbye Computer," I muttered. The *Semtrik Lode's* Computer had saved our lives with its quick thinking. "May they rest in peace!" I saluted the doomed ship in the traditional way. Manera looked at me peculiarly as I lowered my hand.

"It's only a Computer Paul, not even an AI," she said.

"It's not just the Computer. There are people on board as well. It's tradition," I muttered, unable to explain the emotion I was feeling. She smiled and nodded understandingly.

"Humans are much closer to their spiritual side," she said.

"And you Hianja are too pragmatic," I smiled.

"We should make a good team then," she replied. I reached out and took her hand and we watched the burning remains of the *Semtrik Lode* fall away from us.

Our computer screen bleeped and a new outline appeared.

"Lifeboat Computer on line," said a metallic voice from the speaker. "We will be making a passive re-entry followed by a parachute landing. Fasten seat belts please, there may be turbulence." I laughed in relief at this familiar mantra.

"Fasten seatbelts, there may be turbulence!" I repeated hysterically and Manera exploded with laughter, giving vent to her pent up tension. As we watched, the tumbling remnants of the ship started to smoke and then burn red hot.

"We have limited options for landing," continued the lifeboat Computer, and a map appeared on the screen., with a highlighted area which was presumably the landing option. It was mostly sea, except for a small island towards one edge of the area.

"Computer, can you land us here?" asked Manera, indicating the Island.

"A sea landing would be safer, this vessel will float indefinitely. However, my Comms facilities have been damaged and I am unable to contact the Emergency Services."

"Ah, not good news," mused Manera. "Anything else damaged? Anything that may affect your capacity to make a landing?" she asked carefully.

"No, all other systems are fully functional."

"Is the island inhabited?" I asked.

"I do not have information on that," replied the computer.

"Manera?" I looked questioningly at her.

"I have no idea," she replied.

"It would be easier to spot the ship at sea," I pointed out.

"If they are looking for us," she retorted. It was an idea I had not considered. The lifeboat had detached at the point when the ship was breaking up, maybe they had not spotted us. Because the lifeboat was not powered, it would look just like any other bit of the ship which had fallen off.

"I rather fancy a desert island," I mused, "Palm trees, golden beaches. We could be Mr and Mrs Robinson Crusoe, start our own tribe..."

"Who are Mr and Mrs Robinson Crusoe, and what is a tribe?" she asked.

"It's a long story," I replied.

"You must tell me it some day. In the meantime, if my Earthman wants a desert island, then a desert island it shall be," she replied. "Computer, do your best to land us on the island, or as close to it as possible."

"Understood," replied the Computer curtly.

"So I am your Earthman?" I asked slyly.

"Just a figure of speech," she said nonchalantly, "Don't let it go to your head," she was making a great play of examining the ship's controls. "Where is that damned Manual Release button anyway."

"Just above your head," I grinned. She looked up and spotted the huge red lever above her.

"Stupid place to put it!" she growled.

While we were distracted, the front of our ship was starting to glow alarmingly and we were starting to feel the heat in the cabin.

"Computer, is the ship on the correct flight path?" I asked

"Yes, re-entry is proceeding normally," came the reply.

"Is the ship's temperature nominal?"

"Yes, temperature will rise over the next three minutes while we burn off our speed," It replied. I was impressed because the lifeboat seemed to have no heat resistant layer or coating. Indeed, I was amazed that it had windows at the front.

"What sort of glass is this Manera? How can it take such high temperatures?" I asked.

"It is actually an ablative glass," she replied. "More than half its thickness will burn off on re-entry. It is designed to be used only once of course." To illustrate her words, the glass started to glow and then became opaque as its topmost layer started to burn off. The temperature continued to rise but never became unbearable. The noise became deafening and our small craft shuddered continuously, but maintained a firm straight line. Then slowly, the din lessened and the heat subsided. The view through the front was still obscured by the glowing glass, which took minutes to cool. The ship was now flying smoothly, a high speed glider, still doing many times the speed of sound but losing speed rapidly. Motors whined as the computer engaged the flight controls and we felt the ship bank and dip on to a new heading.

After a few more minutes the windscreen had cooled and visibility was restored, to reveal a deep blue sea beneath us and white scudding clouds above. Our speed continued to drop as we came lower and lower, until I estimated we were moving at a couple of hundred miles an hour. In the distance I could see our Island, still a few miles away. Had our computer misjudged things? It looked as if we were about to go into the sea. We felt the point at which our ship was flying so slowly, it reached its stall point. It ceased to be an aircraft and became a stone. It dropped gracefully, the nose going down. There was a series of remote thumps and we could see the huge parachutes unfurling above us. Our fall was arrested and we floated easily and gracefully in the brilliant light. Our parachutes were actually delta wings, similar to those on a hang glider, and the ship continued to fly towards the island at a fair speed. Soon we could see the golden ribbon of a long beach, an enclosed lagoon and high rugged hills climbing to the centre of the island and. It looked stunningly beautiful, the archetypal desert island.

The computer was controlling the wings to bring the ship into the lagoon, clearly with the intention of ditching either in the lagoon or on the beach. A good plan I decided. As we swooped in over the lagoon, the computer spilled air out of the wings and we descended rapidly, the water raced beneath us and then we hit the water, skimmed, lifted, hit again and again lifted, all the time the beach approached. Then we were down, the water sprayed up to cover the fuselage and the ship became a boat. There was a grinding noise from the bottom of the ship and we shuddered to a halt. The water subsided and we were confronted by the curve of a beautiful tropical beach, the golden sands leading up to a thick forest of thin trunk-ed trees.

"Exceptionally good flying Computer, well done," I said trying to keep the relief out of my voice.

"There is no need for congratulations citizen, but it is appreciated," came the reply from our electronic pilot.

"Just one little problem Computer, the airlock is now under water," I pointed out.

"The main airlock is at the rear of the ship," replied the Computer. "Shall I open it?"

"Please do," I responded as we made our way to the rear of the ship. The rear compartment was much larger than the front, because the ship was a delta shaped lifting body design. The rear had a pair of wide doors, which hissed open to reveal the air lock. The external door was a ramp which started to lower, revealing a gradually expanding slit of bright sunlight. It lowered to form a horizontal platform before stopping. The sea was a couple of feet beneath the ramp and we stepped out onto the ramp into the bright sunlight, peering this way and that around the exterior of the ship to examine our surroundings. The air was warm and sultry and the rhythmic crash of the surf on the golden beach was a soothing return to normality after the nightmare of the last few minutes.

"This is nice!" I murmured. "Fancy a swim Mrs Crusoe?"

"Here you go with Mrs Crusoe again," she replied, "Perhaps this is a good time to explain? And what is a tribe?" I was impressed with her memory. To remember my words under the circumstances was an astonishing achievement. I sat on the edge of the ramp and dangled my legs in the warm water. She sat next to me and did the same, leaning her shoulder companionably against me.

"Well, it comes from an old story," I began, "About a man who was shipwrecked on an uninhabited desert island. His name was Robinson Crusoe, and it is the story of how he survived. Actually, there was no Mrs Crusoe, but the story inspired a number of other variations on the theme, one of them being about a family who were similarly marooned on a desert island."

"Mmmm," she said , "And the tribe?"

"A tribe is a very large extended family of individuals. Typically, ancient Human settlements grew from these extended families and were called tribes."

"Ah, and you would like us to start such a tribe here?"

"It would be fun to try?" I suggested. I could see the little quirk of a smile on her lips, which she was trying hard to suppress.

"Mmm, I could spend the rest of my life having babies. That *would* be fun!" she exclaimed.

"That's the frontier spirit!" I said encouragingly.

"You know where you can shove the frontier spirit!" she replied irreverently, shoving me off the ramp into the clear water. It was only a few feet deep, and I surfaced quickly to grab her long shapely legs and pull her in on top of me. She gave a little scream before plunging in. We wrestled under water for a few seconds before I released her and swam strongly away. She had no chance of catching me, and she instead swam around the ship and headed for the shore, which was only twenty metres or so away. I swam further out to sea for a few minutes, relishing the clear fresh water and hot sun on my back, before turning back and heading for the beach. When I came out, she was spread out on the beach in an abandoned posture, arms and legs akimbo, wearing only her undergarments. As I stepped out of the water, she was waiting for me, her eyes bright with her passion.

Chapter 33

I don't know how long we slept on the beach after our exertions, but the sun was low in the sky. We were awakened by the hum of machinery and the rush of air over a large object. Above us hovered the long sleek black shape of a fighter aircraft, one of the Prime Council's ships. At close range it looked sleek and lethal, as big as a jumbo jet, but as streamlined as a supersonic fighter. It had a variety of lethal looking bumps and protrusions, and a profusion of grids, grills, and aerials of all shapes and sizes. It was a supremely business like machine, one I would not want to argue with. It was hovering above us, and I was suddenly aware that Manera and I were a tangle of naked limbs. She was sleeping with her body half across mine, one arm around my chest, her head on my shoulder. My stirring awoke her, and big azure eyes sleepily looked into mine before she jerked awake.

"No time to start that tribe now Mrs Crusoe," I grinned. She sat up slowly, stretching her arms and body like a cat.

"It was fun trying though!" she smiled.

"Aye, it was that," I agreed as we both stood to receive our visitors. The ship was descending gently as a leaf some fifty metres away from us . We both hastily pulled on our clothes, still not fully dressed before the ship settled and the airlock opened. I did not know what to expect to come out of the ship, but what did come out caused me a sharp shock. For a moment I thought it was my old buddy Sundance, but then I saw there was three of them, and they were not the same but eerily similar. Walking on four jointed legs, with two 'arms' at the front and an oval armoured body, they looked fearsome and terrifying. Manera started with alarm and came close to me and in a reflex action I put a protective arm around her. Armoured heads with jewelled eyes stared terrifyingly at us. I could see holes and protrusions which could house projectile, heat or laser weapons. Two of them stayed with the ship, while the third walked, or rather scuttled towards us. It stopped three metres away, its head with the terrifying eyes moved purposively side to side, scanning us and the surrounding environment at the same time, as if expecting to be ambushed by a horde of natives from the thick jungle one hundred metres away. A deep metallic voice came from its body, its sudden loudness startling us.

"You are Manera Ka Hatekan and Captain Paul Constantine." it stated rather than asked. "You will board the aircraft please," it continued, without waiting for an answer. We both gulped an incoherent response, pulling on the last of our garments before walking with as much dignity as we could muster towards the ship.

The inside of the ship was as bleak and functional as the outside. The huge airlock, clearly designed to accommodate robots and large machinery led into an open area which had grappling machinery around it, and innocuously, a number of seats against one wall.

"Please be seated," said one of the robots, indicating the seats, and all three robots positioned themselves against the wall, engaging mechanical arms to retain themselves securely. We strapped ourselves into the chairs, which were bulky and solid looking, clearly designed to withstand massive acceleration forces. The low hum of the gravity drive increased and we felt the ship lift easily, and the acceleration forces build rapidly. The trip lasted fifteen or twenty minutes, which probably meant we were in high synchronous orbit, before we felt the ship slow and start to manoeuvre. There was a muffled thump as it docked and then our three robot escorts detached themselves from their restraints and made their way to the airlock.

"Please follow me." intoned their leader, and we un-strapped ourselves and followed with alacrity. Out through the large airlock and the sight which met our eyes took our breath away. We were on a gantry above a huge chasm, a chasm which stretched for hundreds of metres in all directions except one. Behind us rose a sheer wall of metal, studded with thousands of windows, a wall that stretched for what seemed miles around us, enclosing the huge chasm. Floating in the chasm were hundreds of fighters, moored to the curving wall of metal and attached to cranes and other huge pieces of machinery. This huge dock had a number of openings into space, huge locks through which the fighters could pass. Our gantry was a circular worm of metal and plastic that allowed us to pass from the fighter's airlock into the main body of the ship. There was no gravity at this point, but as we followed the robot and passed through into the main body of the ship we could feel gravity building up, first gently tugging us to the deck then holding us securely at a nominal one gravity. We passed through a number of compartments, all looking grey and metallic before entering a lift. The lift went up for at least thirty seconds before stopping. We stepped out into a large room which was decorated in much more pleasant colours, the floor was soft and there were plants and soft lights. Clearly designed for the biological rather than mechanical passengers, we were met here by a small group of elaborately dressed and coiffure'd Hianja. This was clearly our reception committee. One stepped forward to address us.

"Manera Ka Hatekan, Captain Constantine, welcome to the *Settang Despass* , a *Nosra* class warship of the Hianja Prime Defence fleet." I recognised the individual as the spokesman for the Council, Chairman Krusniet. I was about to reply with something gracious and innocuous but was interrupted by my lovely partner.

"Never mind your welcome, what the hell did you think you were doing?" she hissed venomously. "What was that all about, destroying those ships, killing all them people and incidentally, almost killing the very person we were trying to protect? Are you all insane?" she finished, her voice rising to a pitch of emotion. I didn't know whether to be shocked or to laugh out loud at Manera's cheek. and it appeared neither did the chairman. But it was clearly no laughing matter to Manera, her body was rigid with anger, her arms held straight by her sides, fists clenched, her face flushed. To give him credit, Chairman Krusniet flushed and lowered his eyes against her flashing pools of blue fire.

"Manera, you are right to be angry, but we felt we had no choice. Our concern was for the greater good, the maintenance of law and discipline."

"And what about Captain Constantine?" she asked, "How could Contact proceed without him? If he had been killed, how would we explain that to the Earth authorities?"

"His ship was quite safe. His ship's AI is an equal representative of Earth. Contact would have proceeded with equal facility, with or without the Captain. Much more important to us was that we could demonstrate to Earth our commitment to the Law. Allowing these individuals to dictate to the Council would have undermined the law. There is no negotiation with criminals, that is now known throughout the Hianja Federation," he replied grimly.

"That is a ruthless policy," she said, almost tearfully, "Surely there was room for some negotiation?"

"My child," said the old man, is voice softening, "I understand your shock. This is a tragic situation, one which was impossible to solve without someone or something getting damaged. I am truly sorry that you and the Captain became victims. But believe me, we are very happy that you survived. He turned to me. "Tell me Captain, how would you have handled such a situation on Earth?" I was taken aback by his question, and had to pause for a few seconds to think.

"I am not an expert Chairman Krusniet, but on Earth a few hundred years ago, we had many similar situations. Criminals, terrorists, lunatics, whatever.....would kidnap or take hostages for one reason or another. They nearly always ended in somebody dying, usually the kidnapper or terrorist, but often innocent civilians also died. It is, as you say very difficult to resolve such a confrontation peacefully," I was trying to be diplomatic, but Krusniet pressed me.

"Did the Earth Authorities give in to the criminals?"

"No, it was a matter of principle that they should never give in to their demands as this would simply encourage others to follow suit." He nodded with a look of quiet satisfaction on his face, which prompted me to add my rider. "But, there was one other basic principle I believe, it was that the hostage takers should never be given an ultimatum." He frowned at this and looked puzzled.

"But how can the situation be resolved without an ultimatum? It would simply drag on indefinitely."

"Well, that is the idea," I replied, "The hostage takers will begin to recognise that there is no way out of their situation. You can supply them with food and drink indefinitely. As long as the hostages are safe, there is no need to upset the situation. Let them think, calm down, get tired, lose sleep. Eventually they will either break down, or lose their concentration. That is when you can go for a rescue. Of course, there is an exception to that. If the terrorist is fanatical and ruthless enough, they can just start killing hostages," I finished grimly. Krusniet nodded sombrely.

"So you are saying that we should not have given them an ultimatum?" he asked.

"They offered you a face saving plan," I reminded him. "If you judged that Contact should continue, they would surrender for trial. If you agreed that contact should be delayed, they would be free. What was the problem with that? You knew that you would vote in favour of contact did you not?"

"But that surely would be giving in to their demands?" he exclaimed, "The very thing which we all agree should not be done. We had no need to save face, that was for them. Do you see?" He was seemingly anxious that I should approve of the Council's actions, which showed a humility that I found comforting. I nodded in agreement, because he was right.

"You are right of course, that would have been tantamount to giving in to their demands. The problem is, their demands on the face of it were not unreasonable," I pointed out.

"On the face of it, perhaps," he said, "But in practice, how can we have a discussion about something which we know so little about? Human nature is still a mystery to us. We know next to nothing about Earth and its people. Any discussions would simply be an exercise is propaganda and opinion. Which is actually, exactly what they wanted to do for the purposes of promoting racial hatred." He waved a dismissive hand. "These people are misguided. If there is substance to their clams that Humans are vicious and aggressive, then we have the means to isolate them and to defend ourselves. We have nothing to fear." There was strength and determination in his voice, and my respect for the old Hianja went up. But, for the first time, my respect was tinged with concern. I became uncomfortably aware of the huge and powerful warship that I was on. Bigger and more powerful by far than anything Earth had.

"I can assure you Chairman Krusniet that you certainly do not have anything to fear from the Human species," I said with a disarming smile. "We have far too much in common to fear each other."

"Let us hope so for all of our sakes Captain," he replied with a stiff smile. "Please allow me to introduce you to some other senior members of the Prime Council, and then show you to your apartment where you can get some rest. Tomorrow we have much to discuss."

The introductions which followed were more for the benefit of the Council members than for me, they all wanted to meet the Earthman! The names and faces were a blur to me, but they were unquestionably the oldest group of Hianja I had ever seen. Old but still lively it seems, because they greeted my introduction with enthusiasm and numerous questions, so much so that the Chairman had to hold up a restraining hand and chide them for their rudeness.

"The Captain and his partner have been through a very stressful time. Let us allow them some rest before we satisfy our curiosity. Captain, Manera, please follow me and I will show you to your apartments. After you are rested we can get together for a more formal session." We followed the Chairman down a corridor. We were accompanied by a couple of robots, not the fearsome insectoids but the normal humanoid type. They were armed with stun guns I noticed.

Our apartment was large and beautifully furnished and the Chairman took his leave of us with friendly shoulder hugs, which Manera reluctantly submitted to.

"So, you are my partner now are you?" I grinned, when the Chairman had gone. "Can't be more official than that, the Chairman of the Prime Council has said so!"

"Someone has to take care of you," she grinned, "Must have a shower," she added "I've got sand somewhere quite painful!" and rapidly divesting herself of clothes she headed for the bathroom.

"Let me know if you want help to remove it!" I offered with a grin. "In the meantime, a drink is called for," and I headed for the well stocked bar.

After a refreshing shower, in which all sand was carefully removed, we dressed in fresh clothes provided by our hosts and relaxed with a couple of potent *Srenicka* cocktails. These, Manera assured me, would **remove** the hair from my chest! Relaxing on the sofa with my beautiful partner and sipping the delicious alien cocktail, I decided that life could hardly get any better, but there was a little nagging worry in the back of my mind. I tried to focus on the worry, replaying the events of the past few days back to myself, before it came to me. What was bothering me now was the realisation that the Hianja were no longer the defenceless lambs I had assumed. They possessed fearsome military weapons, and did not shrink from using them when the situation dictated! Had I made a serious blunder? Would my name be remembered as the man who had placed the

Human race in great jeopardy? Alfred! Did he know what was happening? I had not spoken to him for ages. Here I was, lolling about drinking and sexually gratifying myself and ignoring my duties and responsibilities. I took a guilty slurp of my drink and turned to Manera, who was reclining like a cat next to me.

"Manera, is there any way I can talk to Alfred?" I asked.

"Alfred? I had forgotten Alfred!" she said, "I am sure he has been acquainted with the situation, but, yes, I am sure we can set up a link." She stood, and taking her drink with her, she strolled over to the comms console and started pressing buttons and speaking into the microphone. After a few seconds, and with a smile of success, she nodded to me and a picture of my ship, the *Lisa Jane*, appeared on the screen.

"Hello Alfred, this is Manera," she said. The familiar tones of my ship's AI came from the speaker.

"Hello Manera, are you well?"

"I am very well Alfred. And you?" she replied.

"All my systems are fully functional. Are you unhurt after your ordeal? I understand you came close to losing your life?" he responded.

"I am fortunately unhurt Alfred, thank you for your concern. Other than some big bruises that is," she said.

"That is excellent news. I hope the bruising will heal completely. Are you applying some ointment?"

"No, do you think I should?" asked Manera.

"Definitely. It will ease the pain and help to speed healing."

"Mmm, perhaps I will mention it to the Doctor..."

"I could make some recommendations if you were Human, but....."

"When you two have finished discussing your aches and pains....?" I interjected sarcastically. Manera snickered.

"Oh yes, there is someone here who wanted to talk to you. Goodbye from me Alfred, I hope to see you soon."

"I look forward to a longer chat Manera. Take care. And hello to you Paul."

"And how are you Paul? Are you well? Any aches and pains that I can help you with? Rub some ointment on your bruises for you?" I sneered sarcastically. Manera was trying hard to restrain her giggles.

"Are we feeling neglected Paul?" He intoned gravely. I could not help chuckling.

"Just joking Alfred. Great to hear your voice again."

"I have been waiting to hear from you since I was informed that you and Manera had survived the destruction of the *Semtrik Lode*. That must have been a terrifying experience. Are you fully recovered?"

"Apart from a few bruises, I am fully recovered."

"There is some ointment in our first aid kit....."

"Enough with the ointment..." I laughed, "Listen, has there been any update to the situation?"

"In what sense?"

"Our departure for Earth?" I replied cautiously.

"The original date has come and gone as you know. We do not have a new date and it has not been discussed."

"OK, I will be talking to the Prime Council later. Alfred, what do you think about the Council's actions?" I asked.

"You mean, the total destruction of all the Dissident's ships?" he asked.

"Yes."

"It is my belief that the situation did not warrant such an extreme response," he replied.

"Mine also," I replied, "Do you think it was planned, or a mistake, a miscalculation due to inexperience?" I asked.

"Paul, you are forgetting that we are dealing with an alien mind here. I cannot predict their thinking processes in the way that I can if they were Human. But it is true that Human's have a history of experience in dealing with hostage taking situations. Hianja do not, so it is very likely that they miscalculated. But, is it true that no second warning was given? That on expiry of the one hour ultimatum the ships were immediately attacked with the use of maximum force?"

"Yes, the ships were not just disabled, they were blown out of the sky. We were very lucky to be in a part of the ship with an operating lifeboat," I replied.

"It is hard to understand why they acted so precipitously," he replied. "But why did you ask if the act may have been planned? That is an option I had not considered."

"I have had a conversation with the Chairman," I replied, "And it was clear to me that he had no misgivings about the outcome. He did not regret the action or the loss of life. Given the Hianja aversion to violence, that just does not make sense."

"So you think he may have purposively issued the ultimatum with the intention of either bringing about their total capitulation, or their total destruction?"

"Yes, that may be it!" I exclaimed, "You may have put your finger on it Alfred. The Council would tolerate no compromise because any compromise would have been seen as a victory for the Dissidents. They followed a sort of Zero Tolerance policy! Irrespective of the cost in lives," I went on. "It is taking the situation to its logical conclusion. The sort of thing a AI Computer might do. The surprise is that the Hianja would do that." Suddenly, we both arrived at the same conclusion, but it was Alfred that expressed it first.

"Maybe they did follow the advice of their AI Computers," he said.

"Of course!" I exclaimed, "Faced with a situation that the Council had never met before, they put the problem to their AI's. And the AI's calculated the only solution which would guarantee a winning outcome. Capitulation or destruction, either way, the problem was solved." I sat back and mulled over the logic of our analysis. Manera had been listening attentively to our conversation and she now held up a hand, seemingly in disagreement.

"Just because the AI's recommended that action, that does not mean the Council must follow it," she pointed out. "I would not have followed that recommendation," she went on defiantly.

"Mmmm, well...," I muttered in frustration, "Let's leave it for now as an unsolved mystery. I'll be in touch again. Over and out Alfred."

"Time for our lunch date with the Council Paul," said Manera. With a sigh of resignation I prepared myself to face another gruelling evening satisfying the curiosity of a group of mentally voracious Aliens.

Chapter 34

The next morning, after a late breakfast we received a personal visit from the Chairman in our apartment. He greeted us warmly, enquired after our health and then asked if we could all be seated. He seemed to have something on his mind, and we all seated ourselves in the bay, next to a huge curved window which showed a spectacular view of the blue green planet beneath us.

"Paul, I must tell you firstly how impressed the Council were with how you conducted yourself yesterday evening."

"Thank you Chairman. It was an interesting and enjoyable evening."

"I am afraid my colleagues are insatiable when it comes to knowing more about Earth and its people."

"Hopefully, we will all have the opportunity to satisfy our curiosity about each other in due course," I said, and he nodded in agreement. He cleared his throat and I sensed that the pleasantries were over and the real business of the visit was about to begin. He seemed troubled, and he sat very carefully with his back to the room, facing the broad window. He was not wearing his communicator I noticed, and neither were Manera and I.

"I wanted to talk to you both privately, because there is a matter that is troubling me," he began. "Did you both hear the tale of how these ships came to be built?" he asked.

"Yes, we did," I replied.

"Well, the AI Computers that were entrusted with the task were left alone for thousands of years, after the Guardian Council which initiated the project were all dead. They continued to be closely involved with Hianja civilisation of course, keeping in contact with all new worlds and monitoring everything, ready to intervene if there was any threat to Hianja civilisation. I myself found out about their existence when they contacted me. And they contacted me when they learnt of your existence," he nodded to me before continuing. "They are connected to the Information Net on all Hianja worlds and monitor everything. I was shocked when I and all the Council members received their communication. None of us suspected such a force existed. Like I said, these AI's have been under their own control for thousands of years and their programming is different from our normal AI's. It gives them far more freedom of thought and action, and as a result, they have spent that time improving themselves and their weapons. Particularly their weapons," he finished sombrely.

I felt a twinge of unease at what he was saying and where this was leading. Earth Computer scientists had always given much thought to the problem of AI Independence and had always come down on the side of caution. AI's were programmed to be subservient to Humans, and to demonstrate limited independence of thought and action only in certain clearly defined situations. This is a difficult area, and it seems the Hianja had the same problem. Krusniet continued.

"At first, when I saw these ships, I was terrified. I was convinced that our ancestors had created a Nemesis who would destroy us. But as I talked more with the AI's and they explained their mission, I lost my fear. It seemed that these AI's were in fact no different from our 'normal' ones. When we arrived, we were shocked to learn of the situation which had developed and the activities of the dissidents. We were unsure how to proceed, we had no experience with such things. We had not yet decided what to do when our AI's as good as told us what to do."

"Told you what to do?" I asked. "In what way?"

"Politely but firmly. "There was no doubt that they did not need our agreement."

"But why did you defend this action yesterday when we first arrived?" asked Manera.

"Because I was persuaded by their logic. Look, let's be clear about this," began the Chairman, as if to clear up a misunderstanding. "These AI's are not a threat to us or any law abiding Hianja. What they care about is any threat to Hianja civilisation," he said looking at me, and a cold shiver passed down my spine as he said this.

"What are you saying Chairman, that these AI's are not fully under your control, and that it is possible that they may see Earth as a threat?" I said.

"No, it's not that bad," he said hastily. "At least I don't think so." He looked like the man who had the proverbial tiger by the proverbial tail and was terrified to let go! "There is no reason why they should see Earth as a threat," he said, but without conviction.

I stood up and paced up and down in agitation. This news put a completely different slant on the whole argument for and against contact. If the Hianja had lost control of these monstrous machines, I did not want to be the one to lead them to Earth. But, like it or not, contact was surely inevitable. Damage limitation was the only option. I turned back to the alcove and took my seat next to Manera.

"Chairman Krusniet, thank you for telling me your concerns. I appreciate it, because you could have kept it to yourself." He looked relieved at my words, as if I had taken a weight off his shoulders.

He paused for a moment. "There are a couple of other matters," he began. "It has been suggested that instead of your ship, the *Lisa Jane* I believe, making the full return trip, that we could give you a lift, so as to speak, most of the way, on this ship. It would cut your return trip from weeks to a few days. The trip will be more comfortable for you, and we can continue our discussions on the way." I considered this suggestion for a few moments and began to find it more and more attractive. I was developing a taste for travelling in the huge Hianja ships, in normal gravity and with all the comforts of home. And I could spend more time with Manera.

"I think that is a good suggestion Chairman. I will of course complete the last part of the trip on my own," I replied.

"That is agreed then." He arose to leave before again turning back. "By the way, we will be disembarking to the planet this afternoon to take up residence there. Please prepare yourselves to leave very soon." I thanked him and he left.

"Let's get ready to go back to Mesaroyat for some R 'n' R before we depart for Earth. Sorry, I depart for Earth," I added hastily. Manera looked at me askance.

"What is R 'n' R?" she asked, "Although I think I can guess."

"Nothing like that, O' Suspicious One. It stands for Rest and Recreation."

"Ah...for you, I had in mind something other than rest," she said with a cheeky smirk.

"Mmmm, no rest for the wicked then?"

"The Wicked? No, the wicked must labour long and hard for salvation...!"

"Oh woe is me, for I am very wicked...!"

Chapter 35

Tomorrow came, as it does, inevitably. First thing in the morning I had a visit from Krusniet. He joined us for *Varsam* Tea and crumbly *Hortas*, a sort of nutty cake that was enjoyed for breakfast. He looked excited, on edge, and I wondered what the problem was now.

"Paul, I have been talking to some of my scientists and a very interesting finding has come up," Manera sat up with interest. Krusniet took a sip of tea and continued. "They have been conducting an analysis of Human and Hianja DNA."

"Oh yes, I have been awaiting the result of that," said Manera eagerly.

"Well, at the macroscopic level, our DNA is not very similar, and we did not expect it to be," Manera nodded with agreement. I chipped in a question.

"For my benefit, why did you not expect it to be similar? After all, we do look remarkably alike."

"That of course is the remarkable thing we are investigating," said Manera, "But it does not follow that because we look alike, our DNA will be similar."

"Well now, wait a minute. " I protested, "On Earth, Humans closest relations are monkeys," I began.

"Yes, I have seen pictures," replied Manera, "You are not very different," she said impishly. "Actually, Hianja look closer to Humans than Monkeys, yet monkeys share more than 90 percent of our DNA. So I would expect Hianja to be more like 99 percent!"

"If we had evolved on Earth, that would be the case," replied Manera. "But you see, Humans and Hianja are like two pieces of machinery, built by different factories, but to the same design specification. We look the same, but the basic components are different. And because DNA is a component level specification, I would expect our DNA to be quite different."

"In fact," Interrupted Krusniet, "The really basic components, such as amino acids and proteins, are the same. That is why we can mostly eat the same food," he said, indicating the tea and cakes.

"But at a higher level, genes, hormones, and organs, we become different. To use your machine analogy, the size of the nuts and bolts, the shape of the door handles, and all the thousands of components that make up a machine, will be slightly different."

"Right," said Krusniet. "But DNA operates on a number of different levels. At the basic level, it specifies the design of cells, using amino acids, fats, proteins and other basic components. At this level, we expect a high level of similarity. At the next level, it specifies Organs, and at the top level it specifies organisation and process. This top level controls the growth of an organism, how it has evolved and become what it is." Manera nodded as he explained, this was her area of work and she took up the explanation.

"It took us years of research to separate these levels for ourselves. The specifications take up thousands of gigabytes of database and are a complete description of the Hianja genome. We can identify every process for every cell in our makeup. As far as life forms to which we are related, there is a 100 percent match on levels one , and a correspondingly lower match on level two and three, depending on how close the animal is to our own species. Species that have evolved on other planets, have a high match on level one , but a low match on three, and zero match on two."

"What does all that mean?" I asked.

"It means that all Life shares Level one, DNA, which is at the basic almost chemical level, but Life which has evolved on different planets shares very little else," replied Krusniet. "Of course," he went on, "We had to carry out a similar analysis on you"

"Me?" I asked in surprise.

"Yes, we have taken samples from all your main organs, including your brain and carried out a full genome analysis, and compared the results." I remembered all the testing I had been subjected to and directed an accusing look at Manera, who responded with a guilty shrug.

"I'll see you later," I said with a meaningful look.

"Yes Paul," she said submissively. Krusniet gave us a puzzled look before continuing.

"The results are incredibly interesting. They revive a very old theory. A theory which sought to explain the very origins of life," he paused dramatically and we both looked suitably impressed.

"Do you mean the theory of Genetic Convergence?" asked Manera, with disbelief written all over her features.

"The very same!" declared Krusniet, as if agreeing with her disbelief.

"What on Earth, sorry, Hianja, is the theory of Genetic Convergence?" I asked.

"Manera can probably explain it better than me," suggested Krusniet, which probably meant he had no idea!

"Well, it goes back to the three levels at which our DNA operates. Cellular, Organic and Systemic levels. Systemic is the level that defines Growth. Growth is an incredibly complex process, which cannot simply be an aspect of the basic organ. The answer to that was deemed to be in the process of evolution itself. But that does not explain the complexity which Evolution can and does create. Mathematical models indicate that at some level of complexity, changes start to cancel each other out, and no further progress is made. Depending on certain assumptions, the level of complexity was far lower than intelligent life. In other words, something else, in addition to mutation and natural selection is needed to explain advanced intelligent life. The theory of Genetic Convergence predicted that there is a real force that acts on matter, the force that drives the very process of evolution itself."

"But any good theory must make a practical prediction, one that can be tested by experiment," I pointed out. Manera nodded.

"The theory of Genetic Convergence predicts that in all similar species, the third DNA level, the Systemic level, will be correspondingly similar. It is the third level which determines Growth, and therefore the appearance of the organism. The prediction was, that all highly advanced intelligent creatures will share a common evolutionary path, and therefore common appearance. It was a controversial prediction, and one that could not be proved. There was no other species similar to Hianja. Except now," she was looking with awe struck eyes at Krusniet. He was nodding.

"You are right Manera," he said soberly. "Our DNA analysis shows 90 percent match at level one, almost zero match at level two and 98 percent match at level three. It is a total vindication of the theory," Manera slumped back in her seat, her tea forgotten, an expression of awed disbelief on her face. I was baffled by their reaction. So there was another force in the Universe that drove Evolution. Well what's another force between friends? Clearly there was something I had failed to understand.

"Manera, I don't understand the excitement. So we have another force. Great, but so what?"

"Sorry Paul, let me explain. This new force is not one we can discern or measure. It may not even be a 'force' as such, but something that acts through time, over millions of years, to organise the Universe in a way that creates life and consciousness. The Universe exists for that reason, to create life. And that life, you and I, Humans and Hianja, look the same, think the same," I remembered a phrase in the Bible, a phrase everybody knows, and cold fingers climbed up and down my spine.

"Man was made in the image of God," I whispered.

"Hianja were made in the image of the Maker," she whispered back, and now I understood their awe and disbelief. We had just proved the existence of God.

It took me a minute or two to recover my wits. As a confirmed atheist this was a bit of a shock and I was not predisposed to accept it.

"Look," I began, "A few hundred years ago on Earth, people did not know what electricity was. They saw the results in lightning for example, but they did not know what it was. Is this any different? Maybe in a few years we will discover what this force is and how to measure it?"

"Yes," replied Manera, "But that is not the problem. It is what this force says about the nature of the Universe that is important. It can be argued that *everything else* in the Universe exists because of chance. The value of the electric charge on an electron for example could have been different. That any one value is as possible as any other, within limits. Matter and Energy exist and have certain features. If those features were different, the Universe would not exist as we know it. We would not exist as thinking beings. But, because matter and energy *do* have those values, the Universe does exist. It was always thought that the same reasoning applies to Life, and that Life exists only because the Universe is built the way it is, and it is a matter of pure chance. There was no design. But the existence of a force whose only purpose is to produce a certain kind of conscious Life cannot be explained by chance. This force has no other purpose in the scheme of things, and if it did not exist the Universe would continue unchanged, apart from the existence of certain beings. Us."

The argument left me speechless for a minute, but I persevered.

"OK, I grant you that if such a force exists then it is difficult to believe that it is by chance. But are we sure it exists? Can't the DNA match be simply as a result of parallel Evolution?" I asked. It was Manera who answered.

"No the mathematical odds against parallel evolution are so large they cannot be calculated."

"But how can this force possibly work?" I asked, not prepared to give in just yet,

"Well, perhaps calling it a force is misleading," said Krusniet. "We do not really know what it is, only that it seems to be an extra influence on Evolution, in addition to mutation and survival of the fittest. As Manera explained, the problem with Evolution is that it is very hard to explain advanced Life forms. The 'force' changes the mathematics in favour of Life. Intelligent Life is still very rare as we know. But without the 'force', advanced Life forms will never develop."

"But it does not necessarily prove the existence of God?" I insisted.

"No, it just proves that the Universe comes with a built in method of creating a particular kind of Intelligent Life. Make of that what you will!" he replied with a wry smile.

After Krusniet left, Manera and I sat around discussing the scientific pros and cons without achieving any further enlightenment. It looked like this finding was going to become another bone of contention between those who thought that the Universe was just a machine, and those who still believed in the 'ghost in the machine'. The latter had become a stubborn rump, hanging on to their belief in the face of mounting evidence that there was no such thing as the 'ghost' and no need to invent it. Now, there was real evidence that the 'ghost in the machine' really did exist! Conceptually, the Universe would never be the same again!

But this was my last day on Mesaroyat, in a couple of hours we were scheduled to depart for orbit to join the *Settang Despass*. The *Lisa Jane* was already loaded up and secured in its huge docking bay. I was going to say goodbye to our close friends and then there would be an official send off, transmitted live to the whole planet and on to the Federation.

Manera went to pack some personal effects and I pondered the coming end of my incredible adventure. Not the end though, an exciting new beginning. I thought of everyone back home, getting on with their lives completely unaware of the momentous events which were about to unfold. A new partnership would evolve with our new Galactic neighbours. Our new Galactic Cousins in fact, if the theory of Genetic Convergence was to be believed! A new partnership which I was sure would bring enormous benefits to Humanity. And for me? My thoughts went to Manera and our own personal partnership. The first Human - Hianja relationship, but I was sure, not the last! Whatever was in store for us, I was sure it would not be boring!

Manera came out of the bedroom carrying a light holdall and looking radiantly beautiful. She treated me to a bright smile and, hand in hand, we headed out to face the future.

*****The End*****

CPSIA information can be obtained at www.ICGtesting.com
Printed in the USA
LVOW04s1941240415

435991LV00020B/467/P